Studies in War and Peace

Also by Michael Howard

THE FRANCO-PRUSSIAN WAR

MEDITERRANEAN STRATEGY IN THE
SECOND WORLD WAR

MICHAEL HOWARD

STUDIES
IN WAR AND
PEACE

NEW YORK · THE VIKING PRESS

Contents

In Memoriam

BASIL HENRY LIDDELL HART

Introduction

Apologia pro Studia Sua

An author reprints ephemera at his peril. Journalism by definition does not outlast the day for which it was written, while even the most careful studies and lectures, if they are produced in the first place as occasional pieces, look out of place however skilfully they are transplanted. My only excuse for trying to preserve something out of the mass of papers, lectures, articles and reviews which I have churned out over the last fifteen years is that they provide evidence of a kind of intellectual pilgrimage, if not exactly of progress. All are the outcome of a sustained attempt to bring two lines of inquiry into focus: the traditional study of military history, and the study of international relations in the light of nuclear and missile technology. The first assumes war to be an acceptable and accepted institution in human affairs. The second leads one to doubt whether it can any longer be either.

'Traditional military history', by which I mean the kind of campaign study made popular by Jomini and his followers in the nineteenth century, did not survive even the First World War intact. Outside the official histories, and accounts of such isolated campaigns as the German advance on Paris in 1914, Tannenberg, and Allenby's victory in Palestine, it was almost impossible to view the course of that struggle in purely military terms. Its outcome was decided by a complex of political, social and economic factors as much as military. Even those historians who would argue that the military factors of morale, strategy and leadership were ultimately decisive cannot sustain their case without taking account of these non-military elements. War was no longer a gladiatorial contest between professional forces. It had not been so since the middle of the nineteenth century, but it took a good sixty years for the lesson to sink in.

The lesson was one which anxious propagandists had done their best to teach before 1914. Much of the writing of military and naval history during the pre-war epoch had been blatantly didactic; an attempt to alert national electorates to the requirements of national defence, to warn them of the continuing and inescapable probability of war and to engender the necessary patriotic responses. After 1918 studies of this kind were rare. Outside Fascist countries – admittedly a quite considerable exception – militaristic history sank to the level of juvenilia. The view became current, particularly in Anglo-Saxon countries, that war in itself was politically unacceptable. Its very study became suspect. War was not a problem to be examined but an evil to be shunned, and moral passion – not for the last time – became a substitute for rigorous thought. Even the universities where Chairs of military or naval studies had been founded – Oxford, Cambridge, London – failed to develop serious academic centres for the analysis of the problem of war. Apart from the work of a few solitary figures like Liddell Hart, military history became a study for professionals, isolated from the main stream of intellectual development. To me as a schoolboy in the 1930s the whole idea appeared archaic and repellent. Much more plausible were the views on international affairs of such authorities as the Revd. Dick Shepherd, the Revd. Donald Soper, Mr Beverley Nichols and Mr A. A. Milne.[1] Like Mr and Mrs John Lennon today, issuing their ecumenical blessings *urbi et orbi* from their matrimonial couch, we believed that war was over if we wanted it.

We were of course wrong. The Second World War made necessary a painful process of political and intellectual readjustment, bringing my generation face to face with the disagreeable paradox, that war might be necessary as an instrument of policy to ensure the survival of a society in which it was possible to renounce war as an instrument of policy. Good will and international organisations were apparently not enough in themselves to eliminate violence as an

[1] Nichols's *Cry Havoc* (1933) and Milne's *Peace with Honour* (1934) were pacifist tracts of quite remarkable power. They should be read by anyone wishing to recapture the British mood in the 1930s.

element in international affairs. For five years the question, whether our value-system was to survive the attack of the forces of nihilistic militarism, depended very largely on the skill with which armed forces were deployed and did combat by sea, air and land. It was borne in on us that perhaps war and conquest *had* played a larger part in shaping the past than we had been prepared to concede, and that military skills were not yet negligible factors in social survival. We learned also that military efficiency itself is the outcome of a whole complex of factors of which traditional military historians had not always taken full account, and that the study of military affairs was not only still relevant to the problems of our own times but could still provide new illumination in our study and understanding of the past.

It was thus natural enough that military studies should have survived, and even revived, in universities after the war, and attracted a new generation of students whose backgrounds and instincts were entirely unmilitary. There was little temptation in 1945 to believe that we had abolished war. Too much of it was still going on or seemed impending. The advent of nuclear weapons made war appear yet more terrible, but far from impossible. Demobilised after three years military service and a student at Oxford once more, I often wondered for how many more months I would be able to sleep peacefully between sheets before having to put on uniform again. Peace had come, but what kind of peace? If war recurred, what kind of war would it be? Under such circumstances, the whole-hearted concentration on the problems of the past demanded by my chosen profession of historian was really very difficult to sustain.

In 1953, on the strength of having helped to write my regimental war history, I was appointed to a newly-created Lectureship in Military Studies at King's College, London, at a moment when the world was still trying to digest the implications of the first thermonuclear explosions. My terms of reference were liberally vague, and it was my own inclination and training that confined my teaching at first to purely historical studies; that and the fact that this was the only way I could attract any students. My interest focussed at that time on the changing nature of war; particularly the transformation which occurred between the battle of Waterloo and that of the Somme a hundred years later. The German wars of unification, neglected by British historians for fifty years, seemed fundamental to the understanding of these changes, and for ten years my classes followed me patiently through their *minutiae*. But too much was going on in the outside world for any study of the past to be fully satisfying. I ventured timidly into some of the early controversies about deterrence and disengagement. I made the electrifying acquaintance of Basil Liddell Hart and through him of other British students – at that time almost entirely non-academic – of defence questions. I was invited to the seminal conference in Brighton in January 1957 which led to the foundation of the Institute for Strategic Studies; and thereafter I was able to observe, participate in, and feed back into academic teaching the great debates about international security in the nuclear age which I attempt to describe in the paper on 'The Classical Strategists' reprinted in this volume.

The next ten years saw a voyage of discovery, undertaken almost entirely under the inspired sponsorship of Alastair Buchan, through the evolving concepts of deterrence, disarmament, arms control, limited conflict, crisis management and revolutionary war, which took me far away from even the very eclectic interpretation of 'military studies' with which I had set out. It was necessary to acquire a working knowledge of at least the jargon of various technologies; to explore in some depth the functioning of public administration in order to discover how decisions in matters of defence were made in various societies; to carry out some comparative study of civil-military relations; to become familiar with the rapidly expanding field of international relations; to learn something, if only to evaluate the newly-popular theories of revolutionary war, about sociology; all this without losing touch with the solid ground of historical studies in which there was still so much work to be done. It was hard work, immensely exhilarating but at the same time frustrating. I had to skim the surface of many disciplines without having the chance thoroughly to master any one.

By the middle of the sixties, strategic studies had become a thriving academic industry. In so far as I contributed to it at all, I found that I shared the views of those of my colleagues, expressed most magisterially by Raymond Aron and most pugnaciously by Hedley Bull, that force is an ineluctable element in international relations, not because of any inherent tendency on the part of man to use it, but because the *possibility* of its use exists. It thus has to be deterred, controlled, and if all else fails, used with discrimination and restraint. It was a view common to many Europeans who had lived through the earlier decades of the century, and it was carried to the United States by scholars of the European tradition such as Hans Morgenthau, Klaus Knorr and, in a slightly younger generation, Henry Kissinger. The emphasis which these thinkers placed on military power as a factor in international relations was alien to a native American tradition of studies rooted in abstract concepts of law, right and justice; but it evoked a new and potentially more constructive opposition from scholars who, profoundly and admirably pacifist by temperament, refused to accept the ineluctability of the element of force in international affairs, and hoped that, by applying the techniques of the social sciences and of mathematical analysis, they might find ways of banishing it entirely. Centres for 'conflict analysis' and 'peace research' were founded in the United States at the end of the 1950s; in recent years they have been developing in Europe as well.

The absence from the studies printed here of any discussion of the work of this school will no doubt be noted and commented on unfavourably. It is due to no lack of knowledge of their output or sympathy with their intentions. I must admit that their aims seem to me in some instances to be ludicrously ambitious and in others almost as ludicrously narrow; but between the empire-builders who claim to have discovered a positive science of peace and the craftsmen who go on endlessly refining their analytic techniques there is much interesting and potentially valuable work being done. But I am unrepentently a historian and not a social scientist. I think in terms of analogies rather than theories, of process rather than structure, of politics as the realm of the contingent rather than of necessity. Much of the current work being carried out on conflict resolution I find highly stimulating, but I cannot hope to contribute to it; or trust myself, at this stage, to assess its long-term value.

These studies have however had at least one valuable effect. They have forced us to think in much more rigorous terms than has been usual hitherto about international affairs; and particularly about the meaning of that much used and abused term 'Peace'. This word is so emotive in its overtones, so multiple in its meanings, and normally so blatantly perverted by political propagandists for their own purposes, that social scientists now very properly hesitate to use it at all – except perhaps in soliciting grants from foundations. The use of the same term to describe both a subjective condition of personal calm, and an objective state of equilibrium in international relations, leads to arguments which are at best confused and at worst dishonest. 'Peace' is, in its broadest sense, obviously more than the absence of a formal state of war. Twice in these studies I have quoted Hobbes and I make no apology for doing so. Hobbes's ideas seemed at least as relevant to the middle decades of the twentieth century as they had been to those of the seventeenth. (Happy the generation now growing up in our universities whose natural affinity appears to be rather with Rousseau!) A situation in which recourse to force is such an imminent probability that one's whole life and policy has to be adjusted to it is not, save in the most formal sense, a state of peace. It is for that reason that I equate peace with that unfashionable term 'Order'; an emphasis which probably brands me as a temperamental Tory rather than a temperamental Whig.

But with order goes that equally unfashionable concept, 'justice'; and justice can be translated into the rather more fashionable terms of identification, participation, and consensus. In the domestic affairs of states, the greater the degree of perceived justice in the social and political order, the greater the degree of conscious or unconscious participation in its structure and of identification with the community, the less force is required to sustain it. But the need for residual force to deter and if necessary combat obstinately anti-social elements remains in even the most just and comprehensive of societies. And in an international order the same problem remains. States, or rather groups of men in

control of states, retain the capacity to use violence as a short
cut to the gratification of their perceived needs, and so long
as this potential exists, international security postulates the
existence of appropriate deterrent and protective force. The
elimination of this potential has been the object of disarmament studies throughout this century, and for some five
years, between 1958 and 1963, the entire community of
strategic thinkers concentrated their attention on the problem, with regrettable lack of success. Their failure has forced
us back on a second line of defence: if the use of force cannot
be eliminated altogether, how can it be controlled?

Over the last five or six years the urgent concern for disarmament which was so characteristic of the late fifties and
the early sixties has evaporated with quite remarkable
rapidity. There is little cause for surprise in the failure of the
innumerable studies devoted to the subject of disarmament
to do much more than reveal its complexity. What is more
strange is the equanimity with which that failure has been
accepted by the groups which were once most urgent and
anguished in their pursuit of peace. All but a tiny minority
of those who once marched, demonstrated, and sat down to
ban the bomb have learned to live with it. Their successors
take the balance of terror very much for granted. They are
indeed less concerned now with peace than they are with
justice. Whereas ten years ago the pressure was to abolish
war at whatever cost to international order, today it is rather
to secure justice at whatever cost to international or internal
peace.

The focus of popular controversy has thus shifted in recent
years from problems of international to those of internal
order, from the problem of war to that of revolution. The use
of force between states blends – especially in the case of
revolutionary war – into the use of violence within them.[1]
Radicals who question the legitimacy of the existing order
sometimes cite in justification the fact that it is prepared in
extremity to use force to protect itself. 'The system itself is

---

[1] I have tried to deal with this question in a study 'Changes in
the Use of Force 1919–1969' in *The Aberystwyth Papers: International Politics 1919–1969*, shortly to be published under the
auspices of the University of Aberystwyth.

violent' is a slogan taken to justify the use of counter-violence. All political systems do indeed belong to the category of *animaux mechants* which defend themselves when attacked. It is perhaps the highest compliment that can be paid to our own, that this discovery should come as a surprise to some of its members. The monopoly of force in the hands of legitimate authorities has been achieved only by a long and sometimes painful process of historical development. Those who deny the legitimacy of the established political authority because it rests on an unjust social or political order may use force to overthrow it, just as they will undoubtedly use force to defend and enforce whatever system they establish in its place. But the fact that that authority resorts to force to preserve order does not in itself invalidate its legitimacy.

Thus one is led, from describing the splendours and miseries of the military life, to reflect about the nature of society itself and the forces that hold it together. Both war and peace require the existence of some kind of political order, and order implies the control of force by authority accepted as legitimate. But does the legitimacy of the authority in itself legitimise the force which it uses, or are there further criteria which we must apply? What ethical considerations should limit the use of force, whether by states or by revolutionaries? Do they arise from the political objective aimed at or are they extrinsic to it? These are the questions which force themselves most insistently on the minds of the public; whether they arise from the cool calculations of megadeaths by the nuclear strategists; the use of napalm and defoliants in limited wars; the stockpiling of chemical and research into biological weaponry; or the mass starvation of children as a by-product of Africa's civil wars.

Some of these questions are discussed in the study in this volume entitled 'Morality and Force in International Politics', which was originally delivered as a lecture in a series sponsored by the Faculty of Divinity at Cambridge. It was a terrifying and salutary exercise to be compelled to deal with such a problem before such an audience, but I remain deeply dissatisfied with the result and reprint it only with great hesitation. The fundamental moral dilemma remains for me unsolved. The infliction of suffering is in itself an evil, corrupting the agent as well as harming the patient. The conduct of war consists of deploying armed force so as to inflict, or threaten the infliction of suffering on an adversary – which may mean, under contemporary political and economic conditions, on all members of his society. War thus is in itself inescapably an evil. But those who renounce the use of force find themselves at the mercy of those who do not; and the value-system which enables us to see the infliction of suffering as an evil is in itself the product of a certain kind of society which is as liable as any other social system in history to destruction from without, as it is to corruption and disruption from within. On one horn of the dilemma lies suicide, on the other a moral degradation which may be a more subtle form of self-destruction. There are no easy answers: we have no right to expect them.

This then is the range of issues covered by the studies which follow. My severest critic could not say that they are too narrowly specialised nor my kindest friend that they shed any new light on subjects in each of which there exist specialists far more learned than myself. They represent a process of self-education which has still reached only a very elementary level. But I have no doubt that we will all have learned a great deal more about the problems of war and peace before this century has come to an end.

I reprint as an Epilogue a talk broadcast immediately after the Soviet invasion of Czechoslovakia in 1968; if only because that event forced me to bring into focus some of the ideas which I had been developing about the use of force in politics with the very strong emotions aroused in me by that event. It was difficult under the circumstances to preserve the kind of academic calm needed for cool judgement; but the piece retains a certain historical interest.

All Souls College
Oxford

MICHAEL HOWARD

Studies in War and Peace

1 Jomini and the Classical Tradition in Military Thought

It is universally agreed upon, that no art or science is more difficult, than that of war; yet by an unaccountable contradiction of the human mind, those who embrace this profession take little or no pains to study it. They seem to think, that the knowledge of a few insignificant and useless trifles constitute a great officer. This opinion is so general, that little or nothing is taught at present in any Army whatsoever. The continual changes and variety of motions, evolutions, etc., which the soldiers are taught, prove evidently, they are founded on mere caprice. This art, like all others, is founded on certain and fixed principles, which are by their nature invariable; the application of them can only be varied: but they are themselves constant.

With these words Henry Humphrey Evans Lloyd began, in 1766, his *History of the Late War in Germany*.[1] It can almost be said that he opened also a new age in the history of military thought.

By the middle of the eighteenth century students of every aspect of human knowledge had almost completed their slow emancipation from the authority of traditional concepts handed down, usually through the medium of the Church, from classical antiquity. The tide of rational enquiry and scientific method which had begun to creep in in the days of Bacon and Galileo and had been brought to a stand in the seventeenth century, as rival orthodoxies divided Europe in their struggle for dominance, was now in full flood, washing round and past those bastions of orthodoxy, the churches and the universities, bringing with it a new attitude, not only towards the phenomena of the universe, but to the organisa-

---

[1] *The History of the Late War in Germany between the King of Prussia and the Empress of Germany and her Allies.* By a General Officer (London, 1766), I, Preface, p. 5.

tion and activities of man himself. The laws by which the universe operated and by which men regulated their societies could no longer be attributed to the dictates of an omnipotent Deity transmitted through an ecclesiastical corporation whose authority was enforced, sometimes with sadistic enthusiasm, by the secular authorities. But that some such laws must exist was self-evident to a society which had learned, after two centuries of near-anarchy, to value order as the prime social virtue. Newton had revealed them in the natural world – laws of a new kind, arising out of the properties of the matter composing the universe and not imposed on it by external or prescriptive authority. These laws created a pattern of behaviour uniform throughout the world, and by observing a part one could deduce the principles which operated the whole.

But was man not equally part of this universe? Were his activities not equally regulated by fundamental principles arising out of his nature and needs, deducible by observation and universally valid? So thought Montesquieu, whose great work on *L'Esprit des Lois* appeared in 1748 and opened with the precise but revolutionary definition: 'Laws, in their most general signification, are the necessary relations arising from the nature of things.'[1] So thought the authors of the great *Encyclopædia*, at once a manifesto and a *vade-mecum* of the new age, which began to appear in 1750. Education, penology, law, political economy, agriculture, the applied sciences, in all these fields pioneers were working, by the middle years of the century, to establish universally valid principles which would replace unthinking adherence to traditional patterns of behaviour as a guide to action.

One human activity, however, still awaited its Montesquieu, its Newton. Lloyd was not alone in observing that the practice of war was unique in remaining at the mercy of traditional prejudices. Voltaire had observed sardonically that 'The Art of War is like that of medicine, murderous and conjectural,'[2] but did nothing to improve the situation.

[1] Baron de Montesquieu, tr. Thomas Nugent, *The Spirit of the Laws* (New York, 1949), p. 1.
[2] Quoted by J. F. C. Fuller in *The Foundations of the Science of War* (London, 1925), p. 19.

Marshal de Saxe opened his *Reveries de l'Art de la Guerre* with the much-quoted observation 'Every Science has Principles and Rules, only that of War has none';[1] but although his study is packed with wit and wisdom, no principles emerge. Guibert's *Essai Général de Tactique* (1772) opened with a similar plea, but his own work, with its confused and scintillating mixture of political insight and technical minutiae, is the last place to look for them. But Lloyd did more than wring his hands over the lack of any clear scientific thinking about military activity. He tried to do some himself.

In his Preface to the *History of the Late War in Germany*, Lloyd in fact attempted a preliminary sketch for a fuller study of military affairs which appeared fifteen years later in 1781, under the title *Military Memoirs*. In this he pointed out that there were two parts to the art of war, a mechanical part which could be learned, and the application of it which could not. As with poetry and rhetoric, it was not enough to know the rules if one did not possess the talent. He pointed out also that war was not a matter of simple mechanics, for the forces involved were human ones, susceptible to moral pressures and instinctive weaknesses. He therefore devoted quite as much attention to questions of leadership and morale as he did to those of logistics, tactics, and the general conduct of operations. Finally, his discussion of the relationship of government policy and military operations showed, fifty years before the publication of Clausewitz's *Vom Kriege*, a firm understanding of the place of war as an instrument of policy, and the manner in which political considerations affected its conduct.

One can of course always find pioneers before the pioneers; and one can usually find obscure contemporaries whose work paralleled that of the thinkers to whom posterity has given the credit for new inventions. In the writings of the Marquis de Savorgnano in the sixteenth century and those of Montecucculi in the seventeenth we find a systematic analysis of the conduct of war far transcending the accumulation of factual and didactic detail which characterised most of the

[1] *Les Reveries . . . de l'art de la Guerre de Maurice Comte de Saxe* (Berlin and Potsdam, 1763), I, p. iii.

writers of their time.[1] In the work of Lloyd's contemporary,
the Netherlander Colonel Nochern von Schorn, a substantial
section is devoted to strategy, which is there defined as the
art of commanding armies and conducting operations.[2] But
there was in Lloyd's work a succinctness of expression and an
economy of style which gave him a far greater influence than
his more verbose contemporaries and predecessors; the more
so, perhaps, because his conclusions were so entirely in harmony with the general pattern of eighteenth-century thinking. He did indeed deal intelligently with those moral aspects
of war which were to be so much emphasised in the nineteenth century, and the political, which occupy us in the
twentieth; but it was in mathematics and topography, those
most exact of sciences, that he saw the true bases of the art
of war. A firm grasp of these, he maintained, would always
enable the commander so to manœuvre his army as to attain
his objective; and the objective would normally be the occupation of territory which would be of political value. If
manœuvre failed, battle might be necessary; but Lloyd considered, as had Saxe before him, that an able general should
be able to attain his objective without fighting one. Further,
in reducing operations of war to an exact science, Lloyd laid
the foundations of the vocabulary of strategic analysis which
is still in current use. He coined the phrase 'line of operations' to describe the path by which an army moved from its
starting-point to its ultimate destination; and armed with it
he laid down certain elementary strategic principles. The
line should be as short and as direct as possible. Its protection against the enemy should be a prime consideration in all
strategic planning; the harassing of the enemy line of operations should be another. The line must lead to some really
essential objective, and the selection of the correct line of
operations might well determine the outcome of the campaign.

[1] Mario Savorgnano, *Arte militare terreste e maritima* (Venice
1599). *Memorie del General Principe di Montecucculi* (ed. Heinrich von Huyssen, Cologne, 1704).

[2] *Idées raisonnées sur un système général et suivi de toutes les
connaissances militaires* . . . (Nuremberg, 1783). See Max Jähns,
*Geschichte der Kriegswissenschaften, vornehmlich in Deutsch-
land* (Munich, 1891), III, 1,775.

Two distinct schools of military thinkers can thus trace their ancestry to Lloyd. There were those who tried to follow him in establishing firm principles of strategy based on quantifiable geographical and logistic data; and there was the school which stressed primarily the moral and political aspects of war which made it impossible to treat its conduct as an exact science. Outstanding as an exemplar of the first school was Heinrich von Bülow, whose *Geist des neueren Kriegssystem* was published in 1799. Bülow added further terms to the strategic vocabulary. The destination of the Army he defined as its *Objekt*. The magazine or depot from which it set out he termed its *Subjekt*; and the line linking the *Subjekts* on which the Army depended he called its *Basis*. The concept of the *Subjekt* did not outlive its creator, but the terms 'objective' and 'base', together with Lloyd's 'lines of operations', moulded military thinking until our own day. But if in this sense Bülow fruitfully developed the ideas of Lloyd, in another he took them to lengths of rococo absurdity. He considered that all military operations could be conceived of in terms of a triangle, with its apex at the Army's 'objective' and the other two corners at the outer edges of its 'base'. The angle at the apex, he laid down, should be at least ninety degrees if the operation was to be carried out with safety. Anything less would make the line of operations unduly vulnerable to attack. Armed with this ready reckoner, and basing on it yet more abstruse geometrical calculations, a commander could prepare his operations with the maximum prospect of success.

This extreme formalism, which left the movements of the enemy army out of account altogether, was rejected by the overwhelming majority of Bülow's contemporaries and successors. It is remarkable, indeed, that such a work could be published three years after the first Napoleonic campaign in Italy of 1796. Perhaps Bülow should be seen as the last interpreter of eighteenth-century warfare and eighteenth-century rationalism, at a moment when such rationalism, civil and military, was being swept aside by the *Sturm und Drang* of the revolutionary era. It was Bülow's contemporary Georg von Berenhorst whose *Betrachtungen über die Kriegskunst* (1797) heralded the revolution in military thinking which was to match the revolution in warfare. Bülow followed Lloyd in the 'classical' school of military theorists who sought in the chaos of war for clear, consistent, interdependent principles as a guide to understanding and action. Berenhorst was the standard-bearer of the romantics. How could there, he demanded, be any 'principles of war'? Before the invention of firearms it might have been legitimate to speak of them; but modern weapons introduced so great an element of the contingent, the uncertain, the accidental, the unknown, that to attempt scientific analysis was a waste of a sensible man's time. Great captains like Frederick the Great owed their success not to any system that could be copied by others, not to any grasp of 'principles', but to energy, to genius, and to luck. The artificiality of the Frederician 'system' (which he compared unfavourably and inaccurately with the alleged naturalness and simplicity of the American tactics in the War of Independence), indeed the whole institution of standing armies with their drill and their uniforms, had had its day. To military affairs, in fact, Berenhorst brought a Rousseauite, a Wordsworthian demand for 'simplicity, naturalness, clarity and truth'.[1]

The nineteenth century thus opened with two extreme statements of opposing views in a dialectic whose resolution should be the ambition of every serious military theorist. Bülow and Berenhorst were soon to be displaced by two very much abler and more influential thinkers. The eighteenth-century tradition of precise operational analysis, based on logistical needs and topographical limitations, was to be transmitted to the armies of Europe and North America by General Antoine Henri Jomini (1779–1869); while the emphasis on war as the realm of the uncertain and unpredictable, a matching not so much of intelligence as of will, personality, and moral fibre, was to inspire the work of General Carl Maria von Clausewitz (1780–1831) and his yet more influential successors – Moltke, Foch, and the generals of the first World War.

Both Jomini and Clausewitz were far too experienced as soldiers and wise as thinkers to underrate the arguments of the opposing school of thought. In defining the relationship

[1] Jähns, op. cit., III, 2,130.

of the theory of war to its practice they wrote in much the same terms.

> Of all the theories on the art of war [wrote Jomini][1] the only reasonable one is that which, based on the study of military history, lays down a certain number of regulating principles but leaves the greater part of the general conduct of a war to natural genius, without binding it with dogmatic rules. On the contrary, nothing is more likely to kill this natural genius and allow error to triumph than these pedantic theories, based on the false notion that war is a positive science and that all its operations can be reduced to infallible calculations. Yet the metaphysical and sceptical publications of certain writers succeed no better in persuading us that no rules of war exist, for their writings do absolutely nothing to disprove the maxims based on the most brilliant feats of modern war and justified even by the analyses of those who think they are disproving them.

> As a general rule [admitted Clausewitz],[2] whenever an *activity* is for the most part occupied with the same object over and over again, with the same ends and means, although there may be trifling alterations and a corresponding number of varieties of combination, such things are capable of becoming a subject of study for the reasoning faculties. But such study is just the most essential part of every *theory*, and has a peculiar title to that name. . . . If theory investigates the subjects which constitute war; if it separates more distinctly that which at first sight seems amalgamated; if it explains fully the property of the means; if it shows their probable effects; if it makes evident the nature of objects; if it brings to bear all over the field of war the light of essentially critical investigation – then it has fulfilled the chief duty of its province. It becomes then a guide to him who wishes to make himself acquainted with war from books. . . . It should educate the mind of the future leader in war, or rather guide him in his self-instruction, but not accompany him to the field of battle.

[1] Baron de Jomini, *Précis de l'Art de la Guerre* (Brussels, 1841), I, p. 12. Hereinafter cited as *Précis*.
[2] Carl Maria von Clausewitz, tr. Col. J. J. Graham, *On War* (London, 1949), I, pp. 107–8.

But this acknowledgement of common ground was little more than a salute between two duellists. Each attacked the ideas of the other by implication, if not specifically. Clausewitz gave short shrift to Jomini's basic principles: 'To see the whole secret of the Art of War in the formula, *in a certain time, at a certain point, to bring up superior masses* – was a restriction overruled by the force of realities.'[1] Jomini loftily countered: 'If M. le général Clausewitz had been as often as I have myself in a position to ask these questions and see them answered, he would not have so many doubts about the effectiveness of theories of war based on principles, for theories alone can guide us to such solutions.' Indeed in the whole of Clausewitz's 'scholarly labyrinth', he maintained, he had been unable to find anything except 'a small number of illuminating ideas and noteworthy articles'.[2]

Jomini's taunt was, of course, quite uncalled for. He may have seen more action than had Clausewitz, but not very much more. Clausewitz had weathered the opening campaigns of the Revolutionary Wars in 1792–95 as a young ensign, and the concluding ones in Germany and at Waterloo as Chief of Staff to an Army Corps; but his service had had long interruptions with the eleven-year peace between Prussia and France after 1795, and the six years from his captivity as prisoner of war after the Jena campaign in 1806 to his enlistment with the Czar's armies in 1812. Jomini, having studied Bonaparte's early campaigns from his native Switzerland, had succeeded in exploiting the general disorder of the Napoleonic armies by getting himself attached to Marshal Ney's headquarters in the campaigns of Ulm in 1805, Jena in 1806, Eylau in 1807, and Spain in 1808, rising to the position of Chief of Staff while still retaining his Swiss nationality. He served in the Russian campaign as military governor, first of Vilna and then of Smolensk, and rejoined Ney for the campaign in Germany of 1813. A series of flaming personal rows such as had characterised his entire military service (he resigned altogether some fifteen times) led to his crossing to the allied camp in time for the battle of Leipzig and the subsequent invasion of France in 1814. His opportunities for observing Napoleonic warfare at first hand

[1] Op. cit., I, p. 98.　　　　　　　　　[2] *Précis*, pp. 10, 195.

were thus almost unrivalled; and he was able in his subsequent writings to put them to good effect.[1]

Jomini began to write in 1803. The study of the campaigns of Frederick the Great and of the young Bonaparte had revealed to him, he believed, precisely those fundamental Newtonian principles of strategy for which eighteenth-century theorists had sought in vain. These consisted, first, 'in directing the mass of one's forces successively on to the decisive points in the theatre of war, and so far as possible against the communications of the enemy without disrupting one's own'; secondly, 'in manœuvring so as to engage this concentration of forces only against fractions of the enemy's strength'; thirdly, on the battlefield, to concentrate the bulk of one's forces at the decisive point, or against the section of the enemy line which one wished to overwhelm; and finally to ensure not only that one's forces were concentrated at the decisive point, 'but that they [were] sent forward with vigour and concentration, so as to produce a simultaneous result'.[2]

One has only to compare Jomini's work with that of any of his predecessors – always with the exception of Lloyd – to appreciate the clarity of his insight. He did indeed have some claim to be the Newton for whom the military world had waited for so long. As for his own contributions to the Napoleonic campaigns, since he devoted the rest of a long life to touching up his image for posterity, retailing to credulous disciples how his advice alone had saved Ney and others from repeated disaster and how their ignoring it had consistently led to failure, it is difficult to distinguish truth from auto-hagiography. There is certainly enough independent evidence to indicate that he really did understand Napoleon's mind well enough to anticipate the movements of the French Army both in the Marengo campaign of 1800 and the Jena campaign of 1806, and that his analytic abilities awoke the respect of Napoleon himself.[3] Yet even the most respect-

[1] Ferdinand Lecomte, *Le Général Jomini, sa vie et ses écrits* (Paris, 1869), *passim*.

[2] *Précis*, p. 53.

[3] See, e.g., de Montholon, *Mémoires pour servir à l'histoire de France sous Napoléon* (Paris, 1823), I, and Gourgaud, *Sainte-Hélène, journal inédit* (Paris, 1889). But see also E. Carrias, *La Pensée militaire allemande* (1948) for a more critical view.

ful accounts of Jomini's career cannot conceal his weaknesses; and any contribution that he may have made to the success of French arms must have been counterbalanced by an intellectual arrogance and an inability to co-operate with his colleagues which would have made his presence at a busy headquarters almost intolerable. Jomini attributed the coolness which increasingly surrounded him, and his failure to achieve more brilliant successes, to the personal malice of Berthier, Napoleon's Chief of Staff; but even if such an element was present, it is not difficult to sympathise with the attitude of Berthier, wrestling with the multifarious problems of a huge and swiftly-moving Army, towards the dogmatic over-simplifications of the young Swiss theorist.[1] Armies, to quote Lloyd once more, are composed of *men*: great corporations whose functioning is limited not only by the frictions engendered by administrative shortcomings, natural hazards, inadequate information and human fear, but by rivalries, ambitions and an institutional inertia which it requires great qualities of character to overcome. These factors had – and have – to be understood if they are to be mastered; and it was Clausewitz, not Jomini, who rightly emphasised how essential such knowledge of human weakness must be to those who would conduct war.

It is understandable that the reputation of Jomini should have been increasingly overshadowed by that of his great rival. The Clausewitzian emphasis on *will* accorded well with the romanticism of the mid-nineteenth century. His emphasis on the Battle fitted the Social-Darwinian ideas which became current towards the century's close; while in our own day his reiterated emphasis on war as a political act is particularly relevant to the problems of a nuclear age. Yet in practice the influence of Jomini has been no less than that of Clausewitz; for it is in Jominian rather than in Clausewitzian terms that soldiers are trained to think. His *Précis de l'Art de la Guerre*, first published in 1837, brought together in lucid and compact form the lessons he had scattered throughout his earlier works on the campaigns of Frederick and Napoleon,[2] and it

[1] John R. Elting, 'Jomini: Disciple of Napoleon', *Military Affairs*, xxvii (Spring 1964).

[2] Most of Jomini's histories are comprised in his *Traité des*

is doubtful whether a more methodical and comprehensive guide to the mechanics of military operations has ever been written. Military academies teaching the complicated craft of war would find Clausewitz a bewildering guide for busy young officers; but Jomini's *Précis* provided a ready-made outline for the staff-courses which the development of nine-teenth-century warfare was making increasingly necessary for the armies of Europe and North America. Jomini person-ally shaped the syllabus of the new Military Academy founded in St Petersburg by Nicholas I;[1] his ideas, particu-larly as transmitted through Sir Edward Bruce Hamley's monumental *Operations of War*, provided the starting-point for such British officers as were prepared to interest them-selves in *la grande guerre*; one can trace his categories in the work of many French theorists such as Derrécagaix and Pierron; while as for the United States, according to one authority, 'It has been said with good reason that many a Civil War general went into battle with a sword in one hand and Jomini's *Summary of the Art of War* in the other . . . Jomini's writings were the means by which Napoleonic techniques were transfused into the military thought of the Civil War, which was so important in the development of basic patterns of modern battlefield procedure.'[2]

The *Précis* was, in short, the greatest military text-book of the nineteenth century. It can still be studied with profit, and not by soldiers alone. Like Clausewitz – perhaps indeed in imitation of him – Jomini understood that war was an instrument of policy, and varied in its nature according to the degree of national feeling or interest involved. His first chapter is devoted to this question of *politique de guerre*, the various kinds of war in which a nation can engage: ideo-logical, economic, popular; to defend the balance of power, to assist allies, to assert or defend rights; with all the different demands they each made. In his second chapter he dealt with *politique militaire*, or domestic questions of military

grandes opérations militaires (8 vols., 1804–10) and his *Histoire critique des guerres de la Révolution* (15 vols., 1816–24).

[1] Lecomte, op. cit., p. 238.

[2] Lt.-Col. J. D. Hittle, *Jomini and his Summary of the Art of War* (Harrisburg, Pa., 1947), p. 2.

policy; and on all these matters, so relevant to our own times, his comments are particularly interesting. How does one preserve the *morale* of an Army in peacetime? How does one ensure an adequate expenditure on defence? How should one organise recruitment and reserves? How should wars be financed? Above all, in the absence of a sovereign such as Napoleon or Frederick who could command his own armies, what arrangements should be made for command? A sovereign who lacked military ability should, insisted Jomini, keep well away from his armies, where his presence could only do harm. He would embarrass the field commander, and 'if the Army was outflanked, cut off from its communications and compelled to cut its way out, what sad consequences would result from the presence of the monarch at head-quarters!'[1] In 1870 they certainly did. Rather, command should be given to 'a man of experience and courage, bold in battle and unshakeable in danger', with, as chief of staff, 'a man of great ability, straightforward and loyal, with whom the Supreme Commander can live in harmony';[2] the exact pattern, in fact, of high command as it was to develop in the twentieth century.

The actual conduct of war Jomini divided into Strategy, Grand Tactics (the conduct of battles), Logistics, Engineering (narrowly defined as siege warfare) and Minor Tactics. About the last two he had little to say, and his comments on Grand Tactics are significant primarily in a Napoleonic context. It was his writings on logistics and on strategy which were to have a more lasting relevance. Under 'logistics', which he defined as *l'art pratique de mouvoir les armées*, he included all the responsibilities of the General Staff. They comprised the preparation of all material of war; the drawing up of orders for alternative contingencies; the ordering of all troop movements; the collection of intelligence; the organisation of supply and transport; the establishment of camps, depots and magazines; the organisation of medical and signal services; and the provision of reinforcements to the front line. His stress on this branch of warfare reflected his experiences in the Napoleonic wars. Napoleonic operations, he wrote, 'depended on clever strategic calculations, but their

1 *Précis*, p. 43.   2 Ibid., p. 46.

execution was undoubtedly a masterpiece of logistics'.[1] Allowing for the complicating factor introduced by rail transport, Jomini's analysis remained valid as a basis for a manual of staff duties until the outbreak of the first World War.

It was in the field of strategy, however, that the famous Jominian 'principles' operated. Strategy he defined, indeed, as 'the art of directing the greater part of the forces of an Army on to the most important point of a theatre of war, or of a zone of operations. Tactics is the art of putting them into action at the moment and at the decisive point of a battlefield on which the decisive *choc* must occur'.[2] From this mandatory principle, all strategic calculations flowed. The decisive point must be discerned, and a line of operations chosen leading to it from the Army's base. 'The great art of choosing these lines of operations', he insisted, 'consists in making oneself master of the enemy lines of communication without compromising one's own.'[3] The choice of a line of operations thus depended as much on the dispositions of the enemy as it did on the lie of the land. Various combinations of lines were possible – concentric, eccentric, interior, exterior – according to circumstances. Possible also were various kinds of 'decisive point'. One might aim at the enemy flank and thence at his line of retreat. One might try to break through a weakly held centre. One might advance successively from point to point as had Bonaparte in 1796. And much of the skill in choosing one's line of operations lay in spreading them over as wide a front as possible, so that the enemy could not anticipate where one proposed to concentrate for the decisive blow.[4]

All these observations were simple, practical, and kept down to earth by frequent reference to the campaigns of Napoleon and of Frederick the Great. Unfortunately Jomini's analytic *penchant* led him farther into the field of abstract reasoning than his practical experience of war should have permitted him to venture. It may be legitimate, but it is also dangerous, for a theorist to think of a theatre of war in terms of a 'chessboard'. Round the fairly simple conceptual frame-

[1] Ibid., p. 190. [2] Ibid., p. 228.
[3] Ibid., p. 61. [4] Ibid., pp. 106–7.

work of 'bases' and 'lines of operations' which he had inherited from Lloyd and Bülow, Jomini embroidered a complex pattern of strategic lines, strategic points, objective points, strategic positions, strategic fronts, operational fronts, pivots of operations, pivots of manœuvre, zones of operations and lines of communication, each defined with the precision of a medieval schoolman and fitted into a general synthesis in a manner calculated to baffle the simple and fascinate the worst sort of intellectual soldier. It is not far-fetched to see the influence of this aspect of Jomini's thinking in the ponderous and pedantic conceptions of Halleck during the early years of the American Civil War.

This cumbrous analytic vocabulary is the more unfortunate since it obscures what was perhaps the most important legacy which Jomini left to future military thinkers. Like Clausewitz – indeed like anyone who had lived through those tremendous Napoleonic decades – he rejected the eighteenth-century belief, shared by Saxe and Lloyd, that campaigns could be won without battles. He did not labour the point as did Clausewitz; but in all his strategic analyses the objective of operations is always the enemy army, and all geographical objectives were means to that end, without intrinsic value of their own. On the other hand, unlike Clausewitz and his disciples, unlike, in particular, Moltke, he saw the battle in a broader context than that of a straightforward and massive conflict of forces, a 'bloody and destructive measuring of the strength of forces physical and moral' with whoever has the greater amount of both left at the end being the conqueror.[1] For Jomini it mattered *where* the battle was fought, and *how* the battle was fought. It could be delivered in advantageous or disadvantageous circumstances. It could lead to decisive or indecisive results, depending on the relative position of the respective lines of operation. Above all its conduct, no less than the calculations leading to its engagement, was a matter of skill as well as of resolution – of selecting the decisive moment, and the decisive point, for launching one's reserves, of orchestrating flanking threats with frontal attack. Jomini had seen enough battles to know how difficult this could be. 'Battles', he admitted, 'often escape all scientific

[1] *On War*, I, p. 246.

control and provide us with essentially dramatic acts, in which personal qualities, moral inspirations and a thousand other causes sometimes play the leading part . . . in short, everything that can be termed the poetry and metaphysics of war will always influence their results.'[1] Nevertheless, a sound grasp of elementary principles would always provide a guide through the confusion, and make victory depend no less on wise judgement than on simple resolution and on chance.

This Jominian concept of the battle as intrinsic to operations yet subject to intelligent control was to be eclipsed by the doctrine, which Moltke and others read into Clausewitz, that the opposing army should be an objective which one attacked in the strongest possible force, relying upon greater numbers or greater moral strength to see one through. Moltke defined his strategy for 1870 as being simply 'to seek out the main forces of the enemy and attack them wherever we find them'.[2] The French Army's Plan XVII in 1914 was equally unsubtle. The Schlieffen Plan itself was certainly a manœuvre in true Napoleonic style, aiming as it did at crushing the enemy's flank, seizing his lines of communication and forcing him to battle under circumstances where a defeat would be decisive. Without such a rapid decision Schlieffen had foreseen that the weapons and the military institutions of the twentieth century could only produce bankruptcy and deadlock. So, in a way, had Jomini himself, three-quarters of a century earlier. The Napoleonic campaigns had shown, he pointed out in 1837, that 'distance no longer protects a country from invasion, and States who wish to insure against it need a good system of fortresses and defensive lines, a good system of reserves and military institutions, in short a sound military policy. That is why peoples everywhere are organising themselves into militias to serve as reserves to the active forces, which will raise the strength of armies to an increasingly formidable level; and the greater the number in armies the more necessary will be a system of rapid operations and prompt decisions.'[3]

[1] *Précis*, p. 227.
[2] *Moltkes Militärische Korrespondenz aus den Dienstschriften des Krieges 1870–71* (Berlin, 1896), p. 120.
[3] *Précis*, p. 105.

But the failure of the Schlieffen plan showed that the application of Jomini's principles to an age of mass armies backed by railways and armed with twentieth-century fire-arms presented technical difficulties which no one yet knew how to overcome. The classical principles of war seemed irrelevant to the requirements of trench-warfare. The 'romantic' qualities of moral strength and endurance came, for four long years, into their own. But out of that most tragic of conflicts, in which the Clausewitzian Battle acquired a fright-ful, Moloch-like existence of its own unrelated to strategic or political objectives, the new techniques were born which made it possible to think once more in terms of movement and manœuvre, of battle as an instrument and not an end, of generalship as an intelligent activity requiring skill and subtlety as well as moral resolution and logistical expertise, of war as the servant of policy and not its master. It was time, in fact, for a revival of classical military thinking; and that revival came in England, with the work of J. F. C. Fuller and B. H. Liddell Hart. It was appropriate that the cycle should recommence in the country where, with the writings of Lloyd a century and a half earlier, it had originally begun.

2 Waterloo

'The battle of Waterloo,' wrote the Duke of Wellington within a few months of his victory, 'is undoubtedly one of the most interesting events of modern times, but the Duke entertains no hopes of ever seeing an account of all its details which shall be true.' This authoritative admonition should have effectively deterred historians, but it has not. An account of their conflicts and contradictions, British, French and German, would make a fascinating history in itself. And they are quite right to go on studying it. Many battles have provided better material for the connoisseur of tactics, but few have been more dramatic in their course and even fewer more decisive in their results.

Consider the context. Europe had been torn by revolutionary turmoil and recurrent war for a quarter of a century. Her social system had been shaken to its foundations. Political institutions which had stood firm for a thousand years had been overthrown. Every belief, every authority, every standard had been called in question as the Revolution had swept across the Continent in the wake of the conquering French armies. At last the tide had ebbed. The forces of the old order, reinforced by new national feelings, had rallied. In a two-year campaign the Allied Powers had beaten the French back to their own frontiers and forced their daemonic Emperor into exile; and their statesmen had assembled at Vienna, like village elders after a volcanic eruption, to plan the reconstruction of their devastated community. But their planning was premature. The volcano was not extinct. On 1st March 1815 Napoleon Bonaparte again landed in France, and within a few days, without firing a shot, had re-established the régime which had troubled all Europe.

The returned Emperor professed himself a reformed character. He knew that his power was based less on the enthusiasm of his active supporters than on the sullen acquiescence of an exhausted population – one unwilling and quite unable to face again the sacrifices involved in further campaigns against a Europe in arms. Napoleon had now to assume once more the rôle which had won him support at the very outset of his political career, as the bringer of peace, order, and moderate reform. His professions were greeted within France with wary scepticism; beyond her borders they commanded no belief whatever. Within a fortnight the Powers at Vienna had pronounced Napoleon to be *hors le loi,* and within a month they had reconstituted the Treaty of Chaumont of 1814, and pledged themselves – Great Britain, Russia, Prussia, and the Austrian Empire – each to maintain an army of 150,000 men in the field until Napoleon was overthrown.

The assembling of these forces was no easy matter. The Austrians were campaigning in Italy against that troublesome Napoleonic survival Prince Murat. The Russians were, as usual, quietly suppressing the Poles. The best of the small British force in the Peninsula had been shipped off to deal with the bellicose Americans. Wellington's dismay on his arrival in Brussels in April when he discovered the quality and the quantity of the British force assembling under his command is well known. 'I have got an infamous army,' he wrote to Lord Stewart on 8th May, 'very weak and ill-equipped, and a very inexperienced staff. In my opinion they are doing nothing in England. They have not raised a man; they have not called out the militia either in England or Ireland; are unable to send me anything.' There was no shortage of gilded young men with influence at the Horse Guards to claim positions on his staff, but the total number of British troops at his disposal by June – and those mainly inexperienced depot men – was 31,253. The newly founded Kingdom of the Netherlands provided nearly as many again, but since such of them as had fought at all had done so under the standards of the French Empire, their value had to be considered doubtful. Troops from Britain's client North German States, almost all new levies, brought the total of the troops under Wellington's command to 93,717 – a long way short of the 150,000 guaranteed.

Nevertheless Wellington's letters from Brussels through

April and May breathed an air of complete confidence. The Prussian forces under the courageous and experienced leadership of Marshal Blücher and General Gneisenau were building up on his left, round Namur and Liège, to 120,000 men. 'I am inclined to believe,' wrote the Duke on 8th May, 'that Blücher and I are so well united, and so strong that the enemy cannot do us much mischief.' Beyond the Prussians, assembling in Luxemburg and on the Rhine, was an Austrian army under Prince Schwarzenberg, 344,000 strong; while Barclay de Tolly and 200,000 Russians lay behind them in Germany. These were awe-inspiring figures, and Wellington had some reason to write as he did to Metternich on 20th May: 'With the force which is assembling in all quarters, it appears to me impossible that with common prudence and arrangements we should fail in our military operations.'

Such would have been a reasonable assessment of the situation if the French armies had been commanded by anyone but Napoleon. His forces were limited not only by the time needed to raise and equip them but by the political impossibility of reintroducing his old massive conscriptions. He had to rely very largely on the old soldiers prepared to return to his service, and on younger volunteers; and by April, after garrisoning all the French frontiers, he had only 124,000 troops available for operations in the north. But he had faced such odds before, and his army was composed, like those which had first brought him glory, of fiery enthusiasts. There could be no annihilating victory for him, no Austerlitz or Jena. But a series of brilliant limited victories against detached parts of the cumbrous Allied forces, victories such as he had won in Italy in 1796 and 1797, might have the same effect as had those early successes: reviving the confidence of the French people in his star, and discouraging his opponents sufficiently to accept a reasonable peace. Wellington, indeed, divined Napoleon's intentions very clearly: they were to force the Allies out of Brussels and scatter the restored monarchs both of France and of the Netherlands in undignified flight. 'Ce serait,' wrote the bilingual Duke on 5th April, 'un coup terrible à l'opinion publique en France et ici; et, selon son allure ordinaire, la nouvelle de ses succès serait connue par toute la France, tandis que celle des revers, qui pourraient en suivre, serait cachée à tout le monde.'

But by the beginning of June the Duke was deep in his plans for a massive invasion of France by all the allied armies simultaneously. The fortress barrier along the French frontiers, and the reluctance of the Allies, difficult to understand in our ruthless age, to send cavalry patrols into French territory when there was no formal state of war, enabled Napoleon to concentrate his forces in secrecy a few miles from the Allied outposts. The Duke assumed that any French attack would come along the great road through Mons, which would threaten his communications with his base at Antwerp. In fact Napoleon struck further east, along the road from Charleroi, at the point of junction between the Anglo-Dutch and the Prussian forces. Such a tactic was as simple as it was effective. The Germans a century later were to repeat it, unsuccessfully in March 1918, successfully in May 1940. A British Army operating on the Continent would always, in dire peril, fall back towards the sea. Its allies would fall back equally naturally along their own communications to the interior of their own land. A wedge inserted at the crucial point could split the allied front into two halves, each of which could then be dealt with in detail.

The French Army crossed the frontier north of Charleroi on 15th June, and next day there began a three-day battle in which the defence of the heights of Mont-St Jean on the afternoon of 18th June – the 'Battle of Waterloo' of popular history – was only the climax. It took Wellington twelve hours to divine Napoleon's intentions. Obsessed with the threat to his communications, he first ordered a concentration on his right wing before Mons – orders which the Netherlands troops manning the outposts on his left prudently ignored. Holding the vital cross-roads of Quatre Bras where the Charleroi road crossed the main east–west route for lateral communication between the Allies, the Prince of Orange's forces could see only too well where the French were really attacking. So could the Prussians; and Marshal Blücher, as soon as the news reached him, ordered his entire army to concentrate forward at once to give immediate battle to the invaders. Only in the evening, at the Duchess of

Richmond's famous ball, did a despatch from the governor of Mons, reporting the absence of any French forces on his front, shake the Duke's imperturbability and led him to exclaim, with endearing frankness, 'Humbugged, by God!'

Napoleon had thus secured all the advantages of the offensive, precipitating battle at a point and at a moment of his own choosing. Had he been younger and better served, the result might have been a victory as complete as those of 1796, and he would have entered Brussels in triumph within forty-eight hours. But nineteen years had taken their toll. He tired more easily, took longer to make vital decisions. To transfer these decisions into the necessary orders he no longer had the incomparable Berthier as his Chief of Staff, but only the inexperienced Soult. And of his two principal subordinates, Grouchy, in command of the right wing, was stolidly unimaginative, and Ney, on the left, was as notorious for his lack of tactical and strategical finesse as he was for his blazing personal courage. Gradually over the next three days these four men, through their blunders, miscalculations, misunderstandings and sheer inefficiency were to squander the advantage which they had so unexpectedly gained, until their whole army was swept in a terrific rout from the field of Waterloo.

For the 16th June Napoleon had ordered Ney to seize Quatre Bras while Grouchy on the right pressed the Prussian advance-guard back towards Sembloux. The French were then to concentrate against Wellington, forcing him out of Brussels, away from his allies and back towards the sea. Blücher's decision to accept battle on his forward lines changed all this. Seeing the whole Prussian force concentrate round the villages of Sombreffe and Ligny, Napoleon determined to destroy it on the spot. Grouchy was to attack it frontally; Ney, having cleared Wellington's troops from Quatre Bras, was to fall on its flank and rear. But Ney was curiously slow to move on Quatre Bras, and with every hour that passed more British and Netherland forces came hurrying up to hold this key position. By the afternoon, when Napoleon was ready to fall on the Prussians at Ligny, Ney was pinned down in a confused action which made it impossible for him to carry out the Emperor's orders. When one of his corps commanders, General d'Erlon, set off for Ligny in response to a direct summons from Napoleon, Ney imperiously summoned him back, with the well-known result that the wretched d'Erlon's corps took part in neither battle. In spite of heavy attacks, Quatre Bras remained in allied hands until nightfall, with losses totalling something over four thousand on each side. At Ligny the Prussian forces, subjected to the full fury of the classic Napoleonic assault, stood their ground until half-past seven in the evening, and then their centre gave way. But there was no rout. The wings held firm and withdrew in good order. The dreaded Napoleonic pursuit, more lethal than the battle itself, was not launched. Blücher, brought down and overlaid by his wounded horse, was temporarily missing on the battlefield, but Gneisenau's cool strategic insight did not desert him. Resisting the temptation to fall back eastward along his communications to Liège and Namur, he directed the retreating forces due north towards Wavre, where they could remain in touch with Wellington – a decision which the grateful Duke was later to describe as 'the decisive moment of the century'.

Wellington learned of the direction of his Allies' retreat next morning, 17th June, and at 10 o'clock ordered his own forces to fall back in step with them to the next, and last, defensive position before Brussels, on the ridge of Mont-St Jean some six miles south of the city. Privately he warned his friends in Brussels of his doubts whether he would be able to stand even there, and advised them to get ready to leave. The withdrawal was skilfully carried out. Lord Uxbridge (later the Marquess of Anglesey), whose cavalry brought up the rear, described it as 'The prettiest Field Day of Cavalry and Horse Artillery that I have ever witnessed'. But it was not until the afternoon that the French even began to pursue. Napoleon issued his orders only at 11 a.m., and then they were so ambiguously worded by Soult that Ney still did not move to the attack until the Emperor arrived at his headquarters in person. Grouchy was ordered to pursue the Prussians in the presumed direction of their retreat, eastward to Namur; which he did with a deliberation which must have made any cavalryman who remembered Murat speechless with exasperation. During the afternoon the hot thundery weather broke in a torrential rainstorm which soaked both armies to the skin and made further movement almost impossible. The rain lasted all night. Soaking, cold, sleepless and hungry, the British Army watched from its new positions as dawn broke on Sunday, 18th June; a day which they knew must be decisive for their own fortunes, if not for those of the civilised world.

Of the forces under his command, Wellington had assembled 67,661 men and 156 guns on the battlefield, leaving 17,000 guarding the lateral communications which ran off so vulnerably to his right. Napoleon outnumbered him with 71,947 men and 246 guns; but Wellington had all the advantage of a carefully selected and prepared defensive position to suit the tactics which he had perfected in the Peninsula. He deployed his forces, in his usual manner, on the reverse slope of the crest, where they would be relatively safe from artillery fire, and he protected the right flank and centre of his position by fortifying and strongly garrisoning, with the Brigade of Guards and the German Legion, the farm-houses of Hougoumont and La Haye Sainte. Heterogeneous as his forces were, they contained a precious nucleus of first-rate infantry, artillery and cavalry. He knew that the French tactics depended for their success on the moral impact of their assaulting columns rather than on fire-power or manœuvre; and with such tactics the stolid discipline of his regular forces, their carefully husbanded and directed firepower, above all his own cool head and calculating eye were well fitted to deal. Under the circumstances it was unwise of Napoleon to have attacked at all rather than have manœuvred him out of his position by threatening his vulnerable right flank; and Soult and some other commanders who had served in the Peninsular war tried to warn the Emperor that he was running an unnecessary risk. He even refused, until it was far too late, to recall Grouchy from his leisurely pursuit of the Prussians. 'Because you have been beaten by Wellington,' he told them cuttingly, 'you consider him a great general. And now I tell you that Wellington is a bad general, that the English are bad troops, and that this affair is nothing more serious than eating one's breakfast.'

It is pleasant for the victors to recall such hubristic pronouncements by the vanquished; but the Duke himself was later to confide in his brother: 'In all my life I have not experienced such anxiety, for I must confess that I have never been so close to defeat.' The result was certainly not a foregone conclusion. If the French had been able to attack earlier, if they had displayed as much skill in their assaults as they did courage, if they had committed their reserve at the crucial moment, Wellington's line might have broken; and all that Prussian intervention could have done would have been to ensure him a relatively undisturbed retreat. But the Duke was a lucky general as well as a prudent one. Strokes of unforeseen good fortune and the blunders of his adversaries were to play as vital a part in his victory as did the loyalty of his ally, his own skill on the battlefield and the resolute courage of his men.

The first stroke of good fortune was provided by the weather. The rain had stopped, but the ground was still soaking, and the French artillerymen doubted whether they could manœuvre their heavy pieces over it. Napoleon therefore postponed his assault for four hours, from 9 a.m. until 1 p.m., to give the ground time to dry. Meanwhile, as a diversion, General Reille's corps launched an assault on Hougoumont. But so stubbornly was it defended that the assault drew in an ever-increasing number of French troops, until it was the attacking forces themselves who were being diverted, and who remained diverted the entire day until the triumphant, fire-blackened survivors of the garrison emerged to send them packing in disorderly flight. Elsewhere on the battlefield, Wellington's troops stood to expectantly all morning and when at last the attack began, the troops of General von Bülow's Prussian corps were already beginning to appear on the extreme right of the French position.

It is a common British fallacy that the Prussians reached the battlefield of Waterloo only at nightfall, in time to carry out their victorious pursuit. In fact the Prussians' appearance at Chapelle-St Lambert led to Napoleon postponing, by half an hour, his very first attack on the main Anglo-Dutch positions; and the increasing pressure which they exerted on his right flank as the afternoon wore on affected all his plans for the assault. Of course Grouchy should have taken care of the

Prussians and if possible have prevented them from appearing on the battlefield at all. But Grouchy, as Napoleon had cause to know, needed the most precise of instructions before he did anything. Napoleon himself was aware from reports reaching him the previous evening, that at least some of the Prussian forces had moved north to Wavre and so were in a position to bring help to Wellington; but he did nothing about them until 10 o'clock on the 18th, when he ordered Grouchy to advance on Wavre from Gembloux, 'driving before you the Prussian Army which has taken that route'. This order itself was not very explicit: it did not make clear Grouchy's responsibility for preventing the Prussians from falling back on Wellington, and Grouchy certainly did not read any such meaning into it. The result was that by the evening of the 18th, thanks to Gneisenau's original orders after Ligny and the dynamic energy with which Blücher drove his troops to the sound of the guns, the Allied armies were fighting as a single unit on interior lines, while it was the French who were divided and vulnerable to separate defeat.

At 1.30 p.m. the French artillery at last opened fire on Wellington's line, and the French infantry moved forward to attack. In the day of the smooth-bore musket, frontal assaults were not the murderous and sterile manœuvres which they were to become forty years later, but they had, if they were to be successful, to be carried out with skill. The only infantry formation which ensured control and maintained *élan* during the assault was the column; but a column moving up to assault a defending line was vulnerable to every musket and cannon the defenders could bring to bear, while it could reply with only very few of its own. Such an assault was thus unlikely to succeed unless the defending infantry had first been worn down by prolonged artillery and skirmishing fire; or unless cavalry assaults had compelled them to form square, thus reducing by three-quarters the volume of fire they could bring to bear to the front. Only the careful co-ordination of the three classical arms could ensure the success of an assault against experienced troops.

But when the French assaulted Wellington's line, no such co-ordination was attempted. The preliminary cannonade had little effect on his sheltered troops; and when the French infantry came into the assault, 18,000 strong, they did so in the uniquely clumsy formation of divisional columns – 200 men wide, 24 ranks deep. With their beating drums and enthusiastic shouts of *Vive l'Empereur!* they were an impressive sight; but not in the eyes of the impassive veterans of the Peninsula who had dealt with this kind of thing before. Rising from their cover behind the crest, the British infantry poured volley after volley into the columns, checking them in confusion; and then Sir Thomas Picton's division and Lord Uxbridge's cavalry charged into the great mass of hesitant Frenchmen and sent them back helter-skelter to their own lines. Lord Uxbridge indeed lost control of his high-spirited cavalry – never the best-disciplined of arms – and much strength was dissipated in headlong and reckless pursuit which was to be badly needed a little later.

For Napoleon, increasingly anxious as von Bülow's attacks on his right flank grew heavier, now ordered Ney to settle the matter in short order; and Ney, rashly assuming Wellington's line to be on the point of collapse, did not wait to mount a fresh infantry assault but sent in three divisions of cavalry instead. Again, the sight of these close-packed horsemen bursting through the smoke was terrifyingly impressive. Again, as a tactical manœuvre, it was sterile. Wellington's infantry formed squares, his gunners leaving their pieces to take refuge inside, and the flood of horsemen surged and eddied between them like the sea boiling around the rocks of a promontory. Driven on to the defensive, the British and their allies could have done little at this moment to ward off an infantry assault; but none came in. The French did not even tow away or spike the abandoned British guns; and when eventually the British cavalry was able to chase the French horsemen back to their own positions, the British line reformed as solidly as before, in time to meet, and repulse, the infantry assault which Ney at last sent in.

But the strain on the British line was now beginning to tell as the repeated French attacks took their toll of casualties. 'I felt weary and worn out,' reported one participant, 'less from fatigue than anxiety. Our division, which had stood upwards of five thousand men at the commencement of the battle, had gradually dwindled down into a solitary line of skirmishers. The 27th Regiment were lying literally dead, in square, a few yards behind us. . . . I have never yet heard of a battle in which everyone was killed; but this seemed likely to be an exception as all were going by turns.' La Haye Sainte, the bastion which had for so long protected the British centre, at last fell to repeated assaults and the pressure on this part of Wellington's front became almost unendurable. Ney, from his experience of a score of battles, recognised the signs: his victim was ready for the *coup de grace*, the last great cannonade by massed guns directed mercilessly at the troops least able to endure it, the irresistible assault by the veterans of the Guard kept in reserve for just this moment, and the charge of triumphant cavalry through the gap with sabre and lance to break up the last traces of enemy co-ordination and to transform the battle into a terrible manhunt. He sent an urgent message to Napoleon asking for that most vital of all military decisions to be taken – the commitment of the reserve.

At this crucial moment the Emperor hesitated. He had fourteen battalions of the Guard still uncommitted; troops who considered themselves, with some reason, to be among the finest the world had ever seen. The British centre was crumbling; but so, at the village of Plancenoit, was his own right flank, before the Prussian attacks. How could he deal the *coup de grace* to the British when his own line was in danger of being rolled up? First the situation at Plancenoit had to be restored, and two battalions of the Old Guard were sent off to do it. Then it would be the turn of the British. So Wellington gained another vital breathing space; and it was now, between six and seven in the evening, that the Prussian forces of General Zieten's corps came up to prolong his left wing. The moral effect of the appearance of these fresh troops on the weary British was as great as it was on the no less weary French. Wellington was able to reshuffle his battle line, strengthening his vulnerable centre. The crisis of the battle was passed.

When at last Napoleon did send his Guard in to assault – and he would still spare only five battalions – they had to deal, not with men on the point of collapse, but with troops who, though sorely tried, were now quietly confident of their ability to deal with any further attempts that the enemy might make against them. The last of these assaults, launched by the finest troops the Napoleonic Empire could raise, was the most impressive of all; but no less impressive was the red wall of infantry of which they suddenly caught sight as, at a word from Wellington, the Brigade of Guards rose to its feet from behind the crest where it was lying. There was a moment's pause; then the British volleys crashed out. The French troops checked, tried to deploy, and as they did so the Light Brigade and the guardsmen charged shouting into their confused ranks. The French broke and fled before their bayonets, and over the hillside there echoed the incredulous cry, the death knell of an entire epoch: *La Garde recule!*

This was the moment for which the Duke had been waiting. Away to his left the Prussians were already beginning to drive the French before them. Raising his hat in the air, he gave the signal for his own line to advance, and the British, Dutch and German troops surged down the slopes which they had defended so gallantly. 'This movement,' wrote an observer, 'carried us clear of the smoke and, to people who had been for so many hours enveloped in darkness, in the midst of destruction, and naturally anxious about the result of the day, the scene which met the eye conveyed a feeling of more exquisite gratification than can be conceived. It was a fine summer's evening, just before sunset. The French were flying in a confused mass. British lines were seen in close pursuit and in admirable order, as far as the eye could reach to the right, while the plain to the left was full of Prussians.' The battle was over; now the pursuit could begin; and for this task the Prussian cavalry, with eight years of humiliation to avenge, was eagerly standing by.

The battle had been as murderous as it had been decisive. Wellington had lost nearly a quarter of his entire force, 15,000 men, and as he perused the casualty returns he felt no temptation to rejoice in his victory. Blücher lost 7,000 men in addition to the 16,000 casualties he had suffered at Ligny. As for the French, their losses totalled 25,000, excluding 8,000 prisoners who fell into Allied hands, and even Napoleon realised that there could be no question of fighting on. With the sole basis of his support in France shattered, he abdicated once more, entrusting himself to those of his enemies who had the least cause to be vindictive – the British; who had, however, the best facilities for keeping him, for the rest of his life, out of harm's way.

It fell to Wellington to preside over the restoration of the Bourbons and the enforcement of the new peace. Courteous, dry, commonsensical, he seemed the embodiment of those rationalist certainties of the eighteenth century which men were trying, uselessly, to restore. Waterloo had set him on a pedestal in the eyes of all Europe, but it was his own wisdom that kept him there for thirty-seven more years. The respect and gratitude felt for him, when at last he died in 1852, was no less than it had been when, in 1815, he was greeted as the hero who had banished twenty-five years of nightmare for ever.

3 Wellington and the British Army

In 1814 the Duke of Wellington enjoyed among the victorious Powers in Europe a prestige which in this country is taken very much as a matter of course. Yet to her continental allies the part which Britain had played in the downfall of Napoleon was not altogether evident. The destruction of French fleets and the acquisition of lucrative French colonies seemed marginal if not irrelevant activities to Germans, Austrians and Russians who had had to face the *Grande Armée*. The recurrent failure of British forces to establish themselves in the Low Countries or the Mediterranean could arouse nothing but scorn. But the successes of the Army in the Peninsula, limited as they were and secondary as was the front on which they were achieved, could not be ignored. Wellington's little Army was like a terrier with its teeth firmly sunk in a boar's hind leg: doing no serious damage, but maddening and impossible to shake off. When in 1813 he secured at Vitoria a victory such as no allied force had achieved over a major Napoleonic Army since the Austrian defensive triumph at Aspern in 1809, Britain could again hold up her head, and Wellington entered France with as much right as his allies to a conqueror's laurel crown. He went to Vienna, moreover, as the representative of a Power tainted with no suspicion of duplicity, as was Austria, nor of revolutionary infection, as was Prussia, nor, as was Russia, of territorial ambitions in Europe. At Waterloo he gave the revived monster a dramatic and final *coup de grâce*. Thus it was at his feet that the princes of Europe poured, in enthusiastic token of their gratitude, that treasury of orders, marshals' batons, plate, dinner services, pictures and *objets d'art* which now lies, all too little visited, at Apsley House.

The Duke, to the Powers at Vienna, represented a country which, untouched by invasion and firmly controlling its own civil strife, seems to enshrine all the massive certainties of

the eighteenth century. Courteous, immaculate, humorous
and shrewd, Wellington himself was their very embodiment.
And the army which he led belonged quite as surely to that
age. Napoleon's continental adversaries had been able to
make head against him only by adapting themselves to the
military revolution which the French armies had set on foot.
They also had to adopt measures of conscription, abandoning, with far-reaching political consequences, the small and
expert professional armies of the eighteenth century with
their noble officers and their ranks recruited from the social
misfits of their lands. But the British Army of 1815, though
purged of its greatest abuses by the herculean efforts of its
Commander-in-Chief, the Duke of York, was still in essence
that of 1793. There was no question of it representing a
cross-section of the population in which the sons of the
literate, professional and mercantile classes served side by
side with those of gentry, craftsmen and common labourers.
The ranks were still made up of long-serving volunteers who
had said goodbye virtually for ever to civil life. They were
tempted in by the immediate lure of bounty money; and
once in they endured appalling hardships, not so much on
active service – which must at times have come as a blessed
relief – as in disease-ridden tropical garrisons where they
might languish for twenty years or more, and in the fœtid
squalor of overcrowded barracks at home. Drink was their
only solace and escape, and discipline could be enforced
only by plentiful application of the lash. Service under such
conditions – and they were the normal conditions of the
eighteenth century – attracted only the desperate. The Army
was regarded as a midden fit only for outcasts, and the red
coat was a badge less of honour than of shame.

The officers who commanded these men were neither
skilled professionals nor dedicated idealists. The only qualifi-
cation required for a commission was the money to buy it
and the approval of the colonel of the regiment; and promotion went entirely by the ability to purchase higher rank.
There was some professional improvement as the war pro-
ceeded; but for the majority of officers the regiment was an
agreeable club, a uniformed extension of Bucks' or Boodles',
and a campaign was equally an extension of the fox-hunting

with which they normally passed the winter. It was not a system which lent itself either to professional efficiency or to hierarchical subordination. 'Nobody in the British Army,' complained Wellington in the Peninsula, 'ever reads a regulation or an order as if it were to be a guide for his conduct or in other manner than an amusing novel; and the consequence is that when complicated arrangements are to be carried into execution . . . every *gentleman* proceeds according to his fancy.'

This agreeable Whig anarchy applied not only to the officers but to the regiments in which they served. The colonel owned his regiment, much as the officer owned his commission; and his control of it was all the more absolute in that he was responsible, not to one hierarchical superior, but to a multiplicity of authorities, each of whom dealt with a different aspect of its activities. Questions of discipline and promotion in cavalry and infantry came under the Commander-in-Chief. In the artillery and the engineers they were the business of the Master-General of the Ordnance, whose further responsibilities for the provision of weapons and ammunition to both services were much the same as those, in the Second World War, of the Ministry of Supply. Questions of expenditure were the responsibility of the Secretary at War. Transport and supply – the continental *intendance* – came under the control of the Treasury. Once troops left the United Kingdom they became the responsibility of the Secretary of State for War and the Colonies; while the Home Secretary supervised the auxiliary forces at home – the Militia, the Yeomanry and the Volunteers. The delay and inefficiency which resulted from this chaos of overlapping jurisdictions finds its monument in the melancholy succession of humiliations which the British Army suffered, from the early disasters of the American War of Independence to the notorious expedition to Walcheren. It was a sombre background against which the genius of Wellington was to shine all the more bright.

Yet unsatisfactory as was this force, there was little call, save on grounds of economy, to reform it. Its inefficiency was held to be a better guarantee of British liberties than its strength. English politicians, partly haunted by confused legends of the paid force which James II had accumulated to overawe his subjects, and more immediately fearful of any increase in the patronage at the disposal of the Crown, clung stubbornly to the belief that the country did not need a standing Army. It was a view which Wellington himself shared and repeatedly expressed. The Navy, he once declared to the House of Commons, was 'the Characteristic and Constitutional force of Britain, but the Army was a new force arising out of the extraordinary exigencies of modern times.' Any improvement in the administration and efficiency of the Army was seen by the House of Commons as a further addition to that power of the Executive which had, as Mr Dunning put it, increased, was increasing and ought to be diminished. Nor would that be the only danger. Any simplification must work to the advantage either of the civil element in military administration or of the Commander-in-Chief. The principal civil officer was the Secretary at War, who in 1783 had obtained sole responsibility for military expenditure. The office of Commander-in-Chief was held, from 1798 until his death in 1827, by the Duke of York. To pose so brutally the issue of who should control the Army, Crown or Parliament, would be to open wounds which even after 150 years were not totally healed. The very confusion of military administration enabled the British to evade a decision, and so long as the Navy held the seas, no urgent military necessity forced them to make one.

Such was the Army in which the Duke of Wellington was to pass his life, and he had no illusions about it. When asked how he learned his profession he replied, 'I learned more by seeing our own faults, and the defects of our system in the campaign of Holland, than anywhere else. . . . The infantry regiments, taken individually, were in as good and proper hands as they are now but the system was wretched.' But he did not repine. He worked within the limitations set him, and made such limited improvements as he could. In the Peninsula, where he was able to gather the many threads of 'the system' into his own hands, he made it work with unprecedented efficiency. He accepted the strategic limitations of a pre-revolutionary army, with its need for the most scrupulous attention to supply; an attention which had slowed the campaigns of the eighteenth century to snail's pace, and from which the rough and ready methods of the French had broken triumphantly loose. Wellington, trained in his Indian campaigns to be meticulous about these details, did not attempt to copy his enemies. The French Army starved and Wellington's did not; and 'it is very singular,' commented the Duke acidly, 'that in relating Napoleon's campaigns this has never been clearly shown in anything like its full extent.'

So long as the Army was fed it remained an adequate weapon in Wellington's hands, for all the indisciplined insolence of its officers and the drunken barbarism of its men. The defects of both maddened him. Despatch after despatch from the Peninsula complained of the quarrels, the insubordination and the inefficiency of his officers. 'The croaking which already prevails in the Army,' he wrote in September 1810, 'and particularly about headquarters, is disgraceful to us as a nation and does infinite mischief to the cause'; and he confessed bitterly 'that a part of my business, and not the most easy, is to prevent discussion and disputes between the officers under my command.' The insubordination, reminiscent of the quarrelsome tenants-in-chief of some medieval array, led, as insubordination must, to military ineffectiveness. The British Army, he wrote, after his victory at Vitoria, 'is an unrivalled Army for fighting, if the soldiers can only be kept in their ranks during the battle; but it wants some of the qualities indispensable to enable a general to bring them into the field in the order fit to meet an enemy, or to take an advantage from a victory: the cause of their defects is want of habits of obedience and attention to orders by the inferior officers, and indeed by all. They never attend to an order with an intention to obey it, and therefore never understand it or obey it when obedience becomes troublesome or difficult.' Repeatedly he castigated 'the habitual inattention of the officers of the regiments to their duty' and 'the utter incapacity of some officers at the head of regiments to perform the duties of their situation.'

Yet on reflection he would not have them otherwise. Inefficient amateurs many of them may have been, but they had the virtues of their defects. 'The excellence of our own

Army,' he later declared, 'mainly derives from the circumstance that its officers were gentlemen in the true sense of the word.' Here was a frank espousal of the classic view, that officers should be drawn from a distinct class of society, which had been commonplace in eighteenth-century military organisation and which the ideals and practice of the Revolution had so remorselessly broken down. Such a caste system, believed Wellington, not only made for military harmony: it provided constitutional security as well. It prevented the growth of that most dangerous of all elements in society – a group of professional officers of humble birth, with no fortune save their wits and their swords. On these grounds Wellington, until the end of his days, defended the purchase of commissions, no matter what military disadvantages this brought in its train. 'It brings into the services men of fortune and character,' he commented, 'men who have some connection with the interests and fortunes of the country, besides the Commissions they hold from His Majesty. It is this circumstance which exempts the British Army from the character of being a "mercenary army" and has rendered its employment for nearly a century and a half not only not inconsistent with the constitutional privileges of the country, but safe and beneficial.' It was better that quarrelsome but reliable amateurs rather than efficient but rootless professionals should be in charge of the armed forces of the Crown.

As for the men, the Duke accepted them with all their drawbacks, and saw no chance of getting any better. He never believed, according to his friend and biographer, the Reverend G. R. Gleig, that the ranks could be filled with 'persons of what is called a respectable position in life. He still looked to want of other employment, and to idle habits, as the readiest source of recruitment.' With an army thus constituted any relaxation of discipline, and in particular any abatement of flogging, would be fatal. As it was, even with the savage powers of punishment at his disposal, it was all that he could do to keep them in fighting shape. 'They are a rabble,' he wrote home from the Peninsula, 'who cannot bear success any more than Sir John Moore's Army could bear failure'; and indeed the victories of the Army in the

Peninsula did it almost as much harm as all the counter-strokes of the French. The troops after the Salamanca campaign were, he complained, 'little better than a band of robbers'; and their behaviour at Badajoz need hardly be recalled. Yet Wellington's final verdict, on his troops as on his officers, was more kindly. 'I will venture to say,' he told Croker in 1826, 'that in our later campaigns and especially when we crossed the Pyrenees there never was an Army in the world in better spirits, better order or better discipline. We had mended in discipline every campaign until at last I hope we were pretty near perfect.'

Though he had little hopes of their personal improvement, Wellington was too good a commander to underestimate the importance of the welfare of his troops. 'I know of no [point] more important,' he declared, 'than closely to attend to the comfort of the soldier: let him be well clothed, sheltered, and fed. How should he fight, poor fellow! if he has, besides risking his life, to struggle with unnecessary hardships . . . one ought to look sharp after the young officers and be very indulgent to the soldier.' Within the framework which he regarded as unalterable, the Duke did what he could. In war time he laboured to see the troops properly fed, and in peace he worked equally hard to get them decently housed. Under his governance the squalor of English barrack-room life was mitigated. The troops, who had previously slept four to a crib, obtained a bed apiece. He tried to obtain recreational facilities for them and to improve standards of ventilation and cleanliness in the barracks. But he expressed the fear, typically, 'that there was some danger both of overtaxing the liberality of Parliament and of spoiling the soldier, by first creating for him, and then supplying, wants which before enlistment he had never felt.'

Perhaps it was this fear which restrained him from taking up and developing the reforms with which Sir John Moore had been experimenting before his tragically early death. Moore, had he lived, might have done for the Army what Elizabeth Fry did for the prison system and Jeremy Bentham and his disciples for the law: dispelling the brutality and inefficiency of the eighteenth century with a combination of kindly Evangelical morality and brisk utilitarian competence.

Moore had made his young officers train and drill with their recruits. He had held them personally responsible for the welfare of their men. He had introduced new forms of recreation and exercise into military training; and he had insisted on an entirely new standard of sobriety, courtesy and cleanliness throughout his command. But Moore was a Victorian born before his time: Wellington was a man of the eighteenth century who remained till the end of his life unsoftened by the arguments either of the Evangelicals or of Benthamites. If the Army remained one of the last uncleared sections of the great jungle of British institutions which the disciples of Bentham laboured so heroically to level, the Duke cannot rest entirely free from blame.

In 1818 Wellington relinquished his command in France and returned to England as Master-General of the Ordnance, with a seat in Lord Liverpool's cabinet. It was much a political as a military appointment. Wellington was by now widely regarded as the wisest living Englishman; he was, as he always had been, closely in touch with political life and personalities; and the worried Government, in dealing with the country in the throes of near revolution, needed all the advice, both civil and military, that it could get. But Wellington's military influence was still limited. At the Horse Guards the Duke of York remained Commander-in-Chief and relations between him and Wellington were, and always had been, cool.

I can't say that I owe my success to any favour or confidence from the Horse Guards [Wellington confided to John Wilson Croker in 1826]. They never showed me any, from the day I had a command to this hour. In the first place they thought very little of anyone who had served in India . . . then because I was in Parliament, and connected with people in office, I was a politician, and a politician can never be a soldier. Moreover they looked upon me with a kind of jealousy, because I was a lord's son, '*a sprig of nobility*', who came into the Army more for ornament than use. They could not believe that I was a tolerable regimental officer. I have proof that they thought I could not be trusted alone with a division, and I suspect that they still have their doubts whether I know

anything about the command of an Army, for I dare say
you will be surprised to hear that in all the changes made
since the war in the regulations of the Army, I have never
been in the most trifling or distant degree consulted on any
point.

But in the January of the following year the Duke of York
died and Wellington himself became Commander-in-Chief.
'I am in my proper place,' he declared with open satisfaction, 'the place to which I was destined by my trade.' It was
not a place to which he succeeded as a matter of course, nor
one which on this occasion he held for very long. For a few
days it seemed that King George IV might insist on taking
over the command of the Army in person. Liverpool stigma-
tised the idea as '*preposterous*', and Wellington himself
threatened to 'protest against it in the most formal manner
and with all the earnestness in my power.' The moment
passed. Ministers and courtiers combined to persuade their
eccentric sovereign to confine his military influence to the
sartorial – where he certainly did damage enough – and
Wellington assumed the office, temporarily combining it with
the Master-Generalship of the Ordnance as well. Within four
months, however, rather than serve with the odious George
Canning, he had resigned both appointments. But the lure
of the Horse Guards was too strong for him to absent himself
for long. In August he returned; and when, the following
spring, he accepted the King's commission to form a government, he was openly aggrieved to learn on becoming Prime
Minister that he could not be Commander-in-Chief as well.
'I certainly did not contemplate this necessity [of resigning]
as being paramount,' he admitted. That it *was* paramount
was quickly pointed out both by his colleagues and by the
opposition, and with rather an ill grace the Duke stood down.
To facilitate his resumption of the office his successor, Lord
Hill, assumed the title, not of Commander-in-Chief but,
more cumbrously, of 'Senior General Officer upon the Staff
in Great Britain and Ireland, etc. to perform the duties of
Command-in-Chief.' But with or without the title, Hill remained at the Horse Guards for fourteen years, and it was
only in 1842 that the septuagenarian Wellington was able to

succeed his old subordinate, and enjoy the office for the last ten years of his life.

But whether officially in charge of the Horse Guards or not, the Duke was the most influential soldier in the United Kingdom during the quarter of a century which elapsed between his first assuming the command in 1827 and his death. The principal military officers – Lord Hill, Lord Anglesey, Sir George Murray, Lord Raglan – were his old subordinates of the Peninsula and Waterloo. He was necessarily the principal witness before the various commissions which were set up to investigate Army organisation and discipline as the century wore on. Had he been in favour of radical reform, much would have been achieved: but he was not. He was held back not simply by an innate scepticism and caution; even more influential was his realisation how very little in the way of military improvement the country and the House of Commons was prepared to stand. He was under no illusions about the anti-militarism of the British people: indeed to a great extent he shared it. If he did not participate in the popular mistrust of the military colleges and military clubs, he was profoundly sceptical about their value. No more than the most violent Radical did he approve of the proliferation of uniform in the London streets at the end of the war. No man was more anxious that the Army should not overstep its due constitutional and social limits; and 'he retained to the last a persuasion that the less the Army in its expenditure and general management is brought into public notice, the better.' When in 1828 a proposal was brought forward to increase Army pay, he set his face against it. Any increase in military expenditure, he foresaw, would be declared burdensome to the people; any increase in pay would have to be atoned for by a decrease in numbers; and the numbers of the Army, for the work it had to do, were already ludicrously small.

That work was considerable. First of all there was the obligation to garrison the posts overseas which Britain had been so casually accumulating during the past two centuries. 'The Empire is immense,' commented the Duke in August 1827, 'and includes nearly every important post in the world, whether naval, military or commercial. None of these posts

are occupied even for defence, much less to be able to assist
each other, even if they were within distance. Every service
must be provided in, and proceed from, Great Britain.' So
few were the troops available for garrison service that four
regiments that returned to England in 1829 after twenty-four
years' service overseas found themselves posted abroad again
within five years. With such overseas posts we may include
the garrison in Ireland; and when in 1816 the cry had been
raised to reduce its strength, Sir Robert Peel pointed out all
too truly that 'the gentry in Ireland could not reside on their
estates unless they were secure.'

Secondly, troops had to be found to conduct operations
overseas; and those who think of the period 1815–52 as being
one of undisturbed peace should remember that during these
years the United Kingdom was engaged in nearly a dozen
conflicts in all parts of the world: Nepal, India, Afghanistan,
South Africa, West Africa, Burma, and Canada. They were
usually conducted only by a few battalions, but they imposed
a severe drain on the man-power of an Army whose establishment had fallen between 1814 and 1816 from over 250,000
men to less than 80,500. In 1817 Castlereagh had declared
that there were only 16,000 men available for duty in
England; and the England of Peterloo and the Six Acts was
itself virtually a theatre of war. On returning to the Horse
Guards in August 1827, Wellington received from Sir John
Byng, commander of the forces in the north of England, a
warning that 'the present tranquillity is not to be too much
relied on, for the worst feeling exists between master and
man; and the information given me from all the towns in
Lancashire was, that if the troops were removed, I must
expect in a short time urgent application for their return.'
The formation of the Metropolitan Police two years later –
an innovation for which Wellington, no less than Peel,
deserves credit – relieved the Army of a considerable and
unwelcome responsibility. When next serious public disorder
threatened in London, during the Chartist demonstrations of
April 1848, the old Duke prudently collected a military force
of 7,000 infantry and a dozen guns to deal with it, but he
equally prudently kept that force out of sight. On 10th April,
the day of the great meeting at Kennington Common, not a

soldier was to be seen in the streets. The Duke made all his preparations to deal with an emergency; yet only the police, plentifully stiffened by special constables, were in evidence, and such staff officers as had to appear in public wore civilian clothes. There was no horsed yeomanry to lose their heads and provoke another Peterloo; and the incipient revolt melted harmlessly away.

By discretion, by rigorous economies, Wellington thus kept the Army in being. He believed it impossible to do more. To increase its numbers, improve its conditions, renovate its weapons, all meant money; and money meant Parliamentary debate, Royal commissions, an unwelcome glare of hostile publicity which, with Whig and Radical strength swelling in the House of Commons, might be fatal to the military forces of the Crown. But even these motives do not entirely explain the Duke's persistent and successful opposition to the reform of that military administration of which Sir James Graham, on investigating it after the Duke's death, said, 'there is only one word to describe it – Chaos.' If Wellington was guided by an old Whig desire not to infringe the constitutional liberties of the British people, he was no less careful to uphold the proper prerogatives of the Crown; and his care to do so increased as, to his ageing and pessimistic eye, the forces of Radicalism and revolution grew ever stronger in the land. If the House of Commons had feared Army reform in the eighteenth century because it would increase the influence of the Crown, Wellington feared it no less in the nineteenth because it would increase the influence of the House of Commons. So long as the Army remained unreformed, it could be used as a tool neither of Royal despotism nor of political jobbery. When the possibility was mooted of the Secretary at War assuming control of the Army, he commented grimly, 'Let Her Majesty's Government try the experiment whether they can find an officer *whom the Army would respect and under whose control and command the officers and soldiers would cheerfully submit*, who will consent to be placed in this subordinate situation, under the superior direction of a political officer. . . .' Sir John Fortescue wrote of Wellington that 'He considered that to place [the Army] under the absolute control of a civilian responsible

only to the House of Commons would be injurious to its
discipline. Therein,' he added angrily, 'he was probably
right.'

Right or wrong, Wellington opposed every project for the
major reform of military administration that came up during
his lifetime. He opposed the abolition of the Master-Generalship of the Ordnance, partly because of the value of having
a dispassionate military specialist advising the Cabinet, who
could 'not be supposed to have any political influence as a
bias upon his mind.' He opposed equally the abolition of the
Board of Ordnance, whose work, if combined with that of
any other department, would constitute, he thought, an
intolerably heavy burden for any office; and when, in 1837,
a commission was set up to investigate the possibility of
creating a War Office in which all the scattered branches of
military administration would be combined, the Duke's comment was:

> It has astonished me. I have always understood that it was
> a principle of the Government of this country, that he who
> exercised the Military Command over the Army should
> have nothing to say to its Payment, its Equipment, or even
> the Quartering thereof. . . . The Secretaries of State were
> considered, and were, responsible upon all the larger
> Political questions arising out of the existence of the
> Army, while the Commander in Chief exercised the
> Military Command, and, under their superintendence,
> administered the Patronage; as well for the benefit and
> encouragement of the Army itself, as upon Constitutional
> grounds, in order to keep this Patronage out of the usual
> course of Parliamentary and Ministerial management.

The reforms proposed, he commented, would take

> the Military power of the state totally and entirely out
> of the hands of the Person exercising the Royal Authority,
> and places it in the hands of one Member of the House of
> Commons and of the Cabinet. . . . The change cannot be
> made in this form without injury to the power of the
> Crown.

One cannot contemplate without nostalgia an age when
military questions could be settled entirely on broad grounds

of constitutional desirability, not modified in the slightest degree by any fears for the safety of the realm. It was not that the Duke did not feel such fears. In the 1840s, when French chauvinism was reviving and the development of steam navigation posed an entirely new threat to the security of the British coasts, the possibility of invasion 'haunted him like a nightmare.' 'Excepting immediately under the fire of Dover Castle,' he wrote in 1847, 'there is not a spot on the coast on which infantry might not be thrown on shore at any time of tide, with any wind, in any weather.' But he relied on the militia for the defence of the land. 'I should,' he confessed, 'infinitely prefer, and should have more confidence in, an Army of regular troops. But I *know* that I shall not have these'; and he complained, as have so many soldiers since, of 'the difficulty under which all governments in this country labour, in prevailing upon Parliament, in time of peace, to take into consideration measures necessary for the safety of the country in time of war.'

An almost religious respect for the balance of the constitution thus combined with a practical statesman's appreciation of what was politically possible to strengthen the Duke's natural conservatism in things military. And why should he abandon it? With the British Army, imperfect as it was, he had beaten the greatest captain the world had seen for nearly two thousand years. Little wonder that he was reluctant to change even the armament and uniform of so triumphant a force. Seldom has the truism been so amply illustrated, that victory is more harmful to a nation's military prowess than the most shattering of defeats. Wellington could not see that a system which he himself had mastered might produce, in the hands of less talented successors, humiliations and failures as depressing as those which had been so characteristic of British military activity before his arrival in the Peninsula. After the British Army had been seen in action in the Crimea, a sympathetic Frenchman wrote to an English friend, 'The heroic courage of your soldiers was everywhere and unreservedly praised, but I found also a general belief that the importance of England as a military Power had been greatly exaggerated; that she is utterly devoid of military talent, which is shown as much in administration as in fighting; and that even in the most pressing circumstances she cannot raise a large army.'

These conclusions were shared by an appalled British public which discovered, as it watched the progress of operations in the Crimea, that the Army of Queen Victoria was still in all essentials the Army of George III. The reforms against which the Duke had fought could not be long delayed after the terrible winter of 1854–5. When they came, the Duke's fears were belied. The civil servants of the late nineteenth century had developed administrative techniques unimaginable to those of Wellington's day. The importance of political and royal patronage had disappeared; so had the significance of the Commander-in-Chief's direct responsibility to the sovereign – except, of course, in the eyes of the sovereign and of the Commander-in-Chief. This change in the spirit of the constitution was well under way during the Duke's lifetime, but it could have been detected only by younger eyes than his. In the 1820's and 1830's the dangers which he foresaw were still real, and he was well past seventy before they began to abate. The lessons of the Crimea opened all eyes; but by then the eyes of the Great Duke were for ever closed.

4 William I and the Reform of the Prussian Army

Frowning down the Middle-Western bustle of the Kurfürsten-damm in West Berlin, a grotesque reminder, in the middle of the *Wirtschaftswunder*, of an older, grimmer age, stands the mutilated stump of the Gedächtniskirche; that hideous memorial to the Emperor William I and to the founding fathers of the Second Reich. The noble, heavily whiskered countenance of the Emperor himself dominates the surviving bas-reliefs; the better-known figures of Roon, Moltke, even Bismarck sink to the status of attendant lords.

And well they may. Roon may, as William himself acknow-ledged in 1871, have forged the sword with which Germany cut her way to triumph and unity; Moltke may have wielded it; but it was William who set them their tasks and, in Roon's case at least, defined meticulously what was to be done. Bismarck may have rescued William from constitutional deadlock, if nothing worse, and devised the expedients to get him what he wanted for his Army; but it was William's stub-born demands which precipitated a crisis which only Bis-marck could solve. Lesser figures, Edwin von Manteuffel and Gustav von Alvensleben, may have stiffened the royal resolu-tion during the months of crisis between 1860 and 1863, when abdication seemed to offer escape from a conflict more serious and far reaching in its implications than William could ever have foreseen; but the opinions which they rein-forced and the programme which they supported were his own, and he had worked them out many years before the illness and death of his brother, Frederick William IV, put him in a position to give them effect. These men may have been the architects of the German Empire, that anachronistic edifice whose inherent instability was to have such disastrous consequences for the Germans themselves and for their neighbours; but they worked at the behest of a royal patron who supervised their work in detail and would allow little deviation from the pattern which he had laid down. The genius of the servants must not be allowed to conceal the fundamental responsibility, for good or ill, of the master.

Of this responsibility, William himself was constantly aware. It lay with him to decide, in 1861–2, whether Prussia should go like England, France and the Netherlands, along what Roon called in April 1861 'the path of monarchy by grace of the People . . . [and] compete with Belgium in the material blessings of an unhistorical existence'; or whether it would be led in another direction by 'the assertion of the legally justified Royal will! It unleashes the eagle;' went on Roon rhapsodically, 'the King by the grace of God remains at the head of his people, the centre of the State, the ruler in the land, uncontrolled by ministerial guardians or parliamentary majorities. . . . The way is rough at first, but leads, with all the splendour and all the armed magnificence of a glorious struggle, to the *commanding heights* of life. It is the only way for a Prussian King!'[1] William is unlikely to have been impressed by these Nietzschean visions; but he saw quite clearly that in nineteenth-century Prussia, as in seventeenth-century England, sovereignty lay with the control of military power.[2] The radical majority which was returned to the Landtag by the elections of December 1861 and May 1862 saw it too, and their attacks on the Government's military proposals were as consciously devised as blows at the old political and social order as those proposals were consciously devised to defend it. So significant indeed had the issue become by the autumn of 1862 that although there remained virtually no points of substantive disagreement between the leaders of the Landtag and the military specialists in the Ministry of War, and although both Roon and Bismarck saw that the conflict could be resolved by one simple concession which the Prussian War Ministry had been prepared to make from the very beginning, that concession could not be made, not only because the King himself was adamant, but because to yield would have been to strike the royal colours before

[1] Albrecht von Roon, *Denkwürdigkeiten* (Berlin, 1905), II, p. 48.
[2] See Erich Marcks, *Kaiser Wilhelm I* (Leipzig, 1900), p. 189.

the new, victorious vessel of parliamentary sovereignty. Better that parliamentary government – anyhow planted as precariously in Prussia, as one liberal bitterly remarked, as 'foreign rice'[1] – should come to an end altogether than that the *altpreussisch* tradition should be so shamefully abandoned.

The concession in question was the reduction of the period of compulsory military service from three years to two, or the *de facto* recognition of a situation which had prevailed in Prussia for forty years past. The proposed reduction affected infantry regiments only. It was generally accepted that three-year service with the cavalry and artillery must remain. Virtually all other matters of conflict had already been resolved. Opposition to the transformation of the independent Landwehr into a first-line reserve trained by regular soldiers had rapidly dwindled after the sweeping defeat of that institution's principal defenders, the Old Liberals, in the elections of December 1861. The financial cost of the new reforms, which had appalled even the officials of the Kriegs-ministerium, were swallowed up in the new prosperity of Prussia. Even the action of the King in using the Landtag's provisional grant of 1860 to create thirty-six new infantry and eighteen new cavalry regiments as cadres for the new Army, and marking their very unprovisional character by presenting them with regimental colours as the first official act of his reign – even this might have been accepted, as it was accepted four years later, if the monarch had been prepared to give way over two-year service. His own officials in the Kriegsministerium were prepared to accept it. Bismarck was prepared to accept it. Even Roon was prepared to accept it. Manteuffel, of course, delighted at anything that provoked a conflict with the Landtag, was not prepared to accept anything, but General Stosch reflected a fairly general opinion in a letter of 28th September 1862, when he wrote 'Manteuffel must go, then Bismarck will advise the King to accept two-year service in the infantry, and at last we shall have peace'.[2]

[1] Eugene N. Anderson, *The Social and Political Conflict in Prussia* (University of Nebraska Press, 1954), p. 47.

[2] Albrecht von Stosch, *Denkwürdigkeiten* (Stuttgart, 1904), p. 52.

In fact Stosch was too optimistic. It took Bismarck two years to ease Manteuffel out of the royal entourage, and his disappearance made no difference whatever to the King's views. For him any proposal to reduce the length of service was simply, as he gloomily minuted on a famous memorandum of 10th October 1862, 'a death sentence on the Army'.[1]

In view of the importance which this issue assumed in the constitutional crisis of Prussia – and in view of the fact that within five years of William's death the German Army reverted to two-year service without any noticeable decline in its efficiency – it is worth examining this issue a little more closely. It was one on which William had very early made up his mind, as much on political grounds as on technical. Like so many men of his class and generation, he believed that in 1815 the ghost of the Revolution had been very inadequately laid. In his *wanderjähre*, in the early 1820s, he had travelled in Italy during its spasmodic revolts; he had visited Russia while the reverberations of the Decembrist conspiracy were still echoing through the corridors of St Petersburg; and he lamented the failure, in 1831, to settle with the new French revolution while opportunity offered. '[War] will now become a bloodier matter,' he prophesied gloomily, 'as French armaments increase and as her erroneous teachings spread more widely.'[2]

Thus the Prussian Army, into which he had been commissioned in 1807 on his tenth birthday and in which he was to hold active command uninterruptedly until 1848, had to be considered not only as an effective fighting force but as a bulwark of the established order; and he did not need Roon and Manteuffel to tell him how necessary it was, if the Army was to be preserved, that the nobility from which it drew its officers should be cherished as well. As early as 1843, fifteen years before Roon's famous memorandum of 1858, he was stressing the need to encourage the Junkers by providing free places for their sons in gymnasia and cadet schools. This concern for the officer corps was a sensitive nerve on which both Manteuffel and Roon were, during the crisis, quite

[1] *Militärische Schriften weiland Kaiser Wilhelms des Groszen Majestät* (Berlin, 1897), II, p. 479 (hereafter referred to as *Militärische Schriften*).　　　　[2] Marcks, op. cit., p. 43.

mercilessly to play. Manteuffel warned him, in 1861, that if he yielded to the Chamber 'the Army will gain the impression that Your Royal Highness is no longer in control of its destinies but has abdicated this privilege of the Crown to the Chamber'.[1] Roon was still more explicit. Surrender to the Chamber, he warned, would have the gravest effects 'on that part of the Nation which leads Your Majesty's armed forces and which the All Highest himself has always found to be the staunchest pillar of his throne'; to which the All Highest minuted desperately 'That *I* would never survive!'[2]

It would however be quite wrong to see in William simply a royal political soldier. His attention to military matters was minute and expert, and the respect with which his views on military questions was greeted came not just from his august status, but from his thorough knowledge of his profession. However little he knew about anything else, he knew his army and its problems very well indeed. The problems, throughout his period of active service, were those which had bedevilled and to some extent shaped Prussian military organisation since the days of his great-great-grandfather, Frederick William I. Almost all could be traced to the basic one: how to maintain an army of the size which had won Prussia her place among the Powers of Europe on so Spartan an economy. In solving them the Prussian Government in the early nineteenth century adopted many of the expedients of the eighteenth. Although the traditional liability of all young males to military service had been flamboyantly reasserted in 1814, it was a liability of which the Army, in order to keep down expenditure, took only very limited advantage. In 1852 it was calculated that out of an age-group of 66,000, 28,000 young men escaped altogether. The notorious situation resulted, when the Army was mobilised in 1859, that some 150,000 reservists, most of them married men, were recalled to the colours, leaving their families as a burden on the rates, while 100,000 young men were left undisturbed.[3]

---

[1] Gerhard Ritter, *Staatskunst und Kriegshandwerk* (Munich, 1954), I, p. 358.

[2] Roon, *Denkwürdigkeiten*, II, pp. 48 ff.

[3] Julius von der Osten-Sacken, *Preussens Heer von seinen Anfängen bis zür Gegenwart* (Berlin, 1914), vol. III, p. 1.

As a further measure of economy, the traditional expedient was adopted of sending men on unpaid furlough after their initial training and recalling them only for the autumn manœuvres. First revived in 1820, this system became firmly established in 1832, when the Army settled down again after the mobilisation of 1830–1. Formally, the obligation to three-year service with the colours remained. In practice the recruit was furloughed after sixteen and a half months, at the end of his second summer's training, and in his third year he was recalled for six weeks in August and September.[4] Against this decision William, then commanding III Army Corps, energetically rebelled, deploying arguments which were to remain fundamentally unchanged for thirty years. Some of them, indeed, can still be heard today.

> I will not say [he wrote to his royal father in April 1832] that one cannot complete a man's military training in two years; but in such a short period of service the man will be even more liable than hitherto to be looking forward to his demobilisation and so to consider the military life as some-thing to be got over with, so that he hardly thinks it worth the bother and certainly never gets to the point of seeing it as an occupation in which he could remain for longer . . . The shorter the period of service, the more soldierly spirit is bound to diminish in an Army.

With two-year service, he feared therefore, they would never breed those N.C.O.s and long-serving regular soldiers who were the backbone of the Army. In fact they should give the highest priority to the building up of such a cadre, 'in whom the warrior spirit can flourish and through whom it can be transmitted to the nation's youth'. This would pay political as well as military dividends.

> It is the tendency of the revolutionary or Liberal parties in Europe [the prince stated in the same document] to gradually demolish all the supports which guard the sovereign power and authority and give it security in the moment of danger. It is natural that the Army should still be the foremost of these supports; and the more it is in-spired by a true military spirit, the harder it is to subvert.

---

[1] *Militärische Schriften*, I, pp. 146–7.

But discipline and blind obedience are things which can be engendered and given permanence only by long practice, and it is to these that a longer period of service is relevant, so that in the moment of danger the Monarch can securely rely on his troops.[1]

A year later he was still arguing his case. 'Through the reduction in the period of service the infantry is reduced to the level of other small German armies and one will not be justified in asking any more of our men than of theirs.' The money, he argued urgently, must somehow be found. 'We are standing,' he concluded, his imagery somewhat confused by passion, 'at the turning point of this question, which disturbs me to my inmost being, and with whose solution is bound up the destiny of the Fatherland and the Throne!'[2]

But nobody else felt so deeply about it as did Prince William. To his repeated complaints, the officials both of the Treasury and of the Ministry for War continued to reply that the money simply could not be found. Even when, in 1854, he gained the support of his royal brother Frederick William IV, bureaucratic opposition remained immovable. 'I know,' wrote the King petulantly, 'that the Treasury, against my verbal and written orders, rejected three-year service for the infantry'; and he insisted that it must now be carried through.[3] But the matter was still being debated within the Ministry of War when William took over full powers as Regent in 1858; and this debate he was determined, after a quarter of a century, to bring to a summary end.

With the question of length of service was bound up the yet more contentious matter of the Landwehr, that independent territorial force which was regarded by the Prussian bourgeoisie, much as the English regarded their militia, as the true symbol of the liberties granted with such reluctance by the Hohenzollerns during the *Erhebungszeit*. The small size of the regular Army meant that in any mobilisation it was heavily dependent on the Landwehr to make up its numbers; and since the efficiency and morale of the Landwehr, in William's view, depended on the training which

[1] Ibid., pp. 153–5. [2] Ibid., pp. 177–8.
[3] E. von Frauenholz, *Entwicklungsgeschichte des Deutschen Heerwesens* (Munich, 1941), V, p. 249.

such of them as had served with the regular Army had received with the colours, that was another argument, he
considered, for providing three years' service, whose imprint
would really endure. But he was convinced that far more
sweeping measures of reform would be necessary to make
the Landwehr a truly effective military force. The destruction of the independence of the Landwehr and its subordination, both in training and command, to the regular Army,
was one of the principal points in Roon's Army Bill of 1860;
but precisely these measures had been urged by William
twenty years earlier in a notable exchange of correspondence
with no less a figure than the father of the Landwehr, General
Hermann von Boyen, whom Frederick William IV recalled
from retirement in 1840 to become Minister for War.[1]

In this confrontation between the veteran general and the
middle-aged Prince two generations met and entirely failed
to understand one another. Boyen's arguments, based on the
lessons of 1806, already had an archaic ring. The basic object
of universal service, he recalled, was that 'no class of citizen
could remain neutral when war broke out, and that the
government could be assured of the general co-operation of
the People.' ('Quite correct', minuted the Prince.) The object
of the Landwehr, said Boyen, was to maintain units capable
of taking the field; to preserve the idea of *Landesbewaffnung*
by regular exercises in peacetime; to give its members the
feel of arms without too much disturbance of their civil life;
and to keep alive the knowledge acquired during military
service. This was a task which demanded different techniques
and different standards from those of the regular Army, and
few professional officers and N.C.O.s possessed them. The
Landwehr, he insisted, neither could nor should try to ape
the pattern of the Line. 'Those who lose sight of this fact,
rooted as it is in human nature, in their treatment of the
Landwehr,' he concluded warningly, 'are undermining, perhaps unwittingly, the Landwehr spirit, without which it
cannot survive for long and for which the rigid drill-book of
the Line is poison.'[2]

William would have none of this. 'I know that argument
very well,' he commented, 'but I intend to remain deaf to it,

[1] *Militärische Schriften*, I, pp. 333 ff.   [2] Ibid., I, p. 366.

for it is only put forward in order to give the idea that the Landwehr is something quite separate. It is in fact an Army on furlough, and as an Army it must be identical with the Line.' It must, he insisted, 'be able to drill, manœuvre and shoot like the Line, from whom it has learned how to do so. Obedience, discipline, subordination are common to everyone; these cardinal points of the soldier must be strictly maintained and every patriot must be imbued with them. To conceive of the Landwehr as behaving, under arms, in a way different from the troops of the Line is the first step to a revolutionary Army.'[1] Landwehr officers, he concluded, could be considered effective soldiers only in so far as they achieved an effective 'blending' (*Verschmelzung*) with the Line, and to this end regular officers should be detached to the Landwehr in the largest possible numbers. The enthusiasm of 1813 was not to be expected again; as for the experience of those years, he rather unkindly reminded Boyen, it was something of a wasting asset.

Events were to bear out William's arguments. The showing of the Landwehr in the mobilisation of 1849–50 was, by all accounts, lamentable, especially so far as cavalry, artillery and supply was concerned; and Prussia's evident military incapacity on this occasion led to the traumatic humiliation of Olmütz. General von Bonin, who was later to champion the Landwehr against von Roon, was commanding a division at the time, and complained bitterly about the inadequacy of the officers and the indiscipline, the lack of 'good, blind military obedience' among the men. He concluded 'that the Landwehr in itself and in its present organisation is not to be considered an absolutely reliable and efficient body, that its disbandment and reorganisation is necessary, and together with this should be linked a fundamental reform, in many respects, of the standing Army.'[2]

Two months later William drafted a proposal which contained all the elements of the Roon reforms ten years later.[3] The rapid mobilisation which railways now made possible, he pointed out, made the *immediate* effectiveness of reservists a matter of fundamental importance. They must be organised and officered as if they were companies of the Line. Their

[1] Loc. cit.   [2] Ibid., II, pp. 152–3.   [3] Ibid., II, p. 135.

cadres should be combined with the reserve companies of Line regiments to form fourth battalions of those regiments, which could on mobilisation expand into three Landwehr battalions. They should be put in peacetime, with their linked regular units, under the commander who would lead them in war; and to provide for this new reserve organisation, the number of regular officers and N.C.O.s should be considerably increased.

Six years before he assumed power, therefore, William already knew exactly what he wanted to do. Three-year service must be established; the cadres of regular troops must be expanded; and the Landwehr must be 'blended' with the regular Army. Assuming, with some reason, that von Bonin shared his views, he made him Minister for War in the 'New Era' Ministry which he appointed on becoming Regent in the autumn of 1858, and he addressed to that Ministry a message emphasising the urgency of making the Army 'powerful and respected so that when the time comes, it can lay a heavy weight in the scales'.[1] The mobilisation of 1859 lent emphasis to his words. Though less of a shambles than that of 1850, it showed that the traditional weaknesses were still unremedied. The regular Army was too weak to do without the Landwehr, which took the field partially equipped and undertrained, leaving its families unprovided for and its jobs unfilled, while a substantial number of young bachelors, as we have seen, escaped all liability. William resolved that this should never happen again. On 15th July, four days after the truce concluded between the Austrian and the French Emperors at Villafranca, he laid down principles for a reform of the Army to be accomplished within one year from 1st August 1859.[2] Landwehr cadres and reserve battalions were to be amalgamated; the size of cadres was to be doubled; and the cost, he suggested optimistically, should be swallowed up in the general expense of the mobilisation.

To Bonin and the officials in the Ministry of War, however, the reform did not appear quite so easy. They had been quietly working on the problem themselves, and in certain respects were in whole-hearted agreement with their new

[1] Osten-Sacken, op. cit., II, p. 9. [2] Ibid., p. 17.

Kriegsherr. They were fully alive to the absurdity of an Army so heavily dependent on the older age groups whose military efficiency was declining and whose death or incapacity in a bloody war would, in the words of one official, 'reduce their families to the Proletariat in the worst sense of the word'.[1] They therefore accepted the need for the extension of the call-up, as also for some degree of *Verschmelzung* between Army and Landwehr. But they still believed, as had their predecessors, that financial stringency must set rigid limits to any projected reform. Bonin had already committed himself to a weighty opinion on this question which has a thoroughly twentieth-century ring.

To employ disproportionate quantities of men and resources on normal war preparations, to screw these up beyond the proper level, does not give real strength, but only the deceptive illusion of strength, and inevitably reduces it, if continued for a prolonged period, as the productive capacity of the nation becomes exhausted. But Prussia should not be in a state of outward show alone, but a state of intensive internal strength. The real increase of our military capacity can only keep step with the growing productive capacity of our people. This alone, that is to say the industrial and moral resources of our population, constitutes the solid foundation for our military power, and thereby the lasting influence of the state.[2]

This was all very well, but what it really meant was that, if the call-up was to be extended (as everyone agreed that it must) three-year service was out of the question. Nor was Bonin 'sound' on the question of the Landwehr. In spite of his strictures on the Landwehr's performance in 1850, he was reluctant to contemplate any fundamental transformation of the pattern laid down in 1815, and even more reluctant to pilot any such proposal through a Chamber in which, since the election of 1858, the Liberals enjoyed a commanding majority. When, therefore, on 9th August 1859, he ordered his officials to draw up proposals based on the royal outline of 15th July, he laid it down that there should be 'no

[1] Memorandum of Lieut-Col. von Clausewitz, July 1857, reprinted in *Militärische Schriften*, II, p. 326. See also Osten-Sacken, op. cit., III, p. 4.   [2] *Militärische Schriften*, II, p. 378.

essential alteration of the organisation of the Army in its fundamental principles, that is, any disestablishment of the mobile Landwehr.'[1] Moreover he insisted that 'increased recruiting and rejuvenation of the Army could be achieved by a reform on the basis of the existing Defence Law [Boyen's Law of 1814] without the Landtag being asked for its approval to an increase in appropriations.'[2]

A document based on such principles was unlikely to meet with the Regent's approval. In fact the War Ministry, with some ingenuity, succeeded in producing a scheme which preserved three-year service, but only at the cost of substantially reducing the size, both of peace-time cadres and wartime establishments; thereby transgressing another of the Regent's fundamental principles. It was at this stage, September 1859, that William invited the commander of the 18th Division at Düsseldorf, Albrecht von Roon, to join the discussions.

The previous year William had received from Roon a long memorandum on the Prussian armed forces,[3] and on this memorandum, as is generally known, the Roon reforms were eventually based. But it is hard to detect in this memorandum a single proposal which William had not already determined to carry out. Three-year service; increase of cadres and improvement of career opportunities for regular officers and N.C.O.s; the transformation of the 'politically false' institution, the Landwehr, into a first-line reserve for the Army under the control of professional soldiers – none of this, as we have shown, was new. What mattered was that it mirrored exactly William's own intentions; and William detected in Roon a man who not only shared his own views, but who could be relied on to force them through over the objections first of his more moderate or timorous colleagues, and then of a Landtag in which all the forces of opposition, economic, social and sentimental, would be formidably assembled.

---

[1] i.e. the 'Landwehr of the first call', which could be called out to take the field. The 'Landwehr of the second call', older men reserved for garrison duties, did not come into question.

[2] Osten-Sacken, op. cit., III, p. 19.

[3] Reprinted in Roon, *Denkwürdigkeiten*, II, pp. 521 ff.

This rôle Roon joyfully accepted. He saw himself as the King's man, Kurwenaal to his Tristan, 'a sergeant in the great Company of which the King was captain'.[1] In the discussions which ensued with Bonin and his assistants, he loyally pressed the royal view that the larger establishments were necessary even though they increased the estimated cost of the reforms by a quarter, from seven million to nearly nine million thalers. On the Commission which the Regent set up to study the question, at the end of October 1859, he refused to debate the matter at all, simply taking the line that since the Regent had made up his mind, no further discussion was possible – a view which most of his military colleagues shared. Bonin, false to his *Kriegsherr*, tainted with liberalism, was marked out by Roon and Manteuffel for destruction. Bonin's subordinates indeed bitterly suggested that his adversaries had deliberately brought forward totally unacceptable proposals in order to force his resignation[2] – if not indeed to force a constitutional crisis to wreck the New Era for good and all.

In any case, William made it clear that he could no longer work with Bonin.

You quite rightly point out [he wrote to him on 24th November 1859] that military, economic and financial interests must stand together in a certain harmony; but it is equally true that in a Monarchy like ours the military consideration must not be curtailed by the other two; for the European position of the state, on which so much else depends, rests upon that. Peace itself, without which the welfare neither of individuals nor of the community can be conceived, would be endangered by any restriction on the internal efficiency and readiness of the Army.[3]

Could Bonin honestly declare, asked the Regent, that he accepted these principles and would apply them in driving through the reforms which he now proclaimed as an 'iron necessity'? Naturally Bonin could not. He asked to be relieved of his post and slipped away to the obscurity of a provincial

[1] Ibid., II, p. 151.
[2] Theodor von Bernhardi, *Aus meinem Leben* (Leipzig, 1893), II, pp. 295–6, 309–10.
[3] Östen-Sacken, op. cit., III, p. 26.

corps command. In his place, on 5th December, William appointed Roon.

Was the government now set on a collision-course with the Landtag, as Manteuffel so devoutly hoped? Such a judgment would be premature. The bills which Roon introduced in the Landtag in February 1860 were not impossibly contentious. The need to improve the efficiency of the Army and to rejuvenate it was almost universally recognised. The expense was disagreeable but not intolerable: much could be found by an overhaul of the land tax, to ensure the passing of which William was prepared to swamp the Upper Chamber with newly-created peers, and Roon was prepared to withdraw the most unpopular of the proposed levies on trade. The technical arguments for the abolition of the old-style Landwehr were overwhelming. Only on three-year service did no agreement seem possible – a measure justifiable principally by the political arguments so bluntly advanced by William in his younger days, which threw doubt (or, some might say, light) on the whole underlying purpose of the reforms. The object appeared, as a liberal senior officer complained, to turn the Prussian Army into a *'Partei-Armee'*.[1] Torn between their suspicions of the government's intentions and their recognition of the necessity of the reforms, the liberal majority in the Chamber hit on the indescribably stupid expedient of voting a provisional grant for one year only. The Minister for Finance, von Patow, tortuously explained that the government saw the situation as provisional 'in the sense that within the specified period it would only do what it is able within the existing legal provisions and within the limits of the credits requested; what it is able without encroaching upon the constitutional rights of the representative body'. None of this stopped William from immediately issuing a series of Orders in Council for the creation of new regiments, out of the old Landwehr cadres and line reserve battalions, which effectively provided the framework for the new enlarged and integrated force which was to bring Prussia the dominance, first of Germany and then of Europe; or Roon from carrying these through with a rapidity which enabled William to report on 19th June 1860, after a tour of

[1] Bernhardi, op. cit., III, p. 325.

inspection, 'Although the new structure of the Army was decreed by me only a few weeks ago, I recognise with satisfaction that its foundations are already complete.'[1]

This was not what the Prussian electorate had expected of the New Era. In February 1861 the discontented elements in the Landtag broke away from the Old Liberals, those Establishment moderates who had so cravenly sold the pass, to form the D.F.P., the *Deutsche Fortschritts Partei*, to press for the reforms in which the government appeared so uninterested. 'Can the salaries of civil servants be raised?' demanded one radical with bitter sarcasm. 'Oh no, the Army comes first. How about schools and universities? The Army must head the queue. Arts and crafts, business and shipping? No, the Army! Perhaps great land improvement measures, railways and canals? Barracks first of all!'[2] The provisional grant was renewed until the end of the year, but only by a majority of eleven votes; and in December the electorate made clear its own view of the matter by increasing the total liberal representation from 266 to 333, as against 15 conservatives. In such a house the government could make no headway. It gratefully resigned in January 1862, to be succeeded by a shadowy conservative caretaker régime in which the only outstanding figure was Roon; and Roon made no pretence at regretting the disappearance of colleagues whose political programme he described as 'the surrender of the historic Kingdom of Prussia and the enthronement of parliamentary sovereignty'. His own task he now saw simply in terms of conflict. 'I must seek out the struggle, to that I am compelled by my duty and my conscience. . . . The young David had only pebbles and a brave heart – it is God that gives the victory,' he concluded piously, 'not strength or cunning.'[3] Poor Roon, battling single-handed against the forces of darkness and destruction!

In spite of appearances however, Roon was no fool; nor was he, like Manteuffel, a conspirator deliberately driving tension higher to give an excuse for a royal *coup d'état*. The

---

[1] Frauenholz, op. cit., V, p. 253.

[2] Adalbert Hess, *Das Parlament das Bismarck widerstrebte* (Köln, 1964), p. 20. See also Anderson, op. cit., pp. 88–95.

[3] Roon, *Denkwürdigkeiten*, II, p. 72.

conservatives and the radicals he regarded as being equally 'impossible parties',[1] and the bellicose noises which he made in his letters did not prevent him from maintaining, during this session, an air of courteous reasonableness in the Chamber and, throughout the spring and summer of 1862, exploring with the moderates the possibility of compromise. For as usually happens in revolutions, the appearance of men with more extreme demands drove the moderates, with whom the conflict had started, to consider an accommodation with their original adversaries as the lesser of two evils. Elections in March 1862 strengthened the left still further at the expense not only of the conservatives but of the Old Liberals as well; and to the latter Roon's programme was very much more acceptable than some of the proposals which this group now brought forward, for slashing reductions in the standing Army, for promotion of officers from the ranks and for the conversion of the Landwehr into a Swiss-type militia. The Old Liberals were prepared to accept virtually the whole of the government's measures if it would only make the one concession – the abandonment of three-year service.[2] They could face their electorates with nothing less.

Then an extraordinary thing happened. Roon gave in. On 17th September he announced that the government was prepared to consider a compromise proposal along the lines of that urged by the Old Liberal leaders; the passing of the military budgets in return for the acceptance of two-year service.[3] But hardly had the astonished Chamber digested the news than Roon had the disagreeable duty of telling them that it was all a mistake. The King, more convinced than ever that the Chamber was set on 'ruining the Army, in its state of readiness and in its military spirit and in its training,'[4] refused to consider the idea for a moment. It is still difficult to see why Roon ever thought he could get away with such a flagrant transgression of his royal master's wishes,

[1] Bernhardi, op. cit., IV, p. 114.

[2] Waldemar Graf Roon, *Roon als Redner* (Breslau, 1895), I, p. 191.

[3] Gordon A. Craig, *The Politics of the Prussian Army* (London, 1955), p. 158.

[4] Letter of 30th August 1862, reprinted in *Roon als Redner*, I, p. 320.

or how indeed he reconciled it with the 'conscience' to which in his letters he so proudly referred. It was the kind of blunder which ministries are liable to make in their death-throes. 'After this wondrous episode it will be very difficult for the Ministry to hold on much longer,' observed Bernhardi. 'We are rapidly approaching a Bismarck-Schönhausen ministry, of that there can be no doubt.'[1] They were indeed. Roon's colleagues resigned; the Chamber, on 23rd September, finally rejected the military appropriations in the Budget; and the King, on Roon's advice, turned to Bismarck as the only man with the nerve to ride out the storm.

But that was still not the end of the story. Though Bismarck was prepared to govern without the Chamber if he had to, he was anxious to co-operate with it if he could; and his dispassionate eye saw the absurdity of making the break over a principle which, in the view of many military experts, was no principle at all. Almost his first act was to revive the bait of two-year service, in a form which he hoped would settle the matter for good.[2] The principle of three-year service was to remain, but at the end of the second year the conscript might be released on payment of 'substitution money' which could be used to swell the ranks of the regular soldiers; an open imitation of the system which applied since 1818 in the French Army and which in the Italian War of 1859 had apparently produced excellent results. The argument advanced so often, that two-year service would make it impossible to produce enough regulars and N.C.O.s, was thus to some extent met. Linked with this was a further proposal, of more far-reaching significance. Henceforth the size of the Army should be fixed at a constant percentage – 1.2 per cent – of the population; and defence expenditure should be assessed simply on the basis of the number of troops thus raised. The right of the Landtag to vote the defence budget, which even Roon had never questioned, would thus be quietly abdicated, and this disagreeable conflict need never be repeated again.

This project of a *Pauschquantum*, which was to find its

[1] Bernhardi, op. cit., IV, p. 325.
[2] See Ludwig Dehio, 'Bismarck und die Heeresvorlagen der Konflikzeit', in *Historische Zeitschrift*, CXLIV (1931).

way in a modified form into the constitution of the North German Confederation in 1867, has since been condemned as an 'imposition of military absolutism'.[1] In fact, as Manteuffel was quick to perceive, it would have limited the authority of the Crown no less than that of the Landtag, and for that reason, he persuaded the King, it was entirely unacceptable.[2] But the King cannot have taken much persuading. The proposal involved the surrender of the basic principle for which he was fighting. The reduction of length of service, and with it of the size of infantry units, would lead, he considered, to 'the destruction of all military spirit'. And he sent back the document to Roon with, as we have seen, the blistering comment 'a death sentence on the Army!'[3]

So three-year service remained, and the Army was saved. It was to be on parliamentary government in Germany that the death sentence was pronounced – on that, and a great deal else besides. Is it too much to suggest that, had matters been settled rather differently, the Gedächtniskirche might not today be in ruins after all?

[1] Ibid., p. 35.
[2] Gordon A. Craig, 'Portrait of a Political General: Edwin von Manteuffel and the Constitutional Conflict in Prussia', in *Political Science Quarterly*, LXVI (1951).
[3] See n. 2, p. 81.

5   Lord Haldane
and the Territorial Army[1]

In 1906 Haldane, as Secretary of State for War in Sir Henry
Campbell-Bannerman's great Radical administration, introduced his first Army estimates. In doing so he expounded the
ideas which were to be embodied in the Territorial and
Reserve Forces Act of 1907 and bear fruit in the creation of
a new-modelled Territorial Army. That Army has, during
the past twelve months and amid great public outcry, been
utterly transformed, if not totally dismantled. The moment
thus seems appropriate for a re-examination of the circumstances in which it was founded, and the intentions of its
principal founder; so that, in commemorating the creator,
we may also pay our homage to his creation.

Haldane sketched out his intentions in tentative form in
the speech of 8th March 1906, in which he introduced his
first estimates:

> I do not see why the rifle clubs, cadet corps, volunteers,
> all the different forms of military organisation which we
> have at present should not be encouraged, so that the
> people should be able to organise themselves . . . not only
> to defend their hearths and homes – because I think,
> considering the strength of our Royal Navy, they are not
> likely to be called upon to do that – but to come to the
> assistance of the Regular Army in other ways. . . . You
> might perhaps thus form in time of peace a reservoir into
> which would flow the various streams of people from
> every class who take an interest in rifle shooting and drill
> . . . and you might prepare the machinery by which, on
> the outbreak of hostilities, you could turn the streams
> which had flowed into this reservoir, some of them per-
> haps rather muddy, into pure streams which would give
> support of the Regular Army.[2]

[1] Written in 1966.
[2] House of Commons Debates, 8th March 1906.

What was the context in which these proposals were brought forward? Overall, of course, loomed the familiar problem, of keeping Britain's defence budget within limits which a government dependent on the votes of the taxpayer considered economically desirable and politically feasible. The limit for Army expenditure laid down by Haldane's unsympathetic colleagues was £30 million. 'If we had Army expenditure of £50 million a year to play with I could suggest many things which would be delightful and interesting,' he somewhat apologetically told the House of Commons.[1] His successor today could hardly make the same claim.

Equally formidable, but with implications directly in conflict with the demand for retrenchment, was the evident need for urgent military reform which had been made clear by the virtual breakdown of Army administration during the Boer War. The British Army was organised to deal with minor conflicts within, or on the periphery of, the British Empire: 'small wars' or 'imperial policing', in the jargon of that time, 'limited wars' or 'peacekeeping' in that of our own. The South African conflict had revealed that when confronted by intelligent adversaries armed with modern weapons, it was barely capable even of doing that. Training, equipment, administration, supply, above all the system for supplying trained reservists had been proved quite inadequate. Only by frantic improvisation had it been possible to bring the war to a successful end.

To meet its duties even as an Imperial Police Force the British Army therefore needed a thorough overhaul. Other and yet more formidable duties were beginning to loom ahead. In November 1905 the Prime Minister, Mr Balfour, had warned that 'the extension of railways up to the Afghan frontier has rendered war with a great power a military possibility'.[2] Much of the planning of Haldane's predecessors had been directed to the contingency of a major war with

---

[1] Ibid.
[2] A. J. Balfour to Field-Marshal the Earl Roberts, 20th November 1905. Also his Memorandum on Army Reorganisation, 30th March 1905. CAB 17/13A. I am grateful to Mr N. W. Summerton for this and other references to documents in the P.R.O. and the National Library of Scotland.

Russia in the Indian plains. In January 1906, within a few weeks of coming into office, the Foreign Secretary had sounded out Haldane over the prospects of military support for France in the event of another crisis such as that over Tangier leading to a new Franco-German War.[1] It is true that on 12th July 1906 Haldane reassured the House of Commons: 'Our business is to maintain an expeditionary force just so large as to form a reserve which may enable us swiftly and resolutely to reinforce those forces, which are the outposts of the Empire and which act as its police';[2] but already his Directorate of Military Operations was working on contingency plans for sending that force, not to the outposts of the Empire, but to north-west Europe, to take part in a great European war.[3]

Wherever and however the British Army was employed, in Europe, in India, in Africa or in the Caribbean, it needed an adequate system of trained reserves; and the problem of how to create such a system without some kind of compulsory service is one which, so far as I know, no state in the world has ever satisfactorily solved. Compulsory service had been adopted by all the great powers of Europe after the Franco-Prussian War. Continental armies were cadres through which the young manhood of the nation passed for training, subsequently moving through various categories of reserve and always available on mobilisation. It was a system which satisfied both the nationalism which was becoming increasingly characteristic of right-wing politicians in Europe and the demand for equality of sacrifice which had always characterised the Left. Far more than any formal 'parliamentary democracy' it was the distinctive characteristic of the late nineteenth-century European nation state. It was a pattern which Britain had not yet followed, although from the turn of the century there was an increasing demand that she should.

Britain's military requirements were peculiar. The bulk of her Regular Army had to be employed on standing duties

---

[1] F. D. Maurice, *Haldane* (London, 1937), I, p. 174.
[2] House of Commons Debates, 12th July 1906.
[3] G. P. Gooch and H. Temperley (eds.), *British Documents on the Origins of the War, 1898–1914*, vol. III, pp. 179 ff.

overseas. Involvement on a major scale in continental warfare was, at the turn of the century, barely contemplated.
As for an invasion of the British Isles themselves – fear of
which recurred during this period with remarkable regularity
and no less remarkable strength – forces of a kind were on
hand to deal with it, as we shall see in a moment; but the
general concordance of official opinion was that the best
bulwark against such a threat lay in the strength of the
Royal Navy.[1] Edward Cardwell had attempted by his introduction of short-service enlistment thirty years earlier to
create as large a trained reserve as the preservation of voluntary service would permit, but the results were not spectacular. In 1899 the Regular Army Reserve stood at only 78,000
men; no more than half the size of the home Regular Army
itself.[2]

There were other military forces in Britain which could be
called on in an emergency for home defence. There was the
Militia, 'the Constitutional Force'; today virtually forgotten,
but for three centuries an apparently irremovable element of
the English social scene. Its officers might be described as
the squirearchy in arms; its ranks were recruited from un-
employed or casually employed labourers too young or
unwilling to join the Army. Cardwell had reorganised it,
replacing the control of the County Lords-Lieutenant by
that of the Commander-in-Chief and brigading its battalions
with those of the Line, but it remained a home defence force
without liability to serve abroad, and its chief value was seen
as providing recruits for the Regular Army. This it very
satisfactorily did. At the turn of the century 35 per cent of
its ranks joined the regulars every year; but since another
20 per cent deserted and 25 per cent were discharged before
completing their service, its value for other military purposes
could not have been great.[3] There was also the Yeomanry,
that cheerful collection of mounted landowners and farmers
raised during the Napoleonic Wars and used during the

[1] See for example A. J. Balfour's speech in the House of Commons, 11th May 1905.
[2] J. D. Dunlop, *The Development of the British Army, 1899–
1914* (London, 1938), p. 18.
[3] Ibid., p. 48.

subsequent disturbed years to keep the lower classes in order; and finally there were the Volunteers.

The Volunteers were an astonishing institution; an aspect of Victorian social history that still awaits its historian. Here was the English business-man in arms, military private enterprise at its best. Some units, such as the Honourable Artillery Company, dated back to the 'trained bands' of the sixteenth century, but most of them came into being to repel the French invasion which was so confidently expected between 1859 and 1861. Originally they were exclusive military clubs whose members had to be proposed and seconded, who paid an entrance fee and an annual subscription and provided – and of course designed – their own uniforms. The state provided them in the first place only with arms. These stalwart citizens, organised not only in battalions of infantry but as companies of garrison artillery and fortress engineers, guarded the shores and cities of the United Kingdom for half a century. But during this period their character subtly changed. As was happening in other branches of society, private enterprise became increasingly dependent on state subvention. First a capitation grant was allowed for recruits; then allowances were given for uniform, equipment, general expenses, and an annual camp. By 1902 the Volunteers were receiving over one million pounds from the exchequer;[1] and by then, with the exception of a few London corps such as the Artists' Rifles, the Inns of Court Regiment and the Honourable Artillery Company, the Volunteers had ceased to be clubs for the well-to-do, and had become recruited from the urban proletariat and salariat by small groups of entrepreneurs – one might almost call them *condottieri* – who bore sole financial responsibility for their maintenance and upkeep. 'The unfortunate commanding officer of a Volunteer battalion is an even greater patriot than is popularly supposed,' said Haldane; 'he risks not only his life but his fortune.'[2] Moreover, though the Volunteers were numerous (nearly a quarter of a million strong in 1905) and enthusiastic, their military effectiveness was reduced by the fact that any of them could leave at any moment on giving two weeks' notice. As a result,

[1] *The Times*, 2nd February 1907.
[2] House of Commons Debates, 25th February 1907.

The Times military correspondent observed, 'if a commanding officer is given an order, he may allege that his funds do
not permit him to carry it out, or that if he does his men will
leave.'[1]

An enemy force invading the British Isles would certainly,
therefore, have received a vigorous if somewhat erratic
reception. But no invasion came. Instead the War Office,
having shipped all available regular forces to South Africa to
deal with the Boers, found itself with no trained reserves left
to feed into the conflict, and very few untrained. The Militia
had been bled dry of available officers and men to keep the
regular battalions going; and though all its English units
volunteered for overseas service the units which went, consisting of under-trained officers and under-age boys, could
be used only on the lines of communication. Volunteer units,
improvised *ad hoc*, went out and fought as companies
attached to the Regular Army, and often displayed, as might
be expected, considerable dash. But fewer than 13,000 men
of the Volunteers, out of a total of 230,000, could be found
to come forward for overseas service;[2] evidence not so much
of lack of public spirit but of the maturity of the age groups
from which their members were largely drawn. As for those
who remained at home, Volunteers, Militia or Yeomanry,
they had neither the command structure, nor the administrative and supply services, nor even the weapons to enable
them to deal with an invading army in the absence of the
Regulars. It appeared therefore that Great Britain, at the
zenith of her power and prosperity, was incapable either of
defending herself at home or of conducting a prolonged
campaign abroad, even against an adversary whose military
strength was an insignificant fraction of that of a great power.

The British eventually won the Boer War; but even if
they had lost it the need for radical reform of the Army, and
indeed the entire structure of imperial defence, could not
have been made more obvious. Mr Balfour, during his
Premiership, tackled this task with a seriousness and an
energy which has seldom been fully appreciated. An Army
Council was set up to replace the overloaded office of
Commander-in-Chief, and a properly organised General

[1] *The Times*, loc. cit.　　　　　[2] Dunlop, op. cit., pp. 18, 103.

Staff was created to advise the Army Council. The training and armament of the Army was overhauled in the light of the lessons learned in South Africa; lessons which were not, alas, always to prove entirely relevant to the requirements of Flanders in 1914–18. A Committee of Imperial Defence was established to lay down the broad lines of the policy which the armed forces might be required to implement; and a beginning was made in reshaping the whole system of reserve and auxiliary forces. It was a tedious and unpopular business, as military reform always is. Parliament faithfully reflected national opinion in demanding only a reduction of defence expenditure; while the social groups which were not totally apathetic usually had a strong interest in preserving the *status quo*. Haldane's predecessors, Brodrick and Arnold Forster, were savagely harassed from both sides of the House. Curzon, when it was suggested that he might go to the War Office, replied 'My answer would be No, No, and a thousand times No. There is no reason why one should sacrifice the whole of the best years of one's life for work for which you get no gratitude and are, on the contrary, overwhelmed with ignorant calumny and malignant scorn.'[1] A Liberal Secretary of State for War could expect even less sympathy from the opposition or support from his colleagues. It was with grim humour that Campbell-Bannerman remarked, on appointing Haldane to the office, 'We shall now see how Schopenhauer gets on in the Kailyard'.[2]

Haldane, who had a sense of humour, played up to his reputation. When asked by the Army Council what kind of an Army he had in mind, he tells us 'my answer to them was "A Hegelian Army". The conversation then fell off'.[3] A clue to his meaning can be found in the memorandum which he wrote for the Council's consideration on 1st January 1906. In this he stated: 'The problem of the future reorganisation of the British Army can only be considered as a whole, and ... it is fatal to try to deal with the parts of which one entire

---

[1] Curzon to Sir Ian Hamilton, 12th March 1903. Quoted in John Lydgate, *Curzon, Kitchener and the Problem of Indian Army Administration, 1899–1909*. (London Ph.D. thesis, 1965.)

[2] F. D. Maurice, *Haldane*, I, p. 158.

[3] R. B. Haldane, *Autobiography* (London, 1931), p. 185.

force is made up, without first determining their co-ordination on the broad principles according to which they are to be fitted into one another in the scheme as a whole'.[1] He wanted, in short, to establish a clear idea of the Army, with all its reserves, as a *Ding an Sich*, and this went far beyond the more usual approach of asking what the Army was *for*. The latter question was a familiar one; after all, Benthamism was a hundred years old. As Sir Redvers Buller had tartly remarked, 'this question has been frequently asked, and the only time it was answered the answer was wrong.'[2]

Haldane was happy with the succinct reply given by Cardwell's Localisation Committee in 1872; that the test of any peace-time organisation must be its capacity:

1. To place in the field immediately on the outbreak of war, in the highest state of efficiency, as large a force as is compatible with the peace-time military expenditure.
2. To maintain that force in the field throughout the continuance of hostilities undiminished in numbers and efficiency.[3]

For the past thirty years the War Office had attempted to meet this need by taking the Regular Army as it stood and supplementing it by various categories of reserve. Haldane's answer was more grandiose. He visualised an entire nation in arms; not on the continental pattern, where military service was compulsory and the Regular Army acted as the school of the nation both in military and in moral education, but one of a peculiarly British kind, operating through voluntary service and rooted in traditional institutions. The Regular Army, organised into an efficient 'striking force', would be the cutting edge of a blade forged out of the manhood of the entire nation; and the military training and indoctrination of the nation should be undertaken by a new Territorial Army and by associated training corps at schools and universities.

[1] Haldane Papers, National Library of Scotland, MS 5918, ff. 44–5.
[2] Note to Sir George Sydenham Clarke, 27 March 1904. CAB 17/13A.
[3] Haldane Papers, loc. cit.

In a series of documents he made his intentions clear. In a memorandum of 1st February 1906[1] we find him writing:

The main objects to be kept steadily in view in dealing with the military forces of the state must be the education and the organisation of the nation for the necessities of imperial defence.

Consequently the basis of our whole military fabric must be the development of the idea of a real national Army formed of the people and managed by specially organised local associations. This Army must be capable of evolution with the least possible delay into an effective force of all arms should serious danger threaten the empire.

The military training of the nation will gradually be developed by the associations; the efficiency of the Territorial Army will depend mainly on the spontaneous efforts which the nation is prepared to make to organise itself and its latent resources for the purposes of war.

Three months later the Hegelian concept is adumbrated yet further:[2]

The problem, as it presents itself to my mind, is how to reorganise the military forces of this country in such a fashion as to give the whole nation what is really a National Army, not separated from itself by artificial barriers of caste and class, but regarded by the people as something that is their very own. It is of the essence of such a conception that an Army fulfilling these requirements should have its roots within the people themselves, and should be developed at its summit into that perfection of organisation which can only come to be regarded as an organic whole, existing for the whole purpose of protecting British interests, no matter where in the world those interests are threatened.

This idea, he agreed, would have to grow slowly in the public mind. The process of military education should begin at school, where training should take place under a syllabus prepared by the War Office and issued under the auspices of the Board of Education. On leaving school boys should be

[1] Papers of Field-Marshal Earl Haig of Bemersyde, National Library of Scotland, Box 32A.
[2] Memorandum of 25th April 1906, loc. cit.

encouraged to join a cadet corps; and at the age of 19 they should enlist in the Territorial Army – a body which, he believed, would attract the overwhelming majority of young men between the ages of 19 and 21. One result of this programme, as Lord Esher explained to the King, would be

> the fostering, by means of Cadet Corps and Rifle Clubs, [of] the military spirit of the people, which under a voluntary system . . . is essential, if your Majesty's vast empire is to be properly safeguarded, should an appeal some day have to be made to the manhood of the nation.[1]

The entire concept was frankly militaristic; but militarism was less unfashionable sixty years ago than it is, after two world wars, today. Haldane indeed, explaining to the House of Commons his proposals for establishing Officer Training Corps in public schools and universities, assured them rather oddly that 'You are not in danger of increasing the spirit of militarism there, because the spirit of militarism already runs fairly high both there and in the universities'.[2] Times have certainly changed: not, perhaps, entirely for the worse.

The term 'militarism', however, is indefinite and emotive. It is reasonable to assume – though I have never found any evidence for the assumption – that Haldane was influenced during his student days at Tübingen by the prevailing German *Zeitgeist* of the *Volk im Waffen*, the People in Arms. But German militarism was a complex affair, in which the Hohenzollern tradition of military absolutism was blended with the French Revolutionary concept of the identity of Army and People, and the aspirations of such Liberal thinkers as Scharnhorst and Boyen, to make the Army a school for the moral as well as the military education of the emerging German nation.[3] Such ideas were familiar in Edwardian England, as they were elsewhere in Europe, not least in France. A more immediate influence on Haldane's thought can be traced to the work of Jean Jaurès, the great French socialist thinker who in his book, *L'Armée nouvelle*, was to expound

[1] *Journals of Lord Esher* (London, 1934), II, p. 169.
[2] House of Commons Debates, 23rd February 1907.
[3] See Gerhard Ritter, *Staatskunst und Kriegshandwerk: das Problem des 'Militarismus' in Deutschland* (Munich, 1954), I *passim*, esp. pp. 97–124.

the democratic and left-wing arguments for universal military service.[1] In his speech to the Commons of 8th March 1906, Haldane used almost the exact words of Jaurès in making his ideas acceptable to the Radical majority on the benches behind him:

> I do think that in this fashion [of voluntary organisation on a local territorial basis] you might get control of the people over the military organisation, which would be the best guarantee that no war would be entered upon without the full consent of the people. A nation under arms in that fashion would be a nation under arms for the sake of peace and not for the sake of war.[2]

Certain Conservatives found such professions somewhat alarming. What kind of revolutionary militia were these Radicals intending to create, vowed as they were to the destruction of the property and influence of the landed classes? The King himself was evidently disturbed, for Lord Esher found it necessary to inform him that the committee charged with examining Haldane's proposals for the Territorial Army

> with one exception ... is composed of men who by political conviction, birth, station and education are opposed to the Government now in Office, and whose predilections therefore may be assumed to be strongly in favour of maintaining the authority of the Crown over all armed forces, whether Regular or Auxiliary, and opposed absolutely to anything in the shape of what is generally understood by the term 'citizen army'.[3]

Indeed Haldane, although a radical reformer by conviction, was no revolutionary by temperament. He did his best to conciliate the various interests which his innovations were likely to offend. The committee of which Esher spoke in such emollient terms consisted of 45 members drawn from the Regular Army, the Militia and the Volunteers. They were

[1] Jean Jaurès, *L'Armée nouvelle* (Paris, 1910). See also Richard D. Challener, *The French Theory of the Nation in Arms* (New York, 1954), pp. 71–3.
[2] House of Commons Debates, 8th March 1906.
[3] Journals of Lord Esher, loc. cit.

unable to reach full agreement. The Militia clung grimly to their historic status, refusing either to be grouped with the Volunteers and administered in local units, or to be formally designated as a draft-finding body for the expeditionary Force. There was bitter resistance among Volunteer units to the surrender of their cherished, if expensive, autonomy. Senior regular officers looked without enthusiasm on proposals for a body designed, not to find drafts to supplement the Army, but to fight in formed units – divisions and even perhaps Army Corps – of its own. Several of them openly preferred the alternative for which the National Service League under the veteran Field-Marshal Lord Roberts were pressing, of conscription on the continental model.

Haldane's reasonableness and tact quickly overcame the objections of his colleagues on the Army Council. As Lord Esher wrote in June 1908:[1]

> The officers of the Army realise that he is their friend; he has not worried them, and he has supported them. But among retired officers and among politicians of all shades, he has bitter enemies. Some of these people do not understand the political situation, and that Haldane alone stands between us and Churchill.

It was self-evident that Haldane's proposals were more acceptable than anything which *that* ruthless desperado might cook up. Nevertheless the storms which attended the birth of the Territorial Army were quite as violent and prolonged as any conjured up by its dissolution twenty years later.

In weathering these storms, Haldane was helped, as in all his military reforms, by the staunch support of the Crown, which Esher so assiduously mobilised on his behalf. But the real secret of his success lay in two major administrative innovations. The first was an imitation of the pattern which he had noted and admired in Germany; the separation of the functions of administration from those of training and command.[2] This made it possible to give the War Office that complete control over the training and deployment of all

[1] Ibid., p. 325.
[2] *Memorandum of Events between 1906 and 1915*, pp. 51–2. Haldane Papers, MS 5919.

military formations in the country, regular, reserve and auxiliary, to which it had always, naturally enough, aspired; while preserving the sense of ownership and responsibility which lay at the heart of any citizen force. The War Office would be responsible for command and training; administration would lie with county associations – and here was Haldane's second innovation, and perhaps the most brilliant of all. The term, a piece of grossly inaccurate historicism, seemed to link the new institution with those Cromwellian traditions for which Haldane's generation felt such a strong, and such a curious affection. These associations consisted of the commanding officers of the units concerned, representatives of the General Staff, and the representatives of all great local interests, from the Trades Unions to the Lords-Lieutenant. Their tasks included the recruiting of units, their organisation, finance and administration, and the provision of accommodation and training facilities. Into them the country gentry, if they so desired, could direct the energies which for generations they had devoted to the Militia. Through them the old Volunteer battalions could feel that they were still masters of their own destinies even though ultimate responsibility both for their employment and for their finances now rested with Whitehall. By them the sting of opposition, both in Parliament and in the country as a whole, was very largely drawn.

Thanks to this, and thanks also to the trouble which Haldane took to avoid giving offence where it could possibly be avoided, the Territorial and Reserve Forces Bill introduced into the House of Commons on 25th February 1907 had a surprisingly easy passage. There was little sympathy for the Militia, whose spokesmen had contended to the end for its survival as an independent fighting force. It was transformed into a Special Reserve to keep the Regular Army up to strength – the function which it had effectively performed since the days of Cardwell – and its long, rather bizarre story came to an end. Its place in the second line of the nation's defences was to be taken by a new Territorial Army, organised in fourteen divisions with their own artillery and services, and fourteen mounted brigades; 'as complete in every detail as the first line'.

The function of this force was not, like that of the Volunteers and Yeomanry of old, to be primarily home defence. That was now the concern of the fleet, whose command of the seas would not only enable the striking force – or, as it was renamed to avoid offence to Haldane's more pacific colleagues, the Expeditionary Force – to go overseas wherever it might be required, but would also provide precious time for the Territorials to train up to the standard of a first-class continental fighting force. It was still not considered politically practicable for this Army to be made statutorily liable for overseas service; but it was probable that once embodied, said Haldane, 'they would be ready, finding themselves in their units, to say – "We wish to go abroad and take our part in the theatre of war, to fight in the interests of the nation and for the defence of the Empire"... If given the occasion, I do not know that there is any limit to the spirit of our people when the necessity is upon them. At any rate they will have the opportunity.'[1]

They did indeed have the opportunity; but as we know, Haldane's vision was not to be realised quite as he had conceived it. The six years that elapsed between the creation of the Territorial Army in 1908 and the outbreak of the First World War did not see the conversion of the British people into the Nation in Arms which Haldane had visualised: trained and indoctrinated in military units from their youth up. One may doubt whether, even if war had not come so soon, such an objective could ever have been achieved, given the complex cross-currents in the British social system. But by 1914 the Territorial Army was past its teething troubles. Volunteers had smoothly adapted themselves to being Territorials and welcomed regular instructors even if they chafed at the influx of Army documentation. There is no reason to suppose that the machinery would not have produced the efficient second-line force that Haldane intended; certainly the volunteering for overseas service was as universal as Haldane had hoped. But when war came, Haldane was no longer at the War Office. In his place was a regular soldier who knew nothing of his work and who had all of his profession's contempt for amateurs. Kitchener used the Terri-

[1] House of Commons Debates, 25th February 1907.

torial formations which he already had to hand piece-meal to plug gaps, and launched a new appeal to the nation to join a new force improvised under the auspices of the Regular Army itself. The appeal was answered. Kitchener's armies, grimly baptised in the bloody waters of the Somme, deserved the title of the Nation in Arms no less than those of Carnot and of Scharnhorst. But it was not as Haldane had planned it ten years earlier in 1906.

After the war the pieces were put together again. In 1921 the Territorial and Militia Act re-established Haldane's pattern, with the additional feature that now the Territorial Army was automatically liable, on embodiment, for service overseas. Haldane's vision of the Territorials as the great National Army was never to be recaptured. It was to serve an indispensable purpose, providing a dedicated nucleus of enthusiasts in peacetime capable of rapid expansion on the eve of war; it was to produce units of all arms which were to prove their efficiency in every operational theatre between 1939 and 1945; and it was to serve as a continuing and necessary link between the ordinary citizen and the Regular Army. But it remained always a reservoir of manpower to supply and supplement the Regular Army rather than a force capable of taking the field in its own right; and it remained, engagingly and incorrigibly, the son of its volunteer father: a collection of very good clubs never quite aspiring to the heights for which Haldane had destined it of a Nation in Arms.

But these two concepts were not incompatible. The Territorial Army was in fact a good Hegelian synthesis, of the small, stubborn, intimate, independent Victorian volunteer formations, the military expression of pure capitalist private enterprise, and the somewhat grandiose continental étatism which briefly infected British thinking (as it infected British architecture) in the Edwardian age. If the British were to be educated to arms in peacetime at all, perhaps it could only be through the medium which they had developed and made so peculiarly their own: the club. Bred for generations in intimate, cohesive, mutually suspicious societies of conventicles, chapels and craft unions, of connections, parishes and colleges, unable even to produce an army which was more than a congeries of stubbornly independent regiments for whom tradition often ranked higher than efficiency, we produced a citizen force in our own, idiosyncratic pattern. And in a society where the growth of urbanisation and social mobility has been making it increasingly difficult for such social units to survive and flourish, the Territorial Army has continued to serve a social purpose of undeniable value even after the development of nuclear weapons cast reasonable doubt on the validity of its traditional military rôle.

A study of the origins of that Army and the controversies which attended its institution makes very clear how totally, during the past sixty years, the military problems confronting this country have been transformed, and how irrelevant the arguments which justified its creation have now become. Haldane's reforms broke up a pattern of military organisation which in essentials had changed little since the days of Napoleon – and broke it up just in time. Since then we have lived through greater changes still, and no less radical reforms are needed to meet them. But as the British people took Haldane's proposals and tailored them to fit their own rather curious shape, so it is likely to be with the reforms of Mr Healey. A historian may reasonably ask for a further sixty years' grace before being called upon to pronounce judgment on them.

6 Reflections
on the First World War

Even after fifty years the Great War lies like a dark scar
across the history of Europe, an interruption in the development of western society rather than a part of it. Until 1914
war seemed a natural enough part of the state-system, as of
the feudal and dynastic periods which had preceded it: disagreeable, inhumane, wasteful, but a perfectly effective
means of settling disputes irresolvable by any other means.
Even the Second World War seems a natural and intelligible
conflict over issues on which no compromise was possible.
Those of us who fought in it did so without any illusion that
we were creating a better world: we only knew, rightly or
wrongly, that the world which would develop if we did not
fight it would be intolerable, and that conclusion few of us
have seen any reason to revise. My own generation, aged
seventeen when the war began, twenty-three (those of us
who survived) when it ended, suffered as badly as any, but it
did so for a perfectly clear purpose, which gained rather than
lost its validity as the war went on. Mr Evelyn Waugh's
view, that what began as a crusade turned into a tug of war
between indistinguishable teams of sweaty louts, is idiosyncratic. Most of us did not feel like that. But it is evident that
by the end of the First World War a large number of intelligent people did; and ten years later their doubts had become
general.

What in fact was the First World War about? This is not,
on the surface, a difficult question to answer. Every belligerent in 1914 took up arms, either to repel a direct invasion of
its territory, or to fulfil a precise obligation which could not
be abandoned without shattering consequences to national
prestige, morale, and interests; concepts abstract and absurd
to the sardonic layman, but the raw material of all inter-

national affairs. Is that all there was to it? In Mr A. J. P. Taylor's eyes, yes.[1]

Men are reluctant to believe that great events have small causes. Therefore once the Great War started, they were convinced that it must be the outcome of profound forces. It is hard to discover this when we examine the details. Nowhere was there conscious determination to provoke a war. Statesmen miscalculated. They used the instruments of bluff and threat which had proved effective on previous occasions. This time things went wrong. The deterrent on which they relied failed to deter; the statesmen became the prisoners of their own weapons. The great armies, accumulated to provide security and preserve the peace, carried the nations to war by their own weight.

On a certain level of historical explanation, this is true enough; the level which would explain the French Revolution in terms of the financial difficulties of the *ancien régime*, or the Reformation in terms of Luther's theological differences with the Papacy. The *occasion* for war was certainly a series of events as fortuitous as those which have precipitated any other major historical event. But the historian has to go further, and ask why the circumstances were such that so small a detonation could lead to so devastating an explosion. For the answer he has to look far beyond the diplomatic documents. These are valuable in destroying the legend of the 'war guilt' of either side; but apart from that they really tell us very little.

For the diplomatic historian the reasons for the First World War are the traditional ones: the search for, and collapse of a balance of power, first in the Balkans and then throughout Europe. Austria wished to recoup a position in the Balkans eroded by the two Balkan Wars. Russia would not tolerate the humiliation of her client Serbia. Germany could not risk the further humiliation of her client Austria. It was a situation of a kind perfectly familiar to diplomats before and since. There was nothing about it which could not be settled by compromise, or at very most by a limited *Kabinetskrieg* if the forces for fighting such a localised and limited conflict

[1] A. J. P. Taylor, *The First World War: an Illustrated History* (Hamish Hamilton, London, 1963).

had been ready to hand. There were extremists in both camps – Pan-slavs who wanted to destroy Austria as a power, Austrians who wished to settle with Serbia for good – as there always are; but they were not beyond all power to check. The German commitment to Austria was certainly as vital a part of her policy as was the British guarantee to Belgium; but it could have been – as in Bismarck's hands it surely would have been – a stabilising and not a disturbing factor, a reassurance to Vienna rather than a temptation to adventure. It was precisely because nobody took this crisis seriously, because so many far more serious had been successfully dealt with in the past, that it so quickly became unmanageable, and involved all Europe in ruin.

Because the origin of the war was so insignificant, because the fighting spread to western Europe so quickly and continued there so intensively, it is tempting to see the 'real causes' of the war in the irreconcilable rivalries of the western European nations, particularly that of Germany and Great Britain. But this explanation does not stand up to serious examination. Once at war, British and Germans went for each other with the stubborn fury of berserkers, engaging in a long, slow, horrible death-grapple from which neither was fully to recover. True, for fifteen years before the war British and Germans had regarded each other with mounting distrust and dislike; but it may be doubted whether this rivalry ever reached, let alone surpassed, the level which had been normal in Anglo-French relations – with rare intervals – between Waterloo and the conclusion of the *Entente Cordiale*. Anglo-German colonial rivalries were never so acute as Anglo-French, and even the famous naval race was no greater a factor in embittering relations than had been the far greater naval panics of 1859–61 or 1885–9. The fear of German invasion intermittently alarmed the subjects of King Edward VII, as the fear of French invasion had intermittently alarmed the subjects of Queen Victoria. Bernhardi and von der Goltz wrote menacingly of the day of reckoning with England, as Aube and Charmes had written twenty years earlier. Such combinations do not make peace any easier to preserve, but they do not necessarily lead to war. There is no intrinsic cause why Britain's relations with Germany should not have developed peacefully into the same kind of guarded and grudging co-operation as we have established with the French over the past fifty years.

Yet if one does read Bernhardi or von der Goltz or Treitschke; or Frederic Harrison and Seeley; or Péguy and Psichari; or Mahan and D'Annunzio: or if one explores further and reads the pre-war editorials and the speeches at prize-givings and the pamphlets; or soaks oneself in the military literature of the period; one learns far more about the causes of the First World War than in a lifetime of reading diplomatic documents. The diplomats may have been desperately anxious to avoid a war, as were the businessmen; but (to lapse into Taylorian hyperbole) they were about the only people who were. 'The elder statesmen did their feckless best to prevent war, whilst the youth of the rival countries were howling impatiently at their doors for immediate war;' a fact which the idealistic youth of this country today, bear-led by Miss Joan Littlewood and, in his lighter moments, by Mr Taylor himself, find it remarkably easy to forget.

But if they howled, it was because for a generation or more they had been taught to howl. Listen to Lord Rosebery, by no means a martial figure, addressing the boys of Wellington College in 1909:

> The stress that patriotism will have to bear in days not distant, and perhaps imminent, will be greater than has yet been known in the history of this country (*hear, hear*). There never was a time when men were more needed to speak and act up to their faith (*cheers*). I think that men will have to be more universally armed in the future than they are now (*hear, hear*). . . . There are encroaching opinions which threaten patriotism, menace our love of country, and imply the relaxation, if not the destruction, of all the bonds which hold our empire together (*hear, hear*). I would urge that so far as possible the study of patriotism should be promoted (*cheers*).[1]

Read also the concluding words of Colmar von der Goltz's best-seller, *The Nation in Arms*:

[1] Quoted by David Newsome, *Godliness and Good Learning* (John Murray, 1961), p. 202.

It is necessary to make it clear to ourselves and to the children growing up about us, and whom we have in train, that a time of rest has not yet come, that the prediction of a final struggle for the existence and greatness of Germany is not a mere fancy of ambitious fools, but that it will come one day inevitably, with full fury, and with the seriousness which every struggle deciding the fate of a nation entails ere a new political system receives universal recognition. Bearing this constantly in mind, we must work incessantly, by example, by word, and by our writings towards this end, that loyalty towards the Emperor, passionate love for the Fatherland, determination not to shrink from hard trials, self-denial, and cheerful sacrifice may wax ever stronger in our hearts and in those of our children.[1]

One could multiply such quotations indefinitely, from French, Italian, and American sources as well as from British and German. The children of Europe were being trained for war, and war was regarded as something natural and inevitable. Why? There was the influence of Hegel and Mazzini seeping through all European thought, emphasising that the highest morality of the individual lay in service to the state, vulgarised in a million speech-day addresses like Lord Rosebery's. There was the popular 'social Darwinism' with its creed of the survival of the fittest among nations as among species. There were the technical requirements of mass armies, which coincided conveniently with these philosophical trends. There was an upper class which, with its status rendered precarious by industrialisation, found in military life the security, purpose and prestige increasingly denied it in civil. There was a great mass of uprooted proletariat and urbanised petty bourgeoisie, for whom national pride provided a status and fulfilment lacking in their drab everyday lives. There was that disquieting strain of primitive savagery which composers and artists were beginning to tap during the first decade of the twentieth century. There were the boiling frustrations of deepening class-war. Trends like these are difficult and sometimes impossible to document,

---

[1] I quote from the English translation of the fifth German edition, published in London in 1913. I have not checked whether this sentence appears in the first edition of 1883.

but no study of the war can be complete which does not take them into account.

Mr Taylor does not say very much about them; partly because he is a diplomatic rather than a social historian by training, more probably because he is working to rigid limitations of space. He does mention, without explaining or dwelling on it, the enthusiasm with which the war was everywhere greeted. He also points out quite correctly that this enthusiasm did not begin to ebb until the war had run more than half its course. In 1915, he writes, 'there was hardly as yet a flicker of discontent or discouragement in any belligerent country.' Kitchener's armies displayed on the Somme in 1916 no less ardour than the regular soldiers who had dashed over to France in 1914 for fear of missing the fighting. Mr Taylor rightly points out that 'all imagined that it would be an affair of great marches and great battles, quickly decided.' But no one expected, or asked, that there should not be heavy casualties. There was no cold douche of disillusion after the blood-letting of 1914 or even of 1915: it was what everyone had been led to expect. This, after all, was exactly that trial of patriotism, manliness, and endurance for which the nations of Europe had been preparing themselves for an entire generation.

Thus when Mr Taylor talks about 'the deterrent . . . failing to deter' he is being dangerously anachronistic. Armies were not, except perhaps in the eyes of the diplomats, conceived of as 'deterrents'. They were instruments for fighting a war which was widely regarded – and not by the soldiers alone – as being inevitable, necessary, and even desirable. And once engaged, the peoples of Europe showed themselves in no hurry to disengage. When military deadlock had been reached by 1916, the obvious corollary was a compromise peace; but few historians would claim – Mr Taylor is certainly not among them – that those in favour of such a course represented, in the nations of western Europe, more than a tiny and unpopular minority. Why should the Germans, everywhere victorious, abandon an inch of the soil which they had won at such a cost to adversaries who might use it as a springboard for another and bloodier war? How could the French contemplate peace while the invader still occupied so much of her soil? How could the British acquiesce in a settlement which would leave Belgium in German hands? Only in 1917 did the German Social Democrats, with great political courage, come out publicly in favour of a peace with no annexations or indemnities; but by then the total collapse of Russian resistance was making such wise moderation unthinkable for the Germans in eastern Europe, while the entry of America into the war made it unnecessary for Britain and France to consider any compromise at all. The democracies of western Europe, and of course of North America, were fighting for noble causes – the destruction of 'Prussian militarism', the liberation of the subject peoples of eastern Europe – which could be gained, they believed, only if the adversary, huge, evil, dimly descried through the battle-smoke, was totally overthrown. The flower of British and French manhood had not flocked to the colours in 1914 to die for the balance of power.

Popular emotion, then, goes far to explain why the war, when it broke out, should have been so prolonged and so bloody. For the rest, one must look at the nature of the military machines on which the powers of Europe had for the past forty years been lavishing so much loving care.

The first characteristic to notice about these machines is not the obvious one of their size, but that, no less important, of their inflexibility. Millions of men had to be recalled to the colours, organised into fighting units, equipped with a vast apparatus of supporting arms and services and sent by railway to their points of concentration, all within a few days. The lesson of 1870 was burnt into the mind of every staff officer in Europe: the nation which loses the mobilisation-race is likely to lose the war. Mr Taylor rightly points out that it was only in the German Army that mobilisation inevitably meant war – that general staff plans involved not only the concentration of the armies but, as a necessary consequence of that concentration, their *Aufmarsch* into the territory of their neighbours. But in no country could the elaborate plans of the military be substantially modified to meet political requirements. For the Austrian government a declaration of war was a political manœuvre, for the Russian government a mobilisation order was a counter-manœuvre;

but such orders set in motion administrative processes which could be neither halted nor reversed without causing a chaos which would place the nation at the mercy of its adversaries. Even the British government blithely assumed, on 5th August, that it retained complete freedom of choice where to send the B.E.F. in Europe, if they sent it at all; when every ship, every train, and every wayside halt had in fact been designated years in advance, as they *had* to be, if British troops were to arrive in time, and in condition, to fight. The bland ignorance among national leaders of the simple mechanics of the system on which they relied for the preservation of national security would astonish us rather more if so many horrifying parallels did not come to light whenever British politicians give their views about defence policy today. As it was, the German Chancellor spoke for his civilian colleagues in every nation when he exclaimed in despair 'the situation has got out of hand, and the stone has started rolling. . . .' Armies were juggernauts which even their own generals could hardly control.

Military mechanics thus certainly played their part in dragging Europe into war. More predictably they determined the kind of war it would be. The object of all this conscription, mobilisation, and concentration was to arrive on the battlefield in the greatest possible strength; for it was in battle, and only in battle, that the destiny of the nations would be decided. So much had the general staffs learned from Clausewitz, from Jomini, from Bonnal, and from all other commentators who had laboriously analysed the campaigns of Napoleon and of the great von Moltke. 'The best strategy consists in being very strong, first everywhere and then at the decisive point': Clausewitz had made it as easy as that. Battles were not to be won by subtlety or manœuvre; the decision would go to the commander who displayed the strongest moral fibre, who, undismayed by his own casualties, forced the enemy to exhaust his reserves until the moment came when nerve and resistance snapped, the battle-line broke and the victor was able to surge irresistibly forward to dictate peace in the enemy's capital. The new battlefields would be incomparably vaster than the Napoleonic; the new weapons would inflict far heavier casualties; but few commanders doubted that the pattern of Austerlitz, of Jena, of Sadowa and Sedan would be repeated, on a Brobdingnagian scale.

The conventional wisdom of the military was not so much at fault as has sometimes been supposed. On the eastern front, from East Prussia to Galicia, battles of this kind did occur. Fronts did crumble. The victorious cavalry did pursue. It was on the western front that the unforeseen factors came in. The tactical strength of the defence made it impossible to gain a quick decision in battle. The strategic mobility provided by railways stopped at the railhead. Forward of that, even such tactical mobility as had been enjoyed by Napoleonic armies was slowed to a dead halt by machine-guns. Machine-guns could be overcome only by artillery; artillery forfeited surprise, and itself slowed up the advance; so even when a tactical breakthrough was made, it could not be exploited before the defender's railways could bring up fresh reserves to restore the situation. Even so, this did not, in the eyes of the commanders, change the fundamental lessons which Clausewitz had distilled from the Napoleonic experiences. The battle went on for longer than expected; the casualties were higher than expected; but so long as the enemy reserves were being used up at a higher rate than one's own, all was going well. The more stubborn the resistance, the greater the ultimate victory. All that mattered was not to be deflected from the aim, not to allow the will to be shaken, but to exercise all the qualities of moral fibre and resolution which distinguished the Commander, not only in face of the dogged resistance of the adversary, but against the tempters at home who were constantly urging that there must be some easier path to victory.

It is difficult, even with all the wisdom of hindsight, to see that there was an easier path. So long as railways kept the armies supplied with the blood and treasure of the nations, the armies could not be defeated until the nations themselves were exhausted and begging for peace. The experience of 1870, indeed, had shown that even the most crushing military defeats in the field need not necessarily be decisive, if there was still the political will to fight on; whereas if that will had been sapped sufficiently, the most trifling military defeats

might be decisive. It took only two battles, negligible by
earlier standards, at Salonica and at Vittorio Veneto, to bring
about the collapse of the exhausted central powers in 1918.
The subsequent claim of the German military, that the German Army remained 'undefeated', was an appeal to totally
anachronistic criteria, irrelevant even if it had been true.
Armies were no longer corporations distinct from their parent
societies, engaging in gladiatorial combat. Once the national
will to war had been exhausted, that great reserve of enthusiasm and patriotism and endurance built up over a century
of careful training and squeezed to the last drop by relentless
war-propaganda, the military instruments of that will were
as useless as empty suits of armour.

Mr Taylor's summing up of the struggle is pretty summary. It failed to produce Utopia, he agrees, but

> on a more prosaic level it did rather better than most wars,
> though no doubt the price was excessive. The subjects of
> the Habsburg Empire obtained their national freedom;
> the subjects of the Ottoman Empire started on the same
> path. The war postponed the domination of Europe by
> Germany, or perhaps prevented it. The most practical war
> aim was the one most completely achieved. Belgium was
> liberated.

All true enough. Certainly, the wastage in wealth and even
in human life was quickly made good. Certainly, the great
empires of central and eastern Europe had long been in
decay, and the war only hastened their fate. But the effects
of the war on the peoples who had fought it, whose physical
and moral reserve had been slowly sapped, who had seen
traditional authority discredited for ever and who had
learned that the traditional virtues only led them to the
shambles, cannot be measured in terms of peace settlements
alone.

As for the military, the lesson for them was clear. If the
centre of enemy power lies, not in his armed forces, but in
his civilian population, then that population must be attacked
directly. It must be softened and subverted by propaganda.
It must be starved and enfeebled by blockade. It must be
remorselessly bombed from the air. Its morale must be under-

mined to a point where its capacity for armed resistance is fatally weakened. Only then, with swift armoured thrusts, can the *coup de grâce* be delivered. The vast tomes of Clausewitz and his disciples were removed to the lumber-rooms of military libraries, their place being taken by the works of Douhet, Mitchell, Fuller, Liddell Hart. The art of war had outgrown Passchendaele. It was almost ready for Hiroshima.

7   Hitler and his Generals[1]

It is a truism that the vanquished are likely to learn more from their defeat than the victors from their victory. Their histories, also, are often fuller and more reliable. They will naturally contain a human element of buck-passing and self-exculpation, but the catastrophe is there plain for all to see. There is little left to hide, there is everything to be explained; and in any case catastrophes pose more interesting questions for historians than do triumphs. The fifty-year rule, deplorable as it is, is not the only reason why British historians have produced nothing comparable to the reflections of, say, Hans Delbrück on the First World War, or of Friedrich Meinecke on the Second. Defeat might have shaken the academic moles out of their burrows. Victory enabled them to scuttle happily back, leaving it to journalists, official historians and military autobiographers to study the greatest crisis in the history of Europe, if not of the world.

But the trauma inflicted on Germany was too great for German academic historians to remain blind to the need to make a profound examination of the disaster in which they had all been personally involved. For a decade or so, while German military archives were in the hands of the victors, their studies had to be, like those of Professor Dehio and Professor Ritter, deep analyses of the development of German society over the past hundred years. War history was left, as it still is in this country, to able journalists such as Walter Goerlitz, retired soldiers like General Tippelskirch, and the personal reminiscences of such generals as von Manstein, Kesselring and Guderian. There were no 'official' historians, and there still are none.

But instead the Germans have developed something that we lack in this country, and for which the Cabinet Office Historical Section provides no substitute: a group of academic

[1] Written in 1963.

institutions, part officially and part privately sponsored, which recruit some of the ablest young historians in the country to study and publish the principal documents bearing on the German catastrophe as they become available, and to use them as raw material for works of scholarship whose thoroughness and sheer bulk put everything produced in this country – the Official Histories alone excepted – to shame.

The Institut für Zeitgeschichte, the Arbeitskreis für Wehrforschung and the Gesellschaft für Auswärtige Politik; working in close co-operation with the Bundesarchiv at Coblenz; enjoying the support of such great publishing houses as Bernard und Graefe, Mittler, and Kohlhammer; employing scholars of the calibre of Hans-Adolf Jacobsen, Walther Hubatsch and Jürgen Rohwer: all this constitutes a scholarly community without parallel elsewhere in Europe and one worthy of the academic traditions of nineteenth-century Germany. In the very existence of such a community Germany's former adversaries can take a legitimate pride. No one who contemplates what the alternative would have been in the event of a German victory, what Reichsministerium with what uniformed, docile officials glorifying the Führer to order – one gets an ugly smell of it from some of the Russian works produced in the Stalin era – can doubt that the total destruction of the Nazi régime was worth every drop of allied and German blood that had to be spilt in achieving it.

For these scholars dodge none of the terrible issues which an honest study of the Second World War must force upon the German people. The remarkable collection of photographs and documents which Dr Jacobsen has assembled in the three fat, handsome volumes of *Der Zweite Weltkrieg in Bildern und Dokumenten*[1] includes not only pictures of the German Army heroically in action but also pictures of the mass graves, the death-camps, the destruction of the ghettoes and all the rest of the infernal mechanism of the régime for

[1] *Der zweite Weltkrieg in Bildern und Dokumenten*, edited by Hans-Adolf Jacobsen and Hans Dollinger. Erster Band: Der Europäische Krieg 1939–41. 380 pp. Zweiter Band: Der Weltkrieg 1941–43. 480 pp. Dritter Band: Sieg ohne Frieden 1944–45. 492 pp. Munich: Kurt Desch.

which the German Army fought with such skill and courage, and whose orders it continued loyally to obey.

For the Germans this must be the central problem of the whole war. Why did the Wehrmacht, one of the finest military machines in all recorded history, serve so loyally a régime which its leaders so heartily despised? The German Army prided itself not only on its military skill but also – perhaps to a unique extent – on its 'soldierly honour'. Its leaders retained, at least until the end of 1941, a greater degree of independence than any other body in the state. 'The General Staff', as Hitler himself said, 'is the only Masonic Order that I haven't yet dissolved'; and he declared that 'those gentlemen with the purple stripes down their trousers sometimes seem to me even more revolting than the Jews'. He loathed them as the survivors of an establishment he longed to destroy; he feared them as potential conspirators and rivals; and he retained a twisted remnant of the front-line soldier's contempt for the Staff. 'And just what has your front-line experience been?' he screamed at General Halder, the last survivor of the great Moltke tradition to serve him. 'Where were you in the First World War? To think of you trying to tell me I don't know about the front!'

Much has been written about this unhappiest of marriages, and nothing in English to surpass Sir John Wheeler Bennett's *The Nemesis of Power*. But with the publication of further documents by the scholarly groups referred to above a fuller picture is now beginning to emerge, not only of this relationship but also of the entire conduct of the war at its highest level. Most important is the War Diary of the Oberkommando der Wehrmacht, or O.K.W., edited by the survivor of the two staff officers responsible for keeping it, Professor Percy Schramm.[1] Professor Schramm, himself a professional historian, is directly responsible for the last volume, dealing with the years 1944–5, which, following a well-established tradition, is the first to appear; in many ways paralleling Mr John Ehrman's two Grand Strategy volumes in the British

[1] *Kriegstagebuch des Oberkommandos der Wehrmacht (Wehrmachtführungsstab) 1940–45*. Volume IV: 1st January 1944–22 May 1945, edited by Percy Ernst Schramm. In two parts. 1,940 pp. Frankfurt am Main: Bernard und Graefe.

Official History, although Dr Schramm makes it clear that his work is not only material for the historian and not history itself.

The same can be said of the autobiography of General Warlimont, *Im Hauptquartier der deutschen Wehrmacht, 1939–45,*[1] although this is the fullest first-hand study of Hitler's war leadership that has yet been published. General Warlimont, as deputy to General Jodl, occupied a place in the military hierarchy comparable to that of, say, General Hollis in this country. After Keitel and Jodl he was the senior officer in Hitler's personal *maison militaire*, and he is, as a result, the senior survivor. That he did not share the fate of his superior officers shows that the allied tribunals accepted at their face value the protestations of innocence and inability to influence the course of events which recur throughout these memoirs. Historians will be grateful that they did. For General Warlimont's is a solid and scholarly book worthy of the awe-inspiring events he describes; not, like the memoirs of certain British generals, trivial gossip retailed to journalists interested only in maximising sales.

The same is true of the dry, sparse diary of General Halder, of which only the first volume has so far appeared.[2] Since this deals only with the lightning campaigns of 1939–40, when General Halder was Chief of Staff under General Brauchitsch and not immediately responsible to Hitler himself, it is likely to be of less interest than the second volume which is announced for this year, and which General Warlimont himself freely quotes. This will presumably cover the great controversies of the Russian campaign, Hitler's dismissal of all his senior generals and assumption of direct command of the Army, and the nightmare nine months when General Halder worked directly with Hitler as his Chief of Staff. 'If Halder's presentations, in their knowledge and judgment, their style and approach, represented the highest traditions of the General Staff,' observes General Warlimont,

[1] Walter Warlimont, *Im Hauptquartier der deutschen Wehrmacht, 1939–45. Grundlagen, Formen, Gestalten.* 570 pp. Frankfurt: Bernard und Graefe.

[2] Generaloberst Halder, *Kriegstagebuch.* Band I. Edited by Hans-Adolf Jacobsen. 391 pp. Stuttgart: Kohlhammer.

'Hitler chose to answer them in the character of a People's Tribune.' General Halder himself wrote in July 1942, at the beginning of the summer offensive, 'No more question of serious work. Neurotic reaction to impressions of the moment and total failure to gauge the structure of command and its possibilities are the chief features of this so-called "leadership"' (*Führung*). One wonders only how he stood it for as long as he did.

One might be tempted to discount much of General Halder's and General Warlimont's criticisms of Hitler as a military leader simply as professional jealousy of a successful amateur. General Warlimont writes with almost comic indignation of 'Orders given in form that stifled all independent movement – where He Who Knows Best, wholly satisfied with himself, would shift battalions and divisions to and fro, losing entire armies in the process'. But the results speak for themselves and so do the documents. In Hitler's *Weisungen für die Kriegführung*, edited and annotated by Professor Hubatsch,[1] we can trace for ourselves the decline from the crisp and precise statements of aims and methods which characterise the plans for deployment and operations up till the crisis year 1941, when Hitler was still operating by orthodox staff methods; through the wordy repetitiveness of Directive No. 41, for the 1942 campaign in Russia; to the hysterical appeals for fanatical resistance, devoid of any kind of strategic insight, which he launched during the last year of the war. In his Directive for the Battle of Rome, for example, Hitler ordered: 'The struggle must be hard and ruthless, not just against the enemy *but against all units and commanders which are found wanting in this decisive hour*'. An order which was calculated, as General Warlimont remarks, 'to wither any kind of military discipline at its roots'.

Finally, as a clinical record of the atmosphere in Hitler's headquarters from which these crazy orders were issued, we have now a complete edition of all that survives of the *Lagebesprechungen:*[2] the stenographic reports which Hitler

[1] Walther Hubatsch (ed.), *Hitlers Weisungen für die Kriegführung, 1939–1945*. Dokumente des Oberkommandos der Wehrmacht. 330 pp. Frankfurt: Bernard und Graefe. DM.39.
[2] *Hitlers Lagebesprechungen, Die Protokolfragmente seiner*

ordered to be made of all his staff conferences when he
began to suspect, in the autumn of 1942, that his generals
were disobeying his orders. A brief selection from this repellent document has already been published by Dr Felix
Gilbert under the title *Hitler Directs his War*; but only this
full edition can give the marathon flavour of those dreary
ranting monologues in which politics, strategy, philosophic
reflection and personal abuse were jumbled together, in
which the movement of single divisions was endlessly discussed, in which political and private reminiscence was given
free rein and from which, indeed, only one element was
missing: any clear strategic concept based on a thorough
appreciation of well-authenticated facts, of how the war was
to be waged and won. For strategy Hitler substituted in-
tuition, will-power, and, towards the end, sheer terror. 'Anyone who speaks to me of peace without victory', he amiably
informed his entourage, 'will lose his head, never mind who
he is or what his position.'

As for his military advisers, Hitler had by 1943 destroyed
their hated independence as effectively as that of all the
other 'Masonic Orders', and with it all chance that they
could win his war. 'Generals have got to obey just like the
most junior private . . .', he laid down; 'I am the leader and
everybody must follow unconditionally.' Here was an end to
that principle of flexible operational independence on which
the whole structure of the Army had rested since the days of
Moltke and which was more perhaps than any other element
the foundation of its success.

By 1945 every unit in the whole great machine was
shackled to the will of a dictator who oscillated between
momentary whims and fanatical determination to yield no
inch of ground. By his directive of 21st January 1945, Hitler
made all commanders down to divisional level personally
responsible to himself for all operational decisions, both for
withdrawal and for attack. 'His contemptuous formulations,'
comments General Warlimont bitterly, 'show him openly
venting his hatred of the staff officers of the General Staff and
their spiritually and ethically rooted independence.' It might

Militärischen Konferenzen, 1942–1945. Edited by Helmut Heiber.
Stuttgart: Deutsche Verlags-Anstalt.

be added, however, that after the *Attentat* of 20th July he had some reason to do so.

This peculiar relationship between Hitler and his generals made for a unique command-structure from which it would be unwise to try to draw any conclusions of universal application. When defence organisation is discussed in this country the opponents of increased centralisation often cite O.K.W. as an example of over-centralised control which, by separating planning from execution and power from responsibility, fatally diminished the efficiency of the German Armed Forces. But as General Warlimont and Professor Schramm make clear, O.K.W. was not really an operational headquarters. It was Hitler's personal military secretariat, comparable not to the British Chiefs of Staff but rather to the private office which General Ismay ran in London for the Prime Minister.

Hitler appointed Keitel as its head precisely because Blomberg had recommended him as a good *chef de bureau* who was fit for nothing else. Jodl, Blomberg's most intelligent disciple, had at first seen in O.K.W. an organisation for centralising command of the services, and he gladly accepted service with Hitler to achieve this end. In fact, under Hitler's influence it virtually ceased to be a military establishment, as Jodl testified a little pathetically at Nuremberg. It was, he said,

> a cross between a monastery and a concentration camp.... It was not a military headquarters at all but a civilian one, and we soldiers were there as guests, and it is not easy to be a guest for about five and a half years.

In this atmosphere it was easy to lose touch, not only with the *Stimmung* of the Army – General Warlimont describes with irritation how Jodl always *had his hands in his pockets* at conferences – but also with everything else in the Third Reich, military and civil. Goering ran the Luftwaffe as his private empire. Raeder and Doenitz dealt direct with Hitler over important naval matters, merely keeping O.K.W. informed through their representatives there of what was going on. There was no overall appreciation of the war situation or rational allocation of priorities. The Allied landings in North

Africa, for example, came as a complete surprise, and counter-measures had to be improvised in an atmosphere of total confusion.

As for the Army, Hitler dealt directly with that as well, even before he appointed himself its commander in December 1942. O.K.W. was not consulted at all during the military preparations for the invasions of Austria, Czechoslovakia, Poland, or Russia. The invasion of Denmark and Norway, a three-service operation *par excellence*, was, it is true, planned by a special staff within O.K.W., but this time it was the Army that was left out of consultation: 'better get that on record for the war historians', was General Halder's bitter comment.

The invasion of England was also an O.K.W. responsibility, but one which fell to it largely by default, through Hitler's own lack of enthusiasm for the project. As the war developed, indeed, Hitler increasingly used O.K.W. as a convenient receptacle for matters which were in his view too marginal or too complicated to warrant his own attention. The Baltic, the Mediterranean, the Middle East, relations with allies and satellites, all became O.K.W. responsibilities; not because O.K.W. alone could deal with their far-ranging military-political implications but because they were in Hitler's view secondary – trumpery, almost – in comparison with the struggle on the Russian front. From this last O.K.W. was totally excluded. It was an O.K.H. theatre, and over it Hitler dealt immediately with the Chiefs of Staff to the Army – Halder, Zeitzler, Guderian – until the Russians were at the very gates of Berlin. Only on 25th April 1945 did Jodl achieve an ironical empty triumph, when the armies on the eastern front, in so far as they still existed, were at last put under O.K.W.'s control.

But during the last two years of the war the development of the Anglo-Saxon threat from south and west was making it impossible even for Hitler to regard the O.K.W. theatres any longer as 'secondary'. The collapse of Italy in the summer of 1943 compelled Hitler to give the Mediterranean an over-riding priority in order to safeguard the Balkans, over whose security he displayed throughout the war a quite obsessive zeal. Thereafter, watching the allied preparations for 'Overlord' at the end of that year, he admitted: 'The attack in the west, whenever it comes, will decide the outcome of the war.'

Yet he still did not give O.K.W. the authority it needed to allocate resources to these theatres. The only result was a tug-of-war between O.K.W. and O.K.H., between Jodl and Zeitler, over the rapidly diminishing military resources of the Reich, with himself as the final arbiter. And when Hitler was confronted by problems of priorities which could not be solved by simple calls for fanatical resistance, he showed an indecisiveness and ignorance of strategic principle which deepened the contempt in which the soldiers held his judgment, and embittered still further the hatred which he had always had for them.

Yet it would be quite false to accept the picture, which German soldiers are inclined to paint, of Hitler's interference as being that simply of an ignorant amateur, disrupting plans based on sound military concepts which would inevitably have led to victory. Hitler's interventions in 1940, for example, were usually to support a view being developed within the Army itself, hostile to that of the High Command. His most successful was his sponsoring of Manstein's proposals for invading France through the Ardennes. His most notorious was the famous 'Halt Order' at Dunkirk, which the German generals have depicted as a politically inspired veto on their military plans but which Dr Jacobsen, in his definitive study of the Dunkirk campaign, has shown to have been a similar intervention in a purely military debate. But in any case these interventions raised no large issue of principle. It was only with the planning and launching of the Russian invasion of 1941 that it became clear that Hitler and his generals had very different views of what war was all about; and in the conflicts that followed it is by no means certain that Hitler was entirely in the wrong.

For Hitler did see, probably more clearly than did the heirs of Moltke and Schlieffen, that war in the twentieth century was not a simple contest between armed forces conducted according to the principles of orthodox strategy which nineteenth-century theorists had derived from studying the Napoleonic Wars. The First World War had shown the bankruptcy of this view. Basically, modern war was a

conflict of rival economic systems, which the side with access
to the fullest economic resources was virtually bound to win.
'Modern warfare,' he laid it down, 'is above all economic
warfare, and the demands of economic warfare must be
given priority.'

Not all the triumphs of the Imperial Armies could save the
Germany of 1918 from internal collapse, and this must never
be allowed to happen again: this is the message which ran
through the pages of *Mein Kampf*. The attack on Russia was
not simply an assault on the fortress of Bolshevism; it was the
essential preliminary to the creation of that New Order
which would make the Third Reich self-sufficient and im-
pregnable. The coal of the Donetz basin, the oil of the
Caucasus, the grain of the Ukraine, these were the objectives
for which Hitler fought, as Ludendorff had fought before
him. Deprived of these, and of access to the Baltic, the Soviet
Union, he was convinced, would quickly collapse.

To the German General Staff this was the oldest and most
dangerous heresy in the whole of military thought: the belief
that wars could be won without defeating the enemy armed
forces. Warlimont rebukes Hitler because he 'deviated from
the first and immutable object of the conduct of war – to
eliminate the enemy's vital force – in order to pursue secondary aims'. In the conflict between the generals and Hitler in
summer 1941 over whether to aim at Moscow and destroy
the armies which would certainly mass to defend it, or to
seize first the economic resources without which those armies
could no longer fight, we can hear echoes of the old argument so familiar in British military history. Should we attack
the enemy's trade, or his fleet? Should we seize his colonies
or help our allies destroy his armies? Should we mount a
massive surface invasion or devote our resources to attacking
his economic structure from the air?

We can follow the course of this controversy over what
Jodl rightly discerned to be 'perhaps the hardest [decision]
. . . of the present war' in the successive drafts of the Directives for the Russian invasion printed by Professor Hubatsch.
We cannot tell for certain which side was right. We only
know that the month's delay while the matter was threshed
out, added to the late start of the campaign due to the Balkan

complications of the spring, made it impossible for the German Army to reach *any* of its objectives before the weather broke. The result was the disaster of 1941, the virtual collapse of the High Command, and that personal intervention by Hitler which, it may be agreed, alone saved the Army from total rout. The next year Hitler was to have no rivals in shaping his strategy round the economic objectives of the Caucasus; but if the absence of the generals made strategic planning easier, it was fatal to strategic execution. Hitler may have saved the German Army in 1941, but he lost it irremediably, by his sheer technical incompetence as a commander, in the campaign of 1942.

There was another and more sinister aspect of the war, however, into which Hitler could certainly claim a deeper insight than any of his military commanders. It was a revolutionary war fought against societies radically alien and hostile to the values which the Nazi Party professed. Military victory was a mere preliminary to social and political transformation, and the Army was only one instrument among many in the hands of the political surgeon. In the pluralistic societies of the west this transformation of the defeated enemy to take his part in the new order might be gradually carried out behind the façade of a Quisling government. With a rival totalitarian system, sterner measures would be needed. What these measures would be Hitler outlined in a supplement to his Directive for Operation Barbarossa in March 1941. The political aspects of the invasion, he explained through Jodl, were too difficult to be entrusted to the Army. Instead, 'To pave the way for the eventual political administration the Reichsführer S.S. will be given special tasks within the Army area as a mandate from the Führer. These result from the struggle between two diametrically opposed political systems, which must now be conclusively settled.'

There followed the setting up of the *Sonderkommandos der Sicherheitspolizei*, to carry out the *Sonderaufgaben* or 'special tasks' (we can see them at work in Dr Jacobsen's horrible photographs) and the issuing of the notorious *Kommissarbefehl*. Hitler carefully explained the whole policy to his senior military commanders at a special meeting on 30th

March 1941. No one protested. No one asked any questions. The German military code permitted vigorous and prolonged protest when Hitler dared to violate orthodox principles of strategy: when he declared his intention of violating the fundamental moral and ethical codes which hold human society together, it permitted an acquiescent silence.

General Warlimont gives us the usual assurance that the German Army had no part in these prescribed atrocities, and that when given the chance it fought as cleanly on the Russian front as anywhere else. We can believe him, as we believe the assurance of the defendant that he had no personal part in the murder of the night-watchman during the raid in which he took part, even though he had been told in advance that the murder was to be an intrinsic part of the affair; but he will not expect us, or the Russian people, to be particularly impressed.

This is now past history; though it is easier for us to regard it as such than it is for the peoples on whose territories the atrocities occurred. The political system of central and eastern Europe today rests as much upon the freshness of their memories as it does upon the bayonets of the Red Army. Expiation for the German crimes has been exacted and is still being exacted. But the best expiation, that which leads most fully to reconciliation and forgiveness, is to be found in the works of scholars as honest, clear-sighted and thorough as these, who are prepared both to examine what occurred and to explain how it came to occur. In their work, and the respect which it commands among their countrymen, lies our best assurance that we have not been premature in accepting the new Germany as an ally and the new Germans as our friends.

8 The Mediterranean in British Strategy in the Second World War

The conflict between British and American war leaders during the Second World War over the part which should be allotted to the Mediterranean theatre in their strategy for the defeat of Germany has been very fully treated by writers in both countries. The exaggerated and propagandistic image of Allied unity presented during the war was replaced in the post-war years by an almost equally overdrawn picture of the differences which underlay that smooth façade; differences to which historians sometimes contributed by exaggerated claims for the wisdom of the leaders on whose documents they based their work, or uncharitable attribution of motive, guile, or foolishness to those with whom they were out of sympathy. One image which has gained wide international acceptance has been that of a logical and coherent 'Mediterranean strategy' formulated largely by Mr Winston Churchill, based on political as well as military calculations, which would, had it been accepted by the United States, not only have won the war more expeditiously but have placed the western powers at the end of it in a position of political advantage in east and south-east Europe vis-a-vis the Soviet Union. It is not a picture which stands up to serious study. The place of the Mediterranean in British strategic thinking was a great deal more complicated than that.[1]

The Mediterranean played a major part in British strategy in the Second World War for one very simple reason: British forces were already there, defending British interests which had grown up over many decades. Britain had been a major Mediterranean power since the seventeenth century, and had provided herself with strong *points d'appui* at Gibraltar

[1] The present writer has attempted to outline its essential characteristics in *The Mediterranean Strategy in the Second World War* (London, 1968).

and Malta to enable her to remain one. Her naval strength there had enabled her to bring direct support to her continental allies, and blockade and harass her continental adversaries, during all her great conflicts with France from the age of Louis XIV to that of Napoleon. In the last years of that rivalry, at the end of the eighteenth century, the Mediterranean acquired new importance as the first stage on the route to the Indian Empire from which Great Britain was drawing an increasing proportion of her national wealth. In the nineteenth century, with the decline of the Ottoman Empire and the growth of concern over Russian expansion to the south and east, the British interest spread from the eastern Mediterranean to the entire Levant. In 1878 Cyprus was acquired as a *place d'armes* to provide a staple for British naval power in the east comparable to Gibraltar in the west. A few years later the almost accidental involvement in Egypt led to a massive increase of British influence and responsibility, if not of British power, in the Near East; and that influence and responsibility was to be increased yet further when the Ottoman Empire collapsed in 1918 and Britain, guided by such frank imperialists as Curzon, Milner, and Churchill, moved in to fill the vacuum by establishing her military power and political influence in Palestine, Transjordan and Iraq.

By 1939 the Middle East was one of the two major *foci* of Britain's world imperial power; the Far East complex of India and south-east Asia being the other. French possessions lay adjacent in both regions; but they did not, in the eyes of French political and military leaders, possess a comparable strategic importance. Inexorable geographic necessity compelled Frenchmen to concentrate their resources on defending the land frontiers of their own country. It being Britain's good fortune to be an island, she could devote greater attention to the problem of 'Imperial Policing' and 'Imperial Defence'; and it was in these terms that British military thinking was couched between the wars. The building of the ill-fated Singapore base occupied little less attention in Whitehall than the problem of the air defence of Great Britain itself. When war came, the British Chiefs of Staff had to think in terms of the defence, not of the United Kingdom and her dependencies, but of three widely separated areas: the United Kingdom and her continental allies; a Far Eastern region extending from India's north-west frontier to New Zealand; and a Middle-Eastern bloc on which the entire system was dangerously dependent for essential supplies of oil. Each area was under threat: north-west Europe by Germany, the Middle East by Italy, the Far East by Japan. Their communications depended on the Royal Navy retaining virtually uninterrupted command of the sea. The huge complex of the British Empire which sprawled so splendidly scarlet over the maps of the world was in fact terribly vulnerable; and the vast resources which it controlled had to be used almost entirely in its own defence.

The Mediterranean must therefore be seen, as Britain's political and military leaders saw it, as part of an interdependent global system; and as the war went on, its importance to that system increased. The collapse of France deprived Britain of all help in the Mediterranean and closed that sea to transit shipping, which now had to be routed round the Cape. If the Far East collapsed, Japanese sea power could dominate the Indian Ocean and intercept that shipping off the coast of East Africa. If the Middle East collapsed, the Axis could not only capture the vital oil resources of the Persian Gulf, but threaten India. British Middle East Command in Cairo had not only the spectacular threats to its own security from Axis thrusts in the Western Desert to consider. To the north-east was the Soviet Union, whose collapse would expose Iran to German invasion; in the south-east lay the all-important oil refineries of Abadan; while in the east in Iraq, as in Egypt itself, the British knew that an increasingly vocal part of the native Arab population regarded them as guests who had outstayed their welcome, and would regard their forcible eviction with little regret.

When the war began in 1939 the British position in the Middle East did not appear particularly precarious. Italy was still neutral, and French power was intact. The planning of the British Commander in Chief, General Wavell, and of his allied colleague in Syria, General Weygand, was ambitious and aggressive. The German war effort was known to be very largely dependent on oil obtained from Rumania and, to a lesser extent, on that provided by the Soviet Union under the terms of the Nazi-Soviet Pact of August 1939. Although Hungary and Rumania had fallen within the Nazi sphere of influence, Greece, Yugoslavia and Turkey remained neutral; and if they could be wooed into the Allied camp, the Germans would not only be threatened with a war on two fronts but their vital economic resources would be brought under very severe threat. The eyes of both Wavell and Weygand were very firmly fixed on the Balkans. For them the main contribution they could make to Allied strategy was to pose an offensive threat against the German southern flank.[1]

This aggressiveness survived even the disastrous summer of 1940. The loss of French support was to some extent balanced by the rout of the Italian forces in Africa the following winter. Mussolini's rash adventure in Greece opened opportunities in the Balkan peninsula of which political and military authorities attempted, equally rashly, to take advantage; only to suffer humiliating defeat at the hands of the Germans simultaneously in the Western Desert and Greece. The Axis was able in consequence to establish the Aegean as an outpost of *Festung Europa*. But Hitler remained highly nervous about his Balkan flank, and the British chiefs of staff never lost sight of the advantages to be gained there. Negotiations with Turkey, support to Greek, Jugoslav and Albanian insurgents and plans for bombing the Rumanian oilfields remained a major feature of British planning until a very late stage in the war.

These plans however remained unrealistic until the general war situation took a turn for the better and resources could be made available for implementing them. From the summer of 1941 until the autumn of 1942 the British in the Middle East, like the Russians who had joined them so unexpectedly as allies in June, were forced on to the defensive and had little chance to think beyond it. Until the end of 1941 the attack came only from the west, from the Axis forces spearheaded by Rommel's *Panzerarmee*, and fortunately it was mounted on comparatively small scale. It is interesting to

[1] See John Connell, *Wavell, Soldier and Scholar* (London, 1964), esp. pp. 219–20, and Maxime Weygand, *Memoires, tom. iii. Rappelé au Service* (Paris, 1950), Chapters 1 and 2.

speculate what would have happened if Hitler had been
prepared to allocate resources to this theatre on the scale
urged not only by his Italian allies and his commanders in
the theatre but by his own naval authorities and by General
Halder, his Army Chief of Staff.[1] The Axis interior lines
enabled them to concentrate forces far more quickly than
the British, all of whose reinforcements had to come, with
painful slowness, round the Cape; and once arrived, German
ground forces displayed a marked qualitative superiority
over the British. As it was, Hitler could never be persuaded
of the strategic significance of the theatre, and starved it of
resources in his attempt to obtain a decision on the eastern
front; whereas the British, driven on by a Prime Minister
personally and passionately concerned to obtain military
victory in the only place where British arms could be deployed, strained every nerve to build up a superiority of
strength; a superiority all too often squandered by incapable
commanders in the field.

It has been very plausibly argued that Churchill in 1941 in
fact allocated too high a priority to the Middle East;[2] concentrating resources there to gain victories which, however
spectacular, would have been of secondary strategic significance, while he took unacceptable risks in failing adequately
to reinforce Britain's defences against Japan. Much can be
said on both sides. Of the two theatres, the Middle East was
certainly the more vital to Britain's war effort. Its oil resources
were essential to India if not to the United Kingdom; and it
was not underwritten, as was the Far East, by the massive
power of the United States. Yet its defence might have been
organised more economically, without the attempt to secure
the kind of spectacular success which Churchill insistently
demanded from his generals in the field. But would the resources thus freed have substantially changed the situation
in the Far East? The British collapse in Malaya was due, not

[1] See F. H. Hinsley, *Hitler's Strategy* (Cambridge, 1951), and
Andreas Hillgruber, *Hitlers Strategie: Politik und Kriegführung
1940–1941* (Frankfurt a/M, 1965).
[2] Particularly by Sir Basil Liddell-Hart, *The Military Balance
Sheet of World War II* (Lectures at the University of London,
1960).

to lack of resources only, but to lack of training, lack of proper planning, and lack of leadership. More forces in the area might have only increased the scale of the disaster. At any rate it was a disaster which had repercussions on the Middle East itself; for in April 1942 the Japanese fleet irrupted into the Indian Ocean and added a menace from the south-east to that which Middle East Command faced from the west. Three months later the German thrust to the Caucasus added a third menace from the north, just as Rommel, routing the Eighth Army and overrunning the fortress of Tobruk, stormed forward to the Egyptian frontier. The Chiefs of Staff had to contemplate the dire possibility of abandoning Egypt altogether and falling back on a last-ditch defence of the refineries at Abadan.

As it was, the British defences – like the Russian further north – held firm for long enough for the German thrust to exhaust itself and for the strategic balance of forces to be redressed. And now this could be done on a massive scale. With the Wehrmacht strained unendurably in the Homeric struggle at Stalingrad, little more could be spared for the secondary Mediterranean theatre; while behind Britain now stood the arsenal of the United States. By the autumn of 1942 the British had regained complete command of the air in the eastern Mediterranean and had built up an overwhelming superiority on the ground. They were in a position to challenge Rommel to a battle of attrition, and had in Montgomery a commander who was not afraid to force it through to its conclusion. The result was the victorious battle of El Alamein: the first major victory gained by Commonwealth forces over a German-led Army, and the last which they were to win on their own account.

Two weeks later, on 8th November 1942, British and American forces disembarked in French North Africa, and for the first time the entire Mediterranean became a theatre of war.

Behind this Operation 'Torch' there lay nearly a year of strategic debate. It had opened when, in December 1941, the British Prime Minister and his Chiefs of Staff visited Washington shortly after the Japanese attack on Pearl Harbor, to discuss with their new allies their joint strategy for the conduct of the war. The American Joint Chiefs of Staff had already agreed that, if confronted with war simultaneously against Germany and Japan, they would concentrate their resources primarily against Germany as the stronger of their two adversaries.[1] This decision was now confirmed. Further, they accepted, apparently without debate, the proposals which the British laid before them for the conduct of the war in Europe. These, apart from the provision which they made for maritime warfare, strategic bombardment, subversion and blockade, visualised operations as proceeding by two stages. The first, which would occupy the whole of 1942, would be directed to 'closing the ring' about Germany, by building up the Russian front, arming Turkey, building up strength in the Middle East and gaining possession of the whole North African coast. Operations in the Mediterranean were seen as part of the preliminary investment of the European fortress. The second stage would be the assault in 1943, which might, as circumstances dictated, take place across the Mediterranean, from Turkey into the Balkans, or by landings in western Europe. For none of these alternatives did the British, at this stage, express any preference.[2]

These proposals were entirely acceptable to the Americans, who would in any case need a year to mobilise their forces and transport them to Europe. But since the only base from which their Army and Air Force would be able effectively to operate was the United Kingdom, and the only area where their armies could deploy to engage the Wehrmacht for a decisive battle appeared to be north-west Europe, they had no doubt that when the assault was launched in 1943 it should be across the Channel. In April 1942 General Marshall visited London with firm proposals for such an assault; the build-up operation to take place in 1942 ('Bolero') and the assault ('Round-Up') in 1943. With these proposals the British agreed. The third operation proposed by Marshall, a

[1] Louis Morton, 'Germany First: the Basic Concept of Allied Strategy in World War II', in K. R. Greenfield (ed.): *Command Decisions* (New York, 1959).

[2] J. M. Gwyer and J. R. M. Butler: *Grand Strategy*, III (U.K. Official History of the Second World War, Military Series. London, 1964), p. 669.

small-scale attack to be launched across the Channel that summer with largely British forces, they agreed only to examine; but about the general strategy outlined by the Americans there was no dissent, either from the Prime Minister, the War Cabinet or the chiefs of staff. The Mediterranean should be cleared in 1942, and the assault across the Channel launched in 1943.[1]

It will be seen that this strategy involced, during 1942, no major operations against the Axis except a continuation of those in the Western Desert, and no involvement of American ground forces in Europe at all; a perfectly sound assumption in view of the unreadiness of the American war machine and the heavy pressure being exerted on both allies by the Japanese attacks in the Far East. But it was unwelcome to President Roosevelt. On the one hand the sweeping run of Japanese victories in the Pacific over American forces had enraged public opinion in the United States and strengthened the hand of those within the armed forces who questioned the whole concept of 'Europe First'. On the other, the President had grave doubts about the capacity of the Soviet Union to survive another year of German attacks without either collapsing entirely or being compelled to capitulate; doubts which the Soviet Foreign Minister, M. Molotov, who visited the United States in May 1942, naturally did nothing to allay. The President went so far as explicitly to promise him a 'Second Front' in Europe in 1942; and the following month he gave the order that 'US ground forces must be put into position to fight German ground forces somewhere in 1942.'[2]

There was only one way in which this order could be carried out without wrecking the whole 'Bolero–Round-Up' strategy: by launching the cross-Channel expedition in 1942 in which British forces would play the leading part. But the British military planners who had been examining the operation had come to the conclusion that, with the forces which would be available that summer, the Allies stood no chance

[1] Maurice Matloff and Edwin Snell, *Strategic Planning for Coalition Warfare 1941–42* (Washington, 1953), pp. 187–91.

[2] Robert S. Sherwood, *The White House Papers of Harry Hopkins* (London, 1948), II, p. 607.

of establishing any beach-head which would not be rapidly eliminated by German forces already in the theatre: a conclusion which the Dieppe operation in August was most depressingly to vindicate. But failing that, what else could be done? The Combined Chiefs of Staff were unanimous in rejecting Mr Churchill's proposal for a landing in northern Norway; and that left only French North Africa.

An American landing in Morocco had been briefly considered by the Combined Chiefs of Staff the previous December, when the Eighth Army was engaged in a successful advance which might, it was hoped in London, bring it to the frontiers of Tunisia. The repulse of the Eighth Army the following month, and the chronic shortage of shipping, led to the abandonment of the idea; but it was one which continued to attract the President. The United States had retained links with Vichy France and had many agents in North Africa whose over-enthusiastic reports suggested that the whole area would fall into American hands like a ripe plum. The British naturally favoured an operation which might take the weight off their hard-pressed forces in North Africa – forces whose chances of 'closing the ring' by occupying the entire North African coast appeared, in the summer of 1942, to be very remote indeed. But the British Chiefs of Staff were under no illusion. They knew that a landing in French North Africa, with all the resources which it would absorb in manpower, shipping and assault craft, would so disrupt the arrangements for 'Round-Up' as to make it impossible in 1943, and so did General Marshall. If the target-date for 'Round-Up' was abandoned, all arrangements made for a concentration of resources would have to be changed. The Mediterranean operations would make unpredictable demands; the insistent pressure of commanders in the Pacific could not be ignored; and the entire 'Europe first' principle might have to be abandoned.

When the President overruled the protests of his chiefs of staff and ordered them to co-operate in the North African venture, Marshall and his disappointed staff felt betrayed. They attributed the change of plan to British pressure; and British pressure they attributed to the personal influence of a Prime Minister and officials who aimed at using American power to forward British political interests in south-east Europe and the Middle East. Marshall informed his British colleagues that the North African operation meant the end of the strategy agreed on at Washington the previous December and 'the definite acceptance of a defensive, encircling line of action for the Continental European Theatre, except as to air and blockade operations against Germany.'[1] The Americans loyally co-operated in mounting Operation 'Torch', but for the rest turned their attention to the Pacific, where their attack on the Solomon Islands in August opened the first stage of their long counter-offensive against Japan.

The British were disturbed by the American attitude. The suspicions on which it was based were entirely unjustified. The British Empire did indeed have interests to defend in the Middle East; the Chiefs of Staff were indeed alive to the military opportunities offered in Turkey and south-east Europe, which appeared even greater in Cairo than they did in London; but they and the Prime Minister had supported the North African operation for no other reason than that it was the only one which they considered operationally feasible in 1942. The question now arose: what should be done next? It was necessary to provide a convincing alternative to the American inclination to seal off Europe and turn to the Pacific. Shortage of resources – shipping and assault craft above all – made any return to 'Round-Up' in 1943 out of the question, though this operation, considered the British chiefs of staff, should certainly be planned for 1944.

But it was also out of the question to allow a full year to elapse without any land operations against the Axis at all; a year during which the Soviet Union would continue to bear the full brunt of the war. The British chiefs of staff therefore agreed that, after the North African landings, operations in the Mediterranean should continue so as to turn the whole area into a 'heavy liability' to Germany and in particular to force the collapse of Italy. This would compel Germany to divert forces to the theatre which, it was hoped, would be drawn either from the eastern front, where the pressure would be taken off the Russians, or from the garrisons in France, which would make invasion easier the following

[1] Gwyer and Butler, op. cit., p. 635.

year. Whether these operations would consist in the first place of attacks on Sicily or Corsica and Sardinia, and whether they would lead to invasion of the Italian mainland was as yet undecided. The British were only concerned, when they met their American colleagues at Casablanca in January 1943, to persuade them neither to write off the European theatre altogether nor to suspend all operations there until 1944; but to continue with operations in an area where they could operate effectively and immediately, to bring help to the Soviet Union, weaken the Axis, and pave the way for eventual cross-Channel attack.

Marshall accepted these arguments with the greatest reluctance. He could offer no alternative, but he feared with very good reason that further operations in the Mediterranean would make far greater demands on Allied resources than anyone expected; while some members of his staff still felt that behind the military reasoning lay obscure political motives to which the Americans were unwittingly being harnessed.[1] It was however agreed at Casablanca that the Allies should now aim at the capture of Sicily, while establishing a joint staff to begin detailed planning for the cross-Channel operation which should be launched in summer 1944. The British had been successful in wooing the Americans back to the continuation of offensive operations in the European theatre, and very much on their own terms.

Beyond Sicily the British had, at the time of the Casablanca Conference, no firm plans. The objective in their eyes was to bring about the collapse of Italy; it was not possible to visualise what further measures, if any, would be necessary, and it was difficult to appreciate exactly what this collapse would involve. The Dodecanese, the Greek mainland, the Illyrian coast, the Italian mainland, Corsica and Sardinia all offered possible means of increasing the threat to southern Europe, but none of these possibilities were seriously considered in the spring of 1943. It was however unlikely that the Chiefs of Staff or the Prime Minister would accept the American view that no further operations should

[1] See particularly Albert C. Wedemeyer, *Wedemeyer Reports!* (New York, 1958), pp. 105–6.

take place in the Mediterranean after the fall of Sicily. The British military establishments in the theatre were now enormous; their troops were battle-hardened and successful; their commanders and their staffs were prolific with suggestions on how they could best be employed. Operations had in fact developed an inertia of their own. British planners in Cairo drafted and redrafted schemes for seizing the Dodecanese. The British commanders who led the First and Eighth Armies to victory in Tunisia in April 1943 naturally hoped to carry the war into the enemy's own country and ride in triumph through Rome; a hope which Mr Churchill emphatically shared. The British Joint Planning Staff had also observed the growing flame of revolt in the Balkans, especially in Yugoslavia, over the past six months, and believed with good reason that these partisans, if armed and supplied, might double the number of troops the Germans would be forced to detach from other fronts to cover their southern flank. By May 1943, when the Combined Chiefs of Staff again met in Washington, the British were virtually unanimous in believing that the occupation of Sicily should be followed by an invasion of the Italian mainland.

This was exactly what Marshall had feared: an open-ended commitment which would draw in increasing forces and probably once again make it impossible to attack across the Channel. The British argued in Washington in May, and in Quebec three months later, that the two theatres were not competitive but interdependent. Only by continuing with operations in the Mediterranean, urged General Brooke, could the conditions be created which would make possible a cross-Channel invasion: the wearing down of German ground and air strength and the disruption of their ability to reinforce their defences. The scale of the cross-Channel attack would also be rigorously limited by the number of assault craft available; the forces in the Mediterranean could not be used in Normandy even if the shipping was available to return them to the United Kingdom. Once more Marshall agreed with profound reluctance. Behind the British attachment to Mediterranean operations the Americans were now beginning to see, not devious political calculations, but an unwillingness to commit themselves to large-scale land operations on the Continent;[1] and here they had a very much better case. The British commanders were indeed cautious. As young officers they had been through the Somme and Passchendaele. In the early years of the war they had seen the effect of premature commitment of unprepared troops with inadequate air cover against the Wehrmacht in Norway, Belgium and Greece. They were determined to risk neither a slaughter nor a débacle, and it sometimes seemed to them that the Americans were light-heartedly heading for both.

The compromise agreed in May was that operations in the Mediterranean should continue but only with a limited number of forces. The rest should be returned to the United Kingdom to take part in the cross-Channel attack (now re-named Operation 'Overlord') or else sent out to the Far East. How these forces should be used remained unsettled until, two weeks after the invasion of Sicily had begun, the news came through of the collapse of the Fascist régime in Italy and the arrest of Mussolini. Then Marshall himself proposed that they should launch an invasion of the mainland as far north as fighter-cover would permit, and make a dash for Rome. Churchill, delighted, was able to wire to him: 'I am with you heart and soul.'

The collapse of Italy, though long-expected, took the Allies by surprise. The British had visualised the possibility of a rapid occupation with a German withdrawal to the Appenines. They had also considered occupying only the far south of the country, Calabria and Apulia, and concentrating on sending help to the Yugoslav partisans. What nobody had conceived was that a régime might be established which wanted to surrender but would be unable to do so unless the Allies came to their aid. That however was the situation revealed by the Italian emissaries who contacted the Allies in August, and the month passed in frantic political and military improvisation. The Allies mounted an attack, at Salerno, which had slender chance of success unless the Italians moved fast to paralyse the Germans. The Italians would not move unless they were assured of Allied support

[1] Maurice Matloff, *Strategic Planning for Coalition Warfare, 1943–44* (Washington, 1959), pp. 213–14.

on a quite impossible scale. The armistice announcement was a shambles, and the Salerno operation was very nearly the same. Even after the landings had succeeded and the Germans had fallen back north of Naples the balance of forces remained precarious, and the British continued to protest vigorously at the withdrawal of those units earmarked for Operation 'Overlord'. Marshall had hoped that a rapid descent on Italy would put an end to the Mediterranean commitment. As it was he found himself landed with the open-ended drain on his resources he had always feared.

The British were disappointed that the collapse of Italy did not pay more spectacular dividends, but they had every cause to congratulate themselves on the success of the strategy they had persuaded the Americans to accept at Casablanca nine months before. The forces employed could not, if Marshall had then had his way, have been brought into action again until the following summer. As it was their operations had forced Italy from the war, creating a vacuum into which the Germans had to pour substantial forces. Over forty divisions had been diverted to Italy and the Balkans by the end of the year, but not before the Allies had captured air bases in south-east Italy from which to intensify the strategic bomber offensive against Central Europe, and large stocks of Italian weapons had fallen into the hands of Greek and Yugoslav partisans. The Germans had, it seemed, been badly unbalanced, and the British wanted to keep them unbalanced by maintaining continuous pressure. The Allied forces in Italy should not be left to struggle in the mountains south of Rome: they should, considered the Chiefs of Staff, be given the resources to press their offensive up the length of the peninsula, to exploit the unrest in the Balkans, and maintain the maximum pressure on the German forces, even if this meant further delaying the cross-Channel attack. 'We must not,' they wrote on 11th November 1943, 'regard "Overlord" on a fixed date as the pivot of our whole strategy on which all else turns.'[1]

The Chiefs of Staff still saw the Mediterranean in the context of the wider strategy for the defeat of Germany, which included not only the Russian front and 'Overlord' but the

[1] John Ehrman, *Grand Strategy*, V (London, 1956), p. 111.

pressure of the Combined Bomber Offensive. They were to continue to disagree, at times very bitterly indeed, with their American colleagues about the degree of effort which should be allotted to it, but they never lost sight of the principle, that the object of operations in that theatre was to engage German forces in the greatest strength possible so as to weaken their defences in north-east Europe and divert their strength from the Russian front. Nevertheless during the eight months from the beginning of October 1943 until May 1944, when 'Overlord' was in preparation and the Allied forces in Italy were struggling to continue their offensive against a skilful enemy occupying positions ideal for the defence, the British Chiefs of Staff found themselves always in the position of advocates for the Mediterranean commanders. Their reluctance to deprive a commander in the field of resources he considered essential to his campaign was very natural: but it further deepened the suspicion and irritation in Washington with an ally who seemed incapable of sticking to an agreement once it had been made.

The record was certainly not very good. At Quebec in August 1943 the British had firmly accepted 1st May 1944 as the target-date for 'Overlord'. Within two months they were asking for it to be postponed, to enable General Alexander's forces in Italy to continue their offensive to the Pisa–Rimini Line. This the Americans accepted, at the Teheran–Cairo Conference in November, on condition that Alexander then used his resources to mount an offensive against the south coast of France (Operation 'Anvil') to coincide with 'Overlord'. The British agreed. Yet two months later they were asking for 'Anvil' to be cancelled. Alexander had run into further difficulties, and now doubted his ability even to capture Rome if he had to prepare for 'Anvil' at the same time. The Americans again yielded. 'Anvil' was postponed until after the capture of Rome, even though it thereby lost its *raison d'être* as a supporting operation for 'Overlord'. Finally, once Rome fell, Alexander again demanded the cancellation of 'Anvil', so that he could press his attack into the plains of Lombardy and perhaps even to Vienna. But the Americans had had enough. The Italian campaign, they considered, had served the purpose allotted to it in the Allied grand strategy, compelling the Germans to disperse their forces and making possible the decisive thrust in the north-west. Now all superfluous resources should be concentrated in the major theatre and a decision forced as quickly as possible. With this reasoning even General Brooke found it hard to disagree.

The Prime Minister did not. After the summer of 1943 his strategic appreciations show less of that capacity to grasp the totality of the war, and to see the part which each theatre should play in it, which characterised his great state papers of 1940-2. Perhaps age and fatigue were taking their toll. Certainly there is evidence of his mounting impatience with the junior part which he found his country playing as the American contribution to the war in Europe increased. He could not muster for 'Overlord', an operation for which the Americans would ultimately provide nearly four-fifths of the forces, the enthusiasm which he felt for operations conducted by the veterans of the Western Desert under the banners of the Eighth Army and the command of his favourite general, Alexander. 'There lay at the back of his mind,' wrote General Brooke, 'the desire to form a purely British theatre where the laurels would be all ours.'[1] And in the forefront of his mind there was, as ever, the emotion which his military advisers dreaded but which was as natural to the democratic politician as to the former cavalry officer: the wilful desire for immediate and spectacular success. 'I feel,' he told Roosevelt in October 1943, 'that Eisenhower and Alexander must have what they need to win the battle in Italy, no matter what effect is produced on subsequent operations.'[2] It would appear that Churchill's passionate interest in the Mediterranean in 1943 and 1944 arose very largely from his desire to see there a striking victory under British military leaders which would redress the changing balance in the Grand Alliance.

[1] Arthur Bryant, *Triumph in the West 1943–1946* (London, 1959), p. 71.
[2] Winston S. Churchill, *The Second World War*, V (London, 1952), p. 221.

And what of that other great ally, the Soviet Union? Some historians have suggested that it was primarily fear of her post-war expansion that inspired the whole of the Mediterranean strategy; which would, if properly carried through, have brought Anglo-Saxon armies into central and south-eastern Europe before the Russians could get there.[1] In fact contemporary documents show very little evidence of any such motive before the spring of 1944. Until 1943 what the Allies feared was not Russian expansion but Russian collapse. On the part of their peoples – especially the British people – there was the most profound admiration and gratitude for the magnificent struggle of the Soviet Union, and a sense of angry frustration that more could not be done to bring her help; a sentiment nowhere expressed more strongly than in the speeches, letters and memoranda of the Prime Minister himself. The impossibility of allowing the Russians to fight on alone for another year had been one of the strongest arguments used by the British at Casablanca in urging the Americans to continue operations in the Mediterranean. The growth of Soviet influence in the Balkans began to trouble the Foreign Office in 1943, but it did not yet affect the thinking of the Prime Minister. He told his envoy to Marshal Tito, Brigadier Fitzroy Maclean, that 'so long as the whole of Western civilisation was threatened by the Nazi menace, we could not afford to let our attention be diverted from the immediate issue by considerations of long-term policy. We were as loyal to our Soviet allies as we hoped they were to us.' Maclean's task, he told him, 'was simply to find out who was killing the most Germans and suggest means by which we could help them to kill more.'[2]

But by the summer of 1944 the Prime Minister's attitude had changed. Diplomatic friction between the West and the Soviet Union over the settlement of eastern Europe had increased as the approach of the Soviet armies made the matter increasingly urgent. The British now recognised that the future of Yugoslavia lay in the hands of Marshal Tito and had to accept whatever degree of Soviet influence in that

---

[1] e.g. Hanson Baldwin, *Great Mistakes of the War* (New York, 1950). R. W. Thompson, *The Price of Victory* (London, 1960).

[2] Fitzroy Maclean, *Eastern Approaches* (London, 1950), p. 281.

country he was prepared to admit. But they still felt that their interests lay in supporting the royalist government in Greece against the insurgent, communist-dominated forces of ELAS; while in Poland honour, if not interest, demanded that they should give what support they could to the emigré government in London whose forces had fought so gallantly to liberate, as they hoped, their country. It was the uprising of these forces in Warsaw in August 1944 which brought relations within the Alliance almost to breaking point. Not only did Soviet troops a few miles east of the Vistula make no effort to go to the help of the insurgents, but they refused landing and refuelling facilities to Allied bombers who were prepared to fly from Italy to drop supplies. Between the Germans who were abandoning eastern Europe and the Russians who were entering it it seemed that there might be very little to choose.

This crisis in inter-Allied relations coincided with the final conflict between the Western Allies over the disposition of forces in the Mediterranean. On 7th June, the day after the fall of Rome, General Alexander had asked to be allowed to retain his forces intact for a further assault which would carry him, he hoped, over the Appennines, through the Ljubljana Gap to Vienna. In fixing on this ambitious objective, six hundred miles away through increasingly mountainous terrain, there was no doubt in Alexander's mind an element of political calculation. Certainly there was in that of the Prime Minister, who gave the scheme his powerful support. Yet even at this stage this element should not be overestimated. Alexander and his staff were naturally reluctant to see their theatre sink into obscurity and the team they had trained so successfully broken up. For them Vienna would be the appropriate end of a long road and a fitting crown to their efforts. Churchill saw in Alexander and his men the finest flower of that British Empire whose power and prestige he was determined to uphold – not only against the Soviet Union but against the United States. The forestalling of the Soviet Union was only one factor in his calculations, and that not, perhaps, the most important. Certainly he had no difficulty the following October in negotiating with Stalin a businesslike division of power which accorded to the Russians in eastern Europe the sphere of influence which they regarded as the legitimate reward for all that they had suffered and achieved during the past four years.

It will be seen from this account that the Mediterranean cannot be said to have played any simple and consistent part in British strategic thinking during the Second World War. It was necessary for the British to fight for its control if they were to protect their position in the Middle East; and their presence there enabled them to attack successfully the Italian Empire at a time when all other alternatives were barred to them. Once they were able, with American support, to swing over to the strategic offensive, control of the Mediterranean enabled them to invest Hitler's fortress, administer the *coup de grâce* to his Italian ally, bring a certain amount of help to the guerrilla in the Balkan peninsula, and maintain pressure on the German war machine until the attack across the Channel could be mounted with good prospect of success. Naturally operations in the theatre acquired a momentum, and the commanders there acquired ambitions, of their own; and political considerations, concerning British relations with the United States quite as much as those of the West with the Soviet Union, led Mr Churchill to encourage these to a point where they threatened to diverge totally from the Allied strategy agreed, and indeed very largely devised, by the British chiefs of staff. This divergence did not in fact occur, and the few months in the summer of 1944 when it threatened were exceptional. But they have cast a long shadow before them, which it must be the historian's task to dispel.

9 Bombing and the Bomb[1]

In 1961 the Stationery Office published, in four fat and handsome volumes, the Official History of the Bomber Offensive in the Second World War.[2] Reviewers on the whole were less interested in the massive scholarship of this work than in the controversial nature of its conclusions; and a number of senior officers who should have known better rushed into print to express violent opinions based at best on misunderstanding of the book and more often on simple and inaccurate hearsay. The polite but crushing rejoinders of the surviving author, Noble Frankland, and the opportunity to read the entire work at leisure undisturbed by telephone-calls from Fleet Street, have either reduced these critics to silence or forced them to mature better-founded attacks.

But some controversy was inevitable, and the editors of the series must have known it when they selected the formidably pugnacious Sir Charles Webster to take charge of the work. Behind almost every major decision relating to the air attack against Nazi Germany there lay prolonged conflicts of opinion, the more bitter in that they had to be conducted in deepest secrecy. There was the whole question of the rôle and mission of the Royal Air Force itself between the wars, and the amount of money to be spent on it at the expense of the senior services. There was the balance to be struck between offensive bomber and defensive fighter capacity. There were the conflicting claims of the bomber offensive against Germany, the Battle of the Atlantic, and close support for ground operations. There were disputes over the most effective target systems to attack – oil, transportation, the aircraft industry, or civilian morale. Decisions on these questions,

[1] Written in 1962.
[2] *Strategic Air Offensive against Germany*. Four volumes – I: *Preparation*; II: *Endeavour*; III: *Victory*; IV: *Annexes and Appendices*. Published by Her Majesty's Stationery Office.

like all military decisions, had to be made rapidly, if not hastily, on the basis of evidence known to be inadequate, and historians will debate endlessly whether or not they were right. Certainly the protagonists, determined and able men who did not win their way to the top of their professions by suave self-effacement, do not regard the issues as closed, and they are likely to express themselves the more violently for having been compelled, through loyal discretion, to remain silent for so long.

This is all intensely interesting, not only for professional historians, but for all whose destinies were shaped by the outcome of these controversies. This interest in itself would justify the labours which have gone into the book; and to try to set its conclusions in a wider context and use it as a tool in a type of intellectual enquiry even more ambitious and complex than that which its authors conducted may be unwise. It is perhaps only an idiosyncratic itch which leads me to do anything of the kind, and one better not scratched in public. Webster and Frankland should no doubt he left as a monument of Second World War historiography rather than examined for some light on our present discontents, in an effort to link the bombing with The Bomb. Perhaps the vast politico-technological problem comprised in the words 'The Bomb' is best left to politicians, technologists, and military analysts to solve, uncomplicated by the irrelevant intrusions of historians. On the other hand, if it is a matter of all hands to the pumps, the contributions of the historian are no more irrelevant than those of anybody else to a predicament which is as unique as it is dangerous for mankind: in which academic caution, if maintained for too long, becomes slothful timidity.

In any case, Webster and Frankland trace for us, in their history of thinking about air warfare, a pattern which it is tempting to extrapolate. Air power was preached by its early apostles, Viscount Trenchard foremost among them, as the solution to the deadlock to which war seemed to be reduced in 1914–18, when the capacity of industrial nations to raise, arm, and transport vast armies to the battlefield had been equalled only by the capacity of forces dug in behind field-fortifications and armed with machine-guns to slaughter them. Victory in that war came ultimately not through

Napoleonic triumphs in the field but through the collapse of whole nations strained beyond endurance: a collapse, incidentally, almost as disastrous to the victors as to the vanquished. But if the ultimate objective was not the enemy's armed forces but the morale of his people, why attack his armed forces at all? In 1870 the German invaders of France had decided that the quickest, and ultimately the most humane way to reduce French fortresses was to bombard not the fortifications but the civil population so that they themselves compelled the garrison to surrender. *Mutatis mutandis* the apostles of air power advocated the same thing. The development of flight laid the whole of belligerent territory open to attack. Air power opened a new world, free from the sterile slaughters of generals and the antiquated obsessions of admirals. It could be used with surgical precision in conflicts which, however painful, would be brief and effective. The air forces appealed to the young and adventurous as armies with the record of 1914–18 behind them could never appeal. The *Luftwaffe* was the cherished darling of Hitler's new order; the Royal Air Force in the thirties attracted intelligent young men who had read Wilfred Owen and Siegfried Sassoon and who were determined to escape at least that kind of war. The air forces of the world believed that they could do great things, if only they were given the money and the equipment to do them with.

The first great thing which the Royal Air Force did was to win one of the decisive battles of history in the Battle of Britain. But that victory could hardly have been more ironical. The guiding faith which had inspired Trenchard in his creation of the force was that the bomber would, and must, always get through, and that air defence was not only useless but a positive drawback in that it weakened the forces which could be deployed in attacking the enemy. The civilian population, in the words of Giulio Douhet, must submit to the attacks which the enemy inflicted on it until the enemy forces had been destroyed at their sources and that 'command of the air' secured which was, like command of the sea, indivisible and the truest defence. A natural civilian reluctance to submit to anything of the sort led to the air staff being overruled before the war, and resources being devoted to home defence which made possible the perfection of fighter aircraft and radar devices: developments which invalidated all the assumptions on which Trenchard, and other airmen throughout the world, had worked. The cheering image which the RAF built up for itself in the eyes of the public in 1940, of a handful of stubborn heroes successfully defending the skies and shores of their homeland against the hordes of an all-conquering invader, was very different from the rôle which its founding fathers had planned; and the outcome of the Battle of Britain presaged an air war very different from any they had expected. The very name of that engagement revealed that air power had not rendered battles obsolete: it had only changed their nature and location. An industrial nation subjected to air attack could still provide itself with such effective defences, aided by all the resources of science, deployed with skill, and manned by resolute men, that it could inflict on the attackers a rate of loss above their capacity in aircraft and trained man-power to sustain. Once command of the air was achieved it could certainly be used against the enemy vitals with surgical precision. But it could be achieved only by a process of attrition almost as heart-breaking as that of 1914–1918, from which the airmen hoped they had escaped for good.

The air war between 1939 and 1945 was thus, as Dr Frankland has pointed out in a recent authoritative lecture, not revolutionary, but classical in its conduct. The chiefs of Bomber Command had to develop the qualities – acquiring sometimes almost the physical image, as one can see from their photographs – of the generals of the First World War. They had to remain stubbornly convinced, in the face of tragic losses, that they were inflicting greater damage on the enemy than they were suffering themselves. Like Sir Douglas Haig and his staff in 1916–17, Sir Arthur Harris had no doubt whatever that under a few more blows German morale would, without any question, collapse. And they had to sustain the morale of men whom they were subjecting night after night to an ordeal which they could not share themselves. The bomber offensive, indeed, has been described as the Passchendaele of the Second World War.

We can now see, with all the advantage of hindsight, how wrong they often were in their assessment of the damage they were doing to the enemy. But we can also see that there was no short-cut to victory through air power. Webster and Frankland suggest plausibly that if Sir Arthur Harris had obeyed air staff directives more meticulously during the last half of 1944 the war might have been shortened by a few months; but that is all. The *Luftwaffe* had to be beaten out of the German skies, as the Royal Air Force would have had to be beaten out of British skies, before 'command of the air' was won, and it fought back with no less heroism and ingenuity than had its British counterpart.

Air power, in fact, had not transformed the existing pattern of war: it had conformed to it, with remarkable and depressing precision.

Then came The Bomb. To the eye of the laymen, Hiroshima and Nagasaki seemed only a continuation, or at most a culmination, of all that had gone before. There was little discontinuity between the raids on Hamburg in 1943 which had killed 42,000, the great fire-raids on Tokyo in March 1945 which had killed 84,000, and Hiroshima where 71,000 died. It is only in retrospect that the Hiroshima and Nagasaki raids seem to rear themselves as ugly and isolated acts, like Easter Island images, inexplicable without the preliminary scaffolding which made their erection possible. Yet for the experts on air power these raids were truly revolutionary. The damage done by their predecessors had been possible only at a gruelling, possibly an excessive cost, and it had been wreaked by forces of a size which could only be sustained by nations which had geared all their resources to total war. Now all was changed. The vital factor of attrition was greatly reduced. To inflict crippling damage on an adversary it was no longer necessary to send massive and expensive fleets of bombers, night after night, with a high and constant rate of losses, until his defences were worn down and his cities lay at one's mercy. Now it was enough that a handful of aircraft should get through, and in dropping their bombs they had no need for meticulous accuracy. All the old targets which had competed for attention – oil, transportation, heavy industry, civilian morale – could be shattered in a single attack. Perhaps Trenchard and Douhet had been premature and hailed a false dawn: so much could certainly be argued from the coldly deflating assessments of actual damage done to Germany by the allied bombers which were published by the United States Strategic Bombing Survey after the war. But what they had prophesied for the nineteen-twenties must now, thirty years later, surely come true?

So in spite of their disappointments in the Second World War, the advocates of air power seemed, at the beginning of the 1950s, to have emerged supreme. In America, the United States Air Force secured not only independence from, but for a time, dominance over the other two services. For an impoverished and overburdened Britain, the continued development of a bomber force and the creation of an independent nuclear capacity appeared to be, not an additional and unnecessary luxury, but the most economical way of maintaining her influence in the world and helping to restrain aggression. For officers brought up in the tradition of Admiral Mahan, to believe that the peace of the world in the nineteenth century had been a *Pax Britannica* resting on the Royal Navy's command of the seas, the creation of a new kind of fleet of the air, as dedicated to peaceful purposes as its naval predecessor, ever ready to visit instant and condign punishment on any transgressor, naturally seemed the most effective and economical way of keeping the peace. Bomber Command and, even more, the United States Strategic Air Command, learned to regard themselves as forces devoted to the maintenance of peace and law. But for their constant alertness, their whole-hearted and unwearying attention to their tedious, complicated, and awe-inspiring duties, the world, they believed, would collapse in barbarism and disorder, or else fall prey to an all-conquering Communist terror.

The further technical developments of the 'fifties seemed likely at first to reinforce all these assumptions. The thermonuclear bomb, a thousand times more destructive than the atomic weapon, eliminated the problem of attrition altogether. One aircraft could now carry a greater explosive power than all the bombs dropped on Germany during the Second World War. Air defence was still possible – indeed

the development of supersonic fighter aircraft and of ground-
to-air homing missiles had vastly improved its potentialities –
but 100 per cent effective defence had never been considered
feasible, and now failure by a margin even of 1 per cent was
catastrophic. Civilians were once again adjured – in Britain
by Mr Duncan Sandys in 1957 and 1958 – that they had to
submit to the damage which an attacker could inflict on them
while his war-making power was being destroyed at its roots.
Then the ballistic missile, to which it seemed unlikely that
any counter could be developed, made delivery yet more
inescapable. To Atlas, Thor, Polaris, or Minuteman, once
they were launched, there seemed no more defence than
against a bullet in flight. In the Second World War it had
taken Britain and the United States four laborious years and
an infinity of expenditure before they attained the position of
having their adversary at their mercy. Today we are in that
position in the middle of profoundest peace. And so, incidentally, is he.

This, we may assume, is not quite the situation which the
apostles of air power foresaw. For in fact the two technical
developments noted above affected the situation very considerably. In the first place, the bland request that civilians
should submit with resignation to the damage which the
opposing bomber force could inflict on them was even less
acceptable in the thermo-nuclear age than it had been in the
1930s; and as we have seen, they were reluctant to submit
even then. It was one thing to endure ordeal by high explosive which, however much damage and suffering it might
cause, still left the basic structure of society intact. It was,
and is, another to look forward to the total destruction of
one's civilisation – *pace* Mr Herman Kahn, I speak now in a
British context – beyond hope, so far as one can see, of repair; with the consolation only that the adversary is simultaneously being annihilated as well.

The difference between damage on a thermo-nuclear scale
and that experienced during the last war is qualitative and
not quantitative, and the moral and political justifications
either for inflicting or for suffering it which applied then are
no longer likely to be valid. It is sometimes necessary for
societies to suffer – and perhaps suffer agonisingly – if they

are to survive and grow; and if they flinch from such suffering, their chances of survival are small. But it can never make sense for them, in Bismarck's words, to commit suicide for fear of death.

All this is incontestable. But it is equally incontestable that we still live in a world of sovereign states, and that a world of sovereign states is a world of power politics, and that we must survive in this element until we are wise enough to create an effective world authority or weak enough to acquiesce in some universal world empire. Peace is not simply a matter of repressing 'aggression' but of stabilising and constantly adjusting the balance of power, and among the constituent factors which make up political power, weapons still play a not unimportant part. The balance of nuclear terror may seem a terrifying basis for peace; but the only alternative basis, short of the multilateral disarmament for which we are striving, would be the self-restraint of a power with a monopoly of nuclear weapons which it could use without fear of retaliation. In such a world, sovereign states would be likely to become absorbed into a universal empire; and even if we in Britain – or even we in the West – were prepared to acquiesce, there are other powers less self-effacing, who would be unlikely to follow suit.

Peace thus rests on a balance of deterrence, and about that balance much has been written – not least in the pages of *Encounter*[1] – and need not be repeated here. That the balance should be so far as possible constant through the spectrum of weapons, conventional and nuclear, and that it should be rendered as stable as may be by increasing reliance on second-strike forces seems today generally accepted. That such a balance might still, in strict logic, be vulnerable to an aggressor who was prepared to accept a few score million casualties as the inescapable penalty of launching a surprise attack has been brilliantly argued by Albert Wohl-

---

[1] In which this article first appeared. Cf. P.M.S. Blackett, 'Critique of Some Contemporary Defence Thinking', *Encounter*, April 1961; Alastair Buchan, 'A World With Arms Without War', February 1961 and 'P. M. S. Blackett and War', August 1961; Michael Howard, 'Arms Races and War', January 1961; Oskar Morgenstern, 'Nuclear Stalemate?', June 1961.

stetter and Herman Kahn;[1] but their logic is generally considered – in this country at least – to be that of theorists and not of political life. Finally, it is increasingly recognised that the maintenance of the balance is an essential condition of any measures of multilateral disarmament; a problem which, with the best will in the world, no expert has yet been able to solve. The Americans will not disarm without the assurance given by international inspection that the Russians are doing the same; while the Russians will not accept an inspection which would reveal the whereabouts of their launching sites and airfields to a conceivable surprise attack. This is the situation with which at present we have to deal.

But there are two elements in this situation which it is worth noting here. The first is that the concept of 'balance' is something new in thinking about air power, and reflects a more realistic appreciation of the nature of political life than did the concept, which it replaced, of simple 'deterrence'. It is not in the nature of great powers to acquiesce in the monopoly by their rivals of a major military weapon, if they are in a position to acquire it themselves. Even if Mahan was right in attributing the *Pax Britannica* to the Royal Navy's command of the sea – and it may be doubted whether this time-honoured belief would really stand up to critical examination – the immediate consequence of his analysis was to create a determination on the part of his own countrymen, and even more on the part of the Germans, not to remain thus dependent on the mastery of a foreign power, be it never so moderately exercised, for a moment longer than necessary. A great power, however selfless its policy – and has a great power any *business* to be selfless? – cannot gain acceptance among its rivals, except in very limited circumstances, as an international policeman, on whose self-restraint and wisdom all will rely. No responsible Russian statesman, whatever his political creed, could accept as stable a situation in which SAC bases threatened his country with instantaneous destruction from which no escape, and for which no retaliation, was possible; and no Russian statesman could be expected to

---

[1] Herman Kahn, *On Thermo-Nuclear War* (Princeton, 1960). Albert Wohlstetter, 'The Delicate Balance of Terror', *Foreign Affairs*, January 1959.

believe that this force would be used only in generally-accepted interests of world order and peace.

It takes at least two to keep the peace through air power, and only when they themselves threatened the West with comparably great and inescapable punishment for aggression could the Russians begin to feel, on their part, that the peace of the world was tolerably secure. Today the Russian and the Western deterrent forces are not so much rivals as colleagues, twin caryatids sustaining with great labour, boredom, and discomfort the edifice of international security within which political commerce – which includes limited and ideological conflict as well as more peaceful pursuits – continues to be carried on.

The other element in the situation is this. The existence of national armed forces in a reasonable state of alertness, backed by an adequate military potential, has always been a vital factor in international relations. There is nothing new about military balance and mutual deterrence. But hitherto this military strength has consisted of *fighting* forces: troops capable of encountering and overcoming each other in battle, trained, disciplined, and organised for war. The whole *raison d'être* of the elaborate military machine, with its hierarchy, its uniforms, its special laws and privileges and customs, was that it had to fight. The battle was, ultimately, the pay-off. But what if there is no battle? Here lay the central paradox of the Royal Air Force. It was moulded as a military force, hierarchic and traditional, borrowing all the panache and display of its elder colleagues. It was just as well that it was, for as we have seen it had to endure ordeals by battle which would have broken men not subjected to military authority and strengthened by traditional disciplines and *esprit de corps*. Yet these battles were unexpected. The Royal Air Force was certainly not moulded in the expectation that it would have to fight them; enemy fighter and ground defences were regarded almost as negligible elements in the obtaining of command of the air. If the prophets of air power had been right, need the Royal Air Force have been a military body at all – or at least any more military than the police? And if they are belatedly right, now, what are the conclusions which we should draw?

The problem of deterrence has grown out of traditional and historic military problems, as I have been trying to show. The time may not be far off, however, when it will outgrow them altogether: when its difficulties will be purely technical and political, with very little military content; very little, that is, of tactics and strategy left at all. Increasingly during and since the Second World War the struggle for mastery has been transferred from the battlefields of the land, sea, and air, to the laboratories and factory work-benches. The object was originally to ensure that when the opposing forces met in battle, one's own side should suffer no inferiority in weapons. Military discipline and skills were no less necessary to conduct the battles themselves. Now skills and disciplines will continue to be necessary: ones which will stretch human ingenity and self-sacrifice to the limits. But will they be military ones?

The command of a bomber-force may be self-evidently a military affair, but the command of a missile-base is a different matter. Polaris-carrying submarines may be undeniably naval craft, but what of freight-cars carrying Minutemen? This is not to suggest that the operations of such installations could easily be left to purely civilian services; though the effectiveness with which the Merchant Navy and commercial airlines carry out their arduous and often dangerous duties suggests that this idea is less ludicrous than it may at first appear. But it *is* to suggest that their rôle is quite as distinct from military operations as is that of the police, and the time may not be far distant when this distinction should be made institutional.

Like the police, their function would overlap with the military, and as with the police one would expect close co-operation and interchange of personnel. But also like the police their duty is the non-military one of keeping the peace, and not of fighting wars; like the police their discipline and traditions must be based, not on martial virtues, but on deep political wisdom and self-restraint; and finally, like the police, they need to be securely under civilian control.

Such a separation of the 'deterrent' from the fighting forces, if it were to come about, would not only be natural: it would carry with it certain very definite practical advantages. So long as sovereign states exist in a condition of international anarchy, so long are armed conflicts likely to occur, and military forces be kept on foot to conduct them. But that such conflicts should, in a thermo-nuclear age, be kept strictly limited both in their objectives and in their mode of conduct, is a platitude so obvious that it hardly bears stating. The West would have been prepared to devote a great deal of blood and treasure to saving South Korea from Communist conquest, and the Communists were prepared to spend much to conquer it; but nuclear annihilation, even if it had been mutual, was not a price that either side was prepared to pay.

It is reasonable, if pessimistic, to look forward to the recurrence of such conflicts, either as the result of deliberate policy or of miscalculation; and it is equally reasonable to emphasise that the qualities required to conduct these conflicts successfully, the traditional military skills and virtues, are not necessarily the qualities which are desirable in those who control the strategic deterrent, and that it is particularly desirable when such limited wars are in progress that their control and the control of the deterrent should, under the sovereign power, be in different hands. It is not so much that this would reduce the danger of accident and error of judgment: it is that it would be *seen* to reduce it.

The claim made by the British, that our V-bomber force is a dual-purpose weapon equally effective in a nuclear or in a conventional rôle, is a slightly disquieting one; for if the aircraft were prepared for action in a limited war, the adversary might mistakenly believe that they were intending a nuclear strike and react accordingly. We do not boast that the Metropolitan Police can be used in a military rôle: if they can, the Home Office wisely keeps quiet about it. Nor are those qualities of belligerence, resolution, and deep knowledge of military affairs, at first hand and through study, which characterise the military leader to whom a nation entrusts the conduct of its armed forces, necessarily accompanied by the restraint, the diplomatic experience and the political *coup d'œil* needed for those who control its deterrent.

Such a separation of deterrent and fighting forces would at least provide an additional brake on a mechanism which threatens us all with destruction.

Finally, although the strategic deterrent forces are likely to become increasingly non-military, the technical expertise which they demand is very closely allied to the technical knowledge needed for their control and abolition. We are at last beginning, however slowly, to outgrow the sterile epoch when military specialists and disarmament experts were aligned in hostile camps, knowing little of each other's problems and caring less. We still cling to certain archaic principles: that disarmament, for instance, should be controlled by one ministry and defence by another, that defence-specialists can veto disarmament proposals while disarmament authorities are not consulted over military developments. But the realisation is growing that defence and disarmament are indivisible, dual aspects of the single problem of national security, and that if the maintenance of balanced deterrence is an indispensable element in multilateral disarmament, the progressive stages of that disarmament and probably its subsequent enforcement must be worked out in close consultation with those forces on whom the balance depends. The deterrent forces in fact have at least as much in common with disarmament authorities, and with those who will eventually be responsible for inspection and control, as they have with traditional forces responsible for orthodox military action. It will be from their ranks that any international inspectorate is likely to be recruited; and it will be on them, eventually, that the survival of world order is likely to depend.

The logical development would therefore seem that deterrent and disarmament forces should ultimately come together under a single authority, distinct from the Ministry, or the Department, of Defence; leaving to the latter the organisation of armed forces and the conduct of limited wars. But there is nothing logical about political developments, and service opposition combined with civilian parsimony is likely to make anything of the sort unlikely for many years. Still it is worth thinking along these lines. It would be the natural conclusion of Trenchard's doctrine of air power. He and his disciples might be surprised if they had survived to see it happen; but they might also feel satisfied, that it should after all be their direct successors who were charged with keeping the peace.

10   The Classical Strategists[1]

It may help to begin with a definition of 'classical' strategy. Liddell Hart has provided us with one which is as good as any, and better than most: 'The art of distributing and applying military means to fulfil the ends of policy'. Whether this remains adequate in the nuclear age is a matter of some controversy. André Beaufre, for example, has adumbrated the concept of an 'indirect strategy', to be considered later, which embraces more than purely military means; but even he still gives as his basic definition of the term 'the art of the dialectic of two opposing wills using force to resolve their dispute'. It is this element of *force* which distinguishes 'strategy' from the purposeful planning in other branches of human activity to which the term is often loosely applied. When other elements such as economic pressure, propaganda, subversion and diplomacy are combined with force, these elements may also be considered as 'strategic'; but to apply this adjective to activities unconnected with the use, or threatened use, of force would be to broaden it to such an extent that it would be necessary to find another word to cover the original meaning of the term as defined by Liddell Hart, and as considered in this paper.

It need hardly be said that students of strategy have generally assumed that military force is a necessary element in international affairs. Before World War I, there were few who questioned even whether it was desirable. After 1918, many regretted its necessity and saw their function as being to ensure that it should be used as economically, and as rarely, as possible. After 1945, an even greater proportion devoted themselves to examine, not how wars should be

[1] This paper was read at the Annual Conference of the Institute for Strategic Studies in 1968. The term 'classical' was used to distinguish its subject matter from the 'behavioural' thinkers whose work was dealt with in a separate paper.

fought, but how they could be prevented, and the study of strategy merged into that of arms control, disarmament and peace-keeping. There the 'classical strategists' found themselves working with scholars of a different kind; men who believed that the element of force was *not* a necessary part of international intercourse, but could be eliminated by an application of the methodology of the social sciences. This paper will, however, concern itself solely with the thinkers who assume that the element of force exists in international relations, that it can and must be intelligently controlled, but that it cannot be totally eliminated. Further, it is confined to the men who have primarily used the methodology of history or traditional political science; though it includes such figures as Schelling and Morgenstern, who have made considerable contributions in the newer disciplines as well.

The art of strategy remains one of such complexity that even the greatest contributors to its study have been able to do little more than outline broad principles; principles which nevertheless must often be discarded in practice if the circumstances are inappropriate, and which must never be allowed to harden into dogma. Even when these principles appear self-evident, it may be extraordinarily hard to apply them. In World War II 'command of the sea' as advocated by Mahan and 'command of the air' as advocated by Douhet were certainly necessary preliminaries to the military victory of the Western powers. The problem was how to obtain them with resources on which equally urgent calls were being made for other purposes. The academic strategist could not help the chiefs of staff much, for example, in deciding how to allot a limited number of long-range aircraft between the conflicting needs of the strategic air offensive against Germany, the war against German submarines, interdiction bombing of German railways, the requirements of the Pacific theatre and support for guerrilla activities in occupied Europe. Operational research and systems-analysis could simplify the problem without ever eliminating it. In the last resort the quality termed by Blackett 'the conventional military wisdom'[1] remained the basic factor in making the decision; and

[1] P. M. S. Blackett, *Studies of War* (London: Oliver & Boyd, 1962), p. 128.

that decision was determined by what could be done rather than by what ideally should. The military commander is always primarily conscious of the constraints under which he operates, in terms both of information and of resources. He is, therefore, likely to be impatient with the advice of the academic strategist which may appear to him either platitudinous or impracticable. His decisions must be based at best on educated guesses.

But the academic strategist does have one vital rôle to play. He can see that the guesses *are* educated. He may not accompany the commander to battle, as Clausewitz expressed it, but he forms his mind in the schoolroom, whether the commander realises it or not. In World War II the Allied High Command did operate in accordance with certain very definite strategic principles. It is tempting to link these principles with the names of specific theorists: General Marshall's desire for concentration against the enemy army with Clausewitz, General Brooke's desire to enforce dispersal on the enemy with Liddell Hart, the doctrine of the Allied air forces with Douhet: tempting, but difficult to prove. The name of Douhet was virtually unknown in the Royal Air Force.[1] The most eminent thinkers sometimes do no more than codify and clarify conclusions which arise so naturally from the circumstances of the time that they occur simultaneously to those obscurer, but more influential figures who write training manuals and teach in service colleges. And sometimes strategic doctrines may be widely held which cannot be attributed to any specific thinkers, but represent simply the consensus of opinion among a large number of professionals who had undergone a formative common experience.

Of this kind were the doctrines which were generally held in the armed forces of the Western world in the mid-1940s as a result of the experiences of World War II. It was considered, first, that the mobilisation of superior resources, together with the maintenance of civilian morale at home, was a necessary condition for victory; a condition requiring a substantial domestic 'mobilisation base' in terms of indus-

[1] Sir John Slessor, 'Air Power and the Future of War', *Journal of the Royal United Service Institution*, August 1954.

trial potential and trained manpower. It was agreed that, in order to deploy these resources effectively, it was necessary to secure command of the sea and command of the air. It was agreed that surface and air operations were totally inter-dependent. And it was agreed that strategic air power could do much – though *how* much remained a matter of contro-versy – to weaken the capacity of the adversary to resist. The general concept of war remained as it had been since the days of Napoleon: the contest of armed forces to obtain a position of such superiority that the victorious power would be in a position to impose its political will. And it was gener-ally assumed that in the future, as in the immediate past, this would still be a very long-drawn-out process indeed.

The advent of nuclear weapons, to the eyes of the layman, transformed the entire nature of war. But certain eminent professionals suggested that they made remarkably little difference, at least in a conflict between two powers of the size of the United States and the Soviet Union. These weapons obviously would make it possible to inflict with far greater rapidity the kind of damage by which the strategic bombing offensive had crippled Germany and Japan. But the stockpiles of bombs were small – how small is still not known. The bombers were vulnerable to interception; and they had to operate from bases which had to be protected by land armies which would have in their turn to be supplied by sea. All this was pointed out to the general public by, among others, two scientists with long experience in military plan-ning – the British Professor P. M. S. Blackett and the American Dr Vannevar Bush. Blackett, on the basis of care-ful calculations from unclassified material, concluded in 1948 that 'a long-range atomic bombing offensive against a large continental power is not likely to be by itself decisive within the next five years'.[1] Bush, a figure closely associated with the American military establishment, described in 1949 a conflict barely distinguishable from the last.

The opening phases would be in the air soon followed by

[1] P. M. S. Blackett, *The Military and Political Consequences of Atomic Energy* (London: The Turnstile Press, 1948), p. 56.

sea and land action. Great fleets of bombers would be in action at once, but this would be the opening phase only. . . . They could undoubtedly devastate the cities and the war potential of the enemy and its satellites, but it is highly doubtful if they could at once stop the march of great land armies. To overcome them would require a great national effort, and the marshalling of all our strength. The effort to keep the seas open would be particularly hazardous, because of modern submarines, and severe efforts would be needed to stop them at the source. Such a war would be a contest of the old form, with variations and new techniques of one sort or another. But, except for greater use of the atomic bomb, it would not differ much from the last struggle.[1]

It was along these lines that planning went forward when the framework of the North Atlantic Treaty Organisation was established at the end of the 1940s. Such ideas were legitimate deductions from the then 'state of the art'. NATO planners had to think what could be done with the weapons they had available, not with those which might or might not be developed in ten years' time. But many scientists and academic strategists, particularly in the United States, were already thinking ahead. Because their views appeared to have no immediate relevance, or because of the pressures of inter-service politics, they had little immediate influence on Western policy; and they were usually set out in papers or articles which enjoyed only a limited circulation within the academic world.[2] An adequate account of these seminal discussions would require a separate paper. We can, however, salvage and admire the shrewd insights shown by two thinkers who had already established their reputation in the

[1] Vannevar Bush, *Modern Arms and Free Men* (New York: Simon and Schuster, 1949), pp. 115–16.

[2] As for example Jacob Viner's paper on 'The Implications of the Atomic Bomb for East–West Relations', the influence of which is acknowledged by Brodie and many others. Albert Wohlstetter gave an impromptu account, at the ISS Conference, of the main lines along which these discussions ran. Some account will also be found in Richard G. Hewlett and Oscar E. Anderson, *The New World* (Vol. I of the History of the United States Atomic Energy Commission, Pennsylvania, 1962), and in the early issues of the *Bulletin of the Atomic Scientists*.

pre-nuclear era: Bernard Brodie and Sir Basil Liddell Hart. Both of them, in works published in 1946, made prophecies which twenty years later were to be commonplace of strategic thinking.

In the final chapter of *The Revolution in Warfare*,[1] Liddell Hart suggested that, failing disarmament, attempts should be made 'to revive a code of limiting rules for warfare – based on a realistic view that wars are likely to occur again, and that the limitation of their destructiveness is to everybody's interest'. 'Fear of atomic war,' he wrote, 'might lead to indirect methods of aggression, infiltration taking civil forms as well as military, to which nuclear retaliation would be irrelevant. Armed forces would still be required to fight "sub-atomic war", but the emphasis should be on their mobility, both tactical and strategic.'

The great armies of the past would be irrelevant to the needs of the nuclear age. Liddell Hart did not, at this stage, consider the problems and contradictions of limited war, including the possibility which emerged fifteen years later, that it might be necessary to have large conventional forces precisely in order to keep war limited. Neither did he explore the implications and requirements of deterrence. Brodie, however, with his collaborators in the Yale Institute of International Studies' publication *The Absolute Weapon*, did exactly this, and with remarkable prescience. Much that he wrote was to become unquestionably valid only with the development of thermonuclear weapons, but his insights were none the less remarkable for that. He rejected, for example, the whole concept of a 'mobilisation base'. 'The idea,' he wrote, 'which must be driven home above all else is that a military establishment which is expected to fight on after the nation has undergone atomic bomb attack must be prepared to fight with the men already mobilised and with the equipment already in the arsenals.'[2] More important, he outlined the concept of a stable balance of nuclear forces.

[1] B. H. Liddell Hart, *The Revolution in Warfare* (London: Faber, 1946), p. 87.
[2] Bernard Brodie (ed.), *The Absolute Weapon* (New York: Harcourt, Brace, 1946), p. 89.

If the atomic bomb can be used without fear of substantial retaliation in kind, it will clearly encourage aggression. So much the more reason, therefore, to take all possible steps to assure that multilateral possession of the bomb, should that prove inevitable, be attended by arrangements to make as nearly certain as possible that the aggressor who uses the bomb will have it used against him . . .

. . . Thus, the first and most vital step in any American programme for the age of atomic bombs is to take measures to guarantee to ourselves in case of attack the possibility of retaliation in kind. The writer in making that statement is not for the moment concerned about who will *win* the next war in which atomic bombs are used. Thus far the chief purpose of our military establishment has been to win wars. From now on its chief purpose must be to avert them. It can have almost no other useful purpose.[1]

Not until thermonuclear weapons had been developed and the Soviet Union had shown itself to possess an intercontinental delivery system did the US Joint Chiefs of Staff accept Brodie's logic; though it is significant that shortly after the publication of this work Brodie joined the newly-formed RAND Corporation, where with the support of the US Air Force the full implications and requirements of his ideas, and others current in the United States academic community, were to be exhaustively studied.

The first Western government to adopt the concept of 'deterrence' as the basis of its military policy was that of the United Kingdom in 1952; very largely thanks to the thinking of Marshal of the Royal Air Force, Sir John Slessor, the then Chairman of the Chiefs of Staff.[2] Giving a late account of his stewardship at Chatham House in 1953, Slessor was to say:

The aim of Western policy is not primarily to be ready to win a war with the world in ruins – though we must be as ready as possible to do that if it is forced upon us by acci-

[1] Brodie, op. cit., pp. 75–6. He did not, however, deal with the problem of vulnerability of retaliatory forces, and the consequent dependence of stability on an effective second-strike capability.
[2] Richard N. Rosecrance, *The Defense of the Realm* (New York and London: Columbia University Press, 1967), p. 159.

dent or miscalculation. It is the prevention of war. The bomber holds out to us the greatest, perhaps the only hope of that. It is the great deterrent.[1]

This doctrine of 'the great deterrent' was to unleash within the United Kingdom a debate which foreshadowed that set off in the United States by the comparable 'New Look' strategy which Mr Dulles was formally to unveil there in January 1954. Among its earliest and ablest critics were the men who, four years later, were to be primarily responsible for the foundation of the Institute for Strategic Studies: Rear-Admiral Sir Anthony Buzzard, Mr Richard Goold-Adams, Mr Denis Healey, and Professor P. M. S. Blackett. In its public presentation by Ministers and senior officers, the doctrine of 'massive retaliation' provided its critics in England with an even easier target than it did in the United States. No official distinction was made between the use of Bomber Command as a first-strike force in response to a Soviet 'conventional' invasion of western Europe and as a second-strike force to retaliate after a Soviet nuclear attack. In face of the growing strength of Soviet nuclear-strike forces, the first rôle appeared to lack political, the second technical, credibility. Liddell Hart had already pointed out in 1950 that defence against nuclear weapons would be credible only if accompanied by massive civil-defence measures of a kind which no government showed any sign of being prepared to carry out.[2] Britain's military leaders indeed at first assumed that the civilian population might be induced to grin and bear the nuclear holocaust as cheerfully as they had endured the German blitz. The inhabitants of areas which contained no protected installations, suggested Slessor, 'must steel themselves to risks and take what may come to them, knowing that thereby they are playing as essential a part in the country's defence as the pilot in the fighter or the man behind the gun'.[3] This attitude presumably remained

[1] 'The Place of the Bomber in British Policy'. Reprinted in *The Great Deterrent* (London: Cassell, 1957), p. 123.

[2] B. H. Liddell Hart, *The Defence of the West* (London: Cassell, 1950), pp. 97, 134, 139, 140.

[3] Sir John Slessor, *Strategy for the West* (London: Cassell, 1954), p. 108.

the basis of British official thinking until the acquisition of the Polaris missile system gave the United Kingdom a second-strike weapon which was technically if not politically credible. The validity of this thesis however gave rise to widespread doubts, and not only among the members of the Campaign for Nuclear Disarmament. In a famous lecture to the Royal United Service Institution in November 1959, after Mr Duncan Sandys had, in two Defence White Papers, laid yet greater stress on the importance of 'the deterrent', Lieutenant-General Sir John Cowley was to ask a question unusual for a senior serving officer:

> The choice of death or dishonour is one which has always faced the professional fighting man, and there must be no doubt in his mind what his answer must be. He chooses death for himself so that his country may survive, or on a grander scale so that the principles for which he is fighting may survive. Now we are facing a somewhat different situation, when the reply is not to be given by individuals but by countries as a whole. Is it right for the government of a country to choose complete destruction of the population rather than some other alternative, however unpleasant that alternative may be?[1]

As a coherent theory of strategy in the traditional sense, the doctrine of deterrence by the threat of massive retaliation, in the simple form in which it was set out by the British and American governments in the early 1950s, is not easy to defend, and its exponents tended at times to use the vocabulary of exhortation rather than that of rational argument in their attempts to justify it. But three points should be noted if we are to appreciate their standpoint. First, the British Chiefs of Staff from the beginning saw Bomber Command as a supplement to rather than a substitute for the United States Strategic Air Command, with the task of striking at targets of particular significance for the United Kingdom. Its strategic utility and its credibility as a deterrent were thus to be judged within the context of the Western deterrent force as a whole.[2]

[1] Lt.-Gen. Sir John Cowley, 'Future Trends in Warfare', *Journal of the Royal United Service Institution*, February 1960, p. 13.
[2] Rosecrance, op. cit., pp. 160–1.

Second, it was an attempt, like the American 'New Look' two years later, to solve the problem – and one far more difficult for the United Kingdom than for the United States – of maintaining an effective military force in a peace-time economy. The burden of rearmament assumed in 1950 had proved not only economically crippling but politically unacceptable; and since the political objective of the United Kingdom was the maintenance, *virgo intacta*, of the *status quo* in Europe, a policy which imposed the maximum penalty for *any* violation of that *status quo* was not so irrational as it appeared. For the United Kingdom not one inch of western Europe could be considered negotiable.

Third, as British officials repeatedly said later in the decade, 'The Great Deterrent' existed not to fight but to deter war: 'If it is used, it will have failed.' This argument was open to the rejoinder that a strategy which was not militarily viable was not politically credible, but this rejoinder is by no means conclusive. The concept of 'deterrence' takes us out of the familiar field of military strategy into the unmapped if not unfamiliar territory of political bargaining, where total rationality does not invariably reign supreme. Schelling and others were only then beginning their studies of 'the strategy of conflict'; but even without the help of game-theory techniques, it could be reasonably argued that, even if there was only one chance in a hundred that a political move would really be met by the threatened nuclear response, that chance would be an effective deterrent to any responsible statesman. 'The most that the advocates of the deterrent policy have ever claimed for it,' said Slessor in 1955, 'is that it will deter a potential aggressor from undertaking total war as an instrument of policy, as Hitler did in 1939, or from embarking upon a course of international action which obviously involves a serious risk of total war, as the Austrian Government did in 1914.'[1]

Certainly the British advocates of the 'deterrent policy' in the 1950s did not underrate the continuing importance of conflicts which would *not* be deterred by nuclear weapons. Liddell Hart repeatedly pointed out that nuclear stalemate

[1] Slessor, Lecture at Oxford University, April 1955, reprinted in *The Great Deterrent*, p. 181.

would encourage local and indirect aggression which could be countered only by conventional forces; a lesson which British armed forces tied down in operations from Cyprus to Malaya had no need to learn. Faced with the double burden of deterring total war and fighting small ones, it was natural enough for British strategists to adopt the doctrine later termed 'minimal deterrence'. This was stated with uncompromising clarity by Blackett in 1956:

I think we should act as if atomic and hydrogen bombs have abolished total war and concentrate our efforts on working out how few atomic bombs and their carriers are required to keep it abolished. In the next few years I see the problem not as how many atomic bombs we can afford but as how few we need. For every hundred million pounds spent on offensive and defensive preparations for global war, which almost certainly will not happen, is so much less for limited and colonial wars, which well may.[1]

British strategic thinkers in fact – even Slessor after his retirement – tended to take the existence of stable deterrence very much for granted. In view of the highly classified nature of all information relating to Bomber Command and the absence of any serious intercourse at that time between Ministry of Defence officials and free-lance strategic thinkers, this was not altogether surprising. It enabled them to concentrate, not only on problems of limited wars (Liddell Hart) but on graduated deterrence and restraints on war (Buzzard) and, in the atmosphere of *détente* which followed the Geneva Summit Meeting of 1955, on 'disengagement', disarmament and arms control (Blackett and Healey). When a few years later American thinkers questioned the validity of the doctrine of 'minimal deterrence' they evoked from Blackett a forceful rejoinder,[2] in which he expressed the fear that to depart from such a policy would only lead to an end-

---

[1] P. M. S. Blackett, *Atomic Energy and East–West Relations* (Cambridge: Cambridge University Press, 1956), p. 100.

[2] P. M. S. Blackett, 'Critique of Some Contemporary Defence Thinking'. First published in *Encounter* in 1961, this article is reprinted in *Studies of War*, op. cit., pp. 128–46. See also Blackett's dissenting note in Alastair Buchan: *NATO in the 1960's* (London: Chatto & Windus, 1960).

less and increasing arms race. But by the end of the 1950s it was becoming clear that any doctrine of deterrence depended for its validity on technical calculations which stretched far beyond the orthodox boundaries of strategic thinking; and on which it was difficult for thinkers who did not enjoy access to the facilities available in the United States to pronounce with any degree of authority.

Within the United States the controversy was now well under way. It had been got off to an excellent start by Mr John Foster Dulles, whose definition of the doctrine of 'massive retaliation' in January 1954 had been far more precise and dogmatic than the statements emanating from Whitehall to the same effect during the past two years. This, it will be remembered, announced the intention of the United States Administration to place its military dependence 'primarily upon a great capacity to retaliate, instantly, by means and at places of our own choosing', thereby gaining 'more basic security at less cost'.[1] The rationale behind this policy was of course political and economic: American weariness with the Korean War, and the desire of the Republican Party to return to financial 'normalcy' after what they regarded as the ruinous spending spree of the last four years.[2] It should perhaps be judged, not as a coherent strategic doctrine, but as a political expedient – or even as a diplomatic communication, itself a manœuvre in a politico-military strategy of 'deterrence'. By these criteria the policy must be pronounced not ineffective. But its logical fallacies were too glaring to be overlooked. The assumption of American invulnerability to a pre-emptive or a retaliatory strike was unconvincing in the year in which the Soviet Union first unveiled her inter-continental bombers. Even when that assumption had been justifiable four years earlier, American nuclear monopoly had not deterred the Korean conflict; and in that very year American nuclear power was

[1] Text in *The New York Times*, 13th January 1954.
[2] See the analysis '"The New Look" of 1953' by Glenn H. Snyder, in Warner R. Schilling, Paul Y. Hammond and Glenn H. Snyder, *Strategy, Policy and Defense Budgets* (New York: Columbia University Press, 1962), pp. 379–524.

to prove irrelevant to the conflict in Indo-China. These, and other points, were rapidly made with force and relish by Democrat politicians and sympathisers out of office, by academic specialists, and by members of the armed services which were being cut back to provide greater resources for the Strategic Air Command.

There has perhaps never been a strategic controversy which has not been fuelled by political passions and service interests. It is entirely understandable, and for our purposes quite unimportant, that the US Air Force should have sought every argument to justify the doctrine of massive retaliation while the US Army powerfully supported its opponents. What is significant, however, is that the latter included every strategic thinker of any consequence in the United States; and the failure of the present writer to find any serious academic defence of the doctrine may not be entirely due to unfamiliarity with the literature. Among the first critics was that pioneer of deterrence theory, Bernard Brodie, who published in November 1954 one of the earliest analyses of the place of 'limited war' in national policy;[1] but the first really formidable public broadside was fired by a group of scholars at the Princeton Center of International Studies under the leadership of William W. Kaufmann, in a collection of essays published in 1956 under the innocuous-sounding title *Military Policy and National Security*. In this work Kaufmann himself stressed the need for the United States to have the capacity to meet, and therefore deter, communist aggression at every level;[2] that 'spectrum of deterrence', in fact, which Mr Robert McNamara was to develop, not without some assistance from Dr Kaufmann himself, when he became Secretary for Defense four years later. In the same work Dr Roger Hilsman discussed the actual conduct of nuclear war; both making the distinction between counter-

[1] Bernard Brodie, 'Unlimited Weapons and Limited War', *The Reporter*, 18th November 1954. For an indispensable annotated bibliography of the whole controversy, see Morton H. Halperin, *Limited War in the Nuclear Age* (New York and London: John Wiley, 1963).

[2] William W. Kaufmann (ed.), *Military Policy and National Security* (Princeton, N.J.: Princeton University Press, 1956), pp. 28, 38, 257.

force and counter-value targets in total war, and considering the tactics of war with nuclear weapons fought on the ground;[1] and Professor Klaus Knorr gave one of the earliest published estimates of the kind of civil defence policy which might be feasible and necessary if the United States were really to employ the kind of nuclear strategy implied in Mr Dulles's statement.[2] Finally Mr Kaufmann emphasised the necessity for ensuring that military force should be tailored to the actual requirements of foreign policy: a point which was to be expanded more fully in two important books published the following year.

These were Dr Robert Osgood's study of *Limited War* and Dr Henry Kissinger's *Nuclear Weapons and Foreign Policy*.[3] Neither author had any significant experience of military operations or operational research. Their intellectual training was in the disciplines of history and political science; but with the shift of strategic thinking from the problem of waging war to that of its prevention, this background was at least as relevant as any more directly concerned with military affairs. Both analysed the traditional rigidity of the American attitude towards war and peace, contrasting it with the flexibility of communist theory and, as they saw it, practice. Both emphasised the irrelevance of strategic nuclear weapons to the conduct of foreign policy in peripheral areas. Both stressed, as had Kaufmann, the need to provide the appropriate forces for the fighting of limited wars; and both considered that tactical nuclear weapons should be regarded as appropriate for this purpose – a view shared by Mr Dulles himself,[4] and by the joint chiefs of staff under the chairmanship of Admiral Radford.

Osgood based his belief in the need to use nuclear weapons in limited wars largely on the difficulty of preparing troops to fight with both nuclear and conventional weapons.[5]

[1] Ibid., pp. 53–7, 60–72.   [2] Ibid., pp. 75–101.

[3] Robert E. Osgood, *Limited War: the Challenge to American Strategy* (Chicago: University of Chicago Press 1957). Henry A. Kissinger, *Nuclear Weapons and Foreign Policy* (New York: Houghton Mifflin, 1957).

[4] J. F. Dulles, 'Challenge and Response in United States' Policy', *Foreign Affairs*, October 1957.

[5] Osgood, op. cit., p. 258.

Kissinger, whose study developed out of panel discussions at
the Council on Foreign Relations in which a number of
professional soldiers took part, went into the question more
deeply, discussing both the possible *modus operandi* of
tactical nuclear forces and the kind of limitations which
might be agreed between two belligerents anxious not to
allow their military confrontation to get out of hand.[1] In
doing so he aligned himself with the views of Rear-Admiral
Sir Anthony Buzzard, who was energetically canvassing
before British audiences both the value of tactical nuclear
weapons in making possible graduated deterrence at acceptable cost, and the feasibility of negotiating agreed limitations
on the conduct of war.[2] But Buzzard's views were hotly
contested in England. Slessor gave them general support,
but Liddell Hart was highly sceptical (believing the capabilities of conventional forces to be unnecessarily under-
rated) and Blackett, after some hesitation, came out flatly
against them.[3] In the United States the same controversy
blew up. Brodie, writing in 1959, was prepared to admit only
that there might be *some* circumstances in which tactical
nuclear weapons might be appropriate, but considered that
'The conclusion that nuclear weapons *must* be used in limited
wars has been reached by too many people, too quickly, on
the basis of too little analysis of the problem'. Schelling the
following year suggested that the break between conventional and nuclear weapons was one of the rare 'natural'
distinctions which made tacit bargaining possible in limiting
war.[4] By this time Kissinger himself had had second thoughts,

[1] Kissinger, op. cit., pp. 174–202.
[2] Anthony Buzzard *et al.*, *On Limiting Atomic War* (London:
Royal Institute of International Affairs, 1956); and 'The H-Bomb:
Massive Retaliation or Graduated Deterrence', *International
Affairs*, 1956.
[3] Slessor, 'Total or Limited War?' in *The Great Deterrent*, pp.
262–84. Liddell Hart, *Deterrent or Defence: a Fresh Look at the
West's Military Position* (London: Stevens, 1960), pp. 74–81.
Blackett, 'Nuclear Weapons and Defence', *International Affairs*,
October 1958.
[4] Brodie, *Strategy in the Missile Age* (Princeton, N.J.: Princeton
University Press, 1959), p. 330. Thomas C. Schelling, *The Strategy
of Conflict* (Cam., Mass.: Harvard University Press, 1960), pp.
262–6. But the debate continued. Brodie in *Escalation and the*

and agreed that, though tactical nuclear weapons were a necessary element in the spectrum of deterrence, they could not take the place of conventional forces.[1] Within a year Mr McNamara was to take the debate into the council chambers of NATO, where the advocates of tactical nuclear weapons had already found staunch allies among officials grimly conscious of the unpopularity and expense of large conventional forces. Throughout the 1960s the debate was to continue, in three major languages, about the place of tactical nuclear weapons in the defence of Europe.[2] Only the sheer exhaustion of the participants keeps it from continuing still.

It will be seen that the major American contributions to strategic thinking published in 1956–67 were distinguished by two main characteristics. They attempted to reintegrate military power with foreign policy, stressing, in contradiction to the doctrine of massive retaliation, the need for 'a strategy of options'. And they tended to be the work of academic institutions; Kaufmann's group at Princeton, Osgood from Chicago, Kissinger working with the Council on Foreign Relations. Their authors were thus concerned less with the technicalities of defence (Hilsman at Princeton, a former West Pointer, was an interesting exception) than with its political objectives. Over what those objectives should be, they had no quarrel with John Foster Dulles. Although British thinkers, like British statesmen, had been exploring possibilities of *détente* ever since 1954, in the United States the cold war was still blowing at full blast. The Soviet Union was still, in the works of these scholars, considered to be implacably aggressive, pursuing its objec-

Nuclear Option (Princeton, N.J.: Princeton University Press, 1966) was to argue strongly against what had by then become known as the 'firebreak' theory, and emphasise the deterrent value of tactical nuclear weapons.

[1] Kissinger, *The Necessity for Choice* (London: Chatto & Windus, 1960), pp. 81–98.

[2] The literature is enormous, but three outstanding contributions are Helmuth Schmidt, *Verteidigung oder Vergeltung* (Stuttgart, 1961); Alastair Buchan and Philip Windsor, *Arms and Stability in Europe* (London: Chatto & Windus, 1963); and Raymond Aron, *Le Grand Débat* (Paris: Calmann-Lévy, 1963).

tive of conquest in every quarter of the globe, its machinations visible behind every disturbance which threatened
world stability. As Gordon Dean put it in his introduction to
Kissinger's book, 'Abhorrent of war but unwilling to accept
gradual Russian enslavement of other peoples around the
world, which we know will eventually lead to our own
enslavement, we are forced to adopt a posture that, despite
Russian military capabilities and despite their long-range
intentions, freedom shall be preserved to us'.[1] The strategy
of options which they urged had as its object, not the reduction of tensions, but the provision of additional and appropriate weapons to deal with a subtle adversary who might
otherwise get under the American guard.

Two years later, in 1959–60, the major works on strategy
in the United States showed a slight but perceptible change
of emphasis. As it happened, the most significant of these
were the work, not of full-time academics in universities, but
of men drawn from a wide variety of disciplines – physicists,
engineers, mathematicians, economists and systems analysts
– who had been working in defence research institutes on
classified information, particularly at RAND Corporation.
As a result they analysed the technical problems of deterrence
with an expertise which earlier works had naturally lacked.
These problems appeared all the more urgent to the general
public after the launching of the Sputnik satellite in 1957,
which revealed the full extent of the challenge which the
United States had to meet from Soviet technology. For the
first time in its history the United States felt itself in danger
of physical attack, and the question of civil defence, which
had for some time agitated academic specialists, became one
of public concern. Yet at the same time there was beginning
to emerge in some quarters a new attitude to the Soviet
Union. This saw in that power not simply a threat to be
countered, but a partner whose collaboration was essential if
nuclear war through accident or miscalculation was to be
avoided. It recognised that Soviet policy and intentions
might have certain elements in common with those of the
United States, and that its leaders faced comparable prob-

[1] Kissinger, *Nuclear Weapons*, p. vii.

lems. This attitude was by no means general. For scholars such as Robert Strausz-Hupé and William Kintner the conflict still resembled that between the Archangels Michael and Lucifer rather than that between Tweedledum and Tweedledee. But the concept, not only of a common interest between antagonists but of a joint responsibility for the avoidance of nuclear holocaust, became increasingly evident after the new administration came into power in 1961.[1]

The view which commanded growing support among American strategic thinkers was, therefore, that the 'balance of terror' was a great deal less stable than had hitherto been assumed, but that if it could be stabilised (which involved a certain reciprocity from the Soviet Union) there would be reasonable prospects of lasting peace. The technical instability of the balance was described by Albert Wohlstetter in the famous article which appeared in *Foreign Affairs* at the beginning of 1958, describing on the basis of his classified studies at RAND Corporation, the full requirements of an invulnerable retaliatory force: a stable 'steady-state' peacetime operation within feasible budgets, the capacity to survive enemy attacks, to make and communicate the decision to retaliate, to reach enemy territory, penetrate all defences and destroy the target; each phase demanding technical preparations of very considerable complexity and expense.[2]

The following year the mathematician Oskar Morgenstern was to suggest, in *The Question of National Defense*, that the best answer to the problem as defined by Wohlstetter,

[1] For an analysis of the various attitudes of American strategic thinkers to the question of *détente* see Robert A. Levine, *The Arms Debate* (Cam., Mass.: Harvard University Press, 1963), *passim*.

[2] Albert Wohlstetter, 'The Delicate Balance of Terror', *Foreign Affairs*, January 1958. The article is reprinted in Henry A. Kissinger (ed.), *Problems of National Strategy* (New York and London: Praeger and Pall Mall, 1965). The principal relevant studies were *Selection and Use of Air Bases* (R-266, April 1954) and *Protecting US Power to Strike Back in the 1950s & 1960s* (R-290, April 1956) by Albert Wohlstetter, F. S. Hoffman, and H. S. Rowen. Wohlstetter in a private communication to the present writer has stressed also the significant part played in these studies by experts in systems-analysis such as J. F. Digby, E. J. Barlow, and R. J. Lutz.

and the best safeguard against accidental war, was to be found in the development of seaborne missiles; and that it would be in the best interests of the United States if such a system could be developed by both sides. 'In view of modern technology of speedy weapons-delivery from any point on earth to any other,' he wrote, 'it is in the interest of the United States for Russia to have an invulnerable retaliatory force and vice versa.'[1] Whether Morgenstern reached this conclusion entirely through applying the game-theory in which he had made so outstanding a reputation is not altogether clear. Professor Thomas Schelling, who also brought the discipline of game-theory to bear on strategy, reached the same conclusion at approximately the same time;[2] but even by cruder calculations its validity seemed evident, and the concept of a 'stable balance' was central to Bernard Brodie's *Strategy in the Missile Age*, which also appeared in 1959.[3] This study pulled together all the threads of strategic thinking of the past five years and set them in their historical context. Brodie reduced the requirements of strategy in the missile age to three: an invulnerable retaliatory force; 'a real and substantial capability for coping with local and limited aggression by local application of force'; and provision for saving life 'on a vast scale' if the worst came to the worst.[4] About how, if the worst did come to the worst, nuclear war should be conducted, he did not attempt to offer any guidance beyond suggesting that the most important problem to study was not so much how to conduct the war, but how to stop it.

[1] Oskar Morgenstern, *The Question of National Defence* (New York: Random House, 1959), p. 75.

[2] See particularly his 'Surprise Attack and Disarmament' in Klaus Knorr (ed.), *NATO and American Security* (Princeton, N.J.: Princeton University Press, 1959). Schelling's whole work on the problem of dialogue in conflict situations is of major importance. His principal articles are collected in *The Strategy of Conflict* (Cam., Mass.: Harvard University Press, 1960).

[3] Brodie, *Strategy in the Missile Age*, op. cit., Chapter 8. Brodie and Schelling, like Wohlstetter, were at the time working at RAND Corporation, as also was Herman Kahn. All have acknowledged their mutual indebtedness during this formative period in their thinking.

[4] Ibid., pp. 294–7.

Not all of Brodie's colleagues at the RAND Corporation were so modest. The following year, 1960, saw the publication of Herman Kahn's huge and baroque study *On Thermonuclear War*;[1] the first published attempt by any thinker with access to classified material to discuss the action which should be taken if deterrence *did* fail. The horrible nature of the subject, the broad brush-strokes with which the author treated it, his somewhat selective approach to scientific data and the grim jocularity of the style, all combined to ensure for this study a reception which ranged from the cool to the hysterically vitriolic. Many of the criticisms, however, appear to arise rather from a sense of moral outrage that the subject should be examined at all than from serious disagreement with Kahn's actual views. In fact Kahn basically made only two new contributions to the strategic debate. The first, based on the classified RAND *Study of Non-Military Defense* for which he had been largely responsible, was the reminder that a substantial proportion of the American population could survive a nuclear strike, and that this proportion might be considerably increased if the necessary preparations were made. The second was the suggestion that the United States should equip itself with the capacity to choose among a range of options in nuclear as well as in non-nuclear war; that rather than relying on a single spasm reaction (von Schlieffen's *Schlacht ohne Morgen* brought up to date) the United States should be able to conduct a controlled nuclear strategy, suiting its targets to its political intentions – which would normally be, not to destroy the enemy, but to 'coerce' him.[2] Kahn in fact reintroduced the concept of an operational strategy which had been almost entirely missing, at least from public discussion, since the thermonuclear age had dawned ten years earlier. For smaller nuclear powers any such notion, as applied to a conflict with the Soviet Union, was self-evidently absurd. Between the super-powers it was – and remains – a perfectly legitimate matter for analysis. Kahn may have exaggerated the capacity of the social and

---

[1] Herman Kahn, *On Thermonuclear War* (Princeton, N.J.: Princeton University Press, 1960).
[2] Ibid., pp. 301–2.

political structure of the United States to survive a nuclear holocaust; certainly many of his comments and calculations were oversimplified to the point of naïveté. But it is hard to quarrel with his assumption that that capacity, whatever its true dimensions, could be increased by appropriate preliminary measures; while the position adopted by some of his critics, that even to contemplate the possibility of deterrence failing might increase the possibility of such failure, is hardly one that stands up to dispassionate analysis.

At the beginning of 1961 President Kennedy's new Administration took office and Mr Robert McNamara became Secretary of Defense. Not entirely coincidentally, the great period of American intellectual strategic speculation came to an end, after five astonishingly fruitful years. The military intellectuals were either drawn, like Kaufmann and Hilsman, into government, or returned to more orthodox studies on university campuses. Most of them continued to write. Kahn has produced two further works refining some of the views expounded in *On Thermonuclear War*.[1] Kissinger has remained a sage observer of and a prolific commentator on the political scene, and is at the moment of writing President Nixon's adviser on international security affairs. Osgood, Wohlstetter and Brodie have all produced notable work on synthesis or criticism. Perhaps the most interesting work has been that of Knorr and Schelling, who have broadened their studies to embrace the whole question of the rôle of military power in international relations;[2] a remarkably little-explored field in which a great deal of work remains to be done. It would be absurdly premature to suggest of any of these scholars – many of them still comparatively young men – have no more substantial contributions to make to strategic studies; but they are unlikely to surpass the intellectual achievement for which they were individually and jointly responsible in the 1950s. Between them they have done what Clausewitz and Mahan did in the last century, during times

[1] *Thinking the Unthinkable* (London: Weidenfeld, 1962). *On Escalation: Metaphors and Scenarios* (London: Pall Mall, 1965).
[2] Knorr, *On the Uses of Military Power in the Nuclear Age* (Princeton, N.J.: Princeton University Press, 1966). Schelling, *Arms and Influence* (New Haven: Yale University Press, 1966).

of no less bewildering political and technological change: laid down clear principles to guide the men who have to take decisions. Like Clausewitz and Mahan they are children of their time, and their views are formed by historical and technological conditions whose transformations may well render them out of date. Like those of Clausewitz and Mahan, their principles are likely to be misunderstood, abused, or applied incorrectly, and must be subjected by each generation to searching examination and criticism. Debate will certainly continue; but at least we now have certain solid issues to debate about.

The principles established by the thinkers of the 1950s were to guide Mr McNamara in his work on remoulding American defence policy during the eight years of his period of office in the Department of Defense. 'The McNamara Strategy' had a logical coherence – almost an elegance – which may have commanded rather more admiration among academics than it did in the world of affairs.[1] An invulnerable second-strike force was built up on a considerably larger scale than that considered adequate by the believers in 'minimal deterrence'. These forces were endowed with the capability, even after a surprise attack, of retaliating selectively against enemy forces rather than against his civilian population, so that 'a possible opponent' would have 'the strongest imaginable incentive to refrain from striking our own cities'.[2] Forces for 'limited wars' at all levels were created, armed both with nuclear and with conventional weapons. This involved an increase in expenditure, but it was an increase which was not grudged by Congressmen alarmed by an alleged 'missile gap' and happy to see fat defence contracts being placed within their home states; and the techniques of systems analysis which had also been developed at RAND Corporation were employed to keep

[1] William W. Kaufmann, *The McNamara Strategy* (New York: Harper & Row, 1964) provides a useful if uncritical account. It should be read in association with Bernard Brodie's dry commentary 'The McNamara Phenomenon', *World Politics*, July 1965.
[2] McNamara speech at the University of Michigan at Ann Arbor, 16th June 1962. Kaufmann, op. cit., p. 116.

this increase within bounds.[1] Overtures were made, official and unofficial, to the Soviet Union to establish arms-control agreements based on the principle of a stable balance resting on invulnerable second-strike forces on either side. And plans were put in hand for civil defence projects on a massive scale.

McNamara was able to carry out much of his programme, but not all. The Russians were remarkably slow to absorb the reasoning which appeared so self-evident to American academics. The American public was even slower to co-operate in the sweeping measures necessary to provide effective insurance against holocaust. The ideal of a second-strike counter-force strategy seemed to many critics to be one almost intrinsically impossible of realisation. And America's European allies flatly refused McNamara's requests that they should increase their conventional forces to provide the necessary 'spectrum of deterrence'. The Germans saw this as a diminution of the deterrent to any invasion of their own narrow land, and besides had their own not particularly enjoyable memories of 'conventional war'. The British, struggling to maintain a world presence on their obstinately stagnant economy, could not afford it; while the French had ideas of their own. None of them, perhaps, could produce a coherent theoretical framework to sustain them in their arguments, but they remained unconvinced. Several of Mr McNamara's emissaries received, in consequence, a somewhat gruelling introduction to the refractory world of international affairs.

For the American strategic programme was based on two assumptions which were not accepted by all the major allies of the United States: first, that America was the leader of 'the Free World' and had both the right and the power to shape its strategy; and second, it was in the interests of the world as a whole that the United States and the Soviet Union

[1] See Charles Hitch and Roland McKean, *The Economics of Defense in the Nuclear Age* (Cam., Mass.: Harvard University Press, 1960) for the promise. The performance was examined in *Planning – Programming – Budgeting: Hearings before the Sub-committee on National Security and International Operations of the Committee on Government Operations*, United States Senate, 90th Congress, 1st Session (US Government Printing Office, 1967).

should enter into an ever closer dialogue. Neither of these assumptions was challenged by the British; though not all their countrymen admired the assiduity with which successive British Prime Ministers set themselves up as 'honest brokers' between the super-powers the moment they set foot inside Downing Street. Indeed the most substantial British contribution to the strategic debate in the early 1960s, John Strachey's *On the Prevention of War,* quite explicitly advocated a Russo-American diarchy as the best guarantee of world peace.[1] But on the Continent reactions were different. The Chancellor of the Federal German Republic took a glum view of a Russo-American *détente* which could only, in his view, confirm the division of his country and might even threaten the position of Berlin; and long before Mr Mc-Namara had appeared on the scene the President of the French Fifth Republic had made clear his own attitude to the American claim to act as the leader and spokesman of 'The Free World'.

Too much should not be made of the personality of General de Gaulle in shaping the French contribution to the strategic debate which began to gain in importance towards the end of the 1950s. French military experience during the past twenty years had been distinctive and disagreeable. They had their own views on the reliability of overseas allies as protectors against powerful continental neighbours – neighbours who might in future comprise not only Russia but a revived Germany or, in moments of sheer nightmare, both. The decision to develop their own nuclear weapons had been taken before de Gaulle came into power, though perhaps it took de Gaulle to ensure that they would not be integrated, like the British, in a common Western targeting system. General Pierre Gallois, the first French writer to develop a distinctive theory of nuclear strategy,[2] advanced the thesis that nuclear weapons rendered traditional alliance systems totally out of date since no state, however powerful, would

[1] John Strachey, *On the Prevention of War* (London: Macmillan, 1962).
[2] Pierre Gallois, *Stratégie de l'Age nucléaire* (Paris: Calmann-Lévy, 1960).

risk nuclear retaliation on behalf of an ally when it really came to the point. In a world thus atomised (in the traditional sense of the word) the security of every state lay in its capacity to provide its own minimal deterrence. The more states that did, indeed, the greater the stability of the international system was likely to be.

Extreme as Gallois's logic was, it probably reflected the sentiments of a large number of his countrymen and a substantial section of the French armed forces. In spite of innumerable official expressions to the contrary, there is every reason to suppose that many influential members of the British governing establishment felt very much the same about their own nuclear force. A more subtle variant of this doctrine was presented by General André Beaufre, who argued powerfully in his work, *Deterrence and Strategy*, that a multipolar nuclear balance in fact provided greater stability than a bipolar, since it reduced the area of uncertainty which an aggressor might exploit. So far from atomising alliances, argued Beaufre, independent nuclear forces cemented them, 'necessarily covering the whole range of their vital interests'.[1] He was careful to distinguish between multipolarity and proliferation. 'The stability provided by the nuclear weapon,' he argued, 'is attainable only between *reasonable* powers. Boxes of matches should not be given to children';[2] a sentiment which one can endorse while wondering what Beaufre would define, in international relations, as the age of consent. As for the Russo-American diarchy welcomed by Strachey, Beaufre specifically identified this as a danger to be avoided. 'The prospect of a world controlled by a *de facto* Russo-American "condominium" is one of the possible – and menacing – results of nuclear evolution,' he wrote. 'Looked at from this point of view, the existence of independent nuclear forces should constitute a guarantee that the interests of the other nuclear powers will not be sacrificed through some agreement between the two super-powers.'[3]

[1] André Beaufre, *Deterrence and Strategy* (London: Faber, 1965), p. 93. [2] Ibid., p. 97.
[3] Ibid., p. 140. Beaufre's experience as commander of the French land forces in the Suez operation of 1956 may have had some relevance to his views on this point.

The doctrine of 'multipolarity' was thus one distinctive contribution by French theorists to the study of strategy in the nuclear age. The second was their analysis of revolutionary war: a subject little studied by American strategic thinkers until the Vietnam involvement brutally forced it on their attention. For the French it had been inescapable. For nearly ten years after World War II the flower of their armies had been involved, in Indo-China, in operations of far larger scope than the various 'imperial policing' activities which absorbed so much of the attention of the British armed forces, and one which imposed on the French nation a longer and perhaps even more severe strain than the Korean War imposed on the United States. The war in Indo-China was lost. It was followed by six years of struggle in Algeria which ended, for the French armed forces, no less tragically. The outcome of these wars significantly altered the balance of power in the world, but the strategic concepts being developed in the United States appeared as irrelevant to their conduct as those which guided – or misguided – the French armies during the two world wars. The concepts which *were* relevant of course were those of Mao Tse-tung; those precepts evolved during the Sino-Japanese struggles of the 1930s and developed into a full theory of revolutionary warfare whereby a strongly-motivated cadre operating from a position of total weakness could defeat a government controlling the entire apparatus of the state.

The theories of Mao lie outside the scope of this study, though there is little doubt that he is among the outstanding strategic thinkers of our day. Certainly the French paid him the compliment of trying to imitate him. The literature on the subject is so considerable that it may be only by hazard that the earliest French study to receive widespread recognition was Colonel Bonnet's historical analysis, *Les guerres insurrectionnelles et révolutionnaires.*[1] Bonnet in this work gave a definition which has since been generally accepted: '*Guerre de partisans + guerre psychologique = guerre*

---

[1] Gabriel Bonnet, *Les guerres insurrectionnelles et révolutionnaires de l'antiquité à nos jours* (Paris: Payot, 1955). Important unpublished studies by Colonel Lacheroy were in circulation at the same time.

révolutionnaire.' 'Poser cette équation,' he went on to claim, *'c'est formuler une loi valable pour tous les mouvements révolutionnaires qui, aujourd'hui, agitent le monde.'*[1] On the basis of this definition and their own experiences, French military thinkers, true to their national intellectual traditions, attempted to formulate *une doctrine.* (It is interesting to note that the pragmatic British, whose cumulative experience in counter-insurgency campaigning was certainly no less than that of the French, thought more modestly in terms of 'techniques'.)[2] As worked out by such writers as Bonnet himself, Hogard, Lacheroy, Nemo, and Trinquier,[3] this *doctrine* set out the object, both of revolutionary and counter-revolutionary war, as the gaining of the confidence and support of the people, by a mixture of violent and non-violent means directed both at 'military' and at 'non-military' targets. It was not enough to suppress guerrillas: it was necessary to destroy the basis of their support among the population by eliminating the grievances which they exploited, by giving protection against their terroristic activities and, insisted the French writers, by a process of intensive indoctrination to combat that of the revolutionary cadres themselves.

It would be painful to record in detail where and why these excellent recommendations went wrong. The use of undifferentiated violence by legitimate authority undermines the basis of consent which is its strongest weapon against revolutionary opponents. Indoctrination of a population can be done only by men who are themselves indoctrinated; and since the whole essence of the 'open societies' of the West is virtually incompatible with the concept of ideological indoctrination, the men thus indoctrinated rapidly found themselves almost as much at odds with their own society as the revolutionaries they were trying to combat. In Algeria the French Army applied its doctrines with a fair measure of at least short-term success, but in so doing it alienated the

[1] Ibid., p. 60.

[2] See, for example, Julian Paget, *Counter-Insurgency Campaigning* (London: Faber, 1967) and Sir Robert Thompson, *Defeating Communist Insurgency* (London: Chatto & Windus, 1966).

[3] For a good select bibliography see the excellent and highly critical study by Peter Paret, *French Revolutionary Warfare from Indo-China to Algeria* (London: Pall Mall, 1964).

sympathies of its own countrymen. The main fault of its theorists – and of their imitators in the United States – was to overlook the element of simple *nationalism* which provided such strength for the insurgent forces: a curious failing in the country which was the original home of that immensely powerful force. They accepted the propaganda of their adversaries, and saw the conflict simply in terms of a global struggle against the forces of world Communist revolution. Marxist categories of thought make it difficult for their theorists to accept that the most potent revolutionary force in the world may be not the class struggle but old-fashioned 'bourgeois' nationalism. The French theorists were no doubt equally unwilling to take into account a consideration which boded so ill for their own side. But there is good reason to suppose that the FLN won in Algeria, not because they were Marxist but because they were *Algerian*, and the French were not. *Mutatis mutandis* the same applied – and applies still – in Indo-China. Marx and Lenin may provide the rationale of insurgency warfare; Mao Tse-tung may provide the techniques; but the driving power is furnished by the ideas of Mazzini. It is therefore difficult for foreign troops, however well-intentioned, to apply counter-insurgency techniques with any chance of success among a people which has awoken to a consciousness of its national identity.

In addition to the doctrines of multipolarity and revolutionary war, France has produced yet a third contribution to strategic thinking: the doctrine of indirect strategy. This was not totally novel. A group of American thinkers based on the Center for Foreign Policy Research at the University of Pennsylvania had long been working on the assumption that 'The Free World' and the Communists were locked in a protracted conflict which could end only in the victory of one side or the other and in which force was only one element out of many which might be used.[1] It was an assumption that could certainly be justified by reference to the works of Marx-Leninist theoreticians. But the publications of these writers tended to be as emotional and tendentious as

---

[1] Robert Strausz-Hupé *et al.*, *Protracted Conflict; A Challenging Study of Communist Strategy* (New York, 1959) and *A Forward Strategy for America* (New York, 1961).

those of the Marxists themselves. Certainly they had never formulated their theories with the clarity, reasonableness and dispassionate precision of General André Beaufre and his colleagues at the *Institut d'Études Stratégiques* in Paris.[1] For Beaufre the whole field of international relations constituted a battlefield in which the Communist powers, thwarted in the use of force by the nuclear stalemate, were attacking the West by indirect means. Strategy had progressed from the 'operational' (Clausewitz and Jomini) through the 'logistic' (the great build-ups of World War II) to the 'indirect'. Political manœuvres should therefore be seen as strategic manœuvres. The adversary attacked, withdrew, feinted, outflanked, or dug in, using direct force where he could and infiltration where he could not. The West should respond accordingly, devise a single overall political strategy and use economic, political, and military means to implement it.

The trouble with this is that it is not simply a theory of strategy but also a theory of international relations. If it is correct, Beaufre's recommendations follow naturally enough; but Beaufre states his assumptions rather than argues them, and to most students of international relations they are not self-evident. Such a view leaves too many factors out of account. The world is not really polarised so simply. Communist leaders do not control events so firmly. Whatever the ideologues may say, in practice interests are not so implacably opposed. Strategy must certainly be shaped by the needs of policy; but policy cannot be made to fit quite so easily into the Procrustean concepts of the professional strategist.

Perhaps the most significant conclusion to be drawn from this survey is the extent to which the quality of strategic thinking in the nuclear age is related to an understanding of international relations, on the one hand, and of weapons technology on the other. There is of course nothing new in this dependence. Clausewitz emphasised the first, though he never fully adjusted his purely strategic thinking to take

[1] André Beaufre, *An Introduction to Strategy* (London: Faber, 1965); *Deterrence and Strategy* (London: Faber, 1965); *Strategy of Action* (London: Faber, 1967).

account of the political environment whose overriding importance he quite rightly stressed. The second has been evident,
particularly in naval and air operations, at least since the
beginning of the twentieth century. But strategic thinkers,
from the pioneers of the eighteenth century to Liddell Hart
in his earlier writings, were able to assume a fairly simple
model of international relations within which armed conflict
might occur, as well as a basically stable technological environment. Neither assumption can now be made. No thinking about deterrence is likely to be of value unless it is based
on a thorough understanding of 'the state of the art' in
weapons technology. Any thinking about limited war, revolutionary war, or indirect strategy must take as its starting
point an understanding of the political – including the social
and economic – context out of which these conflicts arise or
are likely to arise. Inevitably the interaction works both
ways. Strategic factors themselves constitute an important
element in international relations: the statesman can never
be a purely despotic law-giver to the strategist. Similarly,
strategic requirements have inspired scientists and technologists to achievements they would normally consider impossible. Increasingly the three fields overlap. That is why
strategic studies owe at least as much to the work of political
scientists at one end of the spectrum, and of physical scientists, systems analysts and mathematical economists at the
other, as they do to the classical strategist. One may indeed
wonder whether 'classical strategy', as a self-sufficient study,
has any longer a valid claim to exist.

11 Strategy and Policy in Twentieth-Century Warfare

The military historian today is bound to wonder whether 'military history' still exists, or should exist, as a distinct field of study. Fifty years ago neither in the United States nor in the United Kingdom would anybody have seriously raised the question. Everyone knew what military history was. It was the history of the armed forces and of military operations. Its subject-matter occupied an insulated arena, with little if any political or social context. The military historian, like the military man himself, moved in a closed, orderly hierarchical society with inflexible standards, deep if narrow loyalties, recondite skills and lavish documentation. He chronicled the splendours and the miseries of man fighting at the behest of authorities and in the service of causes which it was no business of his to analyse or of theirs to question.

This kind of combat and unit history still serves a most valuable function both in training the professional officer and in providing essential raw material for the more general historian. To write it effectively calls for exceptional experience and skills. But it is not surprising that so limited a function attracted very few historians of the first rank. It is more surprising that so many historians of the first rank, for so many years, thought it possible to describe the evolution of society without making any serious study of the part played in it by the incidence of international conflict and the influence of armed forces. So long as military history was regarded as a thing apart, it could not itself creatively develop, and general historical studies remained by that much the poorer. The credit for ending this unhealthy separation was due very largely to scholars of the United States – particularly the group which Professor Quincy Wright collected round him at the University of Chicago and those who gathered under Edward Mead Earle at Princeton. But it is due also to the foresight of the United States Armed Services themselves in enlisting, to write and organise their histories of the Second World War, such outstanding scholars as Dr Kent Greenfield, Dr Maurice Matloff, Dr W. Frank Craven and Professor Samuel E. Morison, to name only the leaders in this gigantic enterprise. The work which they produced is likely to rank as one of the great historiographical series in the world, and its influence on military history has been profound. Today, the history of war is generally seen as an intrinsic part of the history of society. The armed forces are studied in the context of the communities to which they belong, on which they react, and so formidable a share of whose budgets they absorb. And their combat activities are considered, not as manœuvres isolated from their environment as much as those of a football game, but as methods of implementing national policy, to be assessed in the light of the political purpose which they are intended to serve.

The number of wars in modern history in which a narrow study of combat operations can provide a full explanation of the course and the outcome of the conflict is very limited indeed. In Europe from the end of the Middle Ages up till the end of the eighteenth century, the performance of armed forces was so far restricted by difficulties of communications and supply, by the limited capabilities of weapons, by the appalling incidence of sickness, and above all by the exigencies of public finance and administration, that warfare, although almost continuous as a form of international intercourse, was seldom decisive in its effects. When states tried to support military establishments capable of sustaining a hegemony in Europe, as Spain did in the sixteenth century and as France did in the seventeenth, their undeveloped economies collapsed under the strain. More prudent powers kept their campaigns within limits set by a calculation of their financial capacity. Military operations thus came to be regarded as part of a complicated international bargaining process in which commercial pressures, exchanges of territory, and the conclusion of profitable dynastic marriages were equally important elements. The results of the most successful campaign could be neutralised by the loss of a distant colony, by a court intrigue, by the death of a sovereign, by a well-timed shift in alliances, or by the exhaustion of financial credit. There are few more tedious and less profitable occupations than to study the campaigns of the great European masters of war in isolation – Maurice of Orange, Gustavus Adolphus, Turenne, Montecucculi, Saxe, even Marlborough and Frederick the Great; unles one first understands the diplomatic, the social and the economic context which gives them significance, and to which they contribute a necessary counterpoint. Any serious student of American history knows how widely he must read not only in his own historical studies but in the political and economic history of Britain and of France before he is to understand how and why the United States won its independence, and the part which was played in that struggle by force of arms. A study of the campaigns of Washington, Cornwallis, and Burgoyne really tells us very little.

This was the situation up till the end of the eighteenth century. With the advent of Napoleonic warfare, the situation changed radically. During the last few years in the eighteenth century both political conditions and military techniques developed to such an extent that now unprecedented proportions of the manpower of the nation could be called up and incorporated into armies of equally unprecedented size. These armies could be controlled and manœuvred so as to meet in a single battle, or series of battles, which would decisively settle the outcome of the war. With national resources thus concentrated and at the disposal of a single commander, the destiny of the state hung on the skill and judgment with which he deployed his forces during a few vital days. The campaigns of Marengo and Austerlitz, of Jena and Wagram, of Leipzig and Waterloo possessed all the dramatic unities. Forces well matched in size and exactly matched in weapons, operating within rigid boundaries of time and space, could by the skill of their commanders and the endurance and courage of their troops settle the fate of nations in a matter of hours. Military operations were no longer one part in a complex counterpoint of international negotiation: they played a dominant solo rôle, with diplomacy providing only a faint apologetic obbligato in the background.

There were of course many factors involved, other than the purely military, in the growth of the Napoleonic Empire and, even more, in its ultimate collapse; but the fact remained that Napoleon had lived by the sword and he perished by the sword. The study of swordsmanship thus acquired a heightened significance in the eyes of posterity.

Nothing that happened in Europe during the next hundred years was to undermine the view, that war now meant the interruption of political intercourse and the commitment of national destinies to huge armies whose function it was to seek each other out and clash in brief, sanguinary and decisive battles. At Magenta and Solferino in 1859 the new Kingdom of Italy was established. At Königgrätz in 1866 Prussia asserted her predominance in Germany, and by the battle of Sedan four years later a new German Empire was established which was to exercise a comparable prediminance in Europe. Operational histories of these campaigns can be written – indeed they *have* been written in quite unnecessarily large numbers – which, with little reference to diplomatic, economic, political or social factors, contain in themselves all necessary explanation of what happened and why the war was won. Operational history, therefore, in the nineteenth century, became synonymous with the history of war. It is not surprising that the soldiers and statesmen brought up on works of this kind should in 1914 have expected the new European war to take a similar course: the breach of political intercourse; the rapid mobilisation and deployment of resources; a few gigantic battles; and then the troops, vanquished or victorious as the case might be, would be home by Christmas while statesmen redrew the frontiers of their nations to correspond to the new balance of military profit and loss. The experience of the American Civil War where large amateur armies had fought in totally different conditions of terrain, or the Russo-Japanese War which had been conducted by both belligerents at the end of the slenderest lines of communications, seemed irrelevant to warfare conducted in Europe by highly trained professional forces fighting over limited terrain plentifully provided with roads and railways.

The disillusioning experience of the next few years did not

at first lead to any major reappraisal of strategic doctrine by the military authorities of any of the belligerent powers. The German High Command still sought after decisive battles in the east while they encouraged their adversaries to bleed themselves to death against their western defences. The powers of the Western *Entente* still regarded their offensives on the Western front as Napoleonic battles writ large: prolonged tests of endurance and will-power which would culminate in one side or the other, once its reserves were exhausted, collapsing at its weakest point and allowing the victorious cavalry of the opponent to flood through in glorious pursuit. From this view the United States Army, when it entered the war in 1917, did not basically dissent. The object of strategy remained, in spite of all changes in weapons and tactics, to concentrate all available resources at the decisive point, compelling the adversary to do the same, and there slug it out until a decision was reached. To this object all other considerations, diplomatic, economic and political, had to be subordinated.

But paradoxically, although military developments over the past hundred years had established the principle, indeed the dogma, of the 'decisive battle' as the focus of all military (and civil) activity, parallel political and social development had been making it increasingly difficult to achieve this kind of 'decision'. On the Napoleonic battlefield the decision had to be taken by a single commander, to capitulate or to flee. It was taken in a discrete situation, when his reserves were exhausted or the cohesion of his forces broken beyond repair. He could see that he had staked all and lost. And since the commander was often the political chief as well, such a military capitulation normally involved also a political surrender. If it did not, then the victor's path lay open to the victim's capital, where peace could be dictated on his own terms. But by 1914 armies were no longer self-sufficient entities at the disposal of a single commander. Railways provided conduits along which reserves and supplies could come as fast as they could be produced. Telegraph and telephone linked commanders in the field to centres of political and military control where a different perspective obtained over what was going on at the battlefield. If by some masterpiece of tactical deployment an army in the field could be totally annihilated, as was the French at Sedan or the Russian at Tannenberg, a government with sufficiently strong nerves and untapped resources could set about raising others. Armies could be kept on foot and committed to action so long as manpower and material lasted and national morale remained intact. Battles no longer provided clear decisions. They were trials of strength, competitions in mutual attrition in which the strength being eroded had to be measured in terms not simply of military units but of national manpower, economic productivity, and ultimately the social stability of the belligerent powers. That was the lesson, if anybody had cared to learn it, of the American Civil War. European strategists had studied and praised the elegant manœuvres of Jackson and Lee, but it was the remorseless attrition of Grant and the punitive destruction of Sherman which had ultimately decided the war. And once war became a matter of competing economic resources, social stability and popular morale, it became too serious a business to be left to the generals. Operations again became only one factor out of many in international struggle, and a 'military' history or a combat history of the First World War can give only a very inadequate account indeed of that huge and complicated conflict.

For with the increasing participation of the community at large in the war there went the broadening of the political basis of society. The necessary efforts would not be made, and the necessary sacrifices would not be endured, by populations which were merely servile or indifferent: that had been the lesson Napoleon had taught the Prussians in 1806, and they had learned it well. Popular enthusiasm had to be evoked and sustained. A struggle in which every member of society feels himself involved brings about a heightening of national consciousness, an acceptance of hardship, a heroic mood in which sufferings inflicted by the adversary are almost welcomed, and certainly stoically endured. If more men are needed for the armies, they will be found, if necessary from among 15–16-year-olds. Rationing is accepted without complaint. Sacrifice and ingenuity will produce astonishing quantities of war material from the most unpromising economic and industrial base. Necessity and scientific expertise will combine to produce ingenious new weapons systems. And as the long process of attrition continues, at what point can it be 'decided' that the war is lost?

By whom, moreover, is the decision to be made? The situation may deteriorate. The Army may fight with flagging zeal; statistics of self-mutilation and desertion may show a shocking increase; but the Army does not break and run. Factories may work spasmodically and slowly, turning out increasingly inferior products: but they do not close their doors. The population grows undernourished and indifferent, absenting itself from work whenever it can safely do so, but it does not revolt. A staunch government can endure all this and still carry on, so long as its police and its military remain loyal. Open dissent is, after all, treasonable. The emotional pressures no less than the political necessities of a wartime society create an environment in which moderation, balance, and far-sighted judgment are at a discount. Few men were more unpopular and ineffective in France, Britain, and Germany during the First World War than those courageous souls who pressed for a compromise peace. Resolution and ruthlessness are the qualities which bring men to the front as leaders in wartime, and if they weaken there will be others to take their place. Ultimately nothing short of physical occupation and subjugation may prove adequate to end the war. That was what we found with Germany in 1945, and so I suspect the Germans would have found with Britain five years earlier. One of the most distinctive and disagreeable characteristics of twentieth-century warfare is the enormous difficulty of bringing it to an end.

After the First World War, the classical strategic thinking came under attack from several quarters. There were the thinkers, in Britain and Germany, who hoped to replace the brutal slaughter of mutual attrition by new tactics based on mobility and surprise, which, by using armoured and mechanised forces instead of the old mass armies, would obtain on the battlefield results as decisive as those of Napoleon's campaigns. In the blitzkrieg of 1939 and 1940 it looked as if they had succeeded. The armies of Poland and France – not to mention those of Denmark, Norway, Holland,

Belgium and Great Britain – were destroyed or disrupted so rapidly that the political authorities were left literally defenceless, and could only capitulate or flee. But this proved a passing phase in warfare, applicable only under temporary conditions of technical disequilibrium and effective only in the limited terrain of Western Europe. When the German armed forces met, in the Russians, adversaries who could trade space for time and who had developed their own techniques of armoured defence and offence, battles became as strenuous, and losses as severe, as any in the First World War.

Then there were the prophets who believed that it might be possible so to undermine the morale and the political stability of the adversary with propaganda and subversion that when battle was actually joined he would never have the moral strength to sustain it. This doctrine was based on a grotesque over-estimate of the contribution which Allied propaganda had made to the collapse of the Central Powers in 1918. It appeared justified by the rapidity with which the French armies collapsed in 1940 and the apparent equanimity with which France concluded peace with her conqueror and her hereditary foe. But propaganda and subversion, although very valuable auxiliaries to orthodox military action, cannot serve as a substitute for it. The British were to rely very heavily on these methods in trying to undermine the Nazi Empire when they confronted it on their own in 1940 and 1941; but it was only when the United States entered the war, when Allied armed forces were deployed in strength in the Mediterranean and when the Russians were beginning to beat the Germans back from Stalingrad that these political manœuvres began to show any signs of success.

Finally there were the prophets of air power, of whom the most articulate was the Italian Giulio Douhet who believed that surface operations could be eliminated altogether by attacks aimed directly at the morale of the civilian population; a population who would, if their cities were destroyed around them, rise up and compel their governments to bring the war to an end. This doctrine, as we now know, over-estimated both the destructiveness of high-explosive bombs and the capacity of aircraft to deliver them accurately and

in adequate numbers to their targets in the technological
conditions then obtaining; while it equally underestimated
the capacity of civilian populations to survive prolonged
ordeals which previously might have been considered unendurable. Bombing, in its early stages, in fact did a great
deal to *improve* civilian morale. It gave a sense of exhilara-
tion, of shared sacrifices, a determination not to yield to an
overt form of terror. It engendered hatred, and hatred is
good for morale. In its later stages, bombing did indeed
result in increasing apathy and war weariness among the
civilian populations of Germany and Japan; but it produced
from them no effective and concerted demand that the war
should be brought to an end. It was only one form, if the
most immediate and terrifying, of the pressures being
brought to bear on their societies to force a decision which
their leaders stubbornly refused to take.

So the Second World War, like the First, was a conflict of
attrition between highly organised and politically sophisticated societies, in which economic capacity, scientific and
technological expertise, social cohesion and civilian morale
proved to be factors of no less significance than the operations of armed forces in the field. The disagreements between
British and American military leaders over grand strategy
arose primarily from the British belief that much attrition
could be to a great extent achieved by indirect means – by
bombing, by blockade, by propaganda, by subversion;
whereas the United States Army believed that there could
be no substitute for the classical strategic doctrine of bringing the enemy army to battle and defeating him at the
decisive point: and that could only be, as it had been thirty
years earlier, on the plains of northwest Europe, in the kind
of prolonged slugging match which Grant had taught it to
endure but which Britain, after the Somme and Passchendaele, had learned, with some reason, to dread. The Americans had their way. Yet in the battles in France there was no
clear decision; there was only a slow ebbing of moral and
material forces from the German armies until retreat imper-
ceptibly became rout, and military advance became political
occupation. Then it was seen that the strength of the German
nation had been drained into its armed forces – much as that

of the Confederacy had been eighty years before; and the destruction of those armed forces meant the disappearance of the German State.

When the object in war is the destruction of the adversary's political independence and social fabric, the question of persuading him to acknowledge defeat does not arise. But the states of the modern world – certainly those of modern Europe – have seldom gone to war with so drastic an objective in mind. They have been concerned more frequently with preventing one another from pursuing policies contrary to their interests, and compelling them to accept ones in conformity with them. Wars are not simply acts of violence. They are acts of persuasion or of dissuasion; and although the threat of destruction is normally a necessary part of the persuading process, such destruction is only exceptionally regarded as an end in itself. To put it at its lowest, the total elimination of an adversary as an organised political entity, his destruction as an advanced working society, normally creates a dangerously infectious condition of social and economic chaos – as the Germans found with the Russian Revolution of 1917. It is likely to increase the post-war political and economic troubles of the victorious side – as the Allies found after 1945. Normally, it makes better sense to leave one's adversary chastened and submissive, in control of his own political and social fabric, and sufficiently balanced economically, if not to pay an indemnity in the good old style, then at least not to be a burden on the victors and force them to pay an indemnity to him. This means that, although the threat of destruction must be convincing, it is in one's interest to persuade the adversary to acknowledge defeat before that threat has to be carried out – a truism which loses none of its force in the nuclear age. In making war, in short, it is necessary constantly to be thinking how to make peace. The two activities can never properly be separated.

What is making peace? It means persuading one's adversary to accept, or to offer, reasonable terms – terms in conformity with one's own overall policy. Broadly speaking, there are two ways in which this persuasion can be carried out. First it can be directed to the enemy government or régime itself, as is normally the case in so-called 'limited wars'. In such wars it is not part of one's policy to disrupt the social or political order in the enemy country. The existing régime, misguided as its policy may be, is probably the best that can be expected in the circumstances, and one does not want to see it replaced by wilder men or crumble into total anarchy. Alternatively, one may despair of men in power ever being brought to acknowledge defeat, as we despaired of Hitler; and even if they were to acknowledge defeat, of being relied on to abide by any agreement thereafter. Then one must seek to replace them by a more pliable régime. This can consist either of members of the same governing group seizing power by *coup d'état*, as the Italian Army did in 1943 and the anti-Nazi conspirators tried to do in July 1944. Or one may aim at a fundamental social and political revolution – or counter-revolution – which will sweep away the old order altogether and instal a government which is ideologically sympathetic to one's own.

Any one of these methods involves persuading significant individuals or significant groups in the opposing community, either those who already possess power or those who are capable of achieving power, that they have nothing to gain from further resistance, and a great deal to lose. In achieving such persuasion, there is, to borrow a famous phrase, no substitute for victory. It was not until defeat stared them in the face that substantial groups, in the Central Powers in the First World War or the Axis Powers in the Second, began to take effective measures to bring the war to an end. But the victor must still realise the enormous difficulties which will confront these groups in wartime from within their own society – in democracies from public opinion, in totalitarian societies from the secret police. If they are to carry public opinion with them – or opinion within their own élites – it may be necessary for the victor to make concessions to provide them with incentives as well as threats. It may be clear to them that peace at any price is better than continued and inescapable destruction, but peace with some semblance of honour provides a better basis for post-war stability, both on an international basis and within the domestic framework of the defeated power. Strategy and policy have to work hand

in hand to provide inducements as well as threats to secure
a lasting settlement.

Everything that I have said so far applies to wars between
states – organised communities fighting over incompatible
goals. But most of the conflicts which have occurred since
1945 have not been of this kind at all. One can call them wars
of liberation, guerrilla, insurgency or partisan wars, revolutionary wars, or, to use the rather charming British under-
statement, 'emergencies'. In all of them, the object on both
sides has been the same. It is, by the judicious use of force or
violence, to compel the other side to admit defeat and abandon his attempt to control certain contested territories. In
this conflict the traditional method of destroying the armed
power of the enemy is not sufficient, or sometimes even
necessary: of yet greater importance is the maintenance, or
the acquisition, of the positive support of the population in
the contested area. The capacity to exercise military control
and to prevent one's opponent from doing the same is clearly
a major and probably a decisive factor in gaining such support; yet if a guerrilla movement, in spite of repeated defeats
and heavy losses, can still rely on a sympathetic population
among whom its survivors can recuperate and hide, then all
the numerical and technical superiority of its opponents may
ultimately count for nothing.

In this kind of struggle for loyalties, military operations
and political action are inseparable. In a more real sense
than ever before, one is making war and peace simultaneously. The guerrilla organisation is a civil administration as
much as a fighting mechanism. It acquires increasing political
responsibilities with its increasing military success until
ultimately its leaders emerge from hiding as fully-fledged
heads of state and take their place among the great ones of
the world. The established régime, on the other side, is concerned to keep operations within the category of policing,
to maintain its own law and order, and to preserve the image
of legitimate power which gains it the support of the uncommitted part of the population. In this struggle schools
and hospitals are weapons as important as military units.
Defeat is acknowledged, not when one side or the other
recognises that the destruction of its armed forces is in-

escapable, but when it abandons all hope of winning the sympathy of the population over to its side. In such a struggle it must be admitted that a foreign power fights indigenous guerrillas under disadvantages so great that even the most overwhelming preponderance in military force and weapons may be insufficient to make up for them. In such wars, as in those of an earlier age, military operations are therefore only one tool of national policy, and not necessarily the most important. They have to be co-ordinated with others by a master hand.

In Vietnam today, the United States faces two tasks. It has to help the government of South Vietnam to attract that measure of popular support which alone will signify victory and guarantee lasting peace; and it has to persuade the government of North Vietnam to abandon – and to abandon for good – its interference in the affairs of its neighbour. In tackling the first of these tasks it has to solve the difficulties with which both the French and the British wrestled in their colonial territories, with varying degrees of success, for the past twenty-odd years. In carrying out the second it faces what one can now call the traditional problem of twentieth-century warfare: how to persuade the adversary to come to terms without inflicting on him such severe damage as to prejudice all chances of subsequent stability and peace. Although armed force is, regrettably, a necessary element in its policy, that force must be exercised with precision and restraint; and its exercise, however massive, will be not only useless but counter-productive if it is not integrated in a policy based on a thorough comprehension of the societies with which it is dealing, and a clear perception of the settlement at which it aims.

Operational histories of the Vietnam campaign will one day be produced, and we can be sure that, in the tradition of American official histories, they will be full, frank, informative and just. But they will be only a part of the history of that war. The full story will have to spell out, in all its complexity, how the struggle has been waged, for more than twenty years, and between many participants, for the loyalties of the Vietnamese peoples. Such a study will show how policy and strategy have or have not been related. It is unlikely to distinguish clearly between military history on the one hand and social, political and economic history on the other. But it will shed much light on the problem which is of central concern to all mankind in the twentieth century, and to whose study the military historian – however we may define him – must try to make some contribution: Under what circumstances can armed force be used, in the only way in which it can be legitimate to use it, to ensure a lasting and stable peace?

12 Military Power and International Order

In his inaugural lecture in the Chair of Military Studies at King's College, London, in January 1927, Sir Frederick Maurice chose as his subject 'The Uses of the Study of War'. These uses he saw as twofold.

> The first, which most concerns the citizen, is to promote peace by promoting an understanding of the realities of war and of the problems which may lead to war. The second, which most concerns the professional, but also does or should concern the citizen, is to ensure that war, if it comes, is waged in the best possible way.

For, he pointed out,

> A struggle between nations in which vital interests are involved is not merely the concern of professional soldiers, sailors and airmen, but affects directly every citizen and calls for the whole resources of the nation. We have learned that statecraft, economics, the supply of raw material, science and industry, are factors which are of prime importance to the issue, and we realise that the tendency is for the importance of the last two to increase . . .
>
> Above all [he concluded] we have learned that war is a great evil.

The course of the Second World War was to bear out everything that he said. Its outcome was determined as much in the factories and shipyards and laboratories as on the battlefield itself. Its historians have to study the development of weapon-design and production, and problems of political, economic and industrial organisation, at least as deeply as the operations of the armed forces themselves. Yet it is quite clear that the development of weapons during the last twenty years has effected so drastic a change in the nature of war that Sir Frederick's lecture can now properly be read only as a historical document from a previous era. Only by considering the context in which it was delivered and assessing the extent and significance of the changes which have since occurred can we take his words as a guide to our own studies and policies in the second half of the twentieth century.

What was this context? It was that of the age of struggles between 'Nations in Arms' which had opened with the French Revolutionary Wars, developed through those great mid-century conflicts between nascent industrial communities, the American Civil War and the Franco-Prussian War, and reached its climax in the two World Wars which dominated the first half of this century. During this period, the development of the political authority and administrative expertise of the state made it possible to place at the disposal of the armed forces the entire resources of the nation in man-power, technical skill and industrial productivity. The development of science, engineering and industry made equally available to them, in great quantities, weapons of unprecedented destructive power. Equipped with these weapons, making full use of all developing means of transport by land, sea, and, ultimately, air, and drawing on national man-power to the point of exhaustion, the armed forces of the great nations of the northern hemisphere were able to pursue on a gigantic scale the classical objectives of warfare: the defeat of the opposing forces, in order to disarm the enemy and confront him with the alternatives of annihilation or surrender; or at least a sufficient probability of defeat to make it sound policy for him to come to terms.

As the twentieth century progressed the means of achieving this objective grew even more complex and sophisticated, but the object itself remained unaltered. The hopes expressed by inter-war theorists, that direct military confrontation might be avoided or mitigated by direct assaults on the morale of the enemy population, whether by propaganda, by blockade or by air attack, bore very little fruit. Command of the air could not be won without first destroying the enemy air force in a subtle and long-drawn-out battle of attrition; and without command of the air it was not possible to strike effectively either at the enemy population or at his sources of economic strength. Without command of the sea the economic base of maritime nations was hopelessly vulnerable; and command of the sea was the reward of a weary struggle, not simply between capital fleets as Mahan and his disciples had believed, but between submarines, escorts, aircraft and surface-raiders, equipped with the finest aids science could provide but ultimately dependent on the courage and skill of the men who manned them. Armies were still needed to seize or defend the bases on which command of the air or the sea depended and to exploit the opportunities which these advantages gave them; and even without these advantages skilful leadership, good weapons and stubborn troops could still inflict heavy losses and impose heartbreaking delays.

For all these reasons, and in spite of the growing complication of war in three elements, one can still trace in the Second World War the basic characteristics of the conflicts waged by Napoleon, by Ulysses S. Grant, by Moltke, and by Ludendorff and Haig. There was the mobilisation of the resources of the nation, involving a transformation of the peace-time pattern of the national economy. There was the conversion of those resources into effective military power; and there was the deployment of that power by military specialists, according to classical principles of strategy, for the defeat of the enemy armed forces.

It is of course an over-simplification to talk of the age of mass-warfare as 'beginning' in 1792. Eighteenth-century habits of military thought and organisation lingered long into the nineteenth and even the twentieth centuries – perhaps longer in this sheltered country than anywhere else. Very few of Goethe's contemporaries could have understood what he meant by observing that a new age had opened when the French volunteers stood firm under the Prussian cannonade at Valmy on 20th September 1792. But there was no lack of would-be Goethes to proclaim the beginning of a new era on 6th August 1945 when the first atomic bomb was dropped on Hiroshima. In the short run they were wrong, just as Goethe was wrong. The atom bombs of 1945, for all their unprecedented power, were not immediately accepted by military planners as being, in themselves, decisive weapons of war. Their process of manufacture was so slow and expensive that it was several years before the United States had a stockpile sufficient to devastate a rival as large as the Soviet Union; while such bombs as were available could be transported to their targets only in sub-sonic, short-range manned bombers, vulnerable to fighter attack and anti-aircraft fire. When the world began to rearm again in 1950 the atom bomb was considered an ancillary and not a decisive weapon in a conflict which, in the view of responsible defence specialists on both sides, was likely to differ little in its basic requirements from the Second World War. The year 1945, like 1792, only provided a foretaste of what might come when the new technology got into its stride; that is, when thermonuclear replaced atomic explosives, and manned bombers were supplemented by ballistic missiles.

It is tempting to draw from this development sweeping and premature conclusions. There are still very few nuclear powers in the world, and it seems unlikely that their number will increase very rapidly. A conflict today between, say, China and India, or between two African states, might well conform to the general pattern of European warfare over the past hundred years. But for the great industrial nations of the northern hemisphere, that pattern is now radically altered. In order to confront one's adversary with the alternatives of annihilation or surrender it is no longer necessary to mobilise major forces and deploy them according to classical principles of strategy. It is unlikely that there will be either the need or the time to apply the techniques we learned in two world wars for the switching over of the national economy from a peacetime to a wartime footing. Those powers which possess sufficient wealth, scientific expertise and industrial capacity have developed weapons-systems which poise the threat of inescapable and unacceptable destruction over the heads of their rivals even in time of deepest peace; and for nations so threatened military security can no longer be based on traditional principles of defence, mobilisation and counter-attack. It can be based only on the capacity to deter one's adversary by having available the capacity to inflict on him inescapable and unacceptable damage in return.

So much is now generally accepted, and the dimensions of this new situation have been studied with encyclopaedic brilliance by a group of American scholars whose work must be the starting point for any student of military affairs today. They have patiently unravelled the problems of the technical and political requirements of deterrence. They have discussed the possible nature of a nuclear war, the alternative forms into which international conflict might be channelled, and the political measures needed to control the military forces we can now unleash. But many things remain unclear: not least of them the effect which this transformation in the nature of war is likely to have on that international order in which armed sovereign states peacefully coexist; always assuming that they remain armed and that they remain sovereign – two assumptions which at present it seems not unreasonable to make.

In offering some tentative remarks on this subject I shall consider briefly the nature both of war and of the international order within which it arises. I shall not, in dealing with the first, adopt the view that war is a disease of the body politic, a pathological condition which can be traced to abnormalities in the social or economic structure, or to the racial characteristics of particular peoples. One could list many such explanations of the causes of war, from 'aggressor nations' or the machinations of armament-manufacturers to particular kinds of ruling class – whether monarcho-feudal, as the Cobdenites believed a hundred years ago, or bourgeois-capitalist, as the socialists believed fifty years later. All take as their starting point the assumption that peace is the natural condition of mankind, as health is of the human body. Such a view is understandable enough. It is a commendable re-action, not simply against the evils of war in themselves, but against the doctrines which were so widespread in Europe during the nineteenth and the earlier part of this century, that war is necessary to the health of the race, that it is an intrinsic part of the dialectical mechanism of progress or the biological mechanism of the survival of the fittest, a test of manhood to be strenuously prepared for and welcomed when it comes. The generation of Rupert Brooke had still to learn the lesson, on which Sir Frederick Maurice was to insist in 1927, that 'war is a great evil'.

But the historian and the political scientist cannot discuss war in terms of good or evil, normality or abnormality, health or disease. For them it is simply the use of violence by states for the enforcement, the protection or the extension of their political power. Some wars, under some circumstances, may be rational acts of policy; under others they may not. Power, in itself, is something morally neutral, being no more than the capacity of individuals or groups to control and organise their environment to conform with their physical requirements or their code of moral values. The desire for, acquisition, and exercise of power is the raw material of politics, national and international, and violence may sometimes prove an effective means to secure or retain it. Within well-organised states groups can seldom achieve power by violence, save in a marginal or covert way; and power which is so achieved will be of a most transitory kind until it is transformed by prescriptive exercise or rational consent into effective authority. Yet in spite of the aspirations of internationalists since the sixteenth century, in spite of Hague Conferences, Kellogg Pacts, League Covenants and United Nations Charters, the use of violence remains among sovereign states as an accepted if rarely exercised instrument for the extension or protection of their power.

But the inhibitions on the use of violence between states are considerable. They are not grounded simply on humanitarian considerations, or on any formal respect for international law. Fundamentally they rest on the most naked kind of self-interest. The use of violence, between states as between individuals, is seldom the most effective way of settling disputes. It is expensive in its methods and unpredictable in its outcome; and these elements of expense and unpredictability have both grown enormously over the last hundred years. The advent of nuclear weapons has only intensified an aversion to the use of violence in international affairs, which has, with certain rather obvious exceptions, increasingly characterised the conduct of foreign policy by the major powers since the latter part of the nineteenth century.

For this aversion there was little historical precedent. In most of the societies known to history, war has been an established and usually rather enjoyable social rite. In western Europe until the first part of the seventeenth century warfare was a way of life for considerable sections of society, its termination was for them a catastrophe, and its prolongation, official or unofficial, was the legitimate objective of every man of spirit. Even in the seventeenth and eighteenth centuries war, elaborate and formal as its conduct had become, was an accepted, almost an indispensable part of the pattern of society, and it was curtailed and intermittent only because of its mounting expense. If war could be made to pay, as it did for the Dutch merchants in the seventeenth century and the English in the eighteenth, then its declaration was as welcome as its termination was deplored. Habits of mind formed in days when war was the main social function of the nobility and a source of profit to the merchants survived into our own century, even though new weapons had rendered aristocratic leadership anachronistic if not positively dangerous, and the City of London confidently predicted ruin and bankruptcy when war threatened in 1914. Such atavistic belligerence was fanned by the jingoistic enthusiasm of the masses in the great cities of western Europe, where gusts of emotion greeted every war from the Crimea to that of 1914.

But by 1914 governments and peoples were largely at cross-purposes. Since 1870 the size and expense of the war-machines, and the uncertainty of the consequences of war for society as a whole, made violence an increasingly unusable instrument for the conduct of international affairs. Defeat, even at the hands of a moderate and restrained adversary, might mean social revolution, as it nearly had for France in 1870 and Russia in 1905; while even a successful war involved a disturbance of the economic life of the nation whose consequences were quite unforeseeable. Clausewitz in his great work *On War* had suggested that 'policy', the adaptation of military means to political objectives, could convert the heavy battlesword of war into a light, handy rapier for use in limited conflicts; but the mass armies of 1870, of 1914 and of 1939 could not be wielded as rapiers in the cut and thrust of international politics. Indeed, so great was the expense of modern war, so heavy were the sacrifices that it entailed, that it was difficult to conceive of causes warranting having resort to it at all. Could the national resources really be mobilised and the youth of the nation really be sacrificed in hundreds of thousands for anything short of national survival, or some great ideological crusade?

So at least it appeared to the great western democracies in the 1930s; and it was this sentiment that Hitler exploited with such superb and sinister skill. Mass war, as Britain and France had learned to fight it between 1914 and 1918, was not a rational instrument of foreign policy. French and British statesmen were naturally and properly unwilling to invoke it for such limited objectives as the preservation of the Rhineland from re-militarisation; or the prevention of the *Anschluss* of an acquiescent Austria with Germany; or to prevent the German population of the Sudetenland being accorded the privileges of self-determination which had been granted to other peoples in Central Europe; and there appeared to be no other instruments they could use instead. To suggest that Hitler could not have been planning for war because in 1939 the German economy was not fully mobilised nor the armed forces at full battle strength is to apply the standards of 1914 to a different situation. Hitler had not armed Germany, as Britain and France had systematically armed since 1935, for a full-scale, formal Armageddon. He had every hope that it might be avoided. But he had the means available to use violence as an instrument of policy in a limited but sufficient degree, and he had no more inhibitions about using it in foreign than he had in domestic affairs. The Western democracies, committed to a policy of total violence in international affairs or none at all, could only watch him paralysed; until they took up arms on a scale, and with a crusading purpose, which could result only in the destruction of Germany or of themselves, and quite conceivably of both.

We should not, therefore, overestimate the change brought about in international relations through the introduction of nuclear weapons. The reluctance to contemplate the use of such weapons, which is fortunately so characteristic of the powers which at present possess them, is a continuation, although vastly intensified, of the reluctance to use the older techniques of mass war. Even as the statesmen of the 1930s found it difficult to conceive of a cause urgent enough to justify the use of the massive weapons of which they potentially disposed, so, *a fortiori*, is it still more difficult for us to foresee the political problem to which the destruction of a score of millions of civilians will provide the appropriate military solution. It is for this reason that political influence does not necessarily increase in direct proportion to the acquisition of nuclear power. Similarly, there is no cause to suppose that the capacity to use nuclear weapons will be any more effective as a deterrent to, or even as an agent of, disturbances of the international order than was, in the 1930s, the ability, given the will, to wage mass war. Those who wish to use violence as an instrument of policy – and since 1945 they have not been rare – can find, as did Hitler, more limited and effective forms; and those who hope to counter it need equally effective instruments for doing so.

Perhaps, indeed, it is necessary, in reassessing the place of military force in international affairs, to rid ourselves of the idea that if such force is employed it must necessarily be in a distinct 'war', formally declared, ending in a clear decision embodied in a peace treaty, taking place within a precise interval of time during which diplomatic relations between the belligerents are suspended and military operations proceed according to their own peculiar laws. We reveal the influence of this concept whenever we talk about 'the next war', or 'if war breaks out' or 'the need to deter war'. If an inescapable *casus belli* were to occur between nuclear powers, there *might* follow a spasm of mutual destruction which the survivors, such as they were, would be justified in remembering as the Third World War; but such an outcome is by no means inevitable, and appears to be decreasingly likely. It seems more probable that a *casus belli* would provoke threats and, if necessary, execution of limited acts of violence, probably though not necessarily localised, probably though not necessarily non-nuclear; all accompanied by an intensification rather than a cessation of diplomatic intercourse. Instead of a formal state of war in which diplomacy was subordinated to the requirements of strategy, specific military operations might be carried out under the most rigorous political control. It will certainly no longer be enough for the statesman to give general guidance to a military machine which then proceeds according to its own laws. Politics must now interpenetrate military activity at every level as thoroughly as the nervous system penetrates the tissues of a human body, carrying to the smallest muscle the dictates of a controlling will. The demands on the military for discipline and self-sacrifice will be great beyond all precedent, and the opportunities for traditional honour and glory negligible. Regiments will bear as their battle honours the names, not of the battles they have fought, but those that they have averted.

The maintenance of armed forces for this rôle creates many problems. Such conflicts must be waged with forces in being, and the task for which they are recruited is a thankless one. The standard of technical expertise, already high, may become still more exacting; military commanders will need exceptional political wisdom as well as military skill; but they must refrain from attempting to shape the political world to their military image, as the French Army tried to do, so tragically, in Algeria. Indeed, the tendency which has been so general during the past fifteen years of regarding all international relations as an extension of warfare, and the description of national policy in such terms as 'national strategy' or 'Cold War' betrays a dangerous confusion of categories and a fundamental misunderstanding of the nature of international affairs, even in an age of bitter ideological conflict.

On the other hand, statesmen now require a deeper understanding of military matters, of the needs and capabilities and limitations of armed forces, than they have ever needed in the past. Only if there is complete mutual understanding and co-operation between civil and military leaders, only if there is effective functioning of the mechanism of command and control, only if there is entire discipline and obedience in every rank of military hierarchy can military power serve as an instrument of international order at all, rather than one of international anarchy and world destruction.

The order which exists between sovereign states is very different in kind from that which they maintain within their borders, but it is an order none the less, though precarious in places and everywhere incomplete. There does exist a comity of nations, an international community transcending ideological and other rivalries. Its activities in many fields – those of commerce and communications, of health and diplomatic representation, of use of the high seas and of the air – are regulated by effective and precise provisions of international law, which are for the most part meticulously observed. But even in those aspects of international relations which international law does not regulate, order still obtains. It is preserved by certain conventions of behaviour established and adjusted by a continuing and subtle process of communication and negotiations, with which not even the most revolutionary of states – neither the United States in the eighteenth century nor the Soviet Union in the twentieth – has ever found it possible to dispense for very long. This order is based on no system of positive law, nor of natural justice, nor of clearly defined rights, nor even of agreed values. It has never been very easy for sovereign states to agree about such things. Even if the differing pattern of their international development does not lead them to adopt divergent and conflicting ideologies, states are bound by their very nature to regard the maintenance of their own power as the main criterion of all their actions and to pursue that, whatever their noble professions to the contrary. International order is based rather on recognition of disagreement, and of the limitation on one's own capacity to secure agreement. It is based on the understanding by nations that their capacity to impose and extend their own favoured order is limited by the will and effective ability of other states to impose theirs. The conduct of international relations must therefore always be a delicate adjustment of power to power, a mutual exploration of intentions and capabilities, so as to find and preserve an order which, though fully satisfying to nobody, is just tolerable to all.

The power which states exercise in international affairs is compounded of many attributes, economic, diplomatic, cultural and ideological as well as military. But military power, the capacity to use violence for the protection, enforcement or extension of authority, remains an instrument with which no state has yet found it possible completely to dispense. Indeed, it is not easy to see how international relations could be conducted, and international order maintained, if it were totally absent. The capacity of states to defend themselves, and their evident willingness to do so, provides the basic framework within which the business of international negotiation is carried on. That this framework should be as wide and as flexible as possible hardly needs arguing; but if no such limits existed, if it were known that there were no extremes of surrender and humiliation beyond which a state could not be pressed, the maintenance of international order would surely be, not easier, but incalculably more difficult. It is significant that nearly every one of the new states which has emerged since the Second World War has considered it necessary to create at least a token military force, even when the strategic need has been as negligible as the financial capacity to support it. Such a force is not purely symbolic. The ultimate test of national independence remains in the nuclear what it was in the pre-nuclear age: whether people are prepared to risk their lives in order to secure and preserve it.

The thesis that military power is an intrinsic part of the structure of international order is not one which will meet with unanimous approval. Attitudes towards the place of armed forces in international relations fall somewhere between two extremes. On the one hand is the view that armed forces constitute a purely destabilising factor on the international scene, and that their abolition would lead to greater stability among nations. The arguments in favour of such a view are familiar and formidable, for it is true that the weapons which a nation considers necessary to its own defence will always be likely to appear to its neighbours as an actual or potential threat to themselves. The military preparations carried out by the Triple and Dual Alliances in pre-war Europe were inspired almost wholly by considerations of self-defence, but they appeared to offer reciprocally an intolerable threat, to be countered only by yet more intensive armament. It is no doubt as difficult today for the

Soviet Union to believe in the purely defensive intentions of the bombers and missiles which ring her territory, and whose devastating powers our political and military leaders frequently extol, as it is for us to believe that the powerful units with which the Soviet Union could strike at western Europe will never be used for aggressive purposes. In any case the 'balance of terror' is never wholly stable. It is maintained only by constant effort, heavy expense and the dedicated work of military specialists. Those specialists must constantly be thinking of the worst possible case, and it is not always easy under the circumstances to retain a sense of proportion and to realise that this may be the least probable case. It is simpler to judge the political intentions of a possible adversary according to his military capabilities; but the actions, writings and speeches stemming from such a judgment are likely to engender reciprocal alarm and bellicosity on the other side. The result is likely to be one of those arms races which inevitably, we are told, end in war.

Much of this is unfortunately and undeniably true. Yet there is all too little evidence to show that military impotence in itself leads to stability and order. The examples of China in 1931, of Abyssinia in 1935, of Czechoslovakia and her allies in 1938, and of Western empires in the Far East in 1941 are not encouraging. Violence can appear a perfectly rational instrument of policy to a state which stands to gain important strategic, economic or political advantages from the domination of helpless and disorganised neighbours; and the experience of the 1930s suggests that under such circumstances only the prospect of immediate and effective counter-violence can make it appear irrational.

At the other extreme we have the belief that military power is not merely one element of national power and international order, but the basic factor; and that no cheque in international politics can be honoured unless there is a full supply of military power in the bank to meet it. But such a view is really no more tenable than its opposite. There are many reasons which deter even the most powerful and ruthless states from attacking their neighbours; not least the inherent drawbacks of violence as an instrument of policy which we have already considered. In certain areas of the world – Scandinavia for nearly two hundred years, and now at last perhaps western Europe – social bonds have been forged between nations which make their military power increasingly irrelevant; while many states – our own not least – have exercised an influence in world politics out of all proportion to their military strength.

The rôle of military power in international order is in fact as difficult to define as is the rôle of gold in economic transactions; and the controversies in the economic sphere parallel very closely those in the military. Those who believe in the primacy of military considerations in international affairs have their parallel in those economists who insist that a sound currency is the only basis for a healthy economy and who pursue policies of sound finance at whatever short-term cost in social distress. Those who deny the need for military power at all have much in common with the thinkers who would maintain that the gold standard is a shibboleth contrived by financiers for their own profit, and that a workable economic system, based perhaps on some form of social credit, if not on simple inflation, can be devised without reference to it at all.

To a large extent this economic controversy has died down, or at least is conducted rather more intelligently than it was thirty years ago. The thunderings of the orthodox have been muted since Lord Keynes showed how far governments could carry economic manipulation without incurring disaster. The arguments of the reformers sound less persuasive after twenty years of chronic balance-of-payment problems. We have learned that although man is not the slave of economic forces, neither is he their master; that he can sail closer to the wind than was ever thought possible, but must still take account of it; and that there are limits to what even the most accomplished sailor can do.

All this was learned – and is still being learned – not only through the hard experience of treasury officials and business men, but by the reasoning, study and debate of academic economists. Today all these three groups work, if not always in harmony, at least in fairly fruitful dialectic. But in the field of military affairs we are still in the pre-Keynesian era. Pronouncements about military power and disarmament are still made by public figures of apparent intelligence and considerable authority with a naïve dogmatism of a kind such as one finds in virtually no other area of social studies or public affairs. The concepts and presuppositions on which defence policy are based are seldom subjected in this country to academic analysis of a really serious kind, and the suggestion that they should be is usually received in Whitehall with a certain lack of enthusiasm. But it is for the academics to show first that they have something to contribute; that academic habits and techniques really are relevant to the understanding of the part played by military power in international order. It is for us to prove that the studies which we are now developing in the fields of strategic theory and military history, in the social and economic aspects of defence questions, in the military aspects of international relations and international law, in the structure of military establishments and their political and constitutional relationship with civil society, do not represent simply a passing intellectual fashion but that they are both academically reputable and socially relevant. Unless their roots within the university are deep and well-nourished, they can never bear any fruit for the outside world.

13 Disarmament and the Military Balance[1]

Nearly twenty years have passed since the USSR and the powers of the West began their attempt to rebuild the world-order which had been shattered by the Second World War, and to incorporate in that order dependable provision for the control, if not the abolition, of national armaments, both nuclear and conventional. They have been years of fruitless negotiation, which have been all the more frustrating in that at least once they have seemed about to succeed; and every failure has tended to make each side more bitter at the apparent perversity of the other and more pessimistic about the chances of ultimate success. When negotiations undertaken in good faith result repeatedly in such complete and humiliating failure, the natural reaction is to blame the stupidity or ill-will of one's opponents – especially when the negotiations are public and the destiny of mankind may be involved. Certainly neither side can be acquitted of short-sightedness or even hypocrisy at certain stages of the negotiations; yet their failure cannot be attributed to this alone. The reasons must be sought at a more profound level, in the nature of the states involved in negotiations – indeed in the nature of the state itself.

Negotiations and agreements between states cannot be equated with those between any other form of corporation. Agreements between private parties are negotiated against the background of security and enforcement which the state provides. That minimal degree of mutual confidence necessary before any agreement can be concluded is not difficult to achieve in the settled condition of human relationships of which the existence of the state is a symptom, and without which the condition of man is nasty, poor, solitary, brutish, and short. Agreement between states themselves rests on a carefully-negotiated framework of self-interest and a grow-

[1] Written in 1964.

ing body of accepted international practice which makes it
possible to conclude, with little difficulty, agreements on
matters of such common concern as trade, reciprocal rights
of natives and aliens, communications, investigation and
extradition of criminals, and cultural interchange. None of
this affects, or need affect, the fabric of the state structure
itself. But the statesman must always, even in dealing with
his oldest ally and his most friendly neighbour, bear in mind
that there rests on his shoulders a burden of responsibility
for the security and independence of his people that no one
else, however friendly their intentions and common their
aims, can be relied upon to underwrite. If his nation is small,
he may be forced to link its interests with those of more
powerful neighbours. If it is suitably situated he may maintain a precarious independence by steering a middle course
between major rivals. But if his nation qualifies as a great
power, however that term is defined, he will seek security
and independence only in his own national strength, which
is in the last resort the ability to defend himself in a major
war; and that great power status, by attracting dependent
minor nations to the shadow of its protection, gives him a
responsibility for allies as well as for his own people.

In the past it has been taken for granted that the whole
foundation of order in a world of international anarchy has
been a balance of military power: great powers checking one
another, clients relying on their protection and neutrals on
their rivalry. That creed is one which, basically, the statesmen of the world still hold; and it is not for those who have
never felt the weight of their responsibilities to say that they
are wrong – that the whole pattern of international affairs
has been based on a monstrous hoax and that the belief in
the need for military strength arises, not from the necessary
relations of sovereign states subject to no supra-national
arbiter, but from a mass delusion. Even if it is a delusion,
there seems, at present, no escape from it: the leaders of the
great powers feel that the security of their peoples and the
protection of their allies remains, in the last resort, a question
of military power. Any question affecting the amount and
efficacy of that power is therefore one which concerns the
very essence of the nation's being. Agreements affecting a

nation's economic welfare can be concluded fairly easily; but agreement on armaments may be a question of the nation's very life.

It is sometimes suggested that the continuing concern over defence and the failure to reach agreement upon arms control is due in large measure to the vested interests of those whose careers and fortunes depend upon the continued existence of military establishments and the maintenance of a booming armaments industry. Certainly it requires an unusual degree of dispassionate self-effacement to admit that any activity on which one is lucratively engaged is not only unnecessary but may be positively harmful. Soldiers like war no more than most men, but they do not take kindly to the suggestion that the armed services to which, in frequent discomfort and occasional danger, they devote their lives, are socially undesirable. The manufacturers of armaments and their employees feel that they are doing a public service, as well as earning an honest living, in providing the best possible weapons for the national defence; and it would be hard to convince them that any sudden and complete cessation of manufacture, with no phasing, no compensation, and no alternative orders provided, was not a grave error of national policy as well as a personal disaster for themselves. These groups may display a considerable inertia where disarmament is concerned but this inertia is not decisive in the formation of national policy. The redeployment of economic and industrial resources devoted to armaments certainly presents considerable, perhaps major, administrative problems, and perhaps cannot be accomplished at all without some temporary dislocation and hardship. But they are problems which no government would shrink from tackling if disarmament seemed possible on other grounds. The decisive reluctance is to be found among those governmental groups most directly responsible for the destinies of the nation over which they preside: not simply the military experts who tender informed advice as to the equipment and posture which they regard as essential to national security, but the statesmen and civil servants who feel themselves bound to accept that advice if they are to fulfil the responsibility which rests on their shoulders.

Nobody who has been brought into contact with that inner group of civil and military specialists who are responsible for the security of this country can fail to notice the almost physical pressure exerted on them by that responsibility, affecting their processes of thought (and often their manner of speech) in much the same way as the movements of a man are affected when he tries to walk in water. There are certain actions which he simply finds impossible; and the impatient onlookers, who have never themselves been plunged into that element, cannot understand why. His direction of movement is distorted, his speed of action is slowed, weights and pressures negligible on dry land become almost intolerable. It is not to be wondered at that they share a common scepticism as to the possibility of disarmament, or indeed of the creation of any effective international authority to whom they can turn over any portion of their responsibilities. They wish as devoutly as the rest of us that such things were possible. The ritual invocations of the spirit of universal peace which were for so many years a feature of the annual presentation of his estimates by the Minister of Defence are not rendered by their ritual nature any less sincere. So with equal conviction do we on Sunday mornings acknowledge that we have erred and strayed from our ways like lost sheep, without our conduct during the following week being noticeably affected by the sincerity with which we lamented our behaviour of the week before. Our actions continue to be guided by the apparently uncontrollable inertia of our personalities; and a comparable inertia leads the men on whom we lay the responsibility for guiding us, to accept the need for international control of armaments in principle but to shy away from it in practice and devote very little of their collective energies to bringing it about. Lord, they pray, make me chaste: but not yet.

How can we blame them? On their discretion and judgment depends the entire fabric of social and political organisation, of law and of order, which makes the whole daily miracle of civilisation possible at all. Men look to the state for protection: to whom can the state look in its turn? The best form of international organisation that we have yet been able to contrive still consists only of a loose association of sovereign states, each of whom will consult its own interests before deciding whether to fulfil its obligations or not. Under these conditions, a statesman could reasonably be accused of betraying his trust if he hazarded the survival of his nation on agreements which he could not be sure that his nation's rivals would permanently observe, and which, under fore-seeable circumstances, it might seem to be to their interests *not* to observe.

Thus in the event of an agreement for total disarmament enforced by no reliable measures of inspection and control – and how many questions that word 'reliable' begs! – a government might feel itself compelled by the highest motives to retain secretly some residuary arms because it cannot know for certain that the other party to the agree-ment is not doing so as well – or that a régime might not come into power there which would secretly take the decision to reverse the policy of its predecessor. The risk of being caught defenceless is one which few statesmen are prepared to take. In the nuclear age the problem has become more difficult than ever before. Up till the Second World War the military preparations of one's neighbours, if they were to be dangerous, were bound to be obvious. The building of strate-gic railways, the training of manpower, the redeployment of heavy industry, all the measures needed for the creation of an effective war machine, were not activities which could be entirely concealed from the world outside. Germany's so-called 'secret' re-armament between the wars was no secret to the French *Deuxième Bureau* or to the intelligence service of the United Kingdom; and although foreign intelligence estimates of the war potential of the Soviet Union in 1941 proved hopelessly inaccurate, it would have been difficult for her to have concealed the very existence of her war-machine from foreign eyes. It is easy to over-estimate the change which has occurred during the past twenty years. The manufacture, movement, siting and manning of nuclear missiles are complicated processes, and the preservation of strict secrecy is not easy. But it is considerably easier than the concealment of war preparations involving armies of millions and air forces of thousands; and in totalitarian states it is rather easier than elsewhere. It would not be a simple business for a state, starting from scratch, to build up a weapons-system capable of annihilating its rivals; but to retain and conceal such a system once it has been created is now a distinctly practical possibility.

It is thus difficult to believe that a world of disarmed nations is possible at all without an armed international controlling authority, or, if it were possible, that such a world would not be at least as insecure and as riddled with mutual mistrust as that in which we live today. After all, we cannot create a 'model' of international organisation, consisting of regenerate states washed in the blood of the Lamb. There would still exist all the pressures of emerging nationalism, increasing populations, racial hatred and ideological rivalry which at present compel 'responsible statesmen' to engage in that arms race which all in theory so much deplore. The Communist and the Western worlds would still each believe that the other lived under a political system which was not only mistaken, oppressive, and doomed to ultimate collapse but which was dedicated to contriving the downfall of the other. So long as this mistrust continues, neither party is likely to see in the adherence of the other to a sweeping disarmament agreement very much more than a step in a programme to deceive the other and obtain world domination: indeed in the past the very readiness of one party to accept concessions has been sufficient justification in the eyes of the other for at once withdrawing them. Moreover the existence of such mistrust will make it equally difficult to create any supra-national authority with effective powers of enforcement for fear that it may become simply the tool of one's adversary. When nations so closely linked by geography, history and culture as those of western Europe find the creation of an effective supra-national authority a matter of apparently insuperable difficulty, there is little prospect that Russia, America and China, the governing élites of which all regard themselves as being in a peculiar sense the guardians of the future of mankind, will do any better.

It is perhaps worth considering some of the practical difficulties which are likely to be encountered by any international inspectorate which may be set up as a result of arms-control agreements between these states. To avoid bias let us call them 'Northland' and 'Southland', and discount internal differences of political structure. Let us assume the recruitment of an arms-control organisation, under United Nations auspices and on an international basis, with permanent posts at all major airfields, railway junctions and factories, with complete rights of unrestricted access to all parts of the inspected country and power to examine all national and private documentation and industrial plant. It is to the integrity and efficiency of this body, to its political trustworthiness and to its technical capacity to scent out any breach of the initial agreement that the governing élite is required to abdicate its ultimate responsibility for the safety of the nation. The government may decide to do so; it may make the decision politically acceptable to the peoples it governs; but even in the most efficient of totalitarian states there will be left widespread powerful prejudices against the decision, which are likely to find influential leaders to express them. The more effective the powers of the inspectorate, the more genuinely international its background, the less popular is it likely to be. Northland will suspect it (containing as it does so many representatives of the Southland bloc) of conniving at evasions on the part of Southland; the reliability of the Northlanders on the organisation, expatriates who have abandoned their primal loyalties, are likely to be continually under attack, openly or covertly, in their own homeland. The organisation will have teething troubles which may justify some of the suspicion of its adversaries; and even were it staffed by angels equipped with infallible techniques of detection, would it be any better trusted?

Consider two not improbable instances. The inspectorate reports that Northland is breaking the agreement. Northland's so-called police forces, it alleges, are paramilitary units; its new refining processes are producing fissile material of military value. Northland hotly denies the accusation, and a long, highly technical wrangle develops. It is not unlikely that Northland would end by denouncing the agreement altogether; and even if she did not, would not the statesmen of Southland be under irresistible pressure to take their own precautions? Or let us assume that the inspectorate, after careful study, decides that the initial reports were false and that Northland is not in breach of the agreement. The government of Southland may accept this judgment, but in so doing it will have to overrule the elements in its own community which suspect that the verdict is based either on inefficiency or on outright connivance on the part of the inspectors. In the western democracies these elements are likely to find strong support in press, Congress and Parliament; in the east they are no less likely to make their voices more privately heard. And when one remembers that other sources of international tension between major states are likely to be continuing unabated: that the struggles of 'the cold war' are still being fought: it is hard to believe that these pressures would not be strong enough, on one side or the other, to destroy the inspectorate at its first real test.

Yet the conclusions to be drawn from this argument are not necessarily totally negative. The image which many of us hold subconsciously, of 'the next war' as a fixed point to which we come nearer as arms increase, and from which disarmament will enable us to back away, is misleading. The experiences of the 1930s suggest that refusal to arm can sometimes increase international tensions. Conversely, the experiences of the last ten years have shown that the development of certain kinds of weapons and weapons-systems can lead to a greater degree of stability rather than less. The creation by the super-powers of truly invulnerable second-strike missile delivery systems capable of retaliating inescapably to any surprise attack can breed and to some extent has bred as much confidence, and made possible as great a degree of détente, as one might expect from the most sweeping measures of disarmament. The Russian development of an intercontinental missile capability, the American development of Polaris-carrying submarines, has created a strategic balance which, even though military specialists on both sides may fear it to be more delicate than it looks, has contributed an atmosphere in which political leaders are negotiating with an entirely new kind of confidence. A stage has been reached – perhaps a unique one in the history of international relations – when neither side believes that it can buy greater security by any increase in its arms budget, and when both sides share a common fear, which they do not hesitate to express, that further technical developments are likely to lead only to a more precarious situation from which each stands only to lose.[1]

So through the polemics about general and complete disarmament, which sometimes strike one as being simply war conducted through other means, the outlines of a new kind of international dialogue are beginning to emerge, as statesmen seek, not to transform the world, and escape from their nuclear predicament, but to adjust themselves to it: to underpin the balance on which we have stumbled with such undeserved good fortune, and to eliminate its more dangerous aspects. The Test Ban Treaty was significant primarily as a declaration of common interest: not in disarmament, in the classical sense of the word, but in limiting the dangers inherent in the existence of nuclear armaments – the poisoning of the atmosphere and the indefinite extension of the nuclear club. The agreement which followed, to abstain from stationing weapons of mass destruction in outer space, was equally a declaration of a common interest in checking developments of a kind from which neither side could expect to gain any decisive advantage and from which both would be likely, in the long run, to suffer. The establishment of direct communications between Washington and Moscow, the lack of which had become dangerously obvious during the Cuba crisis in autumn 1962, reflected a common interest of a slightly different kind, in eliminating the danger of misunderstanding, miscalculation, and accidental war. And it is in areas of this kind – mutual inspection in frontier areas to give reassurance again surprise attack, mutual sponsoring of non-nuclear zones, and other steps to discourage proliferation of nuclear weapons – unilateral budgetary reductions and the abolition of surplus stocks – that we can, without undue optimism, expect genuine progress to be made.

The maintenance of the balance – or to be more precise, the maintenance of the conviction on both sides that there *is* a balance and that the use of military force will never appear

[1] The initiation of Strategic Arms Limitation Talks between the super-powers six years after these words were written suggest that such technical innovations as MIRVs and ABMs have not fundamentally changed the situation.

to its adversary as a rational choice – is therefore an essential prerequisite for disarmament, and an essential condition for it continuing throughout the entire process, if it ever comes about. Both sides have recognised this by their agreement that a certain missile force, a 'minimal deterrent', should be retained by each until the disarmament process has been completed, as an insurance against cheating of any kind. But it is not evident that it will be any easier to maintain the balance in a partially disarmed world than in a fully-armed one; and the results of its de-stabilisation are likely to be disastrous at any stage. Neither side has yet been able to bring forward proposals for disarmament which do not appear likely, in the eyes of the other, to upset the balance. The Russian proposals for a closing down of all foreign military bases; the Western requirements for on-site inspection; the Russian rejection of any supra-national peace-keeping authority; the Western insistence on one; all seems, to the other side, to be likely to create a less stable, more disorderly, and in consequence a more dangerous situation than that which obtains at present. The more closely the difficulties of the disarmament process are analysed, the greater becomes the inclination to re-examine the existing position and see whether the true path to safety does not lie in the prosaic course of accepting and learning to live with it; as the most sensible course for the individual man is usually that of recognising his own imperfections and neuroses and learning to live with them with such patience as he can muster, rather than seeking some violent and spectacular cure.

But as for the individual man such acceptance must be preceded by total self-knowledge, so, in international relations, we must be under no illusions whatever about the dangers with which we must learn to live, and which no amount of diplomatic magic can ever conjure completely away. War by accident or by miscalculation; aggression by a nuclear power unafraid of retaliation; escalation of a minor conflict; the proliferation of nuclear weapons among small and disorderly states; technical innovations upsetting the present 'balance of terror'; these and other possibilities present very precise threats to world peace, and we all have a common interest in finding ways of dealing with them. In finding such ways, a mutual confidence may be built up which will gradually, over decades, erode the bitter conflicts of the cold war which have made disarmament conferences, until now, little more than polemical exercises. Without such confidence, the general and complete disarmament to which we all pay lip-service will remain a dream; to quote von Moltke out of context, not even a beautiful dream. With it, armaments would become as irrelevant to national security as are frontier fortifications between the states of western Europe today.

14 Problems of a Disarmed World[1]

Through all the discussions and negotiations about disarmament which have taken place since the Second World
War, and to which the development of thermonuclear
weapons has given an understandable urgency, there has run
a common assumption which is seldom dispassionately
examined. It is that a disarmed world is likely to be a more
peaceful place than an armed world; that 'peace' and 'disarmament' are different words to describe a single state of
affairs; that the major problems which face us are the technical and political ones of how to disarm, rather than the
political ones, of how to run an organised and orderly society
in a world in which major armaments no longer exist. It is not
unusual to ask whether a disarmed world is possible; but it
is unusual to ask whether, if it were possible, it would be
desirable – that is, whether men as individuals and the
societies in which they live would be more secure, or happier,
or more self-confident than they are today.

In examining the problem, we have to make the very
considerable assumption that general and complete disarmament is possible. We must accept that all difficulties
with respect to phasing, verification, inspection, and control
have been solved. Nations will have discarded all weapons
except those needed for the maintenance of internal order.
All military and paramilitary formations, except militias and
domestic police forces, will have been dissolved. The manufacture of armaments will have been discontinued, and the
national resources so liberated converted to peaceful uses.
An International Disarmament Organisation will have been
established and be working without undue friction. Its orders
would be unquestioningly accepted and its officials enjoying
free access to all parts of every nation's territory, all sectors
of industry, all archives of government. We have also to

[1] Written in 1962.

assume – for this is implied in the current disarmament proposals both of East and West – that the political organisation
of the world is still recognisably the same as it is today, with
sovereign national states pursuing distinct ambitions and
interests, and antagonistic ideologies co-existing in an international community, but regulating their affairs by mutual
negotiations under some form of international authority with
powers sufficient to prevent recourse to armed force. If the
proposals presented by the Soviet Government in 1962 were
implemented and disarmament was achieved in four years,
there could be little if any alteration in the present pattern
of world politics. The same statesmen, the same bureau-
cracies, the same great ideological and much the same great
economic pressures which mould international affairs today
would still prevail. Even the eight or nine years foreseen as
necessary to implement the Western proposals would hardly
be enough to witness any substantial transformation in the
nature of international intercourse. The military element
would be to a large extent removed – though not entirely,
for reasons which we will consider further below: but it is
unlikely that, for example, East and West Germans, Chinese
and Formosans, or Arabs and Israelis would regard one
another with any greater amity; or that the United States
would look with any greater benevolence on Dr Castro; or
that the Communist world would cease to expect the final
disintegration of its capitalist adversaries, and lend that disintegration, if occasion arose, a helping hand.

In order to determine whether such a world would be
'peaceful' in any recognisable sense, we must be quite clear
in our minds in what sense we use the word 'peace'. It is so
emotive a term, one which lends itself so easily to political
propaganda and abuse, that if it is to be used as a tool in
intelligent discussion – especially intelligent international
discussion – it must be precisely defined. It certainly implies
absence of war; yet even more it means social and political
order, absence of anarchy, and escape from that miserable
civil chaos of which Thomas Hobbes wrote: 'In such condition, there is no place for industry, because the fruit thereof
is uncertain, and consequently no culture of the earth; no
navigation, nor use of the commodities that may be imported

by sea; no commodious building; no instruments of moving, and removing such things as require much force; no knowledge of the face of the earth; no account of time, no arts, no letters; no society; and which is worst of all, continual fear, and danger of violent death; and the life of man solitary, poor, nasty brutish and short.' Peace, in short, is the maintenance of an orderly and just society: orderly in that man is defended against the violence or extortion of his neighbour, and just in that he is defended against the arbitrary violence or extortion of his rulers. There can be lasting peace neither in anarchies nor in despotisms. Indeed peace is more likely to be found within a well-ordered society at war with its neighbours than in a community which, although formally at peace, has relapsed into barbarism and civil war. Should any reader doubt this, let him ask himself whether he would prefer to have lived in London in 1941, or in Algiers twenty years later.

The first characteristic of peace, then, is social and political order; and if such order is to be effective and continuing, it must be freely accepted by all politically-conscious members of the community where it prevails. An order which is felt to be imposed by an alien group – alien in terms of race, class, or social caste – may be accepted as a lesser evil, when the alternative is subjugation by a yet more odious group or perhaps total social disintegration; but it is unlikely to remain stable for long. Economic developments, the contagion of ideas, the general flux of history, perpetually create situations in which the political patterns and mechanisms which were thought by an earlier generation to be adequate to the maintenance of a peaceful life appear in their new context, to a significant and articulate élite, as obstacles to a truly just political and social organisation and in consequence obstacles to, rather than instruments of, peace.

This impermanence applies not only to the internal structure of states: it involves equally their very existence in the world community. Empires disintegrate under the pressure of dissident nationalist minorities; new nation-states are formed, divide, coagulate, or become empires in their turn as they extend their influence over technically retarded or politically immature communities. Those international thinkers and lawyers who wish to create or stabilise an international order on the pattern of a domestic order, with sovereign states playing the parts of individuals within it, entering into mutual contacts and accepting a common jurisdiction, inevitably find the analogy applicable only within very narrow limits. States are not, like men, finite. They bear less resemblance to men than they do to cells, splitting, reassembling, and forming new entities. This process of division and coagulation, under the pressure of emergent nationalism or social revolution, has been one of the principal causes of international conflict over the past 150 years; and there are no signs that it is anywhere near its end. When the leaders of the Communist world declared, at their meeting in Moscow in November 1960, that 'national liberation wars' were bound to continue, they were doing no more than stating an evident fact about international society. They were at fault only in implying that at some stage in the future a world order would emerge so just, so wise, and so balanced, that such struggles would cease. It is not out of place to observe that only one such war of 'national liberation' has been waged in Europe since 1945. It took place in Hungary in 1956. The Communist world is no more likely to be immune from them than is the West.

The history of Europe since the close of the Middle Ages, with the possible exception of the period 1870–1914, gives little ground for supposing that the tensions produced by rival armaments-systems have been the sole, or even the principal cause of international conflicts; and the history of North America, whose greatest war arose between two communities which at its outset were virtually unarmed, gives even less. The factors making for war over the centuries have been complex and it is dangerous to oversimplify: but there are two very basic ones, which are as strong today as they ever were.

The first consists in the absorption – economic, political and cultural – of weak, passive or politically impotent communities by their better organised or more dynamic neighbours – a process today condemned as 'imperialism' but one without which no great state in the contemporary world would exist at all: neither the state which originated in the expansion of the Grand Duchy of Muscovy, nor that which, planted on the western coasts of the North Atlantic, absorbed or eliminated the primitive tribal communities which had previously subsisted on the North American continent. This process of expansion and absorption ceases only when two equally positive and expanding cultures meet. The result of this meeting may be conflict, as it was when the French and the Spanish met in Italy at the end of the fifteenth century, or the French and the British met in North America at the end of the seventeenth, or the Slav and the Austrian met in the Balkans at the end of the nineteenth; or it may result in an uneasy balance such as that struck by the British and the Russians in Central Asia in the nineteenth century. We are faced by a similar confrontation between two dynamic cultures in the contemporary world; and the tensions and rivalries which result are not to be eliminated by a purely military disarmament.

This type of rivalry, between major powers, can be kept under control so long as each power conducts its affairs in a rational manner. The gains from overt military conflict today would be so negligible compared with the damage which would be suffered, that only the adventurist or the desperate are likely to provoke it; although it cannot be denied that within our lifetime we have seen such men seize power in at least two of the major states of the world. The great powers, by exercising rational self-control, might keep the peace, and avoid overt conflict, in a disarmed world, as they have in an armed. Moreover, even if they did not, direct clashes of interest are usually susceptible of arbitration and compromise under the aegis of an international authority.

It is questionable, however, whether the same can as confidently be said about conflicts provoked by dissident, revolutionary elements within states, whose activities may call the jurisdiction and even the existence of those states in question. This, the second category of forces making for international instability, is perhaps even more dangerous than the first. The activities of these elements, élites inspired by nationalist or social ideas incompatible with the political framework within which they are compelled to operate, have been the principal source of internal and international conflict over the past hundred years. Active revolutionary minorities inspired by national ideas destroyed the Europe created by the Congress of Vienna; they destroyed the Habsburg Empire and in so doing precipitated the First World War. They destroyed the British and the French Empires; and there is no sign that these and similar movements have either lost their force or would be likely to do so in a disarmed world.

Indeed, dynamic nationalism is likely to increase rather than diminish in the foreseeable future, irrespective of whether disarmament is achieved or not. The increase of education will bring about an increase in political self-consciousness on the part of hitherto dormant minorities, even within recently independent states, and to this inherently fissiparous process there is no logical end. The suppression of such minority desires for independence requires both political ruthlessness and military power. The great powers indeed, rather than repress these tendencies, have increasingly preferred to encourage them, hoping to acquire the newly-independent states as their *protégés*, or at least keep them from entering the political systems of their rivals. The fact that the new states have technical and administrative needs for beyond the capacity of the original revolutionary élites which created them to provide, forcing them to turn to larger and wealthier powers for loans, advice and technical expertise, creates the continuing danger that new nationalism may, in spite of itself, provide fuel for the older pattern of imperialism which we have already examined. Nor is there any reason to suppose that the new states which are emerging today will be more distinct and permanent in their form that were the empires out of whose ruins they were born. They may be so small and non-viable that they must depend on strong protectors to save them from unwelcome absorption by powerful and historically uncongenial neighbours. They may be as liable to disintegration as is the Congo, or as was the Yugoslavia which emerged from the First World War. It would be a bold man who prophesied that the frontiers on maps of Asia and Africa today will remain unchanged at the end of the century, or that the changes will come peacefully by mutual consent – disarmament or no disarmament.

It is not easy to see why either of these great forces making for conflict and change – the clash of cultures, and the internal revolution – should cease to operate in a disarmed world. Disarmament would, it is true, eliminate the strategic factor in international mistrust. A Russia with no cause to fear irruption from the west might take a less direct interest in Central Europe, and vice versa. A relaxation of world tension might make possible the dismantling of alliance-structures which each side at present considers necessary for its security against the threat presented by the other. The great powers might be thus less liable to pressure from their most vulnerable allies. But the effect even of this must not be overestimated. Military forces reflect political tensions as much as they create them. Even in a disarmed world, Great Britain would be alarmed if the oil-bearing states of the Middle East entered into a close association with the Soviet Union and adopted her political system. The United States would feel even more strongly about Central and South America; and it is not probable that the Soviet Union would acquiesce without some protest if the states of Eastern Europe joined a Common Market administered from Brussels – or if Outer Mongolia transferred its allegiance to Peking. It may be that the purely strategic element in international affairs, even in an armed world, is so little decisive that its total abolition would have surprisingly little effect on the pattern of international relations.

Indeed the possibility must be examined that the effect of the abolition of major military force would be to embitter certain aspects of international relations, even if it improved others. The brooding fear of war today acts as a brake on national and ideological ambitions. It holds back the great powers from forwarding their interests and exploiting the weakness of their rivals to the fullest extent of which they are capable. The Western world might be doing far more than it is to encourage counter-revolution and dissident nationalist movements in Eastern Europe and the Baltic States. The Communist powers might exploit far more ruthlessly the anti-western nationalism of the Asian and African states, besides encouraging activities subversive of the existing governments in the West. It is no secret that in both camps strong pressure is constantly being exercised in this direction; pressures held in check by the understanding among the responsible statesmen that the deliberate exacerbation of world tensions, is, in a thermonuclear age, too dangerous an activity to be freely indulged. If those fears were to be removed by general and complete disarmament, the checks might also be removed on the deliberate exploitation by major powers of the weaknesses of minor ones and of each other – exploitation of a kind which no international authority or 'peace-keeping force' would be able to check. To wonder whether, under such circumstances, the world would remain disarmed for very long, is to go beyond the bounds imposed at the beginning of this paper. But one can reasonably ask whether such a world would be, in any meaningful sense, any more stable, peaceful and secure than that in which we live today.

It is, of course, often argued that even if disarmament failed and mutual rivalries, mistrust and recrimination led to rearmament, we would be no worse off than we are now; that we have therefore nothing to lose by disarmament, and everything to gain. But this is not self-evident. The present situation is dangerous, but it is not unfamiliar. The statesmen and diplomats of the world have been living with these dangers for a long time and have acquired certain techniques of dealing with them. The declaratory policies of both sides may appear irreconcilable, occasional *gaffes* and miscalculations may make us shudder with horror, but a perceptible tact has grown up on both sides of the Iron Curtain as to what questions are negotiable and what questions are not, which declarations are to be taken seriously and which are designed for domestic consumption, how far pressure can be applied and at what point it begins to be dangerous. In a disarmed world, the art of international dialogue would have to be re-learned, in an unfamiliar environment where rivalries and ambitions, might, as we have seen, be intensified rather than abandoned. Hostility might be exacerbated to the point when rearmament became inevitable, in an atmosphere far more bedevilled with mutual exasperation and hatred than exists today. This hypothesis may appear far-fetched, yet a simple return to the *status quo ante* is certainly not to be looked for; and an unsuccessful attempt at disarmament, for the failure of which each side would certainly loudly and plangently blame the other, would have contributed little to mutual tolerance and understanding.

All these dangers would, of course, be reduced by an effective supra-national Authority, with the will and the power to intervene swiftly, and with an overwhelming preponderance of force, to settle international conflicts. Existing plans for a disarmed world all recognise the need for national states to retain police forces and militias; and the legitimate requirements for these might be considerable. Large states could keep on foot forces tens of thousands strong – not an excessive number for their internal needs, but a powerful military weapon if concentrated. States with turbulent frontier-areas might reasonably demand military aircraft as the most economical way of keeping the peace. Iraq is a case in point; and if Iraq possessed such aircraft, could they reasonably be denied to Israel? In the presence of such powerful neighbouring 'police forces', no states could be expected to abandon the right and power of self-defence without the assurance that their interests and independence would be protected by the supra-national Authority as sedulously and swiftly as they would protect them themselves. The effectiveness of such assurance would depend not only on the size, efficiency and swift action of the force at the disposal of the Authority, but on the will unhesitatingly to use it. The Authority would need to be immune from political pressure by majority or minority interest groups. Its officials would need in fact to possess a degree of power for immediate and drastic action far exceeding anything entrusted to those of the United Nations – a power indeed such as few sovereign states today have shown themselves prepared to grant. The risk that an Authority armed with such powers might fall into the hands of their political adversaries is no doubt responsible for the understandably cautious attitude adopted in the Soviet disarmament proposals towards the whole question of an international force; yet no statesman could consider risking the very survival of the society for whose welfare and independence he was responsible, by entrusting it to the mercies of a body whose capacity to protect it might, at the crucial moment, be paralysed by indecision, timidity, or political intrigue. Until this elementary dilemma is solved, a disarmed world is likely to present as many occasions for mutual distrust as an armed one; and many more temptations to limited aggression by unscrupulus powers.

This preoccupation with minor conflicts and local revolutionary situations may appear trivial at a time when the main threat to world survival seems to spring from the damage which the great powers can inflict on each other and on the world in the course of a major struggle. If the great powers can agree to disarm, it may be argued, the quarrels of minor powers will be insignificant brawls of little consequence to the peace of the world. Such a hope does not stand up to serious analysis. The relations of great powers with one another are conditioned to a very large extent by their attitude towards, and interest in, their smaller neighbours: and this interest is not a purely strategic one. Even in a disarmed world – which would be a world, as we have seen, where there would still be a considerable amount of military force available – Russia would be unlikely to stand aloof from a quarrel between Poland and Germany; or the United States, from one between China and Taiwan; or Great Britain from one between Iraq and Kuwait. Even if they did not intervene directly, they would do their best to aid their *protégés* by bringing their influence to bear in the international Authority; which, subjected to such pressures, would find it no easier to judge impartially and act swiftly than have its predecessors. Only in those cases where the interests of no great power or its *protégés* were involved could rapid action be taken, or alternatively, the conflict be left to burn itself out. Such instances are likely to be few; and such joint action, or abstention, is as possible in an armed world as in a disarmed one.

It does not seem unreasonable therefore to suggest that general and complete disarmament, if it were rapidly achieved, would do little to eliminate world tensions and disorders; and it might even increase them unless it were accompanied by the creation of something indistinguishable from a supra-national state. We must not underestimate the degree of peace and order which obtains in the world today. The actual peace enjoyed in their private lives by the readers of this paper – their domestic security, their confidence in their government, their harmonious relations within society – is not likely to be substantially increased by general disarmament. It is possible that it would be diminished – particularly if they are citizens of small or unstable states. What *would* be reduced would be the risk of mutual annihilation inherent in the politico-military structure on which that peace now depends. The fundamental dangers of our situation, in spite of its placid surface, may be so great that no price is too high to pay in order to escape from it – even international anarchy, chronic disorder, the whole Hobbesian state of nature which the state, with all its panoply of police and armed forces, exists to avert. Better this, perhaps, than the annihilation of mankind: such would be a perfectly rational choice for us to make. Whether such a world could for long stay disarmed, whether an International Disarmament Organisation could really function within it, is open to question. In any case the possibility must be faced, that it may not be possible to have both disarmament, and that degree of peaceful order which, with all its many imperfections, so much of the world enjoys today.

15 Morality and Force
in International Politics

An ethical teaching which takes it for granted that individuals will have an orderly social background against which to work out their destinies is, however coherent and valid in itself, incomplete. Further, an ethical teaching which deals only with the problems which confront an individual who has no personal and immediate responsibility for the lives and welfare of others is also incomplete. Men and women do not usually exist as solitary individuals unless they artificially create the conditions to do so by a deliberate withdrawal from society. They are normally responsible for the welfare of a social group, if only that of their immediate family; and in order to exercise that responsibility they must possess, or obtain, the necessary power. By 'power' I mean the ability to organise the relevant elements of the external world so as to satisfy their needs. The moral man will so use this power as to lead and make it possible for his dependants to lead – to use an evocative if indefinite expression – the Good Life; a life in which he is free to shape his own character.

The greater the responsibility, the greater the power needed to exercise it. Responsibility will extend beyond the family to government of institutions – schools, colleges, corporations, unions, shops, offices, industries – upwards to the executive organ of society, the state itself: that complex of officials with whom final responsibility rests for ensuring that laws are made, and enforced, which reflect the ethical standards of the community; protecting the good man in his virtuous activity, discouraging the backslider from behaviour offensive or harmful to the rest of society, in general keeping the peace. A good community will be one whose laws a good man will wish to obey – in which he can, without offence to his conscience, be a law-abiding citizen. That postulates a law to abide by, and a power to ensure that everyone abides

by it. Such a community is one where, at the very least, a
man can feed his children without stealing, can protect his
family without killing, and can make a living without lying
to conceal his beliefs. Under conditions of tyranny, anarchy,
and certain kinds of class oppression, moral behaviour of this
kind can be self-defeating: in order to retain the power to
exercise his responsibilities, a responsible man may have to
take decisions which, judged by the standards of individual
ethics, would be counted immoral. It is the function of the
state to create conditions in which such terms as 'crime' and
'justice' make sense; in which the Good Life is possible, not
only for the solitary saint, but for the ordinary man with
wife and children to support; in which he is not faced with
the harsh alternatives of being either a hero or a coward.

This is the justification for the absolute claim which the
state makes on its citizens. This is also, as I understand
it, the reason why the Christian Church, in almost all of its
manifestations, has acquiesced in this claim at least since the
days of St Augustine; why it has recognised, sometimes
rather ruefully, the necessity of the secular arm to the
physical and even the moral welfare of its members. As has
been frequently pointed out, the state is a *condition* of ethical
values: it provides the circumstances in which ethical activity
can be carried on at all.[1]

This claim is not uncontested. Among those who question
it are those who, perhaps, take the benefits of an orderly
society for granted. I hope it is not unfair to cite as an
example of this the statement once attributed to Mr E. M.
Forster: 'If I had to choose between betraying my country
and betraying my friend, I hope I would have the guts to
betray my country.' It is difficult not to react sympathetically
to so staunch a confession of faith in personal relationships;
yet how far do such relationships depend on the state to
provide those conditions of social and political security
which make possible their cultivation? The values developed
in England before 1914, which were perhaps both practised
and expounded in their purest form by the friends and
disciples of G. E. Moore in London and Cambridge, were

[1] See for example R. E. Osgood and R. W. Tucker, *Force,
Order, and Justice* (Johns Hopkins Press, Baltimore, 1967), p. 323.

rooted in a society whose stability was unique in a rapidly disintegrating world. When that society is itself threatened with disintegration, there is a strong case for saying that public loyalties should override private. It is, fortunately, only at infrequent intervals that the ordinary citizen is made so disagreeably aware of the vulnerability of the social and political system which makes his life and his values possible. The statesman has to be conscious of it the whole time.

There will always be those who can do without society. To these saints and hermits the world owes an incalculable debt, but their actions and needs can hardly be considered normative. Christian was no doubt wise to flee the City of Destruction, but someone presumably had to support his family in his absence. Nor is a withdrawal from society *en masse* likely to provide the answer – the kind of attempt frequently made in the past to set up a new community, untainted by the vices of the old, exerting none of the pressures and making none of the amoral demands of the state. The history of such Owenite phalansteries is a sadly uniform one of failure, and there is no reason to suppose that the contemporary yearnings of those who wish to escape from, or abolish, a 'system' which they regard as hopelessly corrupt can lead to any more positive result. The criticisms which Dr Marcuse and his disciples level at society today are often valid, but they are not constructive. These thinkers give little indication of any capacity to create a social and political 'system' so radically different from the old that the familiar problems and dilemmas would not promptly reappear. When new societies have been successfully created, either by emigration (the United States, Israel) or revolution (the Soviet Union, the Chinese People's Republic) it has been only at the price of creating new states which sooner or later make demands on their citizens no less exigent than those of the old. The events in China since 1966 indicate an attempt to interrupt this process, to make revolution perpetual and prevent it from hardening into a new state system. At the moment of writing it is not possible to predict its outcome; but it is difficult to see how revolution can be 'institutionalised' indefinitely, or, if it can, how it can then be distinguished from chaos.

It would appear therefore that the existence of the state and the demands which it makes on its members is not the product of peculiar social or economic circumstances, as Marx for one would have had us believe, but a necessary element in all but the most primitive of social organisations. Those who recognise the validity of those demands are always likely to be in a considerable majority compared with groups, such as those considered above, who do not. This may be the result of inertia and unthinking acceptance of tradition; it may equally be a pragmatic recognition that only the existence of the state makes possible the kind of life which most of them, rightly or wrongly, regard as 'good'.

The state then provides law. But it exists in a world without law. International law, in spite of all efforts to extend its authority, remains a system of agreements and conventions based on mutual convenience, without mandatory powers. This absence of mandatory authority is due, not to any lack of enforcement machinery, but to a more elementary cause, which is this: those responsible for the conduct of state affairs see their first duty as being to ensure that their state *survives*; that it retains its power to protect its members and provide for them the conditions of a good life. For the individual, personal survival is not necessarily the highest duty. He may well feel called upon to sacrifice himself to his ideals, his family, or his friends. The state, or those responsible for it, cannot. As Croce put it: 'History does not acclaim as heroes those who have sacrificed their native land to an ideal, but rather condemns them for having subordinated the interests of the state to any other motives, however generous.'[1]

Hence arises the basic dichotomy to which Friedrich Meinecke devoted so much of his thinking: the split between ethics and politics, between right and expediency, between 'natural law and politico-empiricism'. Hence the wry comment attributed to Cavour: 'if statesmen did for themselves what they did for their countries, what rascals they would be'. Hence the dilemmas in which good men holding posts of political authority are liable to find themselves. Should

[1] Benedetto Croce, *Politics and Morals* (Allen and Unwin, London, 1946), p. 131.

they, for example, deal with régimes – totalitarian, dictatorial, racist – which they find morally repellent? Should they pursue the prosperity, or safeguard the security, of their own community at the expense of oppressed groups elsewhere? Should they use force or the threat of force to protect the security and interests of their community? Should they manufacture nuclear, chemical, or biological weapons? Above all, should they use them?

The term 'statesmen' is vague. I shall use it to indicate the professional groups whose function it is to preserve and if necessary exercise the power and the authority of the state: politicians, civil servants, police, diplomats, soldiers. They are groups which sometimes have a bad press in academic circles. Younger members of society tend to be suspicious of them, find it hard to identify with them, see them often as sinister or at best as grotesque. Some of them are. I can think of some students and not a few dons who are as well. With these exceptions we need not concern ourselves. Most of the people of whom I speak are men of good will and exceptional ability, doing their best, among conditions of great difficulty, to make the right decisions. The options open to them are likely to be far more limited than is generally realised. Where the decisions have moral implications they are likely to be complex and obscure. Seldom is a statesman fortunate enough to have a clear-cut choice between an obviously 'good' or innocuous course of action and one equally obviously bad. His choice is likely always to be one between two evils. And for those with whom ultimate powers of direction and decision rest in great modern states, the implications of their decisions may well be vast; not only for their own peoples and their descendants, but for the whole of the world.

Let us consider one example, the decision taken by the government of the United States, against the advice of many of its best-qualified scientific advisers, to go ahead with the development of thermonuclear weapons. The consequences, not only for the United States and its allies, but for the future course of civilisation, were incalculable. The moral position was doubtful. The technical problems might prove insoluble, and if they did a great deal of time, resources, and scarce manpower would have been wasted. President Truman, with whom the final decision lay, reduced the problem to two questions: Can *they* [i.e. the Russians] do it? If so, how can we not? On the basis of his answers to these questions the work was put in hand. Whether the decision was 'morally' correct may be endlessly debated. In the circumstances it was politically justifiable and probably inevitable. What would, however, have been quite unjustifiable would have been a refusal to take a decision. That is what statesmen are for. President Truman reminded himself of the fact by placing on his desk the small, implacable notice of reminder: The Buck Stops Here.

The problem as it presents itself to the moralist, if not to the politician, thus appears to come down to the familiar conflict of means and ends. Can good ends justify bad means? What does one mean by good and what by bad? What, in this context, does one mean by 'justify'? The literature on this topic is immense. I have not mastered it, nor dare I attempt to add to it. I can only suggest an approach which may help avoid some unnecessary pitfalls, considering in particular the most obvious and tragic example of this apparent conflict, the infliction of suffering and death in the course of war.

The possible positions which can be adopted over this question are bounded by two extremes which admit of no argument. There is on the one hand the view that the infliction of suffering and death, by whatever instrumentality and on whatever victim, is an absolute evil which cannot be legitimised by any 'good' end. On the other hand is the view that war legitimises all means, and that suffering, whoever the victims and whatever the scale, must be accepted as inevitable. Both positions have disagreeable implications. The first abdicates power into the hands of men or nations which have no such scruples about using force to gain their ends.[1] The second is likely to modify, and not for the better,

---

[1] Adam Roberts (ed.), *Civilian Defence: Non-Violent Resistance to Aggression* (Faber, London, 1967) is an interesting study of the possibilities of non-violent resistance, but this is a field on which too little work has been done for firm conclusions yet to be drawn. The events in Czechoslovakia since August 1968 are not encouraging.

both the objective aimed at and the entire environment within which the conflict is carried on. The statesman is unlikely to share either of these extreme views. Both involve for him, to a greater or lesser extent, an abdication of responsibility. He is more likely to operate in the wide middle area between the two. The criterion which he is likely to apply is the purely pragmatic one: what measures are *necessary* to attain his objective; that is, an outcome to hostilities which will not result in any reduction of the security of his state?

His answer to this question will depend rather on technical and professional factors than on moral. Let us take the problem presented by the air bombardment of German cities, recently dramatised by Herr Hochhuth in his play *The Soldiers*. The fundamental charge brought against the Allies here was, surely, not that they inflicted suffering on the German population, but that they inflicted *unnecessary* suffering; that they did damage on a scale (and to targets) which was not necessary to secure a satisfactory outcome to the struggle. The destruction of Dresden aroused particular concern because the damage inflicted seems out of all proportion to the military advantage gained. The raids on Hamburg, Essen, and Berlin, industrial or political targets of obvious importance, are less frequently cited. Post-war analysis has indeed confirmed that allied air power could have been no less militarily effective had it been employed with greater precision and humanity. At the time, however, this was far from self-evident. Throughout the first three years of the war there was no way open to the Western Allies of damaging the Nazi war machine except by inaccurate and indiscriminate night bombing. Techniques and devices were then brought into service which made greater precision possible. But what if these had not been available? What if there had really been no alternative means for the Western Allies to attack their adversary except by continuing to strike hard and blindly at his cities? Should they have confined themselves to the Queensberry rules of 'the Just War' even at risk of their own defeat – and more immediately, that of their Russian ally, which for so long appeared imminent? Would the statesmen who took such a decision have been honoured by the posterity of their defeated societies – or even by that of the victors? These may seem to be rhetorical and emotive questions, but I hope they indicate that the problem is not so simple as some of Herr Hochhuth's disciples suggest.

The statesman may thus find that, although the question 'Is it necessary?' provides as clear guidance as any he is likely to get, the answer will be made obscure by the technical uncertainties of his expert advisers; especially in wartime, when accurate information is particularly hard to obtain. He may well get the answer wrong; but that is the question he has to ask. He has further to consider – once again using only the most coldly pragmatic of criteria – whether certain actions are not only unnecessary but positively harmful to the objective he has in view. Military victory is normally not an end in itself but a means to an end, which is usually the establishment of a more stable international system. The manner in which the war is fought may bring military victory closer at the cost of making this ultimate objective more difficult to attain. The scale on which destruction can now be caused by military operations makes this a matter of peculiar significance for our own times. In Vietnam at the present moment the United States is fighting to achieve a classic and, by normal political criteria, a justifiable goal; the creation of political, social, and economic conditions in which the people of South Vietnam can lead the Good Life. In the course of doing so, however, its forces are apparently inflicting such damage on the community they are defending – not only the physical damage caused by the destruction of lives and property, but the social and economic damage caused by the presence of a huge occupation force with a far higher standard of living – that they are making that goal ever more distant. Yet in this matter as in so many others the responsible officials confront only a choice of evils; believing as they do, on very sound evidence, that the alternative confronting the people of South Vietnam in the event of a North Vietnamese victory would be very far from the Good Life, and that the international system would be rendered less rather than more stable by the defeat of the United States and her allies in South East Asia.

If we assume, without further examination, that the indiscriminate slaughter of civil populations is morally wrong, then the two examples cited above indicate that even in war there will be many occasions – possibly the majority – when moral and pragmatic considerations will parallel one another rather than conflict. The practising statesman may claim that they always do; that he and his colleagues have never been faced with a serious moral dilemma; that, as Lord Grey of Falloden allegedly once put it, 'to do the right thing is usually the right thing to do'. Yet there is no cause to suppose that this easy way out will always be available; that the statesman will never find himself in a situation where the safety of the community for which he bears responsibility cannot be safeguarded without the use of means which, in terms of individual ethics, would be considered immoral. History gives us no reason to expect it; neither, so far as I can see, does Scripture. The Old Testament describes with bloodthirsty relish a succession of massacres, deceptions, trickeries, and assassinations which were considered not only innocuous but positively praiseworthy since they forwarded God's purpose for the Children of Israel. The Gospels preached a gospel of love to individuals existing within a society where the rule of law was based on force and conquest, and Christ, explaining to his puzzled disciples that his Kingdom was not of this world, dissuaded them from disturbing it. St Paul was yet more explicit in his acceptance of Roman authority. In accepting whatever secular power structure it finds itself functioning within, the Church cannot be said to have diverged from the example and teaching of its founders.

The Augustinian acquiescence in the necessity of the State is one thing. Active co-operation with the secular authorities, the Thomist synthesis of civil and ecclesiastical authority, is a different matter. The involvement of the Church in the affairs of the state must always carry the risk that the Church appears not only to accept but positively to connive at the amoral acts to which the state may necessarily be driven. This position is not easily defensible. But few people would deny the priest his obligation to shrive the Christian soldier or bomber-pilot; in doing so, he implies no blessing of their cause or their methods. He is doing no more than recognising and condoling with them in their tragic and inescapable situation; providing some reassurance that in accepting the necessities and obligations of the political realm one does not forfeit citizenship in the spiritual.

There is however a school of thought which maintains that even this degree of involvement and recognition is too great and that the Church should renounce it. Recently Professor D. M. MacKinnon brought to our attention the suggestion of the Dutch Augustinian priest, Father Robert Adolfs, that

> the Church which is coming to be is one which will view the whole history of the Christian Church from the fourth century as a kind of collective experience of the far country in which the prodigal spent his inheritance with harlots.[1]

Yet if the Church were to return to the catacombs, what happens to the unfortunate harlots – the statesmen who have to go on doing their job, and who may be members of the Church as well? Do they incur excommunication by continuing to do what is, by any standards, necessary work? They can of course always escape from their dilemmas by resigning; admitting that a certain action may be necessary in the context of the power situation in which they find themselves, but being unable to square it with their ethical principles, and regarding the latter as overriding. Few do. The cynic will attribute this to simple lust for power, but the explanation is seldom as easy as that. The statesman knows that *somebody* has to take the decision, and to refuse to do so is an abdication of responsibilities deliberately assumed. Pontius Pilate is an unattractive figure for Christians, not because he did his duty and firmly took a disagreeable decision, but because he failed to do so; taking water and washing his hands saying, 'I am innocent of the blood of this

[1] Professor MacKinnon referred to this suggestion by Father Adolfs in a Third Programme broadcast on the treatments of the late Bishop George Bell of Chichester by his biographer (Canon R. C. D. Jasper), and by Herr Rolf Hochhuth in his play *The Soldiers* to which I have referred. The complete text of this talk, which touches quite closely on some issues raised in this lecture, appeared in the *Listener* for 21st December 1967.

just person; see *ye* to it.' President Truman, staunchly accepting responsibility for decisions of unimaginable consequence, is likely to occupy a more comfortable part even of the Christian purgatory.

It is easier for the statesman to avoid the dilemma posed by the implicit dichotomy between ethics and politics if he can embrace one of two political philosophies. The first is that which stems from the Hegelian claim that the state is not the *condition* of values, a social organism making possible the Good Life, but itself the fount and origin of values. According to this view there can be no sphere of private morality outside the state, for the service of the state is in itself the highest morality. In a more or less diluted form this doctrine was widespread in Europe at the turn of the century. A strong admixture of Christianity and traditional liberalism reduced its strength in this country, but its elements are recognisable in the pre-1914 public school ethos – the ethos against which Mr Forster was, perhaps, in revolt when he made the statement discussed earlier. It reached its apotheosis in the Fascist movements which dominated Europe thirty years ago. By this philosophy the problem is resolved. Power politics is no longer a disagreeable necessity to make the Good Life possible. It is itself the highest form of ethical activity. The Good Life consists in total and selfless dedication to the service of the state, particularly in its armed conflicts with other states. War is not a problem; it is a challenge to manhood.

This attitude is today, fortunately, out of favour. Another is more widespread. This arises from an opposite assumption, but reaches similar conclusions. It holds, not that the state creates ethical values, but that it has itself been created by and embodies them. Its citizens are therefore not only the population of a particular geographical area, but all who share those values throughout the world. Its statesmen feel an obligation to protect not only their own societies but their ethical values wherever these may manifest themselves; and, where they can, to extend their bounds. The statesmen of Revolutionary France held, for a time, such a view. Today it runs strongly through the communist tradition and inspires intermittently the policy of certain Communist states. It is strongly held by certain groups in the United States and was dominant there during the time of Mr John Foster Dulles. It is not unknown in this country, where the view is widespread that British power should be used everywhere in the world to uphold individual liberty and counter oppression, though those who hold it here are often equally anxious to reduce national power to a level where it cannot effectively be used at all. It was put at its baldest by a contributor to a recent American anthology:

> The teaching of morality amounts to this: we must do everything that needs to be done to insure the survival of ourselves, our friends, and our free principles.[1]

For men – and women – holding such views, it is the Cause, rather than the state, which legitimises activities otherwise regarded as 'immoral'.

Time does not permit a critique of these two approaches, so different in their origins, so similar in their results. For the moment it must suffice to say that neither, certainly if carried to the extremes we have seen over the past fifty years, has justified itself either in terms of domestic or of international stability. The narrower, traditional concept of national self-interest, with its modest ambitions and demands, has at least done less damage than either, and perhaps it is better to accept the moral dilemmas to which it leads rather than attempt to escape them in such ways as these. But to do so cannot be agreeable to anyone with a strong sense of moral values. It involves a kind of moral relativism which he will, very properly, find repellent. The problem of war we have considered, but there are others, less acute but more continuous. To take a current example: friendly relations have to be maintained with régimes which are morally obnoxious; which persecute minorities – or even majorities; which so far from making the Good Life possible for their citizens, make it virtually impossible, if not by the injustice they compel them to commit, then by the injustice at which they compel them to connive. The criterion which the statesman must

[1] Joseph Cropsey in *America Armed*, ed. Robert A. Goldwin (Rand McNally, Chicago, 1962), p. 83. Quoted in Osgood and Tucker, op. cit., p. 246.

apply in determining the nature of the intercourse between his own and other states will be, not moral approval of the régime in question, but the interests, in terms of physical safety and well-being, of the community for which he is responsible. If such régimes possess economic resources requisite to the well-being of his own community, he must trade with them. If they provide strategic advantages, he must utilise them – unless there are equally strong pragmatic reasons against doing so.

This is not just short-sighted selfishness. Even the most odious of régimes, unless they are imposed by foreign conquest, grow from native roots and respond to native needs in ways which foreign observers do not always understand. Foreign pressure, whether military, economic, or moral, is as likely to consolidate as to undermine them – as was shown by the Anglo-French intervention at Suez in 1956, the American intervention in Cuba in 1961, and, so far as the evidence permits a judgment, current British pressures on the illegal régime in Rhodesia. Foreign support for internal opposition groups, however sympathetic their ideas and personalities may be, seldom produces the hoped-for results. The sheer technical difficulty of successfully intervening in the affairs of another state is normally enough to deter prudent statesmen from attempting it; which means that they have to tolerate activities which, by any ethical standard, they find quite intolerable. In such matters the diplomat has to exercise a discipline and self-control comparable to that of the soldier, and for the same reason: he has to act, not as his own values would dictate, but as the policy of his government requires.

The best that a 'moral' statesman involved in such a dilemma can do is to realise that it *is* a dilemma; that he is an actor in the familiar tragedy brought about by a conflict of values; and that though nothing can be gained by renouncing his rôle, that rôle *is* a tragic one.[1] And the Christian may have more compassion for him in his realisation of the incompatibility of the two ethics than he has with the statesman who believes that he has resolved his dilemma by seeing

[1] This point has been brilliantly elaborated by Herbert Butterfield in *History and Human Relations* (Collins, London, 1951).

his ethical values fulfilled in the power of his state or the triumph of his cause. At least he can remember him in his prayers.

NOTE

It has been suggested to me, since this lecture was delivered, that I should have devoted more attention to the problem of nuclear warfare. This may well be so. I can only plead that this problem is not *sui generis* but presents, in a peculiarly acute and agonising form, the general dilemma confronting statesmen who have to harmonise the norms of individual morality with their perception of the well-being of the state for which they are responsible. The dilemma does not lie in a simple choice between, on the one hand, using nuclear weapons, and on the other risking the extinction of one's cultural pattern by political subjugation or nuclear destruction; though that choice in itself would not necessarily be an easy one to make. It lies rather in the choice – one open to very few states – between possessing a nuclear armoury and the evident determination to use it, if only to deter such attacks against oneself; and deliberately depriving oneself of such a possibility, irrespective of what the effect of such self-denial might be on the plans and attitudes of other, potentially hostile states which might not be interested in following one's example. The first course will probably lead to a heightening of international tension and possibly one day to nuclear holocaust. The second is very likely to place one's state in an inferior position *vis-à-vis* those which make no such self-denying ordinance, in exercising influence on the international evironment even in normal times, and may put it in a position of fatal inferiority in a situation of extreme conflict. It would take another course of lectures to explore the full ramifications of this problem. Those moralists who consider the choice to be a simple one are greatly to be envied.

Epilogue

Epilogue

The Invasion of Czechoslovakia

When the news of the invasion of Czechoslovakia came through on Wednesday morning,[1] the shock was none the less great because we had half expected it. For anyone much above the age of forty, the sensation was horribly familiar. We had felt it over Austria in 1938; over Czechoslovakia and Poland in 1939; over Norway, Denmark, Belgium and Holland in 1940; Yugoslavia, Greece and the Soviet Union itself in 1941; and then Czechoslovakia again in 1948, Korea in 1950, and Hungary in 1956. But this time it was even worse. It came like the renewed symptoms of a vile and dangerous disease which we were beginning to think that we had outgrown for good. Oh God, we prayed, not again! And then came the days spent glued to radio or television; the pride in the heroism of those we were powerless to help, the fury at the mendacious insolence of their oppressors, the desperate hope that this time for once, just for once, things would come out all right.

We are still hoping.

But although our emotion is deep and genuine, we must think beyond it. The Russians, after all, are not the only people who have, during the last twenty years, forcibly intervened in the affairs of other countries. Among those in this country who have been most eloquent in expressing their horror at recent events, and who no doubt will do so again when Parliament meets on Monday, are men who bore a heavy share of responsibility for the British attack on Egypt in 1956. Among those in the United States who have expressed their shock and grief are men who were implicated in planning or executing first the unsuccessful coup against Cuba in 1961, and then the successful one against the Dominican Republic in 1963. In these instances too, a great power, operating within what it had come to regard as its

---

[1] This talk was broadcast on 24th August 1968.

own sphere of influence, intervened by force, using the most transparent of political excuses, with no consideration for the wishes of the people concerned, to overthrow governments which they regarded as dangerous to their interests; without, incidentally, considering very deeply what to put in their place.

President Nasser was a leader who enjoyed, in a very different kind of society, as much national support as did Mr Dubček. The British government, and the great mass of the British people, cared no more for what the Egyptian people thought then than today the Russian government, and probably the Russian people also, care for the Czechs. We simply saw a régime whose attitudes and actions threatened interests which we had come to regard as vital. We had, or thought we had, the military power to do something about it, and we acted accordingly. A large number of people still consider that we were absolutely right and that our only mistake lay in not seeing the matter through. An even larger number of Americans, I suspect, feel the same way about intervention in Cuba; but I doubt whether either group contains many people who would press their logic to the point of justifying the Soviet occupation of Prague. It would be surprising if they did. For many of them, Russia is the enemy, in an almost cosmic sense. Anything that extends her power is intrinsically evil. Anything we can do to limit or reduce it is justifiable. I remember a highly intelligent Conservative Member of Parliament assuring me at the time of the Suez affair, that Nasser was known to be a member of the Communist Party. No doubt in Moscow a rumour is now circulating that Mr Dubček is an agent of the CIA. But more important still – and this applies to a far larger number of people in the West, including me – the Czechs are people with whom we can identify. Peaceful, cultured, intelligent, European, their cities like ours only more beautiful, their people like ours only more sensible – when we see these things happening to them, we can imagine them happening to us. It requires a far greater effort of the imagination for us to identify ourselves with the population of Cairo or San Domingo or Havana in the same way that we do with the people of Prague.

But we must note two consequences of this. First, there are probably more people in the world who can identify themselves with Egyptians or Cubans, or come to that with North Vietnamese, than can identify themselves with Czechs. Their representatives at the United Nations will not feel as agonised over all this as we do, and they will not have to be reminded that the powers which are most forthright in their condemnation of the Soviet Union do not come to the conference chamber with entirely clean hands. And secondly, the extent to which we can empathise with the Czechs as a western and bourgeois people in itself goes far to explain why the Russians acted as they did. The very actions and attitudes which we most admire on the part of the Czechs, their attempts to create an open society of the kind we enjoy in the West, are precisely those which the dominant groups in the Soviet Union dislike and fear the most. For them, *we* are the cosmic enemy, the expansion of whose power and influence must be contained, and if possible, reduced. For Czechoslovakia to become an open society would be to increase our influence and ultimately our power, and the chorus of rage and disapproval which has gone up in the West may only, I am afraid, convince the Russians that they were absolutely right to act as they did. To the hard-line communists in Moscow our expressions of shock and horror are likely to sound less like the considered condemnation of the civilised world than like snarls of rage from the thwarted demons of the bourgeois-imperialist hell. Not to all Russians; but that is a matter to which I will come back later.

In harping on the similarity between Russian action in eastern Europe and British action in the Middle East and American action in the Caribbean, I am not being simply malicious; and I hope I am not indulging in the academic illusion of being somehow above the battle. But if we can get this problem into the right perspective, we shall have a very much better idea how to deal with it. I believe that the British and the French statesmen who launched the Suez expedition, like the American statesmen who sponsored the various interventions in the Caribbean, were decent and honourable if misguided and misinformed men, who were acting in what they genuinely regarded as the best interests of their respective nations. I am prepared to suspend judgement about the Soviet leadership; at least until the fate of Mr Dubček and his associates is known. There is certainly good reason to suppose that the Russian, like the Western leaders, acted only with great reluctance and many misgivings; that their troops have strict orders, as ours had in similar circumstances, to avoid provocative acts – orders which they seem on the whole to have observed; and that the fumbling irresolution of the whole operation – and here the analogy with Suez and the Bay of Pigs is very exact – has probably been due to division of counsel at the top. But it is not enough simply to identify these similarities, label all these operations as 'imperialist adventures' and condemn them out of hand. We must consider why great powers, whatever their political complexion, tend to act like this; and then perhaps we can go on to consider what can or should be done about it.

A great power, almost by definition, is one which has the capacity to control events beyond its own borders; and that capacity is usually based on the ability to use military force. Power, as Chairman Mao said, grows out of the barrel of a gun. Why should they wish to control events? For one of two reasons or a combination of them. First, power, whether exercised by an individual or a group, is the ability to control one's environment and ensure that it remains favourable to one's well-being and ultimately one's survival. States seldom feel secure if their power is simply confined to their own borders. If they can extend their influence over their neighbours they do, and if those neighbours are markedly weaker than themselves – and so vulnerable to a stronger adversary – that influence is likely to take the form of military protection. But, beyond that frontier will be other communities which are seen as a menace, either because they are weak or because they are strong. So the expansion goes on, as British power expanded in India and the Middle East, or American power in the Pacific and south-east Asia, or the Russians in eastern Europe: not out of lust for conquest as such, but basically out of insecurity and fear. The greater the power, the greater its responsibilities and the greater its fears. The

rulers of great powers are seldom confident men; more often
– and British statesmen at the height of our Imperial glory
were no exception to this – they are exceedingly worried as
to how to preserve the structure they have created. If it is
threatened at any point – and the larger it is, the more
precarious it is likely to be – they see this as a menace to the
whole and react, or more likely over-react, accordingly.

The second reason for intervening beyond one's own
borders – and it is one which often parallels and reinforces
the first – lies of course in ideological and religious sympathies. One may feel an inescapable duty to assist those,
anywhere in the world, who share one's system of beliefs,
whether religious or political. The cause of liberal democracy
in Greece; of racial equality in southern Africa; of the 'Free
World' in south-east Asia; of Marxist popular democracy
however interpreted and wherever it appears: how can one
stand idly by and watch these just causes extinguished by
racialist or imperialist or revisionist or totalitarian oppression,
when one has the capacity to stop it? There are those, I suspect, who would contemplate with some equanimity a comparable military intervention, if such were possible, to assist
the causes with which they sympathise in South Africa and
Greece. In fact statesmen – even statesmen of great powers –
have learned to discipline such sympathies. But inevitably,
they are going to feel safer if the government of other nations,
especially contiguous nations, is in the hands of men of a
like mind to themselves. If the alternative appears to be the
seizure of power by groups violently hostile to their way of
life, and sympathetic to the enemy, the temptation to help
these like-minded men will be very strong indeed. And if
there are not any like-minded men available, it only shows
how serious the situation is. It may then be necessary to take
control altogether and educate the people, so that the necessary conditions of democracy can gradually develop.

Can such intervention ever be justified? In terms of international law, no. In terms of individual morality, no. But
statesmen, whatever they may profess, tend to use a cruder
and more pragmatic calculus – that of long-term results in
terms of the tranquillity and prosperity of their peoples; and

this, in their eyes, may sometimes justify actions in themselves illegal or immoral. I for one certainly would not argue that there never has arisen, and never could arise, a situation to which military intervention by a great power was the appropriate response; but for that situation, one would have to postulate, not only the utmost military efficiency and restraint (which it is not difficult to obtain from disciplined armies) but a degree of political wisdom, based on an enormous amount of entirely reliable information, such as few statesmen, either east, west or anywhere else, have shown themselves to possess. Statesmen tempted to such intervention should bear in mind Mr Punch's famous advice to those about to get married: Don't. The information on which they have to act is almost certainly incomplete and unreliable, and the consequences of their actions are utterly incalculable. The Bay of Pigs probably did more than anything else to establish Castro firmly in the affections of his countrymen and shake the standing of the United States throughout Latin America. Suez struck a blow at British influence throughout the Arab world from which it has not yet recovered and possibly never will. As for the Russians, they find themselves now in a dilemma so great that one is almost sorry for them. In the entire world, where can they look for support? To their East German puppets; to the cowed Hungarians; to the contemptible Bulgarians; to the Poles, to their lasting shame; and to the Republic of North Vietnam.

But the Soviet Union does have one enormous asset over the open societies of the West. As yet, they have only the rudiments of a domestic public opinion to bother about. May I read you something which I said on this programme four weeks ago?

'If (I said) during the next few days, Soviet tanks roll into Prague as they rolled into Budapest twelve years ago, and have to burn Czech resisters out of their houses as the Viet Cong had to be burned out of Saigon and Hue; the events will not be shown on television screens throughout the Soviet Union. Mass demonstrations to stop the war in Czechoslovakia will not be held on Red Square, and if they are, they will be broken up with something more lethal than water-cannon. To that extent, the Soviet leaders would have their hands free to impose whatever degree of suffering they may find necessary to reduce the Czech people to obedient satellite status, and the Czechs will have to show, by their capacity to endure such suffering, and the price which they exact for it, whether they can achieve the degree of political independence to which they today aspire.'

Events I am afraid, are justifying that prophesy only too well. The television pictures of the Soviet tanks in Prague, and the reaction to them of the Czech population, have been beamed all over the world; except behind the Iron Curtain. The Russian people still happily believe that their troops entered Czechoslovakia at the request of the Czech people, and that they are still being received with the enthusiasm which was deservedly accorded to them twenty-three years ago. One observes with a certain grim enjoyment the attempts of the editorial staff of *Pravda* to maintain this illusion in the face of mounting difficulties.

This is where the analogy with Suez and the Bay of Pigs breaks down. The American and British governments were subject to the constraints of an articulate and well-informed public opinion which could not be indefinitely deceived. Consciousness of this made the Americans reduce their own participation in the Bay of Pigs invasion to an ancillary rôle, but one which did not save them from a blast of outraged protest from their own press and people when that rôle was exposed. As for Suez, if financial pressures had not brought that operation to a rapid conclusion, Sir Anthony Eden would have had on his hands the worst internal crisis in this country since civil war loomed over the Irish question just before the First World War. The Soviet Union, however, does not have either a reserve currency on which pressure can be brought, nor a free press. Its lack of unbiassed information about the outside world certainly leads its statesmen to make colossal miscalculations, but the absence of domestic criticism inevitably makes their task a great deal easier. It is this imbalance which gives the Soviet Union such an advantage in its dealings with the West, and it is far more important than any 'gap' in technology or arms. The Russian leaders know it; that is why they want to preserve it: and that is a major

factor in their attempt to destroy the open society in Czechoslovakia. But none the less, the Soviet Union does profess
certain political ideals no less than do the Western democracies, and a substantial proportion of the Soviet élite must
take them seriously. Hence the agonised acrobatics of
Pravda's editorial staff. If things go on like this much longer,
the gap between principle and practice is going to start
puzzling an increasing number of people in Russia, and we
should do everything we can to ensure that it does. The
general demand now going up for the Soviet Union to be
boycotted seems to me to be simply silly. We should go out
of our way to meet the Russians and their allies. We should
take every opportunity to talk to them and ask what on earth
they think their governments are up to. We should welcome
the Russian musicians and scientists and athletes and
businessmen, but very insistently talk to them. That, after
all, is what the Czechs have been doing to the Russian
soldiers, and to some effect. The Russians may not like it –
that is their problem. If, as a result, they decide not to come,
that is their decision. But this is no moment for us to break
off the developing dialogue between east and west. On the
contrary: it is one for us to develop it still more intensively.

Finally, I believe that the view which is now so widely
prevalent, that we should intensify the Cold War, increase
our defence expenditure and generally put the hawks in
charge seems to me to be not only silly but dangerous. The
Russians, by their recent actions, have not revealed anything
about either their intentions or their capabilities which we
did not know perfectly well already. If there is one aspect of
the crisis about which all the experts seem to be agreed, it is
that the Russians acted as they did because they were
frightened. How will it improve the situation or help the
wretched Czechs, to make them more frightened? An increase in our defence expenditure, which would anyhow take
several years to affect our actual military posture, would only
lead the Russians to respond in kind, and strengthen the
arguments of those among them who are probably already
demanding a full and permanent military occupation of
Czechoslovakia. Of course our defence must be alert, and
any deficiencies revealed in it must be remedied. If the worst

really came to the worst, and a Czech resistance movement developed against a Russian occupation, we would then be in a condition of greater delicacy and danger than perhaps the world has ever known. The utmost moderation and wisdom would be needed then to deal with it.

In general, I believe that the West should not now change course and abandon that policy of 'peaceful engagement' with Eastern Europe on which we are set. And this is certainly no moment to put the hawks in charge. Will American papers please copy?

Acknowledgements

The studies in this book first appeared as follows:

1 'Jomini and the Classical Tradition in Military Thought' in *The Theory and Practice of War: Essays presented to Captain B. H. Liddell Hart on his seventieth birthday*, edited by Michael Howard (Cassell, London 1965)

2 'Waterloo' was printed by the Old Wellingtonian Society to celebrate the 150th anniversary of the battle

3 'Wellington and the British Army' in *Wellingtonian Studies: Essays on the first Duke of Wellington*, edited by Michael Howard (Gale & Polden, Aldershot 1959)

4 'William I and the Reform of the Prussian Army' in *A Century of Conflict*, edited by Martin Gilbert (Hamish Hamilton, London 1966)

5 'Lord Haldane and the Territorial Army' is the Haldane Memorial Lecture delivered at Birkbeck College, London, November 1966

6 'Reflections on the First World War' in *Encounter*, January 1964

7 'Hitler and his Generals' in *The Times Literary Supplement*, 24th May 1963

8 'The Mediterranean in British Strategy in the Second World War' was read to the Conference of the *Comité de l'histoire du deuxième guerre mondiale*, Paris 1969

9 'Bombing and the Bomb' in *Encounter*, April 1962

10 'The Classical Strategists' in *Problems of Modern Strategy Part I* (Adelphi Papers No. 54, Institute for Strategic Studies, London 1969)

11 'Strategy and Policy in Twentieth-Century Warfare' is the Harmon Memorial Lecture delivered at the US Air Force Academy, Colorado, 1967

12 'Military Power and International Order' is the Inaugural Lecture in the Chair of War Studies at King's College, London 1964

13 'Disarmament and the Military Balance' is a Public Lecture delivered at the University of Leeds, 1964

14 'Problems of a Disarmed World' was written for the Pugwash Conference on Science and World Affairs, Cambridge, 1962. It was printed in *Diplomatic Investigations*, edited by Herbert Butterfield and Martin Wight (Allen & Unwin, London 1966)

15 'Morality and Force in International Politics' is a Lecture delivered at Cambridge University, 1968. It was printed in *Making Moral Decisions*, edited by D. M. MacKinnon (SPCK, London 1969)

The Epilogue, 'The Invasion of Czechoslovakia', was broadcast as a talk in the 'Personal View' series on the Third Programme on 24th August 1968 and reprinted in *The Listener* on 29th August 1968.